Believing Hearts

AN ANTHOLOGY OF FICTIONAL STORIES
OF CONTEMPORARIES OF JESUS
AND THEIR CONVERSIONS

KATHRYN W. HALES

Believing Hearts
An Anthology of Fictional Stories of Contemporaries of Jesus and Their Conversions

v5.0

Outskirts Press, Inc.
http://www.outskirtspress.com

ISBN: 978-1-9772-4159-7

Scripture references from the King James Bible

PRINTED IN THE UNITED STATES OF AMERICA

Dedication

To those who encouraged me to fulfill my dreams.

Contents

Author's Note

The Holy Scriptures are filled with wonderful stories of people who encountered Jesus during his mortal ministry. Some believed Him and became faithful followers; others turned away. Among the thousands who heard him, there are only a few stories recorded by the Gospel writers. This book is a fictional work telling possible stories of ten others, including men, women, and youths, who came to accept Jesus as their Savior. There are recognizable names, such as the Twelve Apostles, Nicodemus, and Jairus. Secondary characters from events gleaned from the Gospels were given names and personalities. When they appeared in more than one story, such as Peter's family, different names were selected to portray independence, not continuity. Each character reflects the universal questions that all must face in accepting Jesus as the Christ__ such as wealth, fear, tradition, and pride. Perhaps we see a little of ourselves in each of these characters. In the end, it comes down to acting on faith, relying on the eternal love and grace of Jesus, and having believing hearts.

During the Covid 19 pandemic of 2020-2021 many Believers shared their testimonies, knowledge, and faith. Podcasts, blogs, books, artwork, and music flourished like flowers in a well-watered garden. I have benefitted from many of them and thank the authors, producers, and artists for being a light in a darkened world. I too wish to share my witness of Jesus Christ as our Savior and Redemer.

Thanks for the cover design to Kylie Zimmerman with a scene of a sunset over the Sea of Galilee. This was the perfect picture to remind me of a personal experiece in the Holy Land. Our scheduled boatride was canceled due to a windstorm and turbulent waters, not uncommon to that locale. This brought to mind a similar account recorded in Mark 4:37-39. Fortunatly for us, the weather moderated by evening when we were able to board a little ship. As a bonus, we were blessed with a beautiful sunset with lavender, indigo, and orange hues. Just as the Savior calmed the physical storms with the power of His word, He can calm the storms of our life through these same words__"Peace, be still." I have felt the power of His Spirit in many places over the course of many years. I know He lives and loves each of us with His perfect love.

What Lack I Yet?

TETHERING HIS HORSE to a nearby tree, Alexander inched his way closer to the crowd surrounding Jesus near the borders of Judea across the Jordan from Jericho. It seemed the multitudes followed the man they were calling Master no matter the distance or personal sacrifice. Many were clamoring for his healing touch__ blind women, crippled men, lepers, innocent children afflicted with demons. He was grateful that he suffered from none of these afflictions. Alexander's upbringing in the privileged class of a wealthy merchant had kept him from being exposed to many of the diseases that snuffed out the lives of those less fortunate. He had not come this far for a healing; but it was obvious that he was drawn to the personality of the man known by some as a charlatan, by others as a great teacher. The scribes and Pharisees from Jerusalem accused Jesus of wresting the teachings of the great prophet Moses.

He mostly wanted to hear the words of the Master. Although Jesus often quoted scriptures with which Alexander was familiar, the Teacher gave the words new life and the young man felt as if he was understanding them for the first time.

As a youth, Alexander had been schooled in the Great Synagogue of Jerusalem at the feet of respected rabbis. He knew the lessons of the Torah and could discuss its teachings with the learned men of his day. His mind jumped back to one occasion when as a youth he had definitely over-stepped his bounds in contradicting his teacher. He saw himself seated on a red cushion on the stone floor with his legs crossed under him…

"Alexander," said Rabbi Ben Jotham, "what says the Law about the eating of the showbread in the temple?"

"It is for the priests only."

"That is right. Why is that so?"

"Because the priests are the representatives of the God of Israel here on earth. The bread is consecrated to God's holy work and those who do that work need nourishment to sustain them in their service."

"Well stated, Alexander. In spite of your Greek name, due no doubt to your mother," he muttered under his breath in a derisive tone, "you have been brought up well in the traditions of the Jews."

"May I ask you a question, Rabbi?"

"Yes, boy. What is it?"

"It is recorded in the Chronicles that David and his men went to the Tabernacle which had been moved from Shiloh to Nob, near Jerusalem. They were trying to escape the threats which King Saul had made upon David's life but were hungry. David asked the priest Ahimelech for something to eat. There was nothing but the showbread, which was about to be replaced by a fresh batch according to the weekly custom. The priest gave the holy bread to David and his men to eat. How could a man, guilty of such a sin, still be blessed by the Lord to become our greatest king?"

"That is a good question, Alexander. We must look at it from many viewpoints. First, Ahimilech knew that it was time for fresh bread to be brought to the Tabernacle and that the consecrated bread would soon be removed, so perhaps it might no longer retain its sacred distinction and would become common once again. Or perhaps, Ahimilech also knew of Saul's madness and had sympathy for David's cause. Or other scholars say that David represents the higher spiritual understanding of the Law. Rabbi Ben Achem once said,__"

"Never mind, sir. I get the idea. No one really has the right answer, if

there is even a right answer."

"Alexander! I never expected such impertinence from you."

"I apologize, Rabbi Ben Jotham. I will not ask such questions in the future."

"Very well. But for your rudeness, you must sit here an additional hour and memorize the scriptures necessary for your Bar Mitzvah. Your thirteenth birthday is approaching soon."

"Yes, sir."

I was obedient that day and stayed the required hour, but my mind didn't focus on the scripture memorization as admonished. The frustration roiled inside of me, as it often did at that time of my life, and I had to breathe deeply to control the spiteful words that quickly rose to the surface. Unruly thoughts then shot through my brain: The rabbis are no masters of truth. They are like goatskin bags once used for wine that have been stretched out of shape by the fermentation process and are now only good for carrying water short distances. They are like puffs of wind that swirl about on the dry deserts of Judea, touching down here and there, but are really empty air, circling about with no purpose. Father will be disappointed in me when Rabbi Ben Jotham reports my rudeness today, for I'm sure that he will do so. I must learn to hold my tongue to honor my father, even though I do not believe all that the rabbis say.

Alexander brought his attention back to the present, surveying the crowd as the afternoon sun dipped toward the west. It appeared that people were dispersing, probably to return to their small camps which they'd set up for the night where they might eat. It didn't look like there would be a repeat of the miraculous feeding of thousands, which rumors claimed occurred near the Galilee. Jesus knew that people needed to hear his doctrine more than they needed food, although He himself had declared His words to be the Bread of Life.

Alexander believed these words, although he also understood the implications it would have if he were to become a true disciple and devote all of his time to traipsing around the countryside. Was it not possible to be a Believer and still carry on the lucrative business that had become his inheritance when his father, the well-known merchant Hosea, had lost his life at sea? Alexander had known he would someday take over, but at age twenty-two, he had certainly not been prepared for such a task. Now, two years later, Alexander felt like he had earned the respect of the shrewd businessmen who had intimidated him for his inexperience. He had studied the ledgers and knew which merchandise was selling the best. He had sought the advice of his father's trusted friends as to which ship captains were reliable and which were confederate with pirates. Some of the old camels that transported the goods from the seaport of Joppa had been sold and stronger ones purchased. He knew that he needed to make a trip to Joppa and bargain for the bolts of silk which were being imported from the Far East. Yet, he found himself more than a hundred miles away on the opposite side of the country, all because he was drawn to this unique man, Jesus of Nazareth.

Alexander spoke to himself, *"If I can just get close enough to ask him one question I will be satisfied. With all that I've been taught, there doesn't seem to be the ultimate answer for how I might obtain eternal life. I know the prophets speak of keeping the commandments, and that I have tried to do. But it feels like there is something more, something I'm lacking that prickles away at my thoughts and leaves me feeling that all my learning is inadequate. Is it possible to believe without being one of His camp followers? How can I receive the guidance that I need? Well, that's certainly more than one question!*

Finally, the rich young man was able to edge himself closer to the circle of loyal disciples that always accompanied Jesus. They were trying to keep a group of eager children from pestering the great man, who had a look of weariness about him.

"Go away," said one, trying to shoo them like they were bothersome chickens. "The Master is tired and needs to rest."

Surprisingly, to Alexander as well as the disciple, Jesus rebuked the men and called the children to come to him. "Suffer the little children, and forbid them not to come unto me; for of such is the kingdom of heaven." (Mark 10:14) He knelt down to look them each in the eye, touching a shoulder, holding a hand, or taking a dandelion bouquet that one bright-eyed little girl offered to him. Then sitting upon a large boulder, he took them up in his arms, and laid his hands upon them and blessed them.

"Here's my chance," thought Alexander as he picked his way through the children who were now scampering away, eager to tell their parents of their encounter with Jesus. He had to pick up his feet, almost to the point of running, so that he could get to Jesus before he disappeared into a nearby tent, probably for a much-needed meal or rest.

"Master, Good Master, please. May I ask but one question?" he panted breathlessly as he quickly knelt at Jesus' feet. "What must I do that I may inherit eternal life?" That indeed was the central issue. If he could have an answer for that perhaps the other matters could be resolved.

"Why callest thou me good? There is none good but one, that is God. But if thou wilt enter into life, keep the commandments."

"Which?"

"Thou shalt do no murder; thou shalt not commit adultery; thou shalt not steal, thou shalt not bear false witness; honor thy father and thy mother, and love thy neighbor as thyself."

"All these things have I kept from my youth up; what lack I yet?"

Jesus reached down and gently lifted Alexander to his feet. Alexander gazed into the clear blue eyes before him, feeling like Jesus was seeing into his very soul. But even more powerful was the love from the Master which enveloped him from the top of his light brown curls to the points of his expensive leather shoes. Speechless, Alexander dropped his own gaze, realizing his own sinful state. In a tender embrace, Jesus spoke gently, "One thing thou lackest; go thy way, sell whatsoever thou hast, and give to the poor and thou shalt have treasure in heaven. Then come, take up thy cross, and follow me." (See Mark 10: 17-22)

Alexander dropped his head in shame. He had his answer, but it was not one he wanted to hear. Jesus removed his arms from the young man's shoulders and pivoted toward the outstretched arm of his disciple, who was impatiently ushering him toward the tent. Alexander turned with great sadness and started back to the edge of the camp where he had left his fine bay horse nibbling at the sparse grass. As he walked he heard the words of the Master speaking to his disciples, "How hardly shall they that have riches enter into the kingdom of God." (Mark 10:24)Then not hearing exactly the Aramaic pronunciation, he wasn't sure if Jesus said something about a "camel" or "rope" going through the eye of a needle, but either way, the meaning was obvious: it was impossible for a rich man to enter into the kingdom of God.

The sun was setting as Alexander guided his horse back through the Jordan at the spot known as Joshua's Crossing. Tradition held that this is where the Old Testament successor to Moses had led the Israelites into the Promised Land. The stones retrieved from the river and once built up as a memorial had been torn down long ago, but the story remained. The stream was shallow at this season of the year with most of the snow already melted from Mt. Herman in the far reaches of the territory originally assigned to the tribe of Dan. All of that was ancient history since the Israelites had been conquered by a variety of ambitious and greedy kings over the centuries. Most of the tribes had been carried away into the northern countries by the

Syrians and their existence lost to the knowledge of the remaining two tribes who had inhabited the southern kingdom of Judah before their own exile as slaves to the Babylonians. A remnant had been allowed to return during the time of the Persian ruler Cyrus and rebuild the city of Jerusalem.

It was long past dark when Alexander pulled up to an inn near Jericho that still showed a candle burning in the window. Knocking on the wooden door to rouse the owner, he rubbed the neck of his tired mount.

"Hold your horses, I'm coming," bellowed a deep voice from inside. Alexander chuckled to himself at the literalness of the man's words.

Opening the door a few inches, the bearded innkeeper barked, "What do you want this time of night?"

"I'd like a meal, a room, and a stall for my horse."

"Bah! If'n you'd wanted all that you should have been here hours ago. Best I can do for you is a plate of leftover mutton stew and a cot in the common room. That will be two pence."

Alexander jingled silver coins in his hand outstretched toward the man's face. "I'm sure a denarius would get me what I asked for." It was a statement, not a question.

"Oh, yes, sir. Right away sir," the oily voice responded as the man snatched the offered coins.

"I will rub down my horse while you are warming up the stew. Serve it with a loaf of bread and a mug of ale in my private room."

"Yes, sir. Right away, sir. The stable is just behind the inn. You will find water in the trough and a bucket of oats near the door."

"That's more like it," mumbled Alexander as he guided his horse around the edge of the inn. "Money never fails to get a man the comforts that he needs."

As Alexander sat in his room perched on the side of a bed with a small table drawn alongside, he ruminated on that thought again.

His money had indeed gotten him more comfortable accommodations than he would have had otherwise. *It's still inferior to my villa in Jerusalem where I sleep on a down-filled pallet covered by a silken sheet in the summer and a finely woven woolen blanket in the winter. Even my servants' quarters are better than this place. At least I'm not in a tent across the Jordan, like the followers of Jesus in their make-shift camps.*

That's the kind of life I would have to get used to if I followed his counsel. How can I sell all my possessions, give the money to the poor, and follow him? Even though I believe many of his teachings and have seen his marvelous healing power at work, could I really live like that? I would have to give up so much. Is hope for an ethereal dream beyond this life worth the sacrifice here and now? Alexander shook his head in sorrow as he set the dishes aside on the table, took one last swallow of the weak wine, and loosening his leather belt, stretched himself out on top of the patchwork quilt, hoping it wasn't full of bed bugs. It was a long time before he dropped off to sleep, his mind too full of thoughts that insisted on a mental sword fight.

The next morning he purchased a loaf of fresh bread and a small bag of dried fruit at the market and filled his water skin at the village well before resuming his journey. At least the sun was at his back for now, but it would be far in the west before he reached his destination that evening. Although it was only twenty-five miles between Jericho and Jerusalem, it was all uphill. Jericho was actually eight hundred feet below sea level, while Jerusalem to the southwest was twenty five-hundred feet above sea level.

There were a few scattered watering holes along the trail, but this time of year, they tended to have more mud than water. He hoped he could find enough for his trusted horse Spartan. Mile after mile they climbed, the sun rising to its zenith. Alexander wrapped a silk scarf around his head and face to protect his skin and eyes from the dazzling sunlight. "No wonder there's so much blindness in this cursed land. That sun is enough to fry one's brains," he mumbled to himself. He tried singing a few of the psalms he remembered from his childhood, but his throat was too parched. He recalled some of the scriptures he had memorized as a boy, but they only reminded him more of the teachings of Jesus. *Why can't I be put the thoughts of that man out of my head?*

He purposely called up thoughts of his mother, Ida, who still lived in his childhood home since the death of Hosea. *She is still such a lovely woman with her auburn hair braided like a coronet around her head. Her soft voice and tender touch always calm me even now. No wonder my father was enchanted with this Greek girl he discovered in the Egyptian city of Alexandria so many years ago. She freely admits that she was captivated by the adventurous young sea captain who had come to trade with the merchants of her land. Father knew he was breaking the social mores of his forefathers to marry a Gentile, but at the time the traditions had seemed so old-fashioned. He knew he couldn't be happy with any other woman by his side. He always called her "My Sweet Ida". To Alexander, it seemed that they had an ideal relationship. Or maybe it was because Father was often gone away on business so that the time they had together was always honored.*

Alexander, as the first-born son, inherited his father's business ventures. His younger brother, Silvanus was an apprentice to a ship-builder in Joppa and Alexander hoped to see him soon. He visualized the day when he and his brother would own their own ships and be able to increase their merchandising profits even more. Their only sister, Rebecca, was betrothed to the son of a landowner west of Jerusalem that raised fine grapes for wine. Alexander had been satisfied with the marriage contract that had been drafted last fall as he acted in his father's behalf. His sister's future looked secure and she seemed happy with the young man who had sought her hand. The wedding was scheduled to take place in a few months.

Night was falling as Alexander, weary from his long ride, neared the village of Bethany, a few miles east of Jerusalem. He could have found an inn there, but decided to press on to his own home and sleep in his own comfortable bed. However, his servants were not particularly expecting his arrival on this night, so Alexander decided to hire a link-boy to run the two miles and alert his household of his return. At least then he could be guaranteed a warm meal and a good rub-down for his tired horse. With hardly a thought, Alexander flipped a coin to the young boy who was eager for the job and watched as the youth's long legs sprinted toward the city beyond. The gates would be closed for the night. But again, with a coin to a greedy guard, they would surely be opened for such an important citizen as himself.

Alexander's stay in Jerusalem was brief, but he indulged himself with a bath, followed by a decent meal while chatting with his mother and sister who couldn't stop talking about the wedding plans.

"Alexander," asked Rebecca, "Will you please find me some cloth on your next journey? I would like some soft cotton for undergarments, and of course silk for the wedding canopy."

"Of course, dear sister. Anything to make a bride happy."

She smiled at him under her long dark lashes in a silent message of thanks. Alexander looked again at his sixteen-year-old sister. She was indeed a beauty and of such a sweet temperament. Any man would be lucky to have her as a wife. Then a not-so-subtle look from his mother let him know he should be finding his own wife. He gave a shrug of his shoulders and opened his palms in a gesture of "I know, but what can I do about it now?" kind of look. As he bade his mother farewell, she whispered in his ear. "Don't wait too long, Alexander. The years pass quickly."

When he arrived at his office in Joppa, he found that agents from Antioch had bought up all the silks that had come by camel caravan and that there would be no more coming this season. He was sure that the women of Corinth, Athens, and Thessalonica would soon be arrayed in fine gowns. He was disgusted with himself more than ever for taking that detour to Jericho.

Alexander decided that a journey to Alexandria was necessary in order to secure the cotton fabric that Rebecca had requested. Egyptian cotton had long fibers resulting in a smoothness unmatched by shorter fibers grown closer to Palestine. Perhaps there would be other merchandise sent up the Nile that would interest his Jerusalem customers as well: tropical fruits, peacock feathers, or carved ivory. He sent a message with a courier heading to Jerusalem to inform his family of his plans and bought passage on a ship sailing to the Egyptian port a little over three hundred miles away. It was slightly shorter than going the land route and he hoped it would save time.

The first evening Alexander stood on the deck looking at the familiar stars. It seemed that every mariner had some imagined shape outlined in the constellations with an accompanying name and story. He couldn't remember the difference between the stag and the cup, Andromeda from Venus. He just knew they were beautiful and in a quiet moment of contemplation started a one-way conversation with Jehovah, which he hadn't done for a long time.

"Great God of Heaven and Earth, I give praise and thanks for the wonders of Thy creations. Each star was crafted by Thy powerful hand. Are any of them home to other beings such as ourselves? What is man and why have you created us? For lives of sweat and toil, war and death, perhaps a moment or two of happiness with a loved one? What is our purpose? Why are some, such as I, blessed with riches, and others to poverty__or worse?" His mind became keenly aware of the beat of the drums in the hold below the deck where the slaves plied their strength with the oars.

He had rarely thought of the oarsman on the other voyages that he had taken with his father. They were just,___just there.

Picking up a lighted torch from a nearby post, Alexander walked to the hatch that opened into the hold. The pounding of the drum sounded louder in his ears and the call of the foreman counting out the four-beat cadence: "Forward, drop, back, lift." Neither the drummer nor the foreman broke their pattern as Alexander slowly made his way down the wooden ladder, although both men glanced in his direction.

Alexander gestured for them to carry on, as he tried to breathe in the stink that assaulted his nostrils. The foul smells of unwashed bodies, sweat, and human excrement made him want to gag. Each man was seated on a narrow wooden bench with one leg secured to the side of the ship with a thick chain. Their upper bodies were naked and sweat rolled down their backs. Down here the heat was still oppressive even though the sun had departed and the air on deck was cool. Only a small amount of outside air came through the portals where each of the twelve-foot oars exited the hold, dipping into the waves. The muscles of the slaves' upper arms and backs rippled as they worked in tandem to move the ship forward through the deep waters of the Mediterranean. Most of their heads were bent, paying no attention to the appearance of a stranger in their midst. Two near the center where he stood turned to stare at him with haggard unshaven faces and vacant eyes. It was hard to tell in the near-darkness, but it was likely that the men before him were blind. Had they spent all of their lives in the darkness of the holds of such ships? What crimes had they committed to be sold as slaves? Then a new thought came: *perhaps they aren't criminals at all, but just unfortunate souls who had been in the wrong place at the wrong time. Perhaps they were snapped up as booty gained by the Romans in their conquests throughout the known world. Some of the men have the black skin of the Ethiopians, but not all. I suppose that with a bath and a haircut, that some of the men would be as light-skinned as I am. Why was I blessed with riches and these men with captivity?*

Then the beat of the drummer changed to four sharp staccato taps, followed by eight additional beats gradually slowing down until the rowing stopped. The foreman yelled out, "Change", Alexander unexpectedly saw another two dozen men crawl out from beneath the benches and grab the oar from a partner. A replacement drummer and another foreman also took their places at the bow. A sudden wave of compassion washed over Alexander and he called out. "Give each man a drink of water before you start up." The new foreman gave him a dirty look and asked with a sneer, "And who are you to be telling us what to do?"

"I am Alexander from Jerusalem and Joppa, a merchant well known to the captain and owner of this ship. It has been a hot day and these men are thirsty. Give everyone a drink. NOW!"

"Boy, water," the foreman growled. And for the first time, Alexander noticed a young boy of perhaps seven or eight years of age who had been sitting behind the drummer. He heaved a heavy wooden bucket and started to make his way among the slaves, giving each man a drink from a gourd with a long curved handle.

Some guzzled it down and asked for more. One man spat it out exclaiming, "Putrid and full of vermin, as always." But one glance from the foreman told the boy in no uncertain terms that the man would not get any other to slake his thirst.

"Back to work you filthy slaves. You've had your rest."

Alexander watched as the first crew crawled under the benches, hoping for some sleep. Their replacements each grabbed one of the twelve-foot long oars with two hands and the drumbeat began again.

Alexander turned and climbed the ladder, breathing in the cool fresh air with a new sense of gratitude. He replaced the torch and made his way to his private cabin and laid down on the wooden bunk covered with a straw-filled tick. He contemplated the Phoenicians who had been master ship-builders for centuries, claiming they had traveled far beyond the lands with which Alexander was familiar. *Some say they have sailed for many months across the oceans to other lands with high mountains where snow never melts. Other sailors speak of sights on islands where the sand is black and mountain tops burn with fires that never cease. I had supposed they were just stories made up to pass the time on lengthy voyages. But what if there is some truth to them and navigation to distant lands is a possibility. What is truth, after all?*

He tried to sleep, but the pounding of the drums below rang more loudly in his ears than ever before. Tonight he had become aware of something he had just taken for granted in the past and it troubled him. What kind of God would allow such cruelty? The prayer of praise that he had uttered earlier was trapped in his throat. Now his only feelings were of sorrow and despair for those who were less fortunate than he.

The young merchant slowly walked through the great souk of Alexandria's mercantile district near the seashore perusing the merchandise on display. Built more than three centuries earlier, Alexandria had long been a center for the desert caravans from the East and the ships from the north and west to meet in a great exchange of wares. There were woven rugs from the Orient, carved ebony chairs from the Sudan, woven shawls from Israel, an assortment of livestock, and always the smell of exotic spices. Since the Romans had conquered it a half-century earlier and now controlled the port, it had become the major source of grain for the whole Empire. His father had focused on textiles, with a few standard spices for stability, and that seemed to be the best course for him to follow as well.

There was plenty of competition as it was. Israel's main export was salt, mined or processed from the shores of the Dead Sea. There were more than a dozen merchants dealing in that commodity deemed so precious that is was often used as a unit of exchange itself.

The colorful bolts of silk lay before him on a long wooden table: lavenders reminiscent of distant sunsets, cerulean blues copying the sheen of the Great Sea in sunlight, and yellows imitating the shade of lemons so closely that it almost made him pucker looking at it. He could imagine the elation with which the wife of Pilate, governor of Palestine, would buy some for her royal attire. The wives of Annas and Caiaphas, men who had both ruled as high priests in Jerusalem, would then think they had to have something just as glamorous. The race for female fashion supremacy would be on and Alexander would be all the more wealthy for it. He haggled with the agent over the price for a while, paying more than he wanted, but was sure he would still make a profit.

His eyes then turned to the table with white fabrics__ the finely woven cotton and the silk for the canopy that Rebecca had requested. He paid for it with his own private funds, not from his business account, so that he could present it to her as a gift.

Alexander made arrangements for the fabric to be carefully wrapped in fleece and then canvas, and to be delivered to the docks where it would wait for loading on the ship returning to Joppa, which was scheduled to leave in a few days. He hired a trustworthy-looking young man with a penny, a normal day's wage, to act as a guard for the merchandise, with the promise of another when the packet was safely loaded. One could not be too careful in regards to dock thieves who might rob him of his investment.

Alexander intended to move on to the next order of business, the purchasing of spices that every housewife used in cooking__cinnamon, nutmeg, pepper, cumin, garlic, tarragon, and thyme _when his eyes caught a display of fine ribbon at the end of the textile section. *Those would make a nice addition to my collection of fabrics*, he thought to himself. He moved down the aisle to get a closer look at the strands hanging from a metal frame. Fingering the finely woven silk ribbons in varying widths, he could imagine long strands of it wrapped around the waist of silk robes or sewn onto the hems of togas. There were scroll designs in variegated violets, others with diamond patterns of green and brown or dainty red hearts and yellow stars. They were all so beautiful that Alexander couldn't decide which ones would sell best, so he held them out one by one, examining them more closely. Seated a short distance away behind a table sat a young woman embroidering on a piece of white ribbon. Her face was bent forward, her long golden curls obscuring her face. Alexander watched her slim fingers as she concentrated her efforts in making the precise stitches. Finally sensing that she was being scrutinized, the girl glanced up. "May I help you with anything, sir?" she asked politely.

"I was just admiring your handiwork. I assume you are the creator of such beauty?" Alexander asked politely.

"Yes, Sir." she replied with a demure smile.

"I can't decide," he paused, his forefinger pressing against his lips as he pondered the selection.

"Here, this strand is just completed," she said handing him a fathom's length of white ribbon embroidered with green vines, pink rosebuds, and blue curlicues.

"I've never seen anything so exquisite. You are a maid possessing great skill. How much do you charge for such a treasure?" He imagined the ribbon tied in Rebecca's long dark hair as she stood under the wedding canopy.

"It requires much time and effort, therefore the price is quite high."

"How much?" he again asked, determined to have the ribbon.

"Ten shekels."

"Oh, that is a high price," he said, weighing the decision now that he knew the cost.

"Your wife would value it very much and give you much praise for such a gift, sir."

"That would be true if I had a wife," he replied. "But I had it in mind to give to my sister for her wedding day."

"Your sister would also be grateful for such a unique gift."

"I am not used to dealing with females in business transactions," Alexander said, thinking perhaps he could negotiate a better price with a man. "Is your husband nearby?"

"I have no husband, sir. My father usually oversees the stall, but he has been called away on other business today. I think you will have to deal with me after all."

He had been so focused on the ribbon that he hadn't noticed that the girl, perhaps in her late teens, was leaning on a wooden crutch. He looked into her face, surprised at her loveliness. Blue eyes sparkled under finely arched brows. She had a pert nose and rosy lips that broadened into a wide smile as she held out the ribbon toward him.

"You can see that the workmanship is of excellent quality, even if I must say so myself."

"Did you make all of these ribbons?" Alexander asked, remembering too late that he had already asked that question.

"Yes. As you can see, I am crippled and not able to be of much use in the household. My mother taught me the basic stitches a few years ago, but with practice and ingenuity, I have developed these particular patterns. I don't think you will find anything else like them in all of Alexandria."

"Nor in Jerusalem."

"Is that where you are from, sir?"

"Yes. Let me introduce myself. I am Alexander of Alexandri___I mean, I am Alexander, a merchant from Jerusalem." He was embarrassed over the verbal blunder, but the beauty of the seamstress had him befuddled.

"And I am Helene, daughter of Damion. So which ribbons do you want to buy?" she gestured to the array on the rack.

"I will take the one you have just finished, thank you. For my sister."

"None of the others, sir?"

"Not today."

"They may not be here the next time you come from Jerusalem."

"I know. But I must make some other purchases first," his voice trailed off lamely. "Spices… for the…women …you know."

"I understand," she said, although he could tell she was disappointed that he hadn't bought more of her wares.

"Here's the ten shekels," handing her the coins.

"Thank you, sir. I'm sure that your sister will look beautiful on her wedding day."

Helene rolled the ribbon into a neat circle and tied it securely with a piece of thread so that it would not spiral out of shape.

Alexander looked into her lovely eyes one more time as he took the ribbon and slowly backed away from the vendor's stall. Finally turning to work his way into the mainstream of the customers that packed the market's walkways, he soon lost sight of Helene.

Alexander completed his business in the spice aisle, purchasing several casks of the spices which had been transported by camel over the mountains from the Orient, India, and the deserts of Moab. The cost of the spices always included a surcharge tax imposed by the men of Petra who provided "protection services" against the Arabian bandits who frequently attacked the caravans. The vendors of the market were beginning to close the gates to their shops as the sun dipped toward the horizon. Alexander felt he had accomplished the business for which he had come to this ancient city and planned to be on the next ship to Joppa.

After checking to see that the young man guarding his merchandise on the docks was still on duty, he decided to purchase his supper at an inn he had noticed as he had made his way to the market earlier that day. Tantalizing odors of roasting meat and baking bread filled his nostrils. It was a pleasant relief from the smell of unwashed human bodies that had filled the market all day. As usual, a dozen beggars stood around the entrance to the inn hoping for a coin to be dropped in an outstretched hand. Wrinkling his nose at their foul smell and seeing their ragged tunics, Alexander intended to brush them aside as usual. A reminder of the slaves on the ship penetrated his consciousness. Alexander looked around him again__these were men just as he was. Through their matted hair he could see dark eyes filled with pleading and hunger. "What brought these men to such impoverished circumstances?" he asked himself. In an impulsive move, he withdrew his leather coin pouch from the inside of his tunic and handed each man a coin.

"Thank you sir,"

"May God bless you for your kindness."

"More, more."

He shook his head indicating there would be no more handouts tonight and made his way into the inn. Somehow the roast chicken, chickpeas, sliced cucumbers, and melon tasted better to him that night than ever before. Was it that his own gratitude had increased? Alexander silently expressed his thanks to the God of Abraham, Isaac, and Jacob whom he claimed as his own even though he was half Greek by birth.

He remembered some of the teachings of the Torah from his

days in the synagogue school. *Was not the Lord displeased with those who forgot to acknowledge His hand in their lives? What about the chief butler who forgot the dream that Joseph interpreted for him in the prison? What about the people of Israel who forgot the Lord and started worshipping idols? I do not want to be guilty of such ingratitude. I have indeed been blessed in my business affairs while in Alexandria and will not return to Jerusalem empty-handed.*

The thought of his guard sitting with nothing to eat came into his mind. *What did such guards do for food? I have no idea. Go without I suppose. Or perhaps they have a family member who brings them a loaf of bread.* But with the compassion he had felt earlier still lingering in his heart, he ordered a second meal wrapped in palm leaves which he took with him as he left the inn. The sky was almost dark, so he ordered the assistance of a local torch-bearer to lead him to the docks where he gave the food to his employee.

"You are most kind, Alexander of Joppa and Jerusalem," said the guard. "No one has ever done this for me before. I will relish the food and your good will all through the night."

"See you in the morning," was all the response Alexander gave. To himself he mumbled, *Am I getting soft? Or maybe it was just good insurance that the man would stay on duty all night and not wander off to find food leaving my goods unattended.*

That night as Alexander lay on the bed in the lodgings where he was staying, he wondered what was happening to him. There was an unfamiliar feeling of peace in his heart and it felt good. *What was it that I had heard Jesus preach?__'in me, ye might have peace'. I haven't thought about Jesus for the whole time I've been in Alexandria. Why am I becoming so uncharacteristically generous__handing out coins to beggars and taking food to an employee? If I keep this up, I'll soon be as destitute as the beggars themselves.* After only a few minutes of those latter thoughts, the feeling of peace quickly disappeared.

He tossed and turned throughout the night dreaming of ribbons, their colorful strands swirling to a drumbeat around the maiden Helene who was dancing on top of the clouds. But that couldn't be true; Helene was a cripple.

Alexander strode to the docks shortly after sunrise to check on the sailing schedule of the ship to Joppa. Noticing the activity of the crew on the deck, he marched onto the ship seeking the captain.

"We will leave on the afternoon tide," reported a man who seemed to be in charge "Be on board then, or you'll have a long way to swim."

"I should conclude my last item of business before mid-day. I will be here by the turn of the tide. Make sure that my merchandise has been loaded by your stevedores," he said pointing to the guard still perched on top of the canvas-wrapped fabric.

"That pile there?" asked the grizzled looking seaman.

Alexander nodded in agreement but didn't speak.

"Yes, sir. I'll get my men on it right away."

Alexander picked his way cautiously down the gangplank to the wooden docks which were built on large pylons buried in the sea floor. It was considered a bad omen for a voyage if one were to fall into the salty brine before the ship embarked.

As the merchant approached, the guard stood up rubbing the stiffness out of his back. "I guess they'll be loading your merchandise soon."

"Yes. The ship sails on the afternoon tide. Thank you for your diligence,____. Sorry I neglected to ask your name before."

"It's Cyrus. And thanks again for the meal you brought last night. No one has ever done that before."

"I'll be glad to give your name to anyone I meet that you are a dependable man. Here's the rest of your wages. And I wish you good luck." The two men shook hands and parted.

Alexander watched as the guard sauntered down the dock and he felt better about having made an effort at being a little friendlier. Being a good businessman didn't mean he had to be austere and intimidating.

Alexander again made his way toward the large market with a determination to buy some more of the embroidered ribbons. He was sure that he would be able to sell them to the elite of Jerusalem society that always wanted the latest in fashion, yet still make a tidy profit. Alexander hoped to speak to Helene again but was afraid to admit to himself that that was the main reason he was heading toward the ribbon vendor's stall.

He spied the rack of colorful ribbons, relieved that they hadn't been snatched up by another buyer since the previous afternoon. As he approached, it was apparent that Helene's father had returned and Alexander's hopes of a personal conversation with the young woman dropped like a hod full of bricks. As the young merchant reached out to examine the ribbons, a middle-aged man appeared at his elbow.

"May I interest you in our fine merchandise, sir? All handmade with exquisite detail."

"I know, I was here yesterday and bought a fathom's length for my sister."

"Oh, you must be the merchant from Jerusalem that my daughter told me about."

"Yes, I am Alexander with offices in Jerusalem and Joppa."

"And I am Damian."

"Yes, I spoke with your daughter Helene yesterday and she told me your name." Alexander craned to look over the man's shoulder to see if Helene was anywhere in sight. He was relieved to see her, but she was further to the back of the three-sided tent seemingly absorbed in her work. However, the sound of his voice had alerted Helene to his presence and she looked up from her needlework. She was pleased with his handsome appearance: a striking face with dark eyes and a hawkish nose. He did not have the dark hair and olive skin like other Jews she'd met, for his hair was a light brown that curled lightly upon his shoulders.

"Oh that Helene is a friendly one all right, not shy about talking to the customers like some of my other daughters."

Alexander wanted to keep the man talking, hoping to catch Helene's eye. He had to see those beautiful eyes again before he left this city. "You have other daughters then?"

"Yes, I have been blessed with many children, five daughters, and three sons. My wife and I enjoy each other's company....," the man chuckled and prodded Alexander in the ribs. "You likewise, sir?"

"No, no. I'm not married."

"Ah. Perhaps I can interest you in one of my eligible daughters. Like I say, I have five, but three are already happily married. However, there is my lovely Thea, a virtuous maid, and a good cook."

"I'm sure Thea is a lovely girl if she's anything like Helene, but I really came to buy ribbons."

Ignoring Alexander's protests, Damian went on. "Yes, Helene is probably my most beautiful daughter, but alas, she is crippled and managing a household would be most difficult for her."

"May I ask how she came to be crippled? Has she been so since birth?"

"No, it was an unfortunate accident, right here in this market, but further down in the produce section. An unruly donkey went crazy and started running through the stalls, knocking over tables full of melons and squash. What a mess. One of the tables fell on little Helene who was just a child at the time, breaking her leg. It never healed correctly, so she must now walk with a crutch. But it has been a blessing in disguise because she has used her time to become an excellent seamstress. Did you say that you were interested in buying some of her beautiful ribbons?"

"Yes, that is why I returned to your stall today." At least that's what Alexander said out loud, but inwardly acknowledged his inner feelings of attraction toward the maiden.

"Which one would you like, the brown and green triangles? The dainty red hearts? That would make a lovely gift to a maiden who is the apple of your eye."

"I have no such maiden in my life, sir."

"Ahh," Damian stretched out the word with renewed interest. He caught the look of longing apparent in Alexander's eyes as he gazed at Helene. "Tell me more about yourself, Alexander of Joppa and Jerusalem."

"My father was Hosea, a merchant from Jerusalem who fell in love with a beautiful young woman right here in Alexandria many years ago. So I am half Greek and half Jewish."

"Ahh," Damian repeated himself. Helene scooted her stool a few feet closer to the front of the stall, trying to hide her movement from her father who was staring with even greater attention at the newcomer.

"My father died in a shipwreck at sea a little more than two years ago and I have taken over the responsibility of his merchandising business. We specialize in fabrics which seem to please the wealthy women of Judea." Damian's eyebrows raised and he nodded his chin in silent approval. Alexander continued, "My mother and sister still live in Jerusalem and my brother is in Joppa as an apprentice shipbuilder. Someday I hope to expand our business to include our own ships as well as our camels to transport our merchandise. Judea is a small country and we do not have many exports, although the woven shawls brought to Joppa always sell very quickly."

Alexander looked up at the sun making its way across the

morning sky. "But to get back to business," he pulled his gaze away from Helene to the man standing close by. "I would like to purchase some ribbon and be on my way because the ship sails with the afternoon tide. The captain says I must be on board or I'll have to swim back to Joppa. Not a pleasant thought, eh?"

"No indeed. Although I've heard that your prophet Jonah did something like that one time."

"Yes, that is one of our ancient stories. I'm not sure how true it is...." Alexander let his voice trail off. He glanced back toward Helene, noticing that her eyes were downcast. *Could it be that she was sad at the thought of his leaving so soon? Or was it just modesty of a virtuous woman? Might he hope that she shared an interest in him?*

Damian cleared his throat saying, "Well, back to the business of ribbons, sir, so that you can be on your way."

"Oh...yes...ribbons."

"Which one would you like, Sir?"

"Well.. ...I'd like all of them," his usual sound business sense seemingly evaporated in the hot Egyptian sun.

Helene's facc jerked up, a smile again lighting her face. She was obviously delighted that Alexander was so pleased with her handiwork.

"Of course, of course, Alcxander of Jerusalem and Joppa. Let's see, there are twenty lengths in all," he said quickly taking the ribbons from their place on the rack. "They sell for ten shekels each. That would be two hundred shekels."

"Yes, that is the price that Helene quoted me yesterday. But I'm wondering since I am taking such a large order that we could negotiate a lower price. Say thirteen shekels?'

"No, no," said Damian, starting to hang the ribbons back up. "If you do not have that much money, I can understand, but I cannot sell all of our stock for such a low price."

"Don't be too hasty, man," said Alexander starting to take the ribbons from the rack himself. "I acknowledge their great beauty and the lovely hands that made them. How about fifteen shekels?"

Seeing that there might still be potential for a big sale, Damian eyed the ribbons with a shrewd eye and stroked his short beard, "Seventeen shekels," he said.

"You drive a hard bargain, Damian. However, seventeen shekels it will be, if you will allow me to begin a correspondence with your daughter, Helene."

Damian glanced back at Helene who was looking wide-eyed at Alexander. "Would you agree to such a correspondence, daughter?"

"Oh yes, father," she tried to say meekly, although the look of radiance on her face revealed her true feelings.

"So shall it be then." The two men shook hands to seal the transaction.

Alexander removed his money pouch and counted out the coins, his eyes hardly leaving Helene's face. Damian wrapped the ribbons around a wooden spool and tied them with a thread before handing them to Alexander.

"I shall visit your shop again when I return to Alexandria. Until then, we will have to rely on the excellent postal system that the Romans have established."

"That is one of the few things that has improved since the Romans took over," grumbled Damian. "We will both look forward to another visit in the future."

"I hope it will be soon. But I must go now or I will miss my ship." He clutched the bundle containing his purchases, startled to stumble as he turned to leave, but catching his balance said "Until we meet again." He waved and started running toward the docks.

Looking at his reflection in the full-length mirror made of polished brass, Alexander adjusted the cream-colored stole around his shoulders. His mother who was standing behind him also looked at the image, patted him on the arm, and said, "You look so like your father." Tears sprang unbidden to her eyes. "So handsome."

"I may have inherited his looks and his position on the Council, but his prestige and wisdom it seems I must earn for myself."

"You will with time, my son."

It had been almost a month since he had returned from his voyage to Alexandria and all of the merchandise he'd purchased there had been sold. As he'd hoped, the fabric and ribbon were well received by his loyal customers in Jerusalem. Of course, he hadn't been able to stop talking about the lovely Helene.

"Have you received a letter from Alexandria yet?" his mother asked.

"No," he sighed. He had written four already, but with the sailing schedules as they were, he hoped for a reply soon. "What if she changes her mind and doesn't want to correspond with me? Or what if her father changes his mind and forbids it? Or what if the ship carrying the postal pouch shipwrecks? The waiting is killing me."

"Be patient Alexander. I know how you are pining for her."

"I so want you to meet her, Mother. I'm not sure yet how that can be arranged, but I'm certain you'll love her."

"If you decide to marry this girl I will do all that I can to make her adjustment of living in Jerusalem as easy as possible. I remember the early days of my marriage to your father and coming here as a Gentile. Although I had put away my pagan gods, I always felt like I was on the fringe of society, not one of the Chosen People the Jews are so proud of calling themselves."

"I had no idea you felt like an outsider, Mother."

"I felt bad that I could never fully participate in Passover and or light the Shabbat candles. I think your father thought he had to work extra hard to raise our status in the social hierarchy of Jerusalem society just so people would like me."

"Well, he certainly succeeded in that aspect. And Mother, I know that being part of our family with a bevy of servants would make it so much easier for Helene. She could supervise the household, under your guidance of course, without having to do all of the physical labor with her disability. That handicap is why she is still unmarried."

"That just makes it all the more lucky for you, doesn't it Alexander?"

The young man smiled in response saying, "I'd best be off," and adjusted his stole one more time. He gave his mother a quick kiss on the cheek and left his palatial home built on the side of the Mount of Olives. Making his way through the narrow streets that led to the Temple Mount where the Sanhedrin held their meetings, Alexander contemplated the grandeur of the buildings around him. *Although Herod the Great was known for his vicious madness, he was a great architect and builder. He rebuilt the former Hasmonean fortress, renaming it after his Roman friend, Mark Anthony. He constructed his royal place, a theater, an amphitheater, a stadium, and monumental gates and staircases leading to the Temple Mount. But the grandest of all his edifices was the Temple in Jerusalem. About fifty years ago, tens of thousands of workmen enlarged the Temple courtyards and porticoes. It has been said that whoever has not seen the Temple of Herod has never seen a beautiful building in his life.*

Alexander crossed the outer court, known as the Court of the Gentiles, then climbed fifteen steps and entered through a gateway into the Court of Women. This was a large space surrounded by porticoes where scholars often gathered for debating the various laws of the Talmud, but its corners were set aside for storage of priestly supplies. Authorized persons, of which Alexander was one, could walk up another fifteen curved steps through the Gate of Nicanor to enter the innermost court. This was actually a double court_the

Court of the Men of Israel and the Court of the Priests. On its sides were porticoes, one being the Chamber of the Hearth, where priests on duty could spend their nights, and on the other, the Chamber of Hewn Stone, where the Sanhedrin met. The latter was his destination and he picked up his pace, not wanting to be late for his meeting. Although the province was designated as Palestine by the Romans and was officially ruled by Caesar Augustus, the seventy-one member Jewish Council, known as the Sanhedrin, maintained a considerable amount of power in directing civil and ecclesiastical affairs. However, their powers were not limitless, in that they could not carry out capital punishment or executions.

Entering the chambers made of massive cut stones, he quickly sensed his inadequacy with the priests, scribes, and elders who were milling about. Before he had time to strike up a conversation with anyone, the Chief Priest Caiaphas, signaled for the ram's horn to be sounded and the men quickly took their assigned seats bordering the walls of the room. Alexander's chair was the last in the elongated semi-circle.

"The topic of our discussion today," began Caiaphas," will be complaints regarding one Jesus of Nazareth."

"He's a fraud. We all know that the Messiah will come from Bethlehem, not Nazareth," shouted one of the older men.

"He's a blasphemer," called out one raising his fist in anger.

"He performs his miracles through the spirit of the devil," said another.

"Quiet! Quiet in the chambers. We will discuss the matter in a civilized manner. We will speak in order of seniority."

Alexander sat and listened to the harangue, doubting if he would be allowed a turn to speak. Nevertheless, he had already decided what he would say if he were called upon. It would be an embarrassment to himself and his father's honor if he were to stammer like an unprepared schoolboy. It was obvious that the attitude of the majority of the council was not favorable toward the wandering preacher. The Pharisees and Sadducees had been called hypocrites by Jesus too many times, not because of their strict adherence to the Law, but for neglecting the virtues of mercy, justice, faith and forgiveness.

Before he knew it, all the others had voiced their opinion and he heard Caiaphas announce, "Now we shall hear from our youngest member of the Council, Alexander, son of Hosea."

Alexander stood in front of his seat and once again felt like a lad being quizzed by his Torah teachers in Synagogue School. His throat felt dry and he wasn't sure how to begin, but with almost seventy pairs of eyes glued on him, he knew he had to say something. He glanced at Nicodemus, the member of the Council seated next to him and the older man nodded for him to proceed.

"I thank you for the privilege of speaking to the revered members of the Sanhedrin today. Although I am the youngest among you, I must ask you the question: Have you been in the presence of Jesus yourself or do you form your opinion based on the hearsay and gossip of others?'" Alexander didn't wait for a response. "I for one have been close to him and had him speak to me. He does not take a stand against the Law of Moses; no, he calls upon us to live it more fully. He only wants us to look beyond the ritual and remember the meaning behind the sacrifices. He wants us to show more kindness and compassion to the poor. I, for one, cannot argue against these things."

There was a rustling of robes as the older men shifted uncomfortably, wanting to speak out, but not daring to do so out of turn. Alexander continued. "I have seen some who have appeared to be healed by his touch. I cannot say by what power it is done, whether by the power of the devil or by the power of God. But certainly, the lives of those who have been healed and their families are better off for it.

"Lest you think that I am one of his disciples, I will assure you that I am not one of those in his inner circle. He gave me specific counsel of what I would have to do to be called one of his disciples. I admit that I do not have the courage to follow it, which would mean giving up everything of value to me and my family to follow after him. Nor, do I believe that many others will. Therefore, I think that the movement will die out of its own accord.

"I agree with Nicodemus who has just spoken to you, and recommend that we leave him alone, let him tell his parables to the poor. His pathetic followers will never have the gumption to overthrow Rome, even though some are heralding him as the Messiah. We know that the Messiah will come in power and authority and free us from the bondage of our enemies. Some in the past have risen up and claimed that role, but we can see that nothing has come of it. Let us use wisdom and prudence, and let the whole matter just fade away of its own accord."

Alexander sat down, tuning out the buzz of conversation that Caiaphas allowed to take place for a few moments. "Well stated, Alexander Bar Hosea," commented the man sitting next to him. Again Alexander thought of his teacher who had used those same words long ago. His eyes were drawn to the gleam of jeweled rings on the older man's bony fingers and that the sleeves of his robe were decorated with a familiar-looking green and brown ribbon.

"Thank you Nicodemus. My father often spoke of you with great respect."

Their conversation was interrupted by a call to order by the High Priest. "Since the members of the Council cannot come to a consensus on a course of action, we will wait a while longer before we initiate any charges against this man Jesus. If we try to arrest him, his followers will stir up the Roman soldiers against us. We could be opening up a hive of swarming bees that might overtake us and we would lose our positions. For the time being let us be alert, learn more if we can, and be cautious. The Council is dismissed."

Some of the men spoke favorably to Alexander, clapping him on the back and shaking his hand as he exited the chamber, but others turned their backs on him. Obviously, those had not gotten their own way in this debate. He reveled in the praise of the elders for a brief moment, but somehow as he walked down the steps of the Temple he was downcast rather than elated. He felt the uneasiness that he had somehow betrayed a friend.

Still on the Temple Mount, Alexander spotted a large group of people near the colonnades of Solomon's porch and out of curiosity ambled toward it. In the center of the group a number of Pharisees stood, the long tassels on their prayer shawls and the enlarged phylacteries strapped to their foreheads and left upper arms designating them as pious Jews. On the ground in front of them knelt a woman who was obviously distraught, as her clothes were disheveled and her tangled hair splayed out around her head. Then Alexander spotted Jesus who was stooped beside her tracing his finger in the dust. He moved closer to the onlookers and in a whispered tone asked one, "What's going on?"

The man turned, staring at Alexander in his council robes, then said quietly, "The Pharisees brought this woman whom they said was taken in the very act of adultery. They recited the Law of Moses to Jesus as if he didn't already know it. Then they asked Jesus what he thought. It was obviously a trick to get him to cross his words."

"What did Jesus say?"

"Nothing. He just knelt down and started drawing his finger on the ground as if he didn't even hear them."

The Pharisees continued their badgering. "Thou knowest the Law, this woman should be stoned." The crowd waited in silent anticipation wondering what the Master would say. If he supported the Law as every good Jew should, the woman would be killed. If he excused the woman's behavior, the Pharisees could rightly claim that Jesus was antagonistic toward the Law and they would have more evidence to convict him.

Then Jesus stood and said unto them, "He that is without sin among you, let him first cast a stone at her." Then stooping down, he again wrote on the ground, although no one could discern what he was writing. Not a word was said, but one by one beginning with the eldest, each of the Pharisees slipped quietly away. Jesus and the woman were left all alone in the clearing.

Jesus then stood, and looking around said, "Woman, where are those thine accusers? Hath no man condemned thee?"

The woman raised her tear-stained face and looked at the empty courtyard. "No man, Lord."

Jesus took her by the hand and raised her up saying, "Neither do I condemn thee. Go and sin no more." *(See John 8:1-11)*

The woman looked up with surprise at his gentle words and the kindness in his face. She quickly gathered her shawl about her and ran from the scene. The crowd murmured among themselves. "Why did he forgive her? She was obviously guilty."

"I've heard him claim he has the power to forgive sins. But only God can do that."

"He didn't say he forgave her, just that he didn't condemn her."

"What does that mean?"

"It means he's giving her a second chance. An opportunity to repent and sin no more."

"We all sin."

"I'm sometimes confused by what Jesus says. It's like he talks in riddles."

Alexander, dressed in his cream-colored robes and fine leather shoes, felt out of place among the disciples of Jesus who mostly wore homespun and sandals. He turned to leave and saw Jesus pointing at the sun, "I am the light of the world. He that follows me shall not walk in darkness, but shall have the light of life." (John 8:12)"

On the way home, the rich young man contemplated Jesus' comments. *Whenever I hear the words of Jesus I get a warm feeling. What a contrast to the negativity displayed in the Council meeting. I felt peace when I was compassionate and served others in Alexandria. Is that my answer? Is my wealth a blessing or a curse? Is eternal life beyond my reach? Am I choosing to walk in darkness at mid-day?*

The flickering torchlight cast vibrating shadows off the faces of the wedding guests surrounding the silk canopy that Alexander had recently brought from his travels to Egypt. Everyone was focused on Rebecca and her new husband, Simeon, as they performed the ritualistic circle dance. Only an hour earlier, as the night of a new day was beginning on this Tuesday, considered the luckiest day of the week to begin a marriage, Alexander had marched through the streets with his brother Silvanus, who had come from Joppa for the occasion, and with his new brother-in-law and his companions. Through the darkened streets they walked with torches, singing with a boisterousness that brought neighbors to peer out their doorways and cheer the procession onward.

Meanwhile, Rebecca was waiting with her maidens at her home where she had been clothed in her beautiful wedding garments and the embroidered rosebud ribbon braided into her clean and shiny dark hair. A long silk veil edged with fringe was draped over her head so that her face would not be seen by her bridegroom until the wedding ceremony. It seemed to Rebecca that she had been sitting on the low stool for hours. *Will Simeon never come? What if he has changed his mind? Am I ready to become a wife?* At last came the call, "The Bridegroom cometh!" Ida gave Rebecca a motherly kiss and a final hug, wondering where the past sixteen years had gone. As Simeon escorted Rebecca, all of the wedding guests followed behind, carrying their small oil-filled lamps to light their way to the home of Simeon's uncle where the ceremony and feast would take place.

Alexander thought of a parable about a marriage procession which he'd heard Jesus tell just a few days earlier about ten virgins who waited for a bridegroom to appear. For some unexplained reason, the man's appearance was delayed and the virgins had grown sleepy in the night's shadows. All of a sudden came the cry that the bridegroom was coming and the girls sprang to their feet to join the celebration, But the lights had gone out in their lamps, and five had not had the foresight to bring extra oil. They begged for their friends to share oil with them but were refused lest they too not have sufficient to complete the journey. The five unlucky virgins, whom Jesus had termed 'foolish", had run to the market to buy more oil only to find that all the shops were closed. They finally made their way to the home where the wedding and feast were taking place, but the door was already shut, and they were not allowed to enter. Alexander wondered what the point of the story was: *lack of preparation? Procrastination? What did the oil represent? He was sure that Jesus intended some lesson from this story. Why was it sometimes so hard to understand his teachings?*

The next morning Alexander and Silvanus both with bloodshot eyes complained of headaches from drinking too much wine at the feast. Ida's eyes were also red, not from liquor but from crying. "Don't be sad, Mother," they said as they tried to comfort her. "This is supposed to be a happy time."

"Oh, I am happy for Rebecca. I'm just feeling sorry for myself," blubbered Ida through her tears. "It just means that all of my children are gone and I'm feeling so alone." Alexander and Silvanus looked at each other with consternation; neither had experience in giving comfort to their mother. She was always the one who had wiped away their tears when they had scraped a knee or been teased by older boys calling them 'Half-breeds' because of their mixed cultural parentage.

All of a sudden Alexander had an idea! "Mother, why don't you travel with me to Alexandria when I return there next week? It will give you an opportunity to meet Helene and all of her family."

"Haven't you said many times that you would like to return to the land of your nativity, Mother?' asked Silvanus. "This seems like a perfect time."

Ida opened her eyes with a newly found eagerness at the suggestion. "I always wanted to go back to Alexandria, but it was never convenient. Between your father's business trips and having babies or being here for you children, it never worked out."

"Do you have any family still living there?" asked Silvanus. "I'm sorry I don't know much about that side of our family."

"Yes, I have a sister and a brother, and many cousins."

"Well then, it's settled," said Alexander. "The order of shawls from the weavers should be completed within a few days. I know there will be agents in both Joppa and Alexandria anxious to have our new batch of merchandise and I can see if there is any more silk fabric available for purchase. Our last shipment sold out so quickly, I would like to get more for our Jerusalem customers."

"This is all so sudden," whispered Ida. "I don't know....But it does sound like an ideal time to go. There's nothing to keep me in Jerusalem right now," another sob choking off her last words.

"I will book passage for us as soon as possible then," declared her eldest son grateful that the idea and solution to his mother's sorrow that had so unexpectedly come to him.

More than three months passed and Alexander again stood near the bow of a ship studying the stars that seemed closer than ever. Although the North Star was the brightest, he could easily see the long band of soft gauzy light stretching across the horizon that gave the Milky Way its name. A crescent of a waxing moon was overhead and it glistened off the undulating waves. The steady drumbeat and the swish of the oars were a sad reminder of what was going on below him. He had spoken with the ship's captain about increasing the water supply to the oarsmen in the hot weather. But beyond that, there wasn't anything he could do. As bad as it was, he couldn't change the system. Alexander was too keyed up to sleep even though his lovely wife Helene was slumbering peacefully in their cabin nearby. He had been absent from Jerusalem longer than expected, but it had all worked out for the best. There wasn't any silk available in Alexandria, but he stocked up on several bolts of the cotton that was always a good investment and bought the dozen ribbons that Helene had embroidered in his absence. He told her that she was starting a whole new fashion craze in Jerusalem with her wares. Assured that circumstances had been serendipitous, he was glad for the delay that had resulted not only in his proposal to Helene but the very marriage itself. She had been as eager as he to begin this journey to her new home in Jerusalem.

Putting his thoughts into reverse, he recalled when he was on his way to Alexandria and contemplating the teachings and miracles of Jesus. The thought had come like a flash of lightning, yes, even right here on the same deck that he was now standing on. Of course, why hadn't he thought of it earlier! Jesus could heal Helene's lameness! He had heard of many such miracles happening throughout the Galilee and Judea, so he knew that Jesus had the power. They just had to get Helene back to Jerusalem first and then locate the whereabouts of the Master Healer. But he hadn't brought this idea up right away. He wanted to be sure that Helene truly loved him and wasn't just consenting to a marriage as an indirect way of finding a cure for her disability. He was soon assured of her true devotion to him.

The Greeks were not bound to the traditions of a year-long betrothal period as the Jews were, so the wedding arrangements had been made quite quickly. It was fortunate that his mother had come along on the trip for she had been as delighted with the lovely Helene as Alexander had hoped. Ida had also reunited with her brother and sister and met their grown children which had made the trip even more special for the siblings who had been separated for a quarter of a century. The family of Damian was also known to Ida's kin, and approval was given that they were indeed honorable and respected members of the community.

After a few quiet days in a seaside villa together, Alexander and Helene were on their way to his home in Jerusalem, accompanied by Ida and Silvanus. How grateful Alexander was to have found such a beautiful and willing wife. He hoped to make her happy for the rest of their lives whether she was healed or not. He knew of her great skill with a needle and had given her the option of continuing her trade if she desired, even though it wasn't an economic necessity. He hoped she would soon be included in his circle of merchant friends and their wives and not feel the same sense of exclusion that his mother had felt. There was much more intermingling of Jew and Gentile under Roman domination than there was when Hosea had brought Ida to Jerusalem..

Coming back to the present, Alexander gazed northward toward

Joppa and Jonah came into his mind. That ancient prophet had been called by the Lord to exhort the people of Nineveh to repentance. The Ninevites were known for their immorality and worshipping of pagan gods and Jonah thought there was no way that they would change. So Jonah had refused the call and boarded a ship in Joppa rather than traveling eastward to the capital city of Assyria. A terrible storm soon broke out and Jonah confessed to his shipmates that it was probably his fault for running away from the Lord. Reluctantly, the other seamen threw him overboard with their superstitious hopes of appeasing Jonah's god so that the storm would cease. A large fish swallowed Jonah and the man spent three days inside its belly before being spewed out upon the seashore.

Those three days had given Jonah time to reconsider the call to preach the gospel and he repented of his cowardice. The Lord gave him a second chance to prove his faith. And the people of Nineveh hearkened to the preaching of Jonah and repented, thus saving their lives and their city.

Alexander had always believed this story to be more myth than truth until Jesus himself used it in his teachings to the Pharisees who asked for a sign. Jesus said that the only sign they would receive would be the sign of Jonah. *What did that mean? A second chance? Was the Lord now also giving him a second chance? He, the rich young ruler who had turned away grieving because of the commandment to sell all that he had and give it to the poor?*

Alexander remembered two other stories told by Jesus because they involved merchants. Jesus had likened the kingdom of heaven first to a treasure hidden in a field, which when a man found it made him so joyful that he sold all that he had in order to buy the property. The second story was similar but was likened unto a merchant man seeking goodly pearls, and when he found a pearl of great price, he sold all that he had and bought it. In both stories, the seeker found something so precious that they were willing to give everything else of value so that they might obtain it. Alexander realized that he had experienced peace and joy as he had sacrificed even a small portion of his wealth to bless the lives of those less fortunate. *Is my faith growing? Is there a second chance now for me? There's no denying that I am believing more strongly in Jesus as a prophet. I can't wait to hear him preach again. What will I be willing to sacrifice for Helene, my greatest treasure, that she might be healed?*

On the other hand, he didn't want to disappoint his bride; he had, after all, presented himself as a rich merchant. He couldn't be a chameleon that changed his appearance and lifestyle now that he was married and only offer her a hovel. Would the Master even remember him? The prophet had undoubtedly encountered thousands in his journeys and healed hundreds. Maybe if Jesus didn't recognize him, he wouldn't have to pay such a high price after all.

A burly hand grasped him on the shoulder and Alexander, tensing up from the touch, couldn't help being startled. Turning to face the intruder, he quickly recognized his brother Silvanus even in the dim moonlight. He still couldn't get over how much his brother had grown in the past year. Working outside as a ship-building apprentice, the eighteen-year-old had formed solid muscles and increased in strength. Alexander felt like a weakling beside him.

"Can't sleep?" Alexander asked.

"No, it's too hot. I'm used to being out in the open air most of the time, so the confines of that tiny cabin have me feeling hemmed in." Silvanus bent his back and stretched his arms in the open space of the bow. "The same with you?"

"No, just too much on my mind. I'm so glad you were able to get permission from your master to have a few weeks off to come to my wedding. It meant a lot to me to have you there."

"I'm glad too. I hope someday I can find a woman as lovely as Helene."

"It will happen when the time is right. Just like it did for me."

"I know we've talked about this before, Alexander, but I'm wondering if your feelings about Jesus have changed."

"I'm still struggling with the full commitment that Jesus said I would have to make."

"You can be a disciple without giving up everything. There are several believers in Joppa and they haven't done that."

"I know there are the Ten Commandments from Moses and then some six hundred rules that the Pharisees say we should abide by. Those are general commandments for everyone. But sometimes there seems to be some commandments that are just for us personally. I think that Jesus asking me to sell all my possessions and give my money to the poor is one of those meant just for me. I often wonder why I was asked to sacrifice so much, but I've not been able to get an answer. If I could keep my wealth, I would declare my loyalty to that man without question."

"Do you think he is the promised Messiah?"

"I'm still not sure about that yet. But I do believe he is a Prophet. And I do believe that he has the power to cure Helene if it is his will. I intend to seek him out as soon as we arrive back in Jerusalem. What are your feelings, Silvanus?"

"I too believe he is a prophet. I haven't seen him in person, but many from Joppa have. We meet together on the Sabbath at Simeon The Tanner's home and discuss his teachings. I admit that I believe without seeing."

"You have great faith, brother. I wish I could say the same for myself. You are also blessed to have a group to meet with. I feel so alone in my search. It would be good to have someone else to talk with. I mean someone in Jerusalem. Most of my acquaintances are among those who are trying to get rid of the man."

"Surely there is a group of believers that meet together there."

"Yes, I will search for them too. Even if I don't feel worthy to join, I would like to learn more." Alexander was quiet for a few more minutes and then said, "I think I will try to get some sleep now. We should arrive in Joppa by tomorrow afternoon and I will be glad to have my feet on solid ground once again."

Silvanus just laughed and said "Good Night."

The camels were loaded with their packs and Alexander was relieved in a way that he hadn't found his usual merchandise in Alexandria. Helene had more than doubled the load with all of her clothing and household furnishings. The women were ready to enter the palanquins Alexander had rented for Helene and his mother, hoping to make the trip from Joppa to Jerusalem a little more comfortable for them. The two camels, not used to the feel of the enclosed litters on their backs, were nervously trying to shake them off. Alexander, mounted on Spartan, was anxious to be on his way and yelled at the handlers to get the camels under control. They had been at the caravansary in Joppa a day longer than he had planned already.

Just then Alexander heard a voice calling his name and he looked beyond the stabling area to see Silvanus running toward him and he quickly dismounted.

Out of breath, the younger man stammered, "Alexander,... I'm glad... I caught you... before you left."

"What's the trouble, brother?" he asked with concern in his voice.

"Have you heard the news?"

"What news?"

"That Jesus has been crucified," sobbed Silvanus.

Alexander's jaw dropped and for a moment he was speechless. All of his hopes for Helene were now shattered in an instant. Finally, he asked, "When?"

"It was during Passover."

"You mean three months ago?"

"Yes. It must have happened soon after Rebecca's wedding when you left for Alexandria."

All this time Alexander had been dreaming of bringing his beloved to Jesus and having him lay his hands on her and heal her crippled leg. And the man had been dead all that time. Then he chided himself for his self-centeredness and shifted his sorrow to those who had associated closely with The Healer. "What about his followers?"

"I don't know much. Simeon The Tanner said that they had most likely gone into hiding, probably back to Galilee."

"So Simeon is the one who told you this?"

"Yes, when I saw him near the docks last night. He keeps in close touch with Jesus' disciples, so I think his information is reliable."

"Does he know how it happened?" asked Alexander.

"You know the Pharisees had been out to get Jesus for a long time. Apparently, they were able to arrest him on trumped up charges of treason and took him before Pilate. The Governor gave in to the rabble, trying to protect his own neck, that Scumbag, and ordered his crucifixion."

"Crucifixion. That is the most horrible means of death the Romans have ever devised, although they aren't the first in the world's history to do it."

"There were many of us who thought he was the promised Messiah," groaned Silvanus, "but it was just another false claim, after all."

"All for nothing. All for nothing."

"I must get back to work, Alexander. I'm glad I could be the one to tell you first."

"Thank you, Silvanus," and the two brothers gave each other a parting embrace.

Their return to Jerusalem was bittersweet. Alexander loved showing Helene her new home and she marveled at its size and the exotic furnishings collected from all over the known world. The servants respected her position as the new mistress of the household but weren't quite ready to relinquish their loyalty to Alexander's mother. It was also difficult for Ida to take a back seat when she had managed the household for years. There weren't any bad feelings between the two women__yet, but Alexander knew they were each trying not to step on the other's toes. Helene spent a lot of her time embroidering the ribbons, as that gave her a feeling of accomplishment, although it also made her homesick for her family.

Alexander went about his business duties half-heartedly and attended Sanhedrin Council meetings with even less enthusiasm. One day following a session, he pulled Nicodemus aside and asked about Jesus.

"Did the Council really sanction Jesus' death?'

"Well, the members of the Council who were in attendance sanctioned it. I was not notified of the meeting for obvious reasons," replied the older man.

"You mean it was done without the full body of members?"

"Oh, yes. Hand-picked they were. And at night no less."

"Why, that's illegal."

Stroking his gray beard, Nicodemus nodded, "Of course, and they all knew it. Nonetheless, that is what happened."

"How did they get a charge of treason against him? Jesus has never initiated a revolt against the Romans. In fact, he was always careful to pay their taxes."

"I don't know for sure since I wasn't there. But they convinced Pontius Pilate of it. That man is such a coward; afraid he is going to lose his position here. He even sent Jesus to Herod in hopes that he would settle the case, but Herod just sent him back to Pilate. I do have to give him credit that he tried to talk the Chief Priests out of it by offering another prisoner, Barabbas, in an exchange, but they would have nothing to do with it."

"We had such great hopes for our people. Now they're all gone."

"Come, Alexander. Walk with me out into the Temple courtyard, there is something else I'd like to tell you."

The two men climbed up the steps, passing through the Court of the Gentiles, and then into the Court of Women, finding a bit of shade under Solomon's Porch. Memories of listening to Jesus preach in this very spot flooded Alexander's mind. He felt that part of the guilt for Jesus' death was his own. Not that he had voted for it, nor would he have if he had been present. But by being a merchant, and feeding the greed of the Chief Priests through expensive apparel now left him with a blot on his conscience.

"What is it Nicodemus?" asked Alexander.

Looking around to make sure that no one was within earshot, although the crowds were much thinner now that Jesus was no longer preaching here, Nicodemus still spoke softly. "There's reports come back to the believers that Jesus is alive."

"What?"

"I know it does sound crazy."

"You mean he wasn't really killed?"

"Oh, he was killed alright. I helped Joseph of Arimathea take his body from the cross and prepare it for burial in a tomb that Joseph recently had constructed for his own father."

"Then what do you mean alive? Come back to life?'

"Yes, that is exactly what I mean," said Nicodemus looking Alexander directly in the eyes." Did you hear about Jesus raising Lazarus from the dead?"

"No" he paused for a moment to think. "Perhaps that took place after I left for Alexandria."

"Lazarus is the brother to Mary and Martha___"

"Yes, I met those women before, at one of the campsites, but not their brother."

"While Jesus was preaching in Perea, Lazarus became very sick. His disciples told him, thinking he would immediately leave and return to Bethany where the man lived with his sisters and heal him. The family was such great supporters of him, after all."

"But he didn't go to help his close friends? After he had healed so many others?"

"No," continued Nicodemus. "In fact, he even waited four days after he heard that Lazarus had died before he crossed the Jordan and returned to this area. Four days, Alexander. You know what a corpse smells like after four days."

"Yes, I suppose I do. Are you trying to tell me that Jesus brought Lazarus back to life after he had been dead four days?" (See John 11:8-46)

"Absolutely. There are hundreds of witnesses to the fact."

"I'm sure that was the last straw that broke the camel's back, so to speak, as far as the Pharisees were concerned. There would be no denying his divinity with that kind of an action."

"You're very right, young man."

"So how did they apprehend him? He has slipped away from them so many times."

"This is one of the saddest parts of the whole story," and Nicodemus swallowed hard to keep from choking on his own words. "Judas betrayed him."

"You mean one of his own specially chosen disciples?"

"Yes. The priests negotiated a deal with him for thirty pieces of silver."

"The price of a slave?"

Nicodemus nodded his head in silence. "And it has been said that he identified Jesus to the temple guards by giving him a kiss and calling him Master."

"What a traitor! What happened to him afterward?"

"He couldn't face up to his own guilt and killed himself."

"I never really knew the man, but I still don't understand how someone who had worked so closely with Jesus for three years could do such a thing."

"No one does."

So what about this tale that Jesus is alive again?" asked Alexander getting back to the original point of their conversation.

"The twelve disciples each testify that Jesus has been resurrected; that he has appeared to them on multiple occasions."

"Are they sure it is him? This all sounds so unbelievable."

"They have felt the nail prints in his hands and side. And Jesus has declared that he has risen from the dead."

"He's spoken to them?"

"Oh yes, and eaten food with them."

"Then it's not just a spirit?"

"No, no. His spirit and body have been reunited."

"Why, if that's true, it is wonderful news! Jesus would be able to continue his work and no one could deny that he's the Son of God that he always claimed to be. He can bring about the freedom of bondage from the Romans and the people of Israel can truly be free just as the promised Messiah is supposed to do. They would never be able to kill him again. This changes everything! Where can I find him? I've been wanting to bring my new wife Helene to him in hopes that he would cure her lameness."

"Slow down, young man. Things have changed."

"I don't understand. If he's alive, then__"

"Even though Jesus has appeared to more than five hundred people__"

"Five hundred?" Alexander asked incredulously.

"Yes. But he is no longer here."

"Where did he go? I will go anywhere to find him."

"The disciples say that he ascended into heaven right before their very eyes."

"So he's not here, after all?" asked Alexander with a downcast face.

"No. But he promised that he will return someday. We can only hope that it will be very soon."

"So what happens in the meantime?"

The Twelve__"

"I thought that you said Judas killed himself. How can there be twelve?"

"They chose a new man named Mathias to fill the vacancy in their quorum. They say that Jesus has commissioned them to preach his same gospel to the whole world."

"So Jesus gave them the authority to carry on while he's gone?"

"Yes. The believers are meeting together, but in secret, so as not to raise the suspicions of the chief priests. The work initiated by Jesus is going forward. I myself attend their meetings as often as possible, although I cannot make it public at the present. I feel that I can serve his cause best by remaining on the Council, giving them private information that might alert them to any danger, or such."

"You are a follower of Jesus yourself?"

"Yes, I was baptized by James, who is now called the Bishop of Jerusalem. It is Peter, James, and John who have taken over the leadership and have formed a church."

"So they no longer attend the synagogue?"

"No" he dragged out the one syllable, "They have been excommunicated from all religious and social gatherings. In fact, we meet together on the first day of the week, not the seventh. The leaders say this is a whole new order of things."

Alexander looked at the older man as if he thought Nicodemus might be losing his mind, he was getting old, after all.

Nicodemus seemed to read Alexander's thoughts. "I testify with my whole soul that what I have told you is true, Alexander. And I do it that you might know that all is not lost. There is still great hope for the future when Jesus returns to reign as King of Kings."

"Thank you for your words, Nicodemus. I sense your trust in me and I will not betray that trust. But you have given me more to think about than I can absorb in one day. I must have time."

"Certainly, Alexander. Certainly. When you are ready I will let you know the meeting place."

Helene and Ida sat in the shade of a lemon tree on the roof of their home, trying to catch any breeze that fluttered up from the Kidron Valley below. Both were embroidering, Helene on her ribbons and Ida on a shawl.

"Thank you for welcoming me into your home, Ida. You have been most kind to me."

"It's not hard to be kind to such a sweet young woman. Alexander made a wise choice when he found you."

"It's really rather a miracle that our paths ever crossed."

"Speaking of miracles, what do you think of the miracles performed by Jesus? Do you believe they're true?"

"Yes, I do," answered Helene. "There are too many witnesses for them to all be fabricated stories."

"Then you believe that he was a prophet?"

"I assume that would be a proper title, although I am not too familiar yet with all the terms used by the Jews."

"I can understand your confusion. It took me years to sort it all out."

"But you never converted to Judaism, Ida. May I ask why?"

"You know that I gave up the worshipping of multiple gods as taught by the Greeks many years ago. I suppose it comes down to the idea that I believe that we are all children of one God and that he loves everyone who is obedient to his commandments. I don't go along with the idea of the Jews being the 'Chosen People" and that they are the only ones entitled to God's blessings. I just chose to worship in my own private way here at home when Hosea went out to the Synagogue."

"You have mentioned feeling like an outsider here in Jerusalem. Do you feel that not converting to their religion contributed to that?"

"Absolutely."

"What do you suggest that I do? For Alexander's sake as well as my own."

Ida paused letting Helene know that she was giving the question serious thought before answering. "I feel that one's desires and methods of worshipping are for that person to decide. I see the value in having a congregation to meet with and friends within that congregation, but worshipping God has to transcend social status. Worshipping requires the giving of one's heart and love to an unseen being, and that applies to every religion man has ever devised. No one has ever seen God. He is a mystery that is beyond man's understanding. Yet I believe that he created the earth and that we are here for a purpose, although even after all of these years I don't know what that purpose is."

"Alexander has tried to explain some of the teachings of Jesus to me and they make sense, even though I don't understand all things."

"I wish I had made more of an effort to see and hear Jesus himself when he was alive, and often in this very city. Then perhaps I would have a better feeling about him."

"I wish that I had had that opportunity as well."

"But he is dead," Ida said with a sigh, "so I suppose that will be the end of it."

"Alexander says that his followers are still gathering together, although he hasn't participated in any of their meetings yet. I know that he spends a great deal of time pondering about what little he has heard." There was silence between the two for several minutes as they each weighed their own thoughts. Then Helene added, "I have to admit that I had hopes that Jesus would be able to heal my leg, but that is never going to happen now."

"You've learned to manage quite well, Helene. I'm amazed at all the things you can do in spite of your disability. In fact, I have been giving an idea some thought, but know I need to discuss it with both you and Alexander."

"What's that?"

"That I move to Joppa and help care for Silvanus. He is almost through with his apprenticeship and will need to find new lodgings. He doesn't have a wife, nor any servants to manage a household for him. Perhaps I am needed there more than here, now that you are managing this household so efficiently."

"Oh, Ida. I hope you don't feel that I have taken over your role. This has been your home for many years. All the servants adore you."

"I know. But it is really Alexander's home, not mine. He inherited it when his father died. That's the way of Jewish laws__everything is controlled by the men and women have no legal rights."

"Ida, I love you and so enjoy your company. You seem to understand me, even better than Alexander sometimes. I'm sure it's because of our common background. I would miss you very much."

"Well, it's not something that needs to be decided right away, but I do think it is worth considering. Besides, one of these days, you'll have your own little ones about to keep you company," and Ida raised a questioning eyebrow.

"Not yet, Ida, although I hope to provide an heir for Alexander in the near future," Helene said, her cheeks blushing to a bright red.

"And I can't wait to become a grandmother," said Ida. "That is a position of great respect and honor in Jewish society that I whole-heartedly agree with." Both women laughed and hugged each other in mutual adoration.

Alexander approached the front entrance of his office noticing a familiar form crouched near the door. "Doesn't that beggar have anywhere else to go?" the merchant asked himself. He flipped a small coin in the man's direction, but the beggar missed the catch in his stubby fingers and scrambled on the cobblestones to pick it up. Alexander entered the warehouse where he scanned his shelves, making notes of his inventory. Then a thought hit him like a load of bricks: *What would Jesus have done to the beggar? Surely spoken to him; probably lifted him up; given encouragement, a blessing.* Even though that same man had been at Alexander's door for months, he couldn't recall having ever seen the man's face. *Was he old or young? In fact, the only physical attribute I can remember are the stubby fingers. What brought about this degrading situation? Was he injured? Was he born that way? Was he just lazy?* Alexander tried to shake the niggling thoughts away as he reviewed his accounting ledgers and what merchandise he needed to take on his next journey to Joppa. The stacks of shawls were definitely low and he decided to stop by the weaver's shop that he ordered from on his way home.

Walking through the crowded streets of Jerusalem took longer than usual. Everywhere he looked there were beggars holding out a cup or a hand. When had the population of the poor and needy in the city increased? Or had it always been this way and he had just been blind to it? What could he, one man, do when there were so many? Even if the money from all the rich men in Judea were combined, it would not be enough to take care of the poor in Jerusalem.

Again Alexander thought of Jesus and the promise that he would return in glory and overthrow their oppressors. *With his miraculous powers, he could conjure up food for everyone. Would that be the answer to the problem?*

Alexander turned into the Street of the Weavers and made his way toward the shop of Ezra Ben Mesha at the end of the street. As he got closer, he saw that the familiar hand-lettered sign was no longer swinging above the door. What was wrong? He picked up his pace and soon found himself in front of what remained of the weaver's shop. The building was half-charred and obviously uninhabitable.

"What happened to Ben Ezra?" he called out to a candle maker in the shop next door.

"Oh, 'twas a sad day about one moon ago. Remember when we had that bad thunder and lightning storm? The timbers of the roof caught fire and with the weather being so hot and dry this season, it went up in flames very quickly. Praise to the Lord that mine didn't burn as well. Although I feel sorry for the Mesha family. We have worked side by side for a long time. Let me think, I believe it was first back in the year..."

Alexander interrupted the garrulous man asking, "Do you know where I might find Ezra? He is a supplier of shawls that I often take to Joppa and Alexandria."

"They are trying to carry on in their courtyard for the time being. But that will only last another moon or so before the rains start coming. Yes, we can usually count on the rains soon after the Feast of Dedication. Praise the Lord!"

"Where is Ezra's home? Do you know where he lives?"

"Oh yes, you just go to the end of the street and turn left, west I believe that would be. Yes, west. Then go to the Cheesemaker's Street and turn right. Then..."

"Thanks for your help. I'll get more specific directions as I get closer."

Alexander was on his way while the candle maker was still scratching his beard. "No, maybe you turn right at the Cheesemakers....." The merchant knew that the easiest way to locate the weaver was to hire a linkboy to lead him there. Having money was so useful in so many aspects of his life. He soon located a lad of about ten years of age that assured him he knew the way to the Ben Mesha home and was relieved when the boy took him there without delay.

Alexander knocked on the door and was soon welcomed in by Ezra's wife, Golda. "I was sorry to hear of the loss of your shop," he told the woman. "Was anyone injured?"

"No, thank the Lord, and we were able to salvage some of the spools of thread and a few shawls that had been completed, although they do smell like smoke. We're trying to keep up on the order that you gave us, but Ezra had to build a new loom, and it has slowed us down. He works so hard, day and night."

"May I speak to Ezra?"

"Certainly, if you don't mind coming through the house to the courtyard in back. That way he could continue working while he speaks to you. Please excuse the humbleness of our abode."

"You are most kind, Golda." As she led him through the house, he observed only the most basic of furnishings: a wooden table with two benches pushed against the wall, a cupboard with a few dishes, pots, and cups, a brick oven built into the wall for baking, and a large pot holding about two firkins of water with two smaller jugs on the floor nearby.

"Good afternoon, friend Ezra," Alexander greeted the weaver who sat on a stool, busy sliding a shuttle over and under the threads with an experienced hand. "I was so sorry to hear of the loss of your shop."

"Hello, Alexander. Yes, it was a great sadness for us all. We had been at that location for many years."

"So your neighbor, the candle maker, told me."

"We didn't let you know about the fire because we still wanted to keep your business and I've been trying to make up for lost time. But with only one loom, we are obviously running behind."

"I commend you for your diligence and your concern for me. I have always admired the fine shawls that you have made and they sell well in Joppa and Alexandria." Suddenly an unbidden thought came into the merchant's mind: *You may not be able to help everyone, Alexander, but you can help one.* Alexander looked around to see if someone had spoken, but he knew the words had come into his mind and heart from another source. It was as if Jesus was standing beside him whispering in his ear.

"How many looms did you lose in the fire, Ezra?"

"One large one and two small ones."

"Did you employ other weavers or was it strictly a family business?"

"My two daughters are skilled, but they cannot help now with only one loom."

Alexander knew what Jesus would want him to do, so he plunged forward before he lost the feeling which had overcome him and started counting his pennies. "Ezra, because you are such a skilled craftsman and that I consider you a friend, I would like to propose a possible solution to your problem. I have ample space in my warehouse at present for two or three looms. If you could recommend a good carpenter or two, we could have new ones built before the rainy season starts. You know that you would not be able to keep working out here once the rains come."

Ezra's hands stopped, "That is very kind of you to offer us space. But I can't afford to have two new looms built until I earn sufficient money from the sale of my shawls."

"I can finance the construction of the looms and you can pay me back a little each month at very low interest. In fact, no interest at all."

Alexander couldn't believe the words coming out of his own mouth.

"You would do this for me?" Ezra looked up from his work with tears in his eyes.

"Yes, Ezra Ben Mesha, I will do it for you."

"Your coming is an answer to our prayers, Sir. I can never thank you enough for your generosity."

"Oh, I expect you can, Ezra. Just keep me supplied with your shawls and that will be thanks enough. Let me know when you want to have this loom moved to the warehouse and I can send a cart and donkey to transport it."

"May the Almighty prosper and protect you, Alexander. I never expected someone of your status to be concerned about a common man like me."

"Send a message when you are ready to make the move, Ezra" and the two men shook hands. "We'll talk again soon."

Golda, who had been standing near the back door overheard the whole conversation, and as Alexander turned to leave, she grabbed his hands and kissed them. "Thank you for your mercy to us. We have been praying for an answer, and here you came. God must have sent you."

"I don't make any claim to be his special messenger, Golda I'm just glad that I can help." He didn't want to add that he had certainly felt a divine spirit directing him in what he had just proposed to their family. However, he left the small home and walked up the hill toward his spacious residence feeling happier than he had in a long time.

The rainy season started in the month of Tebeth as usual, but everyone was glad for the moisture as it had been a particularly long and hot summer. Before the rains had come, Alexander and Helene had ventured a few times to the large home of the mother of a young disciple, John Mark, which Nicodemus had told him about. It was the secret location between Bethany and Jerusalem and the Believers met there regularly on the first day of the week. They both wanted to learn more of the teachings of Jesus, however, their arrival always proved awkward. First of all, Alexander had hired litter bearers to carry Helene in a curtained palanquin. But this seemed offensive to others who were of a lower social class, like Alexander was trying to flaunt their wealth and social status. However, when they saw that Helene was crippled, they were a little more understanding. Another time Alexander hired a donkey for Helene to ride, while he rode Spartan. But horses symbolized oppression, war, and political power, so that didn't make a good impression either. Now the unpredictable rain made traveling even those few miles difficult.

Alexander was glad when Jesus's apostle John, no relation to John Mark, started visiting with them and teaching them in their own home. Since the man had been such a close associate of the Master, he had many insights that others didn't know. They especially liked hearing the story of the Samaritan woman that Jesus had met at a well on one of His journeys through that land. Jesus never looked down on anyone based on where they lived or their social status so Helene began to feel that his teachings weren't only for the Jews, but for other people as well.

"I feel that Jesus gave me two chances to follow him," said Alexander. "The first time I turned away from him because of my wealth. The second, on the ship returning from Alexandria, I was reminded of the experiences of the prophet Jonah and felt like I was being given a second chance. But that dream evaporated when I found out that Jesus had already been killed in my absence."

"Don't beat yourself up, Alexander," was John's response. "That is one of the main things that Jesus taught us__repentance is always possible, no matter how many times we might have to start over again. He will never give up on us, and we can't give up on ourselves. I remember a few blunders I made that I've had to repent for. One of them also involved a group of Samaritans that weren't as accepting as the woman at the well. They refused to give us accommodations at an inn for a night simply because we were headed toward Jerusalem and didn't worship at their holy mountain. I wanted to call fire down from heaven upon them for their inhospitality. In fact, when I first met Jesus, he called me and my brother James, Boanerges, which means "Sons of Thunder". Probably because of our zeal and impetuosity."

"You, John? You hardly seem to fit that description now."

"Oh yes, that was in my younger days, and I was among the youngest of the Twelve that Jesus chose. I had a fervor for Him and His work that just burned inside my bones. I was quite overbearing at times. You see, that is what I was trying to tell you about how living the teachings of Jesus can change us. Oh, I haven't lost any of my fervor, but I have learned to express it with a softer voice. I'm probably more like a mewing kitten than thunder." Everyone laughed good-naturedly.

"I might have gotten my disposition from my mother, Salome. Have you met her?'

Alexander and Helene both shook their heads. John continued speaking, "She's a wonderful woman who believed in Jesus almost from the start, as did my father Zebedee. They made it possible for me and James to leave the fishing business my father owned and follow Jesus straightway. But not entirely understanding Jesus's teachings on the nature of eternal life, she one day asked Jesus if James and I could have positions of honor and glory on his left and right hand when he established his kingdom. He said that only his Father could determine who sat in those positions of honor. You can imagine how the other ten disciples felt about us after that. Then Jesus taught all of us an important lesson: that whosoever would be great among us, should be the servant and minister to others."

"Jesus certainly exemplified that in his own life," said Alexander.

"Oh yes, he taught us what it means to love others. In fact, at the last supper in the upper room, the same night he was arrested, he commanded us to love one another as he had done. For there is no greater love than that which is given when a man lays down his life for his friends."

"Didn't Jesus give his life for all of us, not just his friends?" asked Helene.

"Absolutely. His love is as wide as eternity and will never end. I only hope that I can live up to the new nickname which he gave me a short time before his death."

"What was that, John?"

"The Apostle of Love."

Dark clouds were looming overhead, but for now, the rain had stopped. Alexander hustled through the muddy streets hoping to arrive at the Council Chambers before the next shower began. His mood matched the weather. It was becoming more and more wearisome for him to attend these meetings where so much animosity existed. Council business that should be transacted in an hour took two or three. Alexander wanted to honor his father by continuing to have a voice in the affairs of the city, but his practical nature was starting to take precedence over his emotions. Or was it that his emotions were overtaking his once sure sense of duty?

"Hello, old friend," Alexander clamped arms with Nicodemus.

"Glad to see you are surviving this wet weather."

"Barely," coughed the older man. "There are some days I can hardly breathe."

"I hadn't heard that you were ill. I hope that you will improve once the sun returns. If the weather follows its usual pattern, that should only be another week or two. Have you seen a doctor?"

"Oh yes. I found a new physician named Luke that has prescribed some herbs for me that are helping. That is why I felt I had the strength to come to the meeting today." The man paused to cough again. "He's a young Greek fellow. Someone I'd like to introduce you to."

"I would be happy to meet anyone who is a friend of yours, Nicodemus. I don't seem to have many in Jerusalem these days."

"I understand the feeling". He scanned the chambers which were just starting to fill and small groups of men clustered together conversing with one another. "Let's move to the side of the room out of earshot. I understand that you are still studying the words of our "departed friend"," Nicodemus was careful not to utter the name of Jesus too loudly as there was a growing sentiment against the Believers. Many members of the Council had voiced the concern that the number of followers of Jesus had increased rather than declined as they had hoped by getting rid of their leader.

Alexander nodded. "John has been to our home a few times, and Lazarus once, a few others."

"Lazarus, eh?"

"Oh yes. That man either has had the greatest experience ever told or he is the world's biggest fabricator of stories."

"What did he tell you?"

"About the four days his spirit was in what he called paradise, while his mortal body lay in a tomb here on earth. He described it as a place of exquisite beauty and peace where the spirits of the righteous who have departed this life wait for the time of their resurrection."

"I guess that settles the argument, once and for all, between the Pharisees and the Sadducees regarding the reality of the resurrection."

"Yes, if his story is to be believed."

"Anything else?"

"That there was another place which he did not visit which is called the spirit prison, or the place where the unrighteous go to also wait for the resurrection. There is a wide gulf that separates these two places, but that after Jesus's own sacrifice and resurrection, that the gulf would be bridged so that the righteous can cross over into the prison area to teach the wicked the principles of the gospel. It is a wild idea."

"Yes, but it does fit with the idea that God is just and loves all of his children and will give each one a chance to hear and accept the gospel whether in this life or beyond."

"I know that this idea has given great comfort to my mother regarding my father."

"Your mother? Ida?"

"Did you know that sneaky woman sat behind a screen secretly listening to the men who have been coming to teach me and Helene?"

Nicodemus chuckled, "Hosea told me many times how much he loved her."

"I think the feelings between them were mutual. She just never could believe in Judaism enough to convert."

"Speaking of converts, there was a proclamation read last week that I think you will be most interested in, Alexander."

"What's that?"

Nicodemus cleared his throat before continuing. "You know how the Word is spreading beyond Jerusalem, even beyond the Galilee to Antioch, Cilicia, Derbe, Lystra, and other cities."

"Yes, my brother Silvanus has been attending meetings in Joppa."

"Well, there has been a discussion for quite some time among the Twelve as to whether a convert needs to comply with the ceremonial requirements of Judaism before being baptized into the Church that the Lord set up following his resurrection."

"Yes, I am aware of those requirements. It is one of the reasons that Helene and I have not been formally baptized, as she doesn't believe that the purification rituals should apply now if the Law of Moses has truly been fulfilled. Truthfully, I can't argue with her."

"That's just it, Alexander," the old man whispered in a hoarse voice. "The Twelve have stated that any new convert does **not** need to comply with circumcision or the other ceremonies in order to become a member of the Church. They are just counseled to abstain from meats offered to idols and from blood and from things strangled. They don't want to add any other burdens to these new members." (See Acts 15:20)

"That is indeed good news, Nicodemus. I'm sure Helene and my mother will both be glad to hear it."

"Regarding this new directive, the Twelve wrote letters advising the Christians__that's what the Believers are now being called in Antioch, referring to anyone who accepts Jesus as the Christ,___so that all may understand and abide by the same practices. The letters are being carried by Paul and Barnabas to all the cities where they might go on their missionary journey."

"I just wish I knew for sure," Alexander said with a sigh.

"The only sure way to know the doctrine is to **do** it. That's what He taught. It's called living by faith, not knowledge."

"I know; my head is telling me how illogical it all is and my heart is telling me the opposite. I wish the Master were here. It was always easier to believe when I was in His presence."

"That is because of the divine spirit which accompanied him every day of His life. He has promised that we might have that same influence with us to give comfort and guidance until He comes again."

"Sometimes I feel it, but then it always fades away."

"That is because you are not progressing in your faith, Alexander. The Twelve have been given the power to bestow that gift upon you as a constant companion if you obey the commandmen____"

"I know; have faith, repent, be baptized...."

"That's right. Those are the basic requirements and then you can receive the Holy Spirit through the laying on of hands by those who have the authority. It is the only way."

Nicodemus looked Alexander straight in the eyes before asking, "How long are going to try to serve two masters, Alexander? You can't serve God and mammon. I found that out for myself." (See Matt 6:24) Another coughing spasm prevented Nicodemus from any further converation and Alexander looked at the older man with deep concern.

Seventy members of the Sanhedrin stood facing an opening in an excavated cave. They had come to pay their respects to their former member Nicodemus who had died in the third watch of the early morning. The cave had been used by Nicodemus's family for generations, a holding spot for a body for a year's time when the bones would then be removed and stored in an ossuary at the family home. The tomb would then be white-washed in a purification rite, in readiness for the next family member.

Alexander stood at the rear of the group alone in his thoughts and very much alone in his feelings. The other members of the Council pontificated about the contributions Nicodemus had made during his long years of service in the civic affairs of Jerusalem. But Alexander thought they were probably glad to be rid of a man who showed forbearance and patience in dealing with sticky issues.

Alexander felt like he was the only one who truly knew the man's heart. Nicodemus was the one man on the Council that Alexander had trusted and he now felt not only grief at his friend's death but very alone.

A fair-skinned man with golden curls sidled up to Alexander. "I beg your pardon, sir. Are you not Alexander the merchant?"

Startled at being addressed by the stranger, he acknowledged him with a brief nod. "I am. I don't recall that we have ever met."

"No, I'm sure we haven't. I am Luke, a physician from Macedonia, although I have been in Jerusalem a number of times over the years."

"Oh yes, I recall where I've heard your name. From Nicodemus. You were treating his cough, were you not?"

"Yes. Unfortunately, his lungs were so full of fluid by the time that I met him, that my medicines were not that helpful. His age was also a factor that I could not change. I am very sorry for his death nonetheless. I considered him a friend as well as a patient. We had many interesting discussions regarding one whom I consider to be the Master Healer."

Alexander looked in surprise at the man. "You mean you are a follower of ____?"

Luke nodded in silent agreement. "I heard of that great man a few years ago and have been studying his teachings ever since. And you?"

"I have been studying also, but have not committed myself to becoming a full-fledged Believer, although I must admit I am getting closer."

"I was very glad that Nicodemus took the steps to be baptized before he died. I suppose he told you about one of his earliest questions to the Lord, the man he at that time called Rabbi."

"You mean about being born again?"

"Yes," Luke chuckled, "Being born of the water and the spirit. He liked telling that story on himself later when he came to accept___" the man lowered his voice to a whisper, ___ "Jesus as his Savior. He truly was born of water and of the spirit, therefore I suppose that this day he has entered into the kingdom of God as the Lord promised."

Both men stood in silence as Ezekiel, Nicodemus's only son, emerged from the cave and signaled the priests to roll the stone in front of the doorway, sealing the tomb. The chief priest, Caiaphas, extended a hand to Ezekiel and said to the other men gathered around. "Today I welcome Ezekiel, son of Nicodemus, to fill the chair on the Council, once held by his illustrious father and grandfather."

"I guess I shouldn't be surprised at that," said Alexander, "as the same thing happened to me. But I will miss my old friend sitting in the chair next to me." He cleared his throat and discreetly wiped a tear from his eye.

"Well, that's the only thing Ezekiel is inheriting from his father," stated Luke.

Alexander looked at the man in surprise. "Oh yes," Luke continued. "I was with Nicodemus during the last few hours of his life and was a witness to the changes he made in his last will and testament. He called in his personal lawyer and had him write a new will, leaving all of his money and earthly possessions to the Believers of Jesus, with the stipulation that all was to be administered to the poor under the direction of Peter, who is the leader of the Church. Ezekiel will be furious when he finds out."

"I know that Nicodemus's wife died many years ago and that he only had the one son, whom he loved very much."

"Yes, he did love him and tried to reason with him many times about turning his life toward Jesus, but the young man is ambitious, as much to please his wife as himself, I believe. I met both of them on a few occasions when I was caring for Nicodemus as my patient. A prideful sort of man, who I think was hoping for the inherited funds to increase his own social standing. One of the many who can't see the futility of accumulating the wealth of the world. We both saw today, that none of it goes with us into the tomb."

"The Egyptians tried," quipped Alexander. Then trying to conceal his levity on such a sorrow-filled day, apologized to Luke. "I'm sorry. That was not appropriate for this occasion."

"But you are right, Alexander. The Egyptians thought that by burying their wealth inside the pyramidal tombs that it would go with them into the afterlife." Luke clapped his hand on his companion's shoulder, "I don't mean to be overbearing, but I wouldn't wait too long to make your commitment, Alexander. There are dark clouds approaching and the persecution will probably increase." Then drawing away, the physician said, "I hope that we meet again soon."

With that, the two men said goodbye and went separate directions. All the way home Alexander thought about the commitment and sacrifice that Nicodemus had made. *But in the end was it really a sacrifice? Did Nicodemus truly attain the kingdom of God? Do I have the faith to do the same?*

A large crowd of Believers gathered on the banks of the Jordan River near Bethabara where John the Baptist had baptized Jesus about four years earlier. It was a good time to be away from Jerusalem with its crowds that poured in from all around the Empire for the Passover. It had been a year since the death of Jesus, but that is not what they were gathering to celebrate. No, it had also been a year since the resurrection of Jesus and that was well worth celebrating.

Alexander found a smooth spot on the bank and spread out a sheepskin for Helene to sit on. It had been an arduous two-day journey with Alexander walking and Helene riding on the back of a donkey. Being in a company of other travelers for safety and camaraderie, they had actually enjoyed the trip. Many of the Believers now recognized them and were no longer suspicious of their presence. Helene seemed to be smiling and waving to others in the group all along their way, especially when young children had gathered bouquets of wildflowers and presented them to her. They had dressed in their simplest clothing and brought no servants to attend to their needs. Helene had said that if they were going to join the Believers, then they needed to act like them.

The Twelve were circulating among the group, over a thousand strong it seemed to Alexander as he scanned the throng lined up on both sides of the Jordan. He hadn't realized that the Church which Jesus established was growing so much, therefore, seeing this many gathered in celebration was a grand sight. Matthias, the newest member of the Quorum of the Twelve approached Alexander and Helene but motioning them to stay seated, asked if he might join them. "I am Matthias," he said, introducing himself.

"Yes, I know of you," Alexander replied. "The one chosen to fill the vacancy left by Judas."

"That's me. It was an honor to be chosen, not for my own merits, but by the spirit of revelation which is granted to Peter, James, and John."

"Did you know Jesus well?" asked Helene.

"I was just one of his many unnamed followers, but I had been a disciple for quite some time."

"I wish I might have seen Jesus personally," she replied with a pensive sigh.

"Seeing him was no guarantee that you would have believed him. There were many who saw him who didn't believe. You are one who has faith to believe without seeing. How long have you been numbered with the Believers?"

Alexander cleared his throat before speaking. "We're not exactly numbered with them yet."

Matthias looked at them in curiosity. "Yet you made your way on this pilgrimage, obviously at great sacrifice," motioning to Helene's crippled leg.

"We have been studying the teachings of Jesus for quite some time, and decided to take the plunge, literally and symbolically, in the baptismal service planned after the meeting today," answered Alexander.

"Ah, this is indeed a special day for you then. Let me be among the first to congratulate you on your decision."

"Helene has wanted to be baptized for several months. I'm the one who has been holding back," admitted Alexander.

"You say you have been studying for quite some time; may I ask what finally convinced you that it was time to take the step?"

"Last Sabbath, I was attending the Synagogue as I have done for most of my life. I was called upon to read from the writings of the prophets. The priest handed me a scroll opened to the account of the prophet Elijah and the priests of Baal on Mt. Carmel."

"One of my favorite scripture stories," said Matthias.

"Mine too, ever since I was a boy. It was so dramatic with over eight hundred priests who showed allegiance to Queen Jezebel, all dancing around, slashing their bodies with knives trying to get the attention of their god. And Elijah there, representing the true God of Israel, all by himself."

"So what about this story brought you here today?"

Alexander smiled at Helene, then at Matthias. "When I came to the verse that read, 'And Elijah came unto all the people__'" Alexander stopped his recitation commenting, "I guess there must have been quite a crowd watching this contest to see whose god would light the fire and consume the bullock as a sacrificial offering." Then continuing on with the memorized verse, 'Elijah said, 'How long halt ye between two opinions? If the Lord be God, follow him.' (1 Kings 19:21) Those words just seemed to jump off the page, as if they had been written specifically for me. I have been one who has halted between two opinions for too long. I came home and told Helene of my experience and we prayed to know if this was the right time to be baptized. As you can see, we received an answer to our prayers and we are here."

"Some people who have joined the Church of Jesus Christ seem to know almost instantly that it is true. Others like you, give a lot of consideration over a period of time. I am just happy that you have chosen to be numbered among those who believe that Jesus is the Christ, the Savior, and Redeemer of all mankind."

"We still have many questions," said Helene. "But we realize that we must have faith first, and then the answers will come as we move along."

"You have a wise woman to be your wife, Alexander. I recommend that you treat her well."

"Oh, he does, Matthias. I am very blessed to have such a good husband."

"I can see that Peter is signaling me to gather with the rest of the Twelve. It must be time for the meeting to begin"

"Thank you for stopping by to talk to us, Matthias," said Helene. He took her dainty hand in his large calloused one and shook it gently. Then turning to Alexander, gave him a clap on the shoulder, and picked his way through the crowd toward Peter, the man once known as The Big Fisherman.

Alexander was pleased that it was Matthias who stood waist deep in the Jordan, signaling that it was his turn for the ordinance.

He walked barefoot, grasping at the reeds to steady himself as he entered the river. The melting snow on Mt. Hermon in the north made the water cold at this spring season, and Alexander's teeth began to chatter. "You'll get used to it in a few minutes," Matthias assured him. Several of the apostles were performing similar ordinances for other converts nearby. But as Alexander looked into Matthias's eyes, he felt like he was the most important person in the world to the apostle at that moment. The man's eyes were filled with such love.

Then raising his right arm, Matthias said, "Brother Alexander, having been given authority through the power of God, I baptize you in the name of the Father, and the Son, and the Holy Spirit. Amen." Then Alexander bent his knees and laid back until the water rushed over his face. He came up spluttering. "Sorry, I forgot to tell you that you could hold your nose," Matthias grinned before giving the dripping Alexander a bear hug.

"You were right about one thing, Matthias. I don't feel the coldness of the water anymore. I feel as warm as if I were in a Roman bathhouse."

"Well, in that case, why don't you stay in for a few more minutes and help Helene into the water. I don't want her to be unbalanced and go under before I can perform the ordinance. No use of being immersed twice."

After Helene's baptism, they climbed back onto the shore and wrapped woolen blankets around their wet bodies. Their sodden clothes clung to them and water from their dripping hair ran in rivulets down their backs. But Alexander thought he had never seen his wife so radiant. He grabbed the pack they had brought with them and pointed to a make-shift screen of blankets strung on ropes among several trees, which provided a measure of privacy where they could change into dry clothing "You go first Helene," said Alexander, even though he was shivering. As he waited he thought to himself. *I finally did it. Even though I don't know what the future will bring, I know I made the right decision.*

A short time later about fifty newly-baptized converts gathered together in a quiet grove, while others in their company left to prepare food for the feast they would enjoy later. Fire pits had been dug earlier and the smell of roasting lamb was already filling the air. Peter conducted this meeting, explaining the next ordinance, which he called a confirmation. Speaking with authority, the Chief Apostle declared, "Although important and required, the baptism of water is not sufficient for salvation in the Kingdom of God. It is but a gate onto the strait and narrow way. For guidance in staying on that gospel path, one needs to additionally receive a baptism of the spirit, which comes through the Holy Ghost, just as Jesus had taught." Each convert in turn sat on a large rock while the apostles gathered around and placed their hands on the still-damp head of each individual. Women were treated the same as the men, for as Peter taught, they were each a beloved son or daughter of a loving Heavenly Father, who was pleased with their choices to follow His Son.

Peter asked John to be the spokesman, and Alexander felt the power of God flow into him as the words of the prayer were offered and he was invited to receive the Holy Spirit into his life as a lasting gift to guide and comfort him. Then John paused, saying, "And Brother Alexander, I feel that I should give you a special blessing that you might know how much Jesus Christ loves you and is pleased with your decision to finally become a true follower this day. You have been blessed with the gifts of discernment and good judgment, and you will have the opportunity to use those gifts in wisdom as you go forward in His service this day. You will yet have many positions of respect and leadership and be an instrument in the hands of the Lord in building His kingdom here on the earth."

There were tears streaming down his face as Alexander rose and shook hands with the men in the circle. He felt so inadequate among these men, yet he sensed that some of their power had been shared with him. Alexander had assumed that the power used by Jesus when He was on earth had been taken away with Him. But the Lord had given a portion of that power to His apostles so that His work could continue on the earth until He returned again.

Helene likewise received a special blessing during her confirmation. John said, "Your spiritual endowment is the gift of beauty. You see the beauty of the creations of the earth, the goodness in people around you, and you will continue to share your talents of creating beauty with many others. I bless you that you will become a mother in Israel," and with this Helene smiled inwardly. After a year, she was beginning to wonder if she would be barren as Sarah and Rachel of old. In his deep voice filled with love, John continued, "and because of your faith, Helene, from this moment forward you will walk without pain or lameness." Everyone in the group gasped at this announcement, as the apostle concluded the prayer. Offering her a hand, John lifted Helene from her seated position on the rock. She stood straight, looked around the group, and then ran into Alexander's outstretched arms.

One year later

Helene sat embroidering the last few stitches on the long length of a swaddling band. "I'm almost finished, Alexander. And none too soon if the liveliness of this child in my womb is any indication of its readiness to enter this world."

"So you think this son of ours will be a strong runner?"

"Or this daughter of ours will a graceful dancer. But either way, I would suggest you write an epistle to Ida and send it with the next courier to your mother in Joppa. She wouldn't want to miss out on the arrival of her first grandchild."

In response, Alexander reached down to hug his wife saying, "I'm planning on sending some business papers to Silvanus today so I will include a message for mother as well. And whether this child is a son or a daughter matters not, for this child will be received with love."

"You are so right, Alexander. I am so grateful for the two blessings I received the day of my baptism."

"That was a truly special day, wasn't it?"

Helene nodded, tears suddenly filling her eyes, "Sorry, I just seem to get so emotional these days." Then wiping away her tears, she said. "Have you noticed how much easier it is to show love since we became members of Christ's Church? It is as if His spirit of love influences all our interactions with others."

"You have always been a loving person, Helene. But it certainly does help men like me overcome their pride. That's what Jesus was really asking me to do long ago when he said I needed to sell all of my possessions and give the money to the poor. It was not just the issue of wealth, but where my loyalties were and where I would place my faith. It took me a long time to learn that lesson. I guess one of the things I've noticed most since our baptism is the ability to recognize truth. Jesus taught that we should know the truth and the truth would make us free. I always thought he was talking about political freedom from Roman rule. But I now see that truth makes us free from the bondage of sin and error, from superstition and false traditions, and from the vain philosophies of men."

"Joining His Church was the best decision we ever made. Was it hard for you to give up so much?"

"Giving up my seat in the Sanhedrin was easy. It had become a burden rather than a privilege to serve. I hope my father somehow understands."

"What about your home?"

"Absolutely. We were fortunate that we found a buyer for our home so quickly. But Ezekiel was anxious to move up in his social ranking by living in a mansion."

"Was it hard for you to leave your family home, Alexander?"

"Not the house itself, but the memories of my childhood that took place there."

"You will always have the memories."

"I suppose it was easier knowing that Mother had already decided to move to Joppa. I wouldn't have wanted to displace her. And thinking of mother, I'd better get that epistle written right away. You just tell that baby to be content where he or she is until Ida arrives."

Alexander returned to the table in their small apartment where he had several scrolls propped open with stones. There are some days I *miss having my own desk where I could leave out my business ledgers without having to clear off the table every day,* Alexander thought to himself.

When they sold their home, Alexander and Helene willingly contributed all of their funds to the Church. That large sum had been put to quick use building a compound for the members of the Church on the outskirts of Jerusalem. Each family had their own private apartments for sleeping, but the majority of the activity took place in the courtyard where there were designated sections for food preparation, washing and mending clothes, and a play area for young children. All of their meals were served in a central dining hall, which also was used as a school for the boys and weekly instruction from the Brethren. The women took turns with the cooking, getting their supplies from a central storehouse. Everything was shared in common and each family received according to their stewardship and needs.

Alexander was one of the few men who knew how to read and

write in multiple languages, as well as do mathematical computations, and he was grateful that he had been taught these skills in his childhood. He was designated as a purchasing agent where he could use his connections with merchants to buy the textile supplies needed for their commune.

"I must leave for a while and meet with Matthew and Zacchaeus about some financial matters. Will you be all right here, Helene?"

"Of course. I always have work to keep my hands busy." Her contribution to the society was embroidering shawls, wedding ribbons, or swaddling bands. She taught other women these skills, but she was the most proficient and was often asked to do the special projects.

"Who would have thought that publicans like Matthew and Zacchaeus were such honest and agreeable men?"

"An honest publican? Now you must be jesting, Alexander."

"Well, that's how living the teachings of Jesus changes men, isn't it? We're no longer worried about filling our own purses. I use my contacts to purchase the textiles we need for the weavers and tailors to keep busy. And having your father as my agent in Alexandria helps me have a dependable source of good quality cotton. I no longer wait for the caravans to bring in silk from the Orient. It feels good to be providing for the members and their basic needs and not worrying about the fashion whims of the rich. This united order is a great system when we all work together. As Jesus once said there's no rich and no poor, but we are all one."

"It's all about love," they laughingly said in unison. Then giving Helene a quick kiss on the cheek, he left the apartment.

Later that night Alexander made his way up to the flat rooftop as he often did at the close of a busy day. It was a place for contemplation and problem-solving, but more often than not, a place for praying. He had learned that the best prayers were those offered in quiet secret places where one could truly commune with God. No wonder Jesus had often retreated to the mountains away from the multitudes that thronged Him, when He sought respite and communication with His Father.

Feeling the smooth surfaces of the tiles of the parapet, Alexander remembered that carpenters would soon start adding an upper story to the apartments. *The membership of the Believers is growing and the leaders are now calling our Jerusalem group a Branch, meaning a branch of the true vine, which is Jesus Christ. I heard the Twelve speak of Branches being organized in cities as far away as Ephesus and Corinth. I'm especially glad to know that there is one in Joppa which Silvanus and Ida belong to, although they have not formed a commune as yet.*

There was a glow of candlelight in the windows of many of the apartments below him and he could hear the murmur of voices in the background, the laughter of a child, the lullaby of a mother. Helene had already retired to bed, as she needed extra rest these days. But Alexander wasn't sleepy yet. His eyes picked out the familiar North Star, but said to himself, *"I no longer need the light of the stars to guide me. I have the light of the Son. It is hard for me to realize that the mortal man Jesus that I saw and heard is actually the Creator of all the stars in the heavens. He was so much more than we realized at the time. From here the stars look small and I view myself as large in comparison. But, O Lord, who dwellest in the heavens, I suppose that from your throne you have a better perspective__that the stars are great sources of light and I am just a speck, less than the dust of the earth.*

But on the other hand, Lord, thou hast said that every soul is precious to Thee. So precious in fact, that you were willing to pay for every sin and sorrow for every man or woman who has ever lived on the earth. I am sorry for those sins of both commission and omission that I committed. I'm sorry for my stubbornness and slowness to accept Thy Way. But I also believe that because of Thy redemption, that those sins have been remitted. I pray that although I feel inadequate, that I am worthy of thy cleansing power.

I thought I only had one question for you Lord many years ago, but in spite of what I have learned, I still have many questions. I wonder when you come again will there be another star in the night sky that will signal your coming? Will there by wisemen watching for that star? I hope that there will be many wise men. When **will** *you come again? But probably the more important question is, when you come again, will* ***I*** *be ready? I asked once before, Lord what I must do to have eternal life. Your answer was one of truth, although it was a difficult one. It took me a long time to accept and act upon that answer. But as always, Thou knowest what is best for all of God's children here on the earth. So I ask you again in humility, knowing that it may also be an answer I am not ready for yet, but will strive to understand and obey straightaway this time__what lack I yet that I might gain eternal life?*

The Jericho Inn

MERZI HUMMED AS she swept the sandstone and basalt rock wall with a short-handled broom made of scrub oak branches tied to a sturdy handle. Sweeping the rocks was such a thankless task with the constant sand blowing across the desert terrain coating everything with the lightly colored dust. But Naomi had drilled it into her eleven-year-old brain for more than five years that it didn't do any good to wash the bed linens and lay them out to dry on dirt-covered rocks. There was, after all, their reputation of having the cleanest beds of any Jericho inn to uphold.

Merzi, formally named Merziabah (Mer-zee`-a-bah) after her grandmother, laid aside the broom and carefully withdrew a large linen sheet from the woven basket at her feet. She had been at the well before dawn to haul the water up to The Inn of Nine Palms in order to wash the bedding as soon as the overnight guests had departed. Naomi had stressed that no sheets should be left on the beds once a customer had paid his bill and left. No telling what kind of vermin might be transported from one man to another through sleeping in the same sheets. Other inns might not be so picky, but the House of Nine Palms established the practice years ago and both Naomi and her husband James felt that the policy had paid off. They got new referrals from satisfied customers plus their reoccurring business. Jericho was an important stop on the trade routes between

Damascus to the northeast, Jerusalem to the southwest, and onto the Mediterranean ports of Caesarea and Joppa.

Although lying below sea level, and near the Jordan River, Jericho could be unbearably hot. "I wonder when father will return," Merzi asked herself. "He usually makes his rounds with Sebastian's caravan two or three times a year, and it has already been four months since I last saw him. Although I don't see him often, I miss him terribly. And what about Amos? It has been five years since I've seen him. He would be about fourteen now, I think." For the thousandth time, Merzi mourned the loss of her mother Huldah, who had died in childbirth when Merzi was six and her brother Amos was nine. Her father, Jedidiah had been in a conundrum about what to do. His employment as overseer of the camel drovers for Sebastian, the Samaritan merchant, took him away most of the year. He had no other skills to start a new way of life in order to care for his two small children. Besides, he had a wanderlust that urged him to always be on the move and knew he could not settle down in one place.

Saul, one of his young drovers, offered a suggestion. "My parents, James and Naomi, of Jericho, are proprietors of a reputable establishment known as the Inn of Nine Palms".

"I have heard of it," said Jedidiah.

"My brother and I are no longer living at home, and my parents only have my sister Rebekah who is a little older than your Merziabah. Perhaps you could go into a business arrangement with them to care for her as an indentured servant until she becomes of marriageable age."

So that is what Merzi's father had done. A legal document had been drawn stating that she would be indentured to James and Naomi for the period of seven years, during which time she would provide such services as they would require in return for shelter, food, clothing, and an account of one pence per week to be used as a future dowry. A similar arrangement had been made with a shepherd near

Bethlehem for her brother Amos.

Merzi let her mind wander over five of those seven years, which had now passed. The first four of them had been pleasant enough with the company of Rebekah who was two years older than Merzi. They had played the games of childhood and collected pretty rocks from the banks of the Jordan River. And like all good Jewish children, they were taught to obey the Law of Moses, although their attendance at religious services at the synagogue had dwindled over the years. It seems that there were always customers to prepare food for no matter what day of the week. They couldn't very well close up their business for Sabbath observance, reasoned James.

In addition to clean sheets, the Inn of Nine Palms had also gained a favorable reputation as a place to get a good meal. Weary travelers appreciated the tasty food that Naomi was expert in preparing. She knew just the right touch of rosemary to flavor the mutton stew or the pungent cinnamon in the bread pudding that customers raved about. As the business had grown throughout the years, each family member was designated certain responsibilities. In his younger days, Saul had cared for the animals which were sheltered in the rock-enclosed corrals behind the inn. In fact, it had been Saul's brother, Philipp, who had constructed the corrals and developed his skills as a stone mason. Rebekah had become the chief server, carrying the plates from the kitchen and clearing the dishes afterward. She also swept the main serving room and fluffed up the large cushions which supported the bodies of the men while they reclined at the low tables. Merziabah had been assigned to clean the sleeping quarters and wash the bed linens. Naomi was the cook, of course, and James greeted customers, arranged feed for the animals, assigned travelers to desired sleeping rooms, and kept the financial accounts. There was a place for everyone and each knew his duty to his family. Until....

That is, until Philip met a maiden named Sara and desired her for wife. He had the skills to become an apprenticed stone mason and soon became a partner in a business owned by a man named Jude.

Saul, after his many years working with the camels and donkeys in the stabling area of the Inn, wanted to get away from the confines of the dry desert town where he had been raised. Against his father's advice, Saul had hired on as a drover with Sebastian. Within a short time, Saul had proven his skills in dealing with cantankerous animals and Sebastian had promoted him to be an assistant to Jedidiah. The young man was almost like a younger brother to the overseer. The departure of his two sons left James short-handed, so he had decided that since most travelers now left their animals in one of the caravansaries on the outskirts of town, he would no longer offer stabling accommodations, but concentrate on the two-legged travelers. After several periods of cleaning and disinfecting, the corral behind the Inn was now where Merzi did the laundry

That morning she had followed her usual routine with kindling a small fire in the center of the enclosure and set metal tubs on top, filling them with water carried in large pots on her shoulder from one of the city's wells. She scrubbed any of the stained areas with strong lye soap as a means of disinfecting the sheets and left them to soak while she went to sweep and tidy up the rooms. Unfortunately, today there had been no loose coins which had rolled under the straw-filled mattresses laid on the low beds, which were raised up about one cubit from the wooden-planked floors. James said she could keep any of the coins that she found as her own spending money. Her pile of coins was pitifully small.

Merzi went back outside, the bright sun almost blinding her after being indoors. She swirled the sheets through the hot water, then pried them from the soaking tub with a thick pole, dropping them with a thud into another tub filled with cold water. After the fabric cooled enough to handle, she laboriously began to wring the water from the long lengths of cloth, her young arms twisting and turning to squeeze out as much moisture as possible. Then taking each sheet individually, she draped it over the rock wall to dry, the sun bleaching them to a dazzling white. No wonder the customers liked the fresh-smelling clean sheets at the Inn of Nine Palms!

As she hung the last sheet, she observed the skillful workmanship Phillip had exhibited in constructing the wall. Black and white rocks were wedged together tightly and cemented with a limestone mortar that hardened, then stacked and fitted to form the enclosure. She enjoyed it when Philipp, Sara, and one-year-old Jonah came to visit. This was the closest thing to a family she had known for a very long time. Merzi was uncertain about what the future would hold for her. She didn't think that James and Naomi would kick her out when her indenturement was completed in two years. But what would she do?

With the final sheet hung, Merzi breathed deeply with a feeling of relief that the task was completed, but also a certain satisfaction in a job well done. She inhaled the pungent smell of the strong soap and smoothed the wet fabric to ease out the wrinkles. Although it was hard work, Merzi felt pleased with her efforts and liked making both her adopted family and the guests happy.

The Inn was named for the nine palms that framed the entry courtyard. Four large trees on each side provided a modicum of shade for weary travelers. One lone palm stood between the two entrances to the Inn. The arched door on the left led to the dining area, while the one on the right opened into a hallway branching off to the various sleeping quarters. The Inn was constructed of sunbaked adobe bricks like all the buildings in town, a buff-color that blended into the desert surroundings. It was located on the northern end of Jericho, closest to the trail that paralleled the Jordan River leading toward Decapolis and further on to Damascus. She liked the stories of far-away places that Saul told when he returned from his travels with the caravan. Would she ever get to see the great marketplace in Damascus or the Mediterranean Sea?

Merzi recalled the secrets that she and Rebekah used to confide to one another when they nestled together in their own straw mattresses each night. They dreamed of marrying handsome and rich merchants who would lavish them with silken scarves from the Orient, alabaster jars full of perfume from Egypt, or peacock-feather fans from Persia. Lately, Rebekah didn't seem to have time for Merzi. If she had any freedom, she wanted to spend it chatting with the older girls she often met in the market. When male guests were present, she fluttered her eyelashes at each one, whether he was twenty or sixty years old. She brushed her arm lightly along their bodies as they reclined on their elbows at the low tables to dine. Nor did she look away when the men gaped at her developing bosom as she bent low with the serving dishes. Rebekah's flirtatious behavior disgusted Merzi, but no matter what she said, Rebekah would flounce her skirts and give her a condescending look that let Merzi know she was still such a child and a servant at that. Gone was the sisterly feelings they had once shared.

Because of her own housekeeping duties, Merzi didn't often hear the news that travelers shared as they ate an evening meal together in the common dining room. But it was impossible for her not to hear some of the rumors that were flying everywhere regarding one Jesus of Nazareth who was teaching north of Jericho, above the Sea of Galilee. Some said he had miraculous healing powers. Others claimed he was the very Messiah. Many said he was an imposter and should be ignored. Merzi had once heard a bearded man named

John preach as he had passed through Jericho on his way south. His followers declared that he was a prophet like the men of ancient Israel calling the Jews to repentance in no uncertain terms. John did not deny his prophetic calling to prepare the way for the coming of the Lamb of God. Merzi knew her family's religious observance was lax and felt bad about missing synagogue, but there wasn't much she could do about it in her present circumstances.

James said it was more important to be friendly and open to people from all places if he wanted to have anyone use his inn. He called people from many countries and religious persuasions among his friends and customers. Her adoptive father was not a tall man, but built more portly and actually a little shorter than his wife. His once-thick hair was already starting to gray and recede from his forehead. Although not what one would call handsome, his jovial personality seemed to draw people to him like bees to a flower's pollen.

Naomi was also plain in appearance and Merzi wondered what James had seen in her that had prompted a marriage proposal. Did her father supply a large dowry? Maybe her great cooking skills had won James over from the beginning. It was an old saying that the way to a man's heart was through his stomach. And Naomi was a master when it came to selecting the right spice from a myriad on her shelf and with a pinch of one or a shake of another, turned everyday food into feasts once only served to kings. She was starting to instruct Rebekah in the arts of cooking, but Merzi had not been invited to join them.

Now, on this particular morning, Merzi was having an especially difficult time trying to manage the linens as the wind whipped the wet fabric into her face. She stood on a small three-legged stool trying to anchor the sheets to the wall when she heard a deep voice calling her from inside the inn. Recognizing it immediately, she squealed, "Papa, Papa" and tried to untangle herself from the billowing fabric without letting it fall to the ground.

"Merziabah, my darling girl! James said I would find you out here," he responded. "Here, let me help you with this sheet so I can have a proper hug."

With his long arms, Jedidiah held the sheet securely to the wall, while Merziabah placed the rocks at intervals along the top to anchor the cloth against the breeze which was already stirring up the dust. Then throwing herself into her father's arms exclaimed, "Oh, Papa, I've missed you so."

"I know, dear one, it has been a long time. Sebastian's caravan was delayed in Joppa for several weeks awaiting a shipment of goods from Alexandria. My, I think you have grown since I last saw you," pushing her gently away from his body and mentally measured her height.

"I think I have too, Papa. My clothes are all feeling a little tight."

"I will speak to James about that while I am here. That is part of our arrangement that you will be adequately clothed. Are they feeding you well? Do they make you work too hard?"

"I am treated well, Papa. Naomi is an excellent cook. That's probably why I'm growing so much. The work is hard, but I am getting stronger. I have no complaints, except that I miss you and Amos so much."

"I know; I know, child," and he again took her in his arms for another hug. "Let me help you hang up the rest of these sheets and we can sit and talk a bit."

"James or Naomi will probably scold me if I'm not working."

"I'll take care of that with James. He realizes that our visits together are few and far between. He won't mind if you sit with me for a few minutes." Working together, they soon quickly completed the task. Jedidiah brought a wooden bench from the inn into the enclosure, and finding a shady spot near the back door they settled down to talk.

"Have you seen Amos lately? Is he growing too?" asked Merzi.

"Yes, lass. I arranged to take a day off when we were in Jerusalem last week and walked down to Bethlehem to see Amos. You know that it is only a few miles south of the capital city. In fact, the shepherd that he works with supplies the special lambs for the temple sacrifices. And yes, Amos is growing too. I'd say he is about this high," signaling with his hand a height several inches above his daughter's.

"Really?" said Merziabah in wonderment, "I wish I could see Amos again. Even though it's less than thirty miles away, it feels like it might as well be on the other side of the world."

"Poor, Merzi. What a sad thing for you to be separated from your own family all these years," said Jedidiah stroking Merzi's back. "But let me tell you something very interesting that Amos shared with me when I visited with him. He said that the old shepherds have told him of a strange occurrence that happened about three decades ago. One night they were tending the sheep on the hillsides near Bethlehem, and an angel appeared to them."

"An angel? A real angel?"

"That's what the old man told Amos."

"Was it a man angel or a woman angel?"

"I don't know, child. Maybe angels are just angels."

"What did the angel say?"

"Now that is the really interesting part. First of all, the angel said that he, or she, I don't know which, was bringing glad tidings of great joy which should be for all people. The angel said that a Savior who was Christ the Lord had been born that day in the City of David, which is Bethlehem. Then the angel instructed the shepherds to go and see the baby."

"How would they know where to find him?"

"The angel said it would be in a stable and the baby would be wrapped in swaddling clothes lying in a manger."

"Did they go? Did they see this baby who is supposed to be a Savior?"

"Yes, they did. But before they left their flocks, there was a multitude of angels which appeared in the sky singing praises to God."

"That is an amazing story, Papa. Do you think it really happened?"

"I asked Amos the same thing."

"And what did he say?"

"Your brother believes that the shepherd spoke in truthfulness. He has known this man, Haggai, for many years and has never known him to be false with any man. There were others who went with him who verified the story."

"If he's a Savior, does that mean he will deliver the Jews from Roman captivity?"

"That is what some people are saying."

"Do you mean there are people who have seen this person now that he has grown, and are calling him their Savior?"

"Yes, and that is the next part of the story. That same baby born in Bethlehem, whose name is Jesus, is now claiming to be the Deliverer promised by the prophets."

"I have heard of a man named Jesus who is teaching near the Sea of Galilee and performing miracles."

"Yes, I have heard of him too. I hope that when Sebastian's caravan heads north we will have an opportunity to hear more about him."

"I hope so, Papa. Maybe then you would know for sure if he is a Deliverer."

"Sebastian says he has heard this man Jesus preach of kindness and living a higher law than that given by Moses, but that Jesus doesn't seem to be organizing any kind of revolt against Rome."

"That is a very interesting story, Papa. Tell me about some of the other places you have been recently."

"Well, when we were in Caesarea, I saw Pontius Pilate."

"You mean the Roman governor?" Merzi asked with her eyes growing wider.

"Yes, he was with a legion of his soldiers, all of them wearing red cloaks, holding their spears in their hands, riding on horses. It was quite an impressive sight."

"I'm scared whenever I see any Roman soldiers. Sometimes they stop at the Inn for a meal before going on their patrols across the Jordan River."

"I'm sure they would never hurt a child like you."

"Stop calling me a child, Papa. It makes me feel like I'm five years old."

"I'm sorry, Merzi. I guess I will always consider you my child, even when you are a grown woman. That's the way with all mamas and papas, I think," and he gave her another hug.

"Did you see Rebekah when you arrived? I think she is fast becoming a woman."

"Yes, I did. And I agree with you in that regard."

"She still treats me like a child."

"I'm sorry about that. What else would you like to tell me about living here?"

"Well, there's Phillip and Sara and baby Jonah. He is so cute, toddling about….." Merzi went on to share the tidbits of her life that she had been storing up in her heart for months.

A few days later James called Rebekah and Merziabah to meet with him following the noon meal, which was usually the time of day when the Inn was least busy and there were no guests to care for. "Girls," James began with a serious tone in his voice, "Jedidiah, Saul and Sebastian have all issued a warning which we would be wise to heed. They say that thieves abound on all the trade routes around

Jericho. You know there are hundreds of hiding places among the rocks along the trails. It seems that the thieves attack travelers, especially anyone alone, and then disappear back into their hideouts in the hills."

Merzi and Rebekah both raised their eyebrows, somehow questioning James without speaking. The man continued, "You must both be my eyes and ears to protect our Inn from any stealing or violence. Your mother is usually in the kitchen and does not often interact with the guests, but both of you do. Rebekah, be aware of any suspicious-looking men__those with shifty eyes or hands quick to reach for a dagger." And looking directly at his daughter added in a serious tone, "And for heaven's sake, stop flirting with every man who walks through the door. You are much too young for such indecent behavior." Rebekah lowered her eyes in humble submission. "Yes, Papa," she muttered.

"Merzi, be on the lookout for anything you see in the bedchambers which might be suspicious, like heavy-looking money belts or bags, a foreign coin that might fall to the floor. We cannot be too careful in this regard."

"Yes, James. I will try to be more observant."

"And Merzi, your father spoke to me about getting you a new robe as soon as we can. I must admit that I have not been observant enough about that. Since I see you every day, I did not notice how much you have grown, but your father pointed it out to me and I want to be fair to our contract."

"Thank you, James. That is most kind of you."

"And Rebekah, perhaps it is time for you a new robe as well. I think the Inn is prosperous enough that I can order two robes from the seamstress down the street. Perhaps something with a higher neckline would be more appropriate."

Rebekah blushed and meekly said, "Thank you, Papa. I would love to have some new clothes." The two girls quickly hugged each other, the thought of each getting a new robe uniting them in an embrace reminiscent of previous years.

"There's not much choice in colors for robes in Jericho. We're not like the high-minded women of society in Jerusalem. So the usual dun-colored is what they will be. But perhaps we can splurge and allow you to have colored sashes. What colors would you like?" asked James. "Within reason, of course. No purple or scarlet."

"I'd like blue," answered Rebekah.

"I'd like green" added Merzi.

"Two robes__one with a blue sash, one with green__ that's what it will be then. And remember what I said about watching out for thieves and robbers or there will be no money for robes for anyone."

The hot sun beat down mercilessly as the days passed and no thieves were suspected at the Inn of the Nine Palms. James said perhaps it was because their Inn had such a good reputation and that the unsavory characters dared not show their faces to the respectable citizens who frequented their establishment. However, about four weeks after the warning issued by the caravan travelers, shortly before sunset a clamor was heard outside the courtyard. Saul rushed in calling for his father. "Papa, Papa, where are you?"

Recognizing the voice, James slammed his ledger book shut, Naomi quickly wiped her hands on her apron front, and Rebekah set down her serving tray, all rushing to the left door of the Inn. "Here, Saul. What is the matter? Are you all right? Why are you here?" each asked anxiously, their words tumbling into each other like new puppies rolling about in play. Merzi, who had been tidying up one of the bedchambers appeared at the right door of the Inn, peering out in curiosity.

"I am fine, but I..." Saul began trying to catch his breath, "I mean we, that is Sebastian and I, have brought an injured man. Someone we found on the road outside the city." Another brief pause for breath. "He'd been beaten and left lying there in the hot sun. We knew he'd surely die."

Sebastian strode into the courtyard at that moment and James ran to embrace his friend with a kiss on each cheek. "What is this my son Saul is saying, old friend? Can you tell us more?'

"Saul speaks truthfully, James. The caravan had stopped at an oasis not too far north to rest the animals during the heat of the day. We saw an occasional man walking, which isn't unusual, but two of them seemed to be in an extraordinary hurry, which seemed curious at the time, but I did not dwell on the question for long. Based on their clothing, I would surmise that one of them was a Levite and the other a priest. Shortly after we got back on the trail, with the intent of making the caravansary here in Jericho by nightfall, we came upon a man lying in the roadway. He had apparently been robbed."

"Ah, the thieves you warned us of, Sebastian?"

"Most likely. He had been beaten and stripped of most of his clothing and was left as if he were dead. He surely would have been soon if we had not come along when we did. I thought back about the priest and the Levite we'd seen hurrying from the oasis. Surely they both would have recognized the man as a fellow Jew inasmuch as they had traveled that trail such a short time before. I wondered why they had not stopped to help. Nonetheless, I dismounted from my camel and attended to the man as best I could__giving him water to drink, and pouring wine on the cuts to disinfect them and smoothing on a little olive oil to aid in the healing of some of his wounds. I can see no identification about his person, but know that he needs to rest for a few days. Perhaps by then he will regain consciousness and he'll be able to tell us his name and village of origin. But there is a dilemma that now confronts me, James. I have left Jedidiah with the merchandise we are transporting, but I cannot delay my caravan long enough to stay in Jericho to care for this stranger. So who did I think of, but my good friend, James, of course? I would like to leave this man in your care."

James pulled away slightly, cleared his throat, and said, "Why, Sebastian, I don't know if I can spare a room for him for as long as it will take for him to heal."

"Do not worry, James, I will pay for his lodging in advance," reaching inside his dusty robe for the money belt he kept fastened around his waist. Handing the innkeeper two coins, he then added, "And if that is not sufficient payment, I will pay more when I return."

"That is most generous of you, Sebastian," replied James, happy to help now that he knew payment was guaranteed. "I know that you are a good man, but I must ask why you, a Samaritan, would want to help this stranger, who is a Jew? Most Samaritans would have likely spit at a wounded Jew and walked on by."

"I have been hearing some of the teachings of one Jesus of Nazareth in my travels. He is preaching what he calls a new gospel, a gospel of love. I didn't stop to think whether this wounded man was a Jew, a Samaritan, or a Moabite. When I saw he was in need, I just knew that I had to help him. Perhaps the teachings of this Jesus have entered into my heart more than I realized."

"I have heard somewhat of this Jesus also, but have never heard him in person. I hope he will come to Jericho before long and perhaps I can hear his message and judge for myself. But in the meantime, old friend, I will care for this man as you wish. Where is he now?"

"My men loaded him in my palanquin to keep him out of the sun."

James turned toward the arched doorway where his family was in conversation with Saul, who seemed to be retelling the same story with great animation. "Merzi, prepare one of the rooms for an injured guest. Saul, help me carry him in."

"This means a great deal to me, James. I knew you were a man who could be trusted." said the old caravan owner before he and Saul exited the courtyard together. Merzi scurried into one of the guest rooms, making sure there was a clean sheet on the straw-filled mattress.

Merzi was checking on the wounded stranger the next morning according to James's instructions when the man began to mumble something unintelligible and his eyelids fluttered. Merzi knelt down on the floor beside him and touched his shoulder. "Sir," she said, "you are safe. You have been badly wounded, but are now in the excellent care of my master."

"Where, where am I?" muttered the man trying to sit up.

"Be careful, sir. I will help you. You are at the Inn of the Nine Palms in Jericho."

Coming to a sitting position, the man leaned his back against the wall, moaning with pain. "Jericho? How did I get here?"

"You were injured on the road outside of the city. Do you remember what happened?"

The middle-aged man had long curled forelocks and a graying beard that Merzi could see was usually well-trimmed, so she assumed he was a citizen of some importance. "I will get you a cup of water, Sir, if you will just stay still. I will bring my master to you and you can tell him your story."

"Thank you, lass. I hurt too much to be going anywhere."

Merzi hurried next door to tell James that the stranger was

awake. She proceeded to the large pot of drinking water kept near the kitchen door and ladled some of the fresh liquid into a metal cup. When she returned to the bedchamber the man was telling James how he had been attacked by three thieves as he was journeying from Bethany toward the cities of the Decapolis on the eastern shores of the Sea of Galilee.

"I had to take the long road around, as usual, rather than travel through the despicable land of the Samaritans," he was saying when James signaled for Merzi to approach and give the man a drink.

"You may be interested to know, sir, that it was a Samaritan who rescued you and brought you to my Inn."

"What? A Samaritan would stop and help a Jew? That's hardly believable." The man sipped at the cool water, and then wiped his mouth with the back of his hand, wincing with pain as he raised his arm to his chin.

"But it is true," James continued. "My good friend Sebastian, a Samaritan caravan owner, is the one who saw you lying on the road and stopped to help. Apparently, there had been others who had come along, but not wanting to get involved, passed you by."

"I hope that someday I will be able to thank this Sebastian, Samaritan though he is, for saving my life."

"Yea, indeed. By the way, my name is James and I am the proprietor of this Inn, known as the Inn of Nine Palms."

"Thank you for your kindness on my behalf. As you see, I have no funds with which to pay you for this room. But if you are willing to trust me, I will make good on my debt."

"That will not be necessary, sir. I'm sorry that I have not yet learned your name."

"Of course, my good man. I am Jehu, a publican from Bethany. I was on my way to meet a publican of your city, Zacchaeus by name. Then we were going to travel together to the Decapolis. There's strength in numbers, you know," the man attempted a chuckle but ended up coughing instead. "By chance, do you know Zacchaeus?"

"Oh yes," replied James with unmasked disgust in his voice, "everyone knows Zacchaeus the tax collector."

"I perceive that you are not fond of tax collectors," replied Jehu, trying in vain to be humorous.

"Is anyone? We can thank the Romans for that injustice, along with many others."

Jehu continued, although his voice was weakening, "Well, be that as it may; we can't change the system ourselves. But back to my bill here at the Inn, what will I owe you? In spite of your kindness, I hope my stay here won't be long." Jehu started to rise from the mattress but fell back grimacing with pain and weakness.

"Merzi, more water for the publican, please."

Merziabah stepped forward and gave the man another a drink.

"I think I must rest here a little longer than I thought," replied Jehu sinking back onto the bed. Walking quietly toward the door, James said. "It is right that you should rest yourself and recover from your injuries. Do not concern yourself with your bill. It has been paid in advance by Sebastian, the Samaritan." James wondered if Jehu had heard his final words or if the man was already drifting off to sleep.

Jehu slowly rolled to his side testing his strength, then cautiously arose from the mattress to a sitting position, placing his bare feet on the floor. He allowed the dizziness to clear from his brain and wiped his face with his hands, stroking the tangles from his beard. He had appreciated the tender care of young Merzi, who had frequently brought fresh water and rubbed a healing salve into his cuts and bruises with her gentle hands. The nourishing food prepared by

Naomi had helped him regain some strength, even though it had been only three days since he had been brought to the Inn. Reaching his hand to the wall to steady himself, Jehu struggled to his feet and straightened his upper body. "Oh that feels good to be upright again," he said to himself. *But what now? I have no robes to clothe myself since I was stripped to my tunic by the thieves. Nor do I have any sandals for my feet. I cannot go out into public like this.* In discouragement, Jehu lowered himself again to the bed thinking about his problem.

I could send a message to Zacchaeus asking him to temporarily loan me some outer garments and sandals. Yes, as soon as Merzi returns, I will ask her to locate one of the village lads to be my messenger. I assume there are messenger boys here as there are in Jerusalem. I told James that I was on my way to meet Jericho's tax collector and that we were planning on traveling along the eastern side of the Jordan to Decapolis. That is true enough. But what I didn't tell him was that Zacchaeus and I were also planning to go further north, even to Galilee if necessary, in search of the man Jesus. Rumors of his healings and miracles have spread throughout the province, and we want to hear him ourselves. In spite of being looked down upon by the people, we are honest in our dealings with both the Jews and the Romans.

These plans were soon carried out, and with many thanks to James and his family for their kindness, he departed with the local publican. Although much shorter in stature than Jehu, Zacchaeus provided a supportive shoulder on which his friend could lean. As they slowly walked along the dusty streets to the tax collector's home that was not far distant, they talked of their common interest in Jesus.

"Have you heard any more about the Master?" asked Jehu.

"Only that He continues to teach a gospel of love and goodwill. But to the Pharisees and scribes, he is often brutally direct, condemning their hypocrisy."

"What do you think he would say about us tax collectors, whom many classify among the greatest of sinners?"

"I believe that Jesus looks more on a man's heart than on his occupation," replied Zacchaeus.

"Have you heard of any more miracles after the outlandish rumors that he fed five thousand people with only five loaves and two fishes? We all know that that's impossible. Sometimes the tales grow and grow with their re-telling."

"Do you not think that someone who has the power of God could perform such a miracle, Jehu?"

"Well, I suppose if he truly had that power. That is something I don't really understand."

"Nor I," admitted the man from Jericho. "But if you do believe it, perhaps you could also believe the report that he raised a young man from the dead in Nain. The family was on the way to the burial tombs, carrying the corpse wrapped in linen on a litter. Jesus suddenly appeared and spoke quietly to the young man's mother, and then told the dead man to arise."

"Preposterous!" growled Jehu. "These stories are getting more fantastic every day. I wonder how long the Pharisees and temple priests are going to allow this to go on."

"Don't be too hasty in your judgment, old friend. Let us wait a few more days until you have regained your complete strength and then we will go and find this Jesus. Perhaps when we see him ourselves we can determine if he is a charlatan, the devil's tool, or if he is really the Son of God that he claims to be."

Springtime freshness filled the air as the desert came alive with the pink and yellow blossoms of the prickly pear. Snow melting from the heights of Mt. Hermon to the north had widened the Jordan's banks with its rapidly moving stream of water. There was often a mood of optimism at this season, sandwiched in between the dismal winter rains and the blistering heat of the summer. It was also the season for thoroughly cleaning the Inn in preparation for the Passover. In spite of their lack of attendance at synagogue, James and Naomi were faithful Jews and obeyed the Laws of Moses. That Law required the dwelling to be swept and scrubbed from top to bottom. So along with their normal duties, each family member took on added responsibility for sweeping the rafters for cobwebs or the corners of each bedchamber for mouse droppings or cockroaches' nests.

One evening as guests lounged in the dining room, the word was passed around that Jesus was on his way to Jericho and would be arriving on the morrow. James and Naomi were as curious as many of their townspeople to see and hear this itinerant preacher. Originally the plan was to leave Rebekah and Merziabah to proceed with the cleaning and oversee the Inn, if by chance any new guests happened to drop by. But when the time came, James relented to the girls' pleas, locked the doors with a note attached that they would all return by sunset, and the family joined the crowds already filling the streets of Jericho. "Do you think Jesus will do a miracle here like He's done in the Galilee?" Merzi asked James.

"Hard to say, child."

"It looks like the whole district has come out to see and hear Jesus," commented Naomi. "I wonder if I should have stayed home and prepared the evening meal. Perhaps we will have more customers tonight."

"There will still be time to prepare food, Naomi," replied James. "We're not going to be gone long. It's not every day that we get the chance to hear a man like Jesus speak."

The crowd seemed to be moving toward the central market where there was an open area, usually filled with tents of vendors or carts of produce hauled in from the outlying farms. But today all the shops were closed, as every inhabitant of Jericho wanted to hear Jesus. The family moved to the side of the throng as they watched four men carrying a man on a litter. The leader called out, "Make way, we're taking our father to Jesus to be healed." They soon noticed others__one leading a blind man, another carrying a crying child.

"I had hoped we might find shade under one of the sycamore trees, but we would have had to have been here before dawn to do that. I wonder if some of these folks waited here all night," said Naomi scanning the crowded area.

"Look, there are Jehu and Zacchaeus near one of the trees. There seems to be a little space around them," said Merzi, pointing across the public square.

"That's because no one wants to be seen standing near a tax collector, Merzi," said Rebekah in derision.

"But it's still a place to stand out of the sun. I do believe the day is going to become quite warm for the month of Nisan," said Naomi, already fanning herself with the edge of her shawl.

"We have no need to fear either of them," replied James. "In spite of their occupations, they are both upright men. Come, let's go meet them. I'd like to know how Jehu is recovering from his wounds."

They inched their way across the crowded Square until they came to the publicans. James extended his hand to Jehu, "How are you feeling, old friend?" To James, anyone who had ever stayed under his roof was considered an 'old friend.'

"Much better, and I thank you for inquiring. Rest, good food, and good company at both places I've lodged in while in Jericho have benefitted me greatly. I should be well enough to resume my journey soon."

Jehu did not think it necessary to inform James that perhaps the purpose of his journey might not now be necessary since it seemed that Jesus was coming to them.

Zacchaeus strained his neck trying to see around the crowd of onlookers. He always hated to stand in front of the other adults, along with the children. It was so embarrassing for a man of his social standing to be so short in stature.

"Here He comes! Here comes Jesus" the cry went up from the multitude.

"Where? I can't see Him."

"Is He the one in the brown robe? He looks just like any other Jew to me. I thought he'd look like someone extra special."

"Hush, we want to hear the Master."The comments dwindled as Jesus and about a dozen men approached.

"I can't see Him," complained Zacchaeus. "Friends, can you give me a boost up into this tree where I can see better? It will be so embarrassing if anyone should discover me, but I do want to be able to see and hear the Man."

James and Jehu bent their knees, forming a strong platform of their backs. Zacchaeus grasped the hem of his robe and tucked it into his sash, freeing his legs for action. Nimbly, he climbed onto the backs of the two other men and boosted himself onto a sturdy limb of the sycamore tree. Because of the abundance of green foliage, Zacchaeus was not visible to the crowd, but he had a birds-eye view of all that was going on below him. There were hundreds crowded into the Square all vying for a view of Jesus. It seemed to be a sea of brown swirling below him of dusty dun-colored robes and weathered faces blending into the desert landscape.

But for Zacchaeus, the attempted camouflage in the tree did not last for long. As Jesus approached, he looked up and saw the publican. Reaching his arm upward, Jesus said unto him, "Zacchaeus, make haste and come down; for today I must abide at thy house." (Luke 19:5) With a look of chagrin, like a young boy being caught sneaking a handful of dates from a vendor, Zacchaeus blushed with embarrassment and quickly jumped down from the limb that had been his short-lived secret perch. Fortunately, attention soon returned to Jesus as murmuring from the crowd began, "Jesus is going to be a guest with a man that is a sinner?"

"Oh, James," whispered Naomi, "I wish that Jesus had said He would be a guest in our house." She was already taken in by the demeanor of the renowned preacher, who in spite of the bright sunlight seemed to have a light radiating specifically around Him.

Zacchaeus thought to himself: I *should send word back to my household staff to prepare the evening meal for this honored guest. But I see no one whom I might send. I cannot ask Jehu to leave in my behalf, nor can I pull myself away. There is something like a magnetic force emanating from this man drawing us all toward him. How did Jesus know my name? I have never seen Jesus in person before today.*

Again, murmuring words turned Zacchaeus's attention back toward the crowd. "Have not the prophets said that the kingdom of God should soon appear?"

"Is Jesus going to be our King?'

"Down to the Romans!"

"How can we believe what He says, when he deliberately violates the Sabbath?"

"I was cured of my blindness by this man as he walked toward Jericho."

"You can't always believe in miracles. Remember how the priests of Pharaoh matched the miracles of Moses."

Jesus raised his hand to quiet the crowd which had parted, allowing the publican to come into the center of the Square. Zacchaeus bowed before Jesus acknowledging him as a man of great honor. "Lord, the half of my goods I give to the poor; and if I have taken anything from any man by false accusation, I restore him fourfold." (Luke 19:8)

Speaking to the multitude, Jesus spoke, "This day is salvation come to this house, forasmuch as he also is a son of Abraham. For the Son of man is come to seek and to save that which was lost." (Luke 19:9-10)

"I want nothing to do with a man who shows such respect to a tax collector," roared a deep voice from within the crowd. Several from the group turned away, following the agitator down a narrow alley.

"Can you save me, O Lord? I am a lost and fallen man."

"Save us, Son of David."

"Show us one of your miracles."

"Hush, give the man a chance to speak."

Jesus scanned the crowd, drawing every eye to him, then the comments ceased. "I would speak unto you a parable. A certain nobleman went into a far country to receive for himself a kingdom, and to return. And he called his ten servants and delivered them ten pounds and said unto them,' Occupy till I come'. But the citizens hated him, and sent a message after him, saying, 'We will not have this man to reign over us'.

"And it came to pass, that when he was returned, having received the kingdom, then he commanded these servants to be called unto him, to whom he had given the money, that he might know how much every man had gained by trading.

"Then came the first, saying 'Lord, thy pound hath gained ten pounds.' And the nobleman said unto him, 'Well, thou good servant: because thou has been faithful in a very little, have thou authority over ten cities.' And the second came, saying, 'Lord thy pound hath gained five pounds'. And he said likewise to him, 'Be thou also over five cities.' And another came, saying, 'Lord, behold here is thy pound, which I have kept laid up in a napkin. For I feared thee, because'. And the nobleman said unto him, 'Out of thine own mouth will I judge thee, thou wicked servant. Thou knewest that I was an austere man, taking up that I laid not down, and reaping that I did not sow. Wherefore then gavest not thou my money into the bank, that at my coming I might have required mine own with usury?"

" And he said unto them that stood by, 'Take from him the pound, and give it to him that hath ten pounds.' But those men said, 'Lord, he already has ten pounds.'The nobleman answered, 'For I say unto you, that unto every one which hath shall be given; and from him, that hath not, even that he hath shall be taken away from him. But those mine enemies, which would not that I should reign over them, bring hither and slay them before me."(Luke 19:12-27).

Jesus stood quietly, waiting for the people to understand his story.

"I wish someone would give me a pound."

"I don't understand what this parable means. Why can't he speak plainly?"

"This man does not speak justly. Why would he give the one with the most money even more?"

"Who are the enemies that he wants to slay?"

Jesus again scanned the sea of faces before him, and stopping on Jehu, looked the publican from Bethany straight in the eye. Jehu wanted to shrink back into the crowd, to escape the piercing gaze, but he seemed as firmly attached to the spot as Lot's wife who had been turned into a pillar of salt. Jesus raised his hand again and the crowd became silent. "Another parable I would speak unto you. As I spoke unto the people of Jerusalem, so I now speak unto you. 'A certain man went down from Jerusalem to Jericho."

"Ah," interrupted several from the crowd.

"We are so honored that the Lord would speak of our city. Now others will want to come here, eh?"

"Let him finish his story."

Jesus, in patience, began again, "A certain man went down from Jerusalem to Jericho, and fell among thieves, who stripped him of his raiment, and wounded him, and departed, leaving him half dead." (Luke 10: 30)

Jehu cringed and wanted to shrink away. *How did Jesus know what had happened to him? Who had told the Master of his tragic circumstances?* Glancing around, Jehu realized that few in the crowd knew of him or why he had been brought to Jericho. James reached out and touched Jehu's shoulder. "I didn't tell him," he mouthed wordlessly.

Jesus continued, "And by chance there came down a certain priest that way, and when he saw him, he passed by on the other side. And likewise, a Levite, when he was at the place, came and looked on him, and passed by on the other side. But a certain Samaritan, as he journeyed, came where he was, and when he saw him, he had compassion on him. And went to him, bound up his wounds, pouring in oil and wine, and set him on his own beast, and brought him to an inn, and took care of him.

"And on the morrow when he departed, he took out two pence, and gave them to the host, and said unto him, 'Take care of him, and whatsoever thou spendest more, when I come again, I will repay thee. Which now of these three, thinkest thou, was neighbor unto him that fell among the thieves?"

Jehu stepped forth, and answering for all said, "He that shewed mercy on him."

Then Jesus answered, "Go and do thou likewise." (See Luke 10:31-37)

Jehu was speechless. He dropped to his knees in the dusty street as people moved on, not willing to accept the message they had just heard. Still Jehu was motionless as he heard the Master call for those who were sick, lame, blind, or possessed of devils to be brought unto him, so that He might heal them. Jehu didn't move until James came up behind him and asked in a concerned voice, "Do you need help in arising, Jehu?"

The publican shook his head, but nevertheless leaned heavily on the inn keeper's arm, steadying himself enough to stand. "How did he know?" Jehu asked incredulously.

"It seems that Jesus has the power to discern the thoughts of men," answered James.

"I feel his power penetrating my very soul. It was as if he were speaking directly to me, 'Go and do thou likewise.' First I must find the Samaritan who rescued me. James, what did you say his name was?"

"It was Sebastian, a caravan owner, whom I have known for many years."

"Do you think Sebastian may have been the one to tell Jesus what he had done for me?"

"It is doubtful, for he is not a man to boast of his own good works. It is unlikely that Sebastian and Jesus have ever met, but as you say, more probable that Jesus has the power to discern the thoughts of men."

"But I'm sure there is more than a mere expression of gratitude to Sebastian that I am expected to do. I must learn to show mercy to all, and not pass them by."

"I think that is the message for all of us, Jehu. However, It appears that Jesus is through speaking for today. We must return to the Inn and resume our duties. I wish you well, Jehu."

With that, James turned and gestured for his family to follow him out of the public Square. Zacchaeus returned to Jehu saying excitedly. "We must hurry back to my house, Jehu. Jesus will dine with us this evening and we can ask him more. But for now, we must prepare for his arrival." The two tax collectors walked off in the opposite direction of the Inn, Zacchaeus thinking that perhaps being small in stature had today brought him great blessings.

The next fortnight was among the busiest that the Inn of the Nine Palms had ever seen. It seemed there were thousands who joined the pilgrimage to Jerusalem for the biggest festival of the year__Passover. Rebekah's feet ached from serving so many guests, for in addition to her duties in the dining room, Rebekah now made a daily trip to the market buying fresh supplies for her mother. Merzi's arms ached from the washing and hanging of the heavy sheets. Naomi ached all over. James' fingers were almost forming callouses from rubbing the numerous coins that passed through his hands daily.

In spite of the busyness, Merziabah was glad that Rebekah was treating her more like a sister again. Somehow it seemed that everyone under the roof of the Inn of the Nine Palms was acting a little kinder to one another since they had heard Jesus speak in Jericho.

Sebastian's caravan was among those on the road heading toward Jerusalem. It was not only a lucrative season for innkeepers, but for merchants. He was hoping that all those pilgrims in Jerusalem would be eager to buy the fabrics, incense, and spices that he transported to the merchants in the Holy City. He had stopped briefly to settle his account regarding the injured traveler he had left with James a few weeks earlier. The innkeeper refused any additional payment, saying that not only had Sebastian's earnest money been sufficient but that they had been abundantly blessed by going to hear Jesus and hear the Master tell the parable of 'The Good Samaritan'. Sebastian agreed to try and learn more of Jesus's teachings, as he was sure that He would be teaching in the temple during the Passover celebrations. He promised that he would relay any new information back to them. Jedidiah only had a few minutes in which to greet his daughter and promise a longer visit the next time.

But Sebastian's caravan did not return before the news reached them that Jesus had been crucified in the midst of Passover. It was unimaginable that the priests had conspired with the Roman governor to put to death a man who only promoted good. Every heart in

James' household ached with sorrow. They had only seen Jesus once, but there had been such a presence about Him, that He had made a profound impact on their lives in that brief encounter. Even though the sun still shone brightly outside, it was if a cloud now enveloped their lives.

It was two months before Sebastian's caravan returned, having traveled to the western port of Joppa. One evening all the members of James' family gathered in the courtyard trying to catch a hint of a breeze from the heat of the summer's day. Phillip and Sarah had joined them, and Rebekah was playing pat-a-cake with Jonas. Saul was full of tales of the ships he saw in the harbor there, and of people he met from many nations. Merzi snuggled close to her father caressing the folds of a blue silk scarf which he had just presented to her. Jedidiah was pleased to see how the color complemented her dark eyes and hair. But most importantly, Sebastian told them more about Jesus. "The Master was betrayed by one of his own disciples, a man named Judas. The Chief Priest, Caiaphas, was instrumental in getting a charge of blasphemy that is only punishable by Jewish law, changed to one of treason, saying that Jesus claimed to be the King of the Jews. Of course, Pontius Pilate, could not ignore such a threat, for we all know what a power-hungry man the governor is. Although Jesus had taught nothing about overthrowing the Romans, mob rule prevailed and Pilate ordered execution by crucifixion."

"The most horrible way to die," remarked James. Merzi shuddered to think about an innocent man hanging on a cross.

"But I do report some good news, although it may take some time to sort things out. I am good friends with Joseph of Arimathea, a well-known merchant in Jerusalem. This Joseph has been secretly learning more of Jesus's teachings over the past three years, and he says that the followers of the Master are not disbanding, but actually increasing in numbers."

"How can that be?" asked James.

"It is true that Jesus died. But many now testify that on the third day he rose from the tomb."

"What did you say, Sebastian?"

"Joseph of Arimathea offered his own tomb for the burial of Jesus and saw the corpse wrapped in linens, and then sealed with a huge stone. Temple guards were positioned to keep it secure for the next three days."

"Then what happened? Did someone come and steal the body away and now they are claiming he has risen from the dead?"

"It is true that the body no longer lies in the tomb, but angels told some of the women who came to anoint the body with spices on the day following the Sabbath, that He was no longer there but had risen."

Well, you know how women can tell tales," said James glancing at Naomi, then Sara, Rebekah, and Merziabah in turn. "Not that any of you would tell such outlandish stories," he added in an apologetic tone.

"Jesus's apostles claim that he was resurrected, come back to life, and continues to direct his work."

"That is unbelievable."

"At first I felt the same way, but more than five hundred people claim to have seen Him."

"Five hundred? That's a lot of witnesses."

"Yes, indeed, James."

"You said, "at first," you thought it was unbelievable. Do you believe it now?"

"I must admit that I do, James. I have heard Jesus's apostles preach in the Court of the Gentiles myself, and I believe that He is the Son of God that he professed to be."

James looked at Sebastian with a dubious glance but did not say anything.

"They proclaim a gospel based on the teachings of Jesus, and many are flocking to join this new religion. Peter, James, and John, the three who head up this movement, say that Jesus has given them the same power to heal the sick and I have talked to some who were cured of their infirmities. They have a sure witness of this divine power. I myself have observed the same glow of light radiating from them that Jesus did. I feel that the Holy Spirit has touched them and that their message is true."

"But Sebastian, you are a Samaritan. How can you accept a religion directed to the Jews?"

"That is part of the beauty of the teachings of Jesus Christ. It is a message for **all** people. The Master told his disciples to preach the gospel to all the world. I intend to pave the way for them wherever I go."

"It sounds like you are quite converted, Sebastian. Who would have imagined?" James said with a chuckle, "A hard-nosed, coin-biting, camel-loving Samaritan like you."

"I guess if Jesus can change a hard-nosed, coin-biting, camel-loving Samaritan like me, He can change the hearts of every man who is willing to listen. I truly want to be known as The Good Samaritan."

"I think you have blessed me and my household in a new way this day, Sebastian."

Merzi looked up at her father, "I want to learn more about Jesus," she whispered.

"I'm sure you shall, my dear. The old ways are changing."

Merzi knew that things would never be the same at this Jericho Inn.

Five Loaves and Two Fishes

ELI MOANED AND turned over on his pallet near the hearth and his mother knelt nearby to stir the glowing embers into a brighter flame. He knew it must be about dawn, but he wanted a few more minutes of sleep for his twelve-year-old body that needed all the rest it could get.

"Eli," whispered his mother as she shook his shoulder. He groaned, trying to turn away from her. "Let me sleep," he grumbled.

"Eli, wake up now," came the command in a slightly louder tone. "You must go to the fish market while the catch is still fresh."

Eli knew it wouldn't do any good to argue so he threw off the woven blanket, sat up, and reached for his homespun brown tunic which lay on a nearby stool. Then tying the leather thongs of his sandals he arose and stretched his arms, giving a loud yawn.

"Shh, don't wake the other children."

"Yes, mother," he whispered back.

"Your father did not come home last night but he sent word with Uncle Silas that he is staying one more day to listen to Jesus. He wants you to meet Silas at the village well as soon as you can after daybreak. I told your uncle that I would bake some bread to send along for your father. He will undoubtedly be hungry and I doubt he took many coins with him yesterday." As if we had any coins to spare, she thought to herself.

"Here is a farthing. Go to Zebedee's stall. His fish can always be trusted to be fresh. The bread should be finished by the time you return."

Eli tiptoed quietly, stepping over his younger brother who lay on his own pallet on the opposite side of the hearth, and released the leather thong which allowed the door to swing inward, its worn hinges squeaking with the movement. Eli cringed at the noise, but waved to his mother as if to say "it's not my fault" and he silently stepped out into the grayness of the morning. A mist still hung about the shores of the Sea of Galilee, but he could hear sounds of fishing boats being pulled onto the rocky shore and knew that the men were coming in from their night's work.

He picked his way along the smoothly-worn trail to the village of Capernaum, which was situated on the western shore of the Sea, also known as Lake Chinnereth.

"Good morning, Zebedee," called out Eli to an older man who was plucking fresh mackerel from the long net he had used to collect the fish.

"Same to you, Eli. You're up early."

"Mother wants me to get a few fish to take to father."

"Oh, so Nehome stayed in Bethsaida last night to listen to Jesus?'

"I guess that's where he is. Uncle Silas told mother last night that father wouldn't be coming home."

"Well, that's where James and John are as well. Wish I could do the same, but someone has to keep this business running."

"They say hundreds are following Jesus from city to city to hear his message. I am anxious to hear him myself."

"I heard him speak a few weeks ago when he came to Capernaum to rest a few days at Peter's house. I must say I was enthralled with his words as anyone, but as I said, someone must keep this family in business. I don't begrudge James or John for wanting to be near The Master though. That man speaks with a power that I can't explain."

"I'm sorry I can't stay longer and hear what you have to say about Jesus, Zebedee, but Mother is anxious for the fish…"

"Sorry, lad. I'm just an old man who likes to hear myself talk. Comes from spending so much time alone out on the water. Here are three fish for you, fresh as you can get them."

"But I only have one farthing, Zebedee. Surely three fish are worth more than one farthing."

"Well, they're on the small side today. So take them with my blessing."

"Thank you, Zebedee. You are very generous."

"Perhaps you can share with me what you learn from Jesus when you return as compensation for the extra fish."

"I will be glad to do so, Zebedee. Is there any message you would like me to give James and John if I see them?"

"Yes, tell them to learn as much as they can from the Master while He is with us."

Eli took the fish wrapped in a palm leaf and hurried back up the trail to his home, which was really more of a cave with a constructed stone front, one window still shuttered from the night air, and the squeaky wooden door. It was a humble dwelling for a weaver's family. His father's shop was in a shed adjacent to the house, its door still closed. Eli's oldest brother, Ezekiel who was learning the trade, would open the shop later in case there were any customers. His sister, Ruth, who was married to a potter, lived down the street and was expecting a baby, which made his mother very happy. Eli's youngest brother, Reuben at nine years of age, completed his family. It was a lot of mouths to feed on the small income from the shop, and now with his father absent so many days, there wasn't much money coming in. What could they do?

The bread was just coming out of the brick oven built into the side of the hearth when Eli stepped through the door, the tantalizing aroma enveloping him and waking up his stomach, which growled for nourishment.

His mother withdrew a dozen small loaves from the baking tray and tucked five of them into a basket lined with a linen cloth. "Here's another one for your breakfast, Eli, and the rest are for you and your father to eat at mid-day. Did you get any fish?"

"Yes, Mother. Zebedee sold me three for the price of two, saying they were small, but you know he is always generous."

"Yes, a kind man, as are his sons. But I wonder what will happen to his business now that James and John seem to be caught up in following the Preacher Jesus. It seems the whole village is following after this man and the throngs increase daily. I hope you and your father can return by nightfall and give me a full report of what you hear and see."

"I will, Mother."

Rebecca took the fish, expertly gutted them, and then poured a marinade over the top consisting of olive oil, vinegar, salt, turmeric, cumin, and other spices. It would preserve the fish from decay since it wasn't going to be eaten for several hours. "Here, you take two of the fish. You will need the energy for the walk to Bethsaida and back. We will make do here with one for today. I will pull some leeks from the garden, and with fresh cucumbers and goat cheese, we will be able to make a meal here. Now you'd better be on your way. Silas will be waiting."

Eli grabbed a goatskin, which he planned on filling at the well and hung it over his shoulder. He took the proffered basket with one hand, the single loaf with the other and gave his mother a quick hug. "Shalom."

"God go with you, my son. Be careful," replied Rebecca, returning the embrace.

Eli started munching on the warm loaf of bread as soon as he was out the door. The outside was crusty and chewy, while the inside was so soft it seemed to melt in his mouth. The sun had just risen over the eastern hills that lined the shore of the Lake. He hurried down the trail he had just traversed, but instead of heading directly to the shore, took the fork that led into the center of the village. Just as his mother had predicted, his Uncle Silas was waiting at the well. The man was taller than his brother Nehome but had the same dark brown hair, black eyes, and jutting nose of the Jewish race. Eli hurried the last few rods, the empty bag at his side.

"You are late, Eli. The sun has already risen."

"I beg a thousand pardons, Uncle Silas. Mother sent me to the fish market earlier while the bread was baking so that I could take some food for father."

"Your mother is very considerate, Eli, and Nehome is blessed to have her for a wife. Beulah on the other hand…" he gave a shrug of his shoulders, before adding, "I stopped at the baker's shop on my way," tapping a scrip hanging at his side.

Eli filled the goatskin with clear water from the well and then the two of them set off with the sun in their eyes. Word had filtered back to Capernaum that Jesus was teaching in Bethsaida, a nearby village six miles away in the cluster of settlements that hugged the northern shore of the Sea of Galilee.

"Do you think we should take the upper or lower road, Uncle Silas?" asked Eli.

"I know the upper trail is steeper and rockier but it is the shorter distance, so I say we should go that way. I want to hear as much of Jesus's teachings today as possible," replied the older man.

"I am anxious to listen to him also. I have heard so much about him. Do you think it is strange that one as young as I is interested in religion?"

"Not at all, Eli. You have been studying for your Bar Mitzveh, haven't you?"

"Of course, Uncle. But somehow Jesus's teachings seem a little different."

"It's not just his teachings that are wonderful. His whole presence seems to emanate with power."

"Do you think he is the Messiah?" asked Eli.

"I have heard some call him such, but I can't say for myself. He doesn't seem to be seeking political power to overthrow the Romans, although I wish someone would. His power seems to be more of a spiritual nature. There are many who claim he has special abilities to heal the blind and the lame. I have not seen any of his miracles, so they may just be rumors."

"Tell me more about his teachings, Uncle Silas."

"See that small valley below us?" asked Silas, pointing down toward the seashore.

"Yes," answered Eli, shading his eyes against the morning sun.

"Only a few days ago Jesus sat on the side of the mount and taught us new doctrine. He would start by saying, 'It is written', meaning written in the Law of Moses, of course. Then he would go on with, 'but I say unto you,' as if he had greater authority than Moses."

"No one is greater than Moses. At least that's what they teach in the synagogue classes."

"Ah, yes. Bar Mitzvah, eh?"

"Yes, sir. I hope to be ready within a few months."

"Then you are familiar with the teaching that we should love our neighbor and hate our enemy?"

"Of course, so it is written in the Second Reading of the Law, commonly known as the Book of Deuteronomy, written by the prophet Moses," said Eli, defending the venerated Israelite leader.

"That's just it, Eli. This Jesus said 'We should love our enemies, bless them that curse us, do good to them that hate us and pray for them which despitefully use us."

"I don't think I can accept this Jesus as a true prophet then. He must be an imposter. No one should have to pray for those who persecute us."

"Don't judge him too quickly, lad. He went on to say that the Father in heaven maketh the sun to rise on the evil and the good, and sendeth rain on the just and the unjust. Isn't that so?"

"Yes," answered Eli with a little less surety than before.

"Then Jesus went on to say that if we love only those who love us, we are no better than the publicans. Then he commanded us to be perfect."

"How can any mortal man be perfect?"

"Here, let's stop near this cedar tree for a little rest, Eli. My legs are not as strong as yours. I will tell you what Jesus said, how we could become perfect or at least blessed."

"Would you like a drink of water first, Uncle Silas?"

"Oh, thank you, lad. Yes, I am very thirsty." They both guzzled long drafts of the cool clear liquid before Silas continued.

"Jesus used just such a symbol as water to teach us. He said if we would hunger and thirst after righteousness as much as we thirst after water, then we would be filled. He said if we were poor__"

"We certainly are that," interrupted Eli, fingering the coarseness of his brown tunic. "Sorry, I interrupted; go on."

"He meant poor in spirit, then the kingdom of heaven would be ours. If we comfort or give mercy to others then we will receive the same in return."

"And all of these things are supposed to bring us blessings?"

"Yes. If we are peacemakers, we shall be called the children of God."

'If the Jews are the Chosen children of God, it seems like they are persecuted a lot more than any other people."

"I know what you mean. So has it been through the ages. Nonetheless, the prophets been persecuted before us, and Jesus says we should be exceedingly glad, for our reward will be in heaven."

"Somehow that doesn't make it any easier to be a Jew now."

"Let's be up and going before any Romans see us here and call us sluggards," said Silas rising to his feet.

"It is a rotten law, that they can force us to carry their packs or armor for a mile," replied Eli.

"Oh yes, and I've done it many a time. But that is another thing Jesus said. 'If they compel us to go one mile, we should cheerfully do it twain.'"

"This Jesus must be crazy. I'm surprised my father is so taken with him."

"Just wait, Eli. Be open to his spirt before you make up your mind."

With that, the duo continued on the trail toward Bethsaida, Silas telling him more about Jesus and his teachings using the everyday language of salt and candles and cloaks. (See Matthew 5-7)

The day was wearing on and Eli was now the one dragging his feet. His too-small sandals had given minimal protection against the protruding rocks of the mountain trail. The gritty dust coated his feet with several of his exposed toes bruised from stubbing. The water bag now hung limply from his shoulder in its emptiness. He had shifted the basket of food from one arm to another throughout the morning and now both arms ached, although its contents were not large in quantity. The delicious aroma of the fresh bread had dissipated and was now replaced by the tantalizing smell of the fish with its aromatic spices. Eli's stomach yearned for the food; the one loaf he'd eaten hours ago was now long gone and the growling was intensifying. Yet, he dared not eat any of the loaves or fish lest there not be enough when he reached his father.

"Do you think we will find Jesus soon?" asked Eli.

"I would hope so," answered Silas in a weary tone. "We have already come almost five miles from Capernaum. Maybe we can see something over the next rise. Surely a large group of people would be easy to spot."

But their eyes met disappointment as they reached the ridge, for Bethsaida looked as sleepy as an infant in its mother's pack, dozing in the mid-day sun. Silas and Eli were debating about taking the downward path into the city or continuing on the mountain trail further north when a fellow traveler came toward them. Silas raised his hand in the common salutation, while Eli respectfully stepped back, giving the approaching man more space on the narrow trail.

"Greetings, traveler," said the man, addressing Silas.

"Greetings to you as well. By chance, would you know where the Master Teacher might be? We heard he was in Bethsaida."

"He was in the city earlier this morning, but the crowds became so great that they went a few furlongs into the desert beyond. I would guess five thousand men, plus a few women and children."

"That many?"

"He's got the whole country in an uproar with his ideas. Are you one of his disciples?"

"We're just learning at this point," replied Silas, not wanting to express an opinion to a stranger. One never knew who were friends or foes that would report any subversive talk to the Romans.

The man continued, "I don't believe he is the Messiah, but he tells interesting stories which he calls parables. There is no denying he has the power to perform miracles. I've seen him restore sight to the blind and make the lame to walk. Some say he turned water into wine at a wedding in Cana. Now that's the kind of miracle that I'd like to take part in," the man chortled.

"We have walked from Capernaum today in hopes of finding Jesus, so we had better continue on our journey. Thank you for the directions."

"If you keep on this trail, you can't miss them."

"Thank you and God-speed."

"Likewise."

Silas and Eli trudged along, tired, but also glad to know that their destination wasn't much further away.

It was just as the stranger had told them, for as they reached the next ridge they saw a multitude below milling about in the desert area. The sight of so many suddenly made Eli wonder how he would locate his father in such a throng. He could hardly stand from the mountaintop and call down to him like a priest with a ram's horn outside the city of Jericho. Nor could he make all the others disappear with the wave of an Egyptian magician's wand. But maybe some other kind of magic would happen and they would just bump into each other. Surely his father would have been watching for him and Silas throughout the day. Eli hoped it wouldn't be long before they would be reunited.

Silas chose a narrow path that led single file down through the scrub oak and pampas grass that lined the hillside. "Looks like the whole province of Galilee is here today," he said, turning his head back to speak to Eli. As they approached the gathering, Silas halted and pointed to his right. "There's Jesus, Eli. The man in the russet-colored robe."

"Oh yes, I see him. He looks like rather an ordinary man."

"What did you expect? Someone with golden curls and a patrician head like one of the Greek gods?"

"No. Yes. I don't know. I guess I just thought he would look special, especially if he is the promised Messiah."

"Do you not recall Isaiah's description__that he would 'have no form or comeliness, that when we should see him, there would be no beauty that we should desire him.'? Wait until you get closer and can look into his eyes. Then you will know that he is special indeed."

They were almost down the hill when Silas spotted Nehome in a small circle of men gathered around Jesus." Wait here, Eli, and secure us a space to sit where we can see and hear if The Master begins teaching again. I will go down and let your father know we are here. It looks as if the group is breaking up now so I will not have to intrude."

Eli scraped dirt and bird droppings off the semi-smooth surface of a protruding boulder and sat down, drawing his tired knees up to his chest. He surveyed his surroundings__ the haze of the summer day almost obscuring the tallest mountains of the Golan Heights on the far eastern shore. The natural geological narrow wedge that formed the Sea of Galilee was fed by the Jordan River with its clear-stream headwaters located near Mt. Hermon in the north and drained into the heavy salt brine of the Dead Sea twelve miles to the south. Eli remembered that fishermen said it was a furlong deep. How would anyone measure over six hundred fifty feet?

Eli breathed in the smell of the water that kept this area of the country cooler in the summer, one of the reasons that the Roman Governor Tiberius had constructed a fine palace nearby. The rise in elevation toward Jerusalem brought drier air and hotter temperatures. The birds, which usually swooped the shoreline for fish entrails, were now quietly resting in the branches of nearby trees to escape the heat of the afternoon's sun.

Just then a shadow broke through Eli's reverie and the boy looked up with a start. "Shalom, lad. Sorry if I startled you."

Eli looked warily at the intruder; he was not used to being around strangers. "I am Andrew," the man introduced himself. "I believe you are the son of Nehome, the weaver. Am I correct?"

Eli slowly nodded his head, not sure whether to trust the man or not. "I am Andrew, oh, I already said that didn't I? I'm the brother of Simeon, known as the Big Fisherman, from Capernaum. Perhaps you have heard of our father Jonah?"

Eli nodded, recognizing the familiar name. Although his family usually frequented the fish stalls of Zebedee, this village connection made Eli feel a little safer addressing a stranger. Andrew continued, "I am one of the disciples of Jesus, and we are asking if any among this large gathering has any food that we might have."

Eli glanced at the woven reed basket he had dutifully carried all morning. Surely the man could smell the fish, so it would do no good to deny he had some food. "I have only five barley loaves and two fish which my mother sent so my father might have something to eat."

"So you have walked all the way from Capernaum this morning?"

"Yes, sir."

"Then you must be hungry as well. I commend you for controlling your own appetites to serve your father. However, I am now trying to be obedient to our spiritual father, Jesus, who has requested food, however small the amount. Would you be willing to sacrifice your five loaves and two fishes for The Master?"

Eli was reminded of his own hunger and how he had waited all day for this food. His father would undoubtedly be expecting it, as well. But a powerful feeling inside prompted him to trust Andrew and give him the food. Hopefully, his father would understand.

Perhaps Uncle Silas had an extra penny or two he would be willing to loan, even though they were a considerable distance from a village where they might go to buy bread.

Eli slowly handed the basket to Andrew, somehow knowing he had made the right choice. "Bless you, lad. Jesus says sacrifice brings forth the blessings of heaven. Shalom." And with the basket in hand, Andrew disappeared down the trail toward the man Jesus.

"Andrew," called Eli to the retreating figure. The man stopped and turned around.

"Did you change your mind, lad?"

"No. I just remembered that Zebedee sent salutations to his sons."

"Thank you. I will give James and John the message."

Within minutes Eli began to doubt his decision. He was hungrier than ever and his stomach grumbled loudly. *How could I have been so foolish as to give away the food mother entrusted to me? And to a complete stranger? It wasn't as if some poor starving child had asked for it.* Eli felt remorse not only for himself but for his father who would now go hungry as well. *My parents will be so disappointed in me.* Although there were no clouds in the sky, a darkness settled over Eli's heart and mind pushing aside all the pleasant thoughts of the day.

How long he sat there wallowing in his gloom Eli did not know, but at last, he saw both his father and uncle walking up the short path toward him with several others following. Eli respectfully stood, but his head drooped toward his chest and he could not look Nehome in the face when his father reached out to hug him. "I am happy to see you, Eli. But you don't look like you are happy to see me. Why has your countenance fallen?"

"I'm sorry for my foolishness, father," thinking that he might as well get his confession out of the way sooner than later. *It won't do any good to deny I brought food from home; Silas was a witness of that. Nor will it do any good to lie; I know the punishment that can be heaped on liars according to the Law of Moses.*

"What is this about?"

"The loaves and fishes which mother sent for you. I gave them away."

"What? I was looking forward to a morsel of food."

Silas, overhearing the exchange, interrupted, "Eli, you mean that after you carried the basket more than six miles from Capernaum, you gave the food to someone else?"

"Yes, sir."

"We will talk about it later," said Nehome in a stern voice, "pri vately." He then gave his brother a look which said he didn't want any interference in this family matter. "The Master has asked us all to gather into companies for the time being," gesturing toward the dozen or so men who had followed Nehome and Silas up the trail. "They have also been with Jesus for two days and others will probably be joining us until there are about fifty in each group. I do not know the reason, but we are learning that Jesus doesn't always give a reason for his instructions or an explanation of his parables. But we are learning what it does mean to increase in our obedience and faith."

"We might as well sit here and wait," said Silas. "We can have a good view of the proceedings and hear whatever it is that Jesus will say. Perhaps the rest of you can enlighten Eli and me with what you have heard." The rest of the men settled themselves onto rocks, or even the bare ground trying to find some modicum of comfort in the desert area without a shade tree in sight.

One man with a pointy chin exaggerated by his V-shaped gray beard began. "Jesus told a parable about a sower who planted seeds. Some fell in good ground, others in stony places like this area. Some of the seeds sprouted but then shriveled when the hot sun came. I must confess I did not understand his meaning."

Another spoke, "I think the Master's message was more about the kind of soil than about the sower or the seed."

"Might that not apply to people's willingness to accept his word, which can be likened unto a seed?" said another.

The discussion was interrupted by the arrival of additional men, saying that Andrew had sent them this way. The mention of Andrew's name made Eli downhearted all over again.

The multitude all seemed to be seated in the dry grass or on rocks, with their eyes turned toward a cluster of men a little below. "Those are the twelve apostles whom Jesus has specially chosen to assist in his work," explained Nehome to Eli. A tall, broad-shouldered man raised his arms and called for everyone to be quiet. "That one is Simeon whom Jesus now calls Peter," he whispered; the near-by men gave him a dirty look for ignoring the injunction to be silent.

Eli recognized the name; Simeon was Andrew's brother. The thought of Andrew again brought Eli to heap self-reproach upon himself. Would he never be rid of his shame?

"Listen to the Master," directed Simeon Peter, who seemed to be taking charge; then he sat down with the rest of the Twelve. Jesus arose and took a basket in his hand and held it aloft. Eli immediately recognized the basket his mother had woven herself. It was apparent that Jesus was praying, but it was a prayer not intended for the ears of mortal men, but for His Heavenly Father only.

When Jesus finished, he took the bread from the basket and began to break it into pieces, then gave it to his apostles to eat. Eli realized that with only five small loaves and two fishes that even the meal divided among the chosen Twelve would be a scanty one. He watched as the apostles ate the bread and fish, **his** bread and fish, apparently enjoying the meal until they were filled. Eli's anger grew! *How rude for the men to flaunt that they had food while the rest of the multitude looked on with longing eyes and empty bellies.* However, Jesus did not eat with them, nor did he not stop breaking bread. He filled twelve other baskets which had been collected. Jesus did the same with the two fish, breaking them into small fragments.

Eli thought that many others must have contributed as well. His sacrifice wasn't so special after all and the dark feeling intensified. The twelve apostles began distributing the baskets of bread and fish among the twelve companies gathered on the side of the mount. Andrew himself brought one up the path to where Nehome, Silas, Eli, and the others were seated.

"Here men, eat your fill. The Master has provided a meal so that none of you need to go away hungry."

"Where did he get all of this food?" asked the man with the pointed chin. "Did someone go into Bethsaida and buy it?"

"I doubt there would be enough bread in the whole village of Bethsaida to feed this multitude," responded another.

Andrew smiled broadly. "No man here had money enough to buy such quantities of bread, sir. But this young lad sitting with you," he said, nodding toward Eli, "contributed all that he had__five small barley loaves and two fishes." All heads turned toward Eli as the young man ducked his head in embarrassment, his dark curls surrounding his reddened cheeks.

"Did you give your basket of food to Andrew?" asked Nehome.

Eli nodded his head without looking up. How would he ever be able to face his father again?

Andrew continued his explanation, "And with that small sacrifice, the Lord has blessed it and multiplied it bounteously."

"You mean all of this food came from only five loaves and two fishes?" asked Silas suspiciously.

"Yes. That is exactly what I mean," said Andrew. "Our Lord is truly a god of miracles."

"But how?" asked Eli, now looking up. "We only saw him lift one basket toward heaven and say a prayer."

"The Master does not explain how he is able to perform such great works. He only asks that we have faith in him."

"Did not the great Jehovah provide manna for the Israelites in the wilderness?" questioned a scholarly looking man who was sitting nearby. "What do the scriptures say, Rabbi?"

"Bread raining from heaven is spoken of in both the Law and the Psalms," answered a man wearing the skull cap and robes of a Jewish leader. "What happened here wasn't exactly rain, though. We must look to the Pharisees for a proper interpretation of the scriptures."

Andrew turned to leave, "We must look to the Lord for all of our answers," he said with finality.

The group was abuzz with the happenings they had witnessed with their own eyes but did not understand. Nehome spoke quietly to Eli who was still seated beside him. "So it was to Andrew that you gave the basket of food your mother sent?"

"Yes, father. I am not excusing my actions, but I can only say I had this strong feeling come over me that it was the right thing to do. I'm sorry. I hope I can regain your trust."

"My son, you have brought me great honor this day. To think your sacrifice was a part of this great miracle..." Nehome's voice was so overcome with emotion that he could not continue speaking. He promptly encircled Eli in his arms, murmuring, "My son, my son."

Eli felt the darkness evaporate from him and he was again filled with the uplifting spirit he had experienced earlier. It was like going from night to day and unbidden tears trickled down his dusty cheeks.

It was surprising how fast strangers could become friends when they started talking about the teachings and miracles of Jesus. About a dozen of the other men they ate with were heading toward Chorazin and the trio from Capernaum decided that they should also go that way. There was more protection from robbers if they traveled in a group. Nehome said it was too late to go all the way back to Capernaum, so perhaps they could find a night's shelter at the home of Rebecca's sister who lived in Chorazin. As the sun dipped further into the western sky the men took the lower trail nearer the seashore that would be less dangerous than the mountain trail in the dimming light.

"Did you notice how the Master didn't let any of the food go to waste?" asked one man. "Even after we had eaten our fill, they collected twelve baskets full of leftover bread and fish."

"I wonder if it will stink and be full of worms like the manna did when the Israelites tried to collect extra rations and save it overnight." Everyone laughed.

They discussed the nature of Jesus's teachings that were an injunction to live a higher law than the Law of Moses.

"Jesus said that not only should we not kill according to the sixth commandment of the Decalogue, but we should not even become angry with our brothers."

"That would be a hard one to keep if you have a brother like mine," teased Silas, pounding Nehome on the back. "It was such a rascal when he was a lad."

"Don't be giving Eli any ideas," retorted Nehome.

"Jesus also said we should be friendly with the Samaritans," said one man.

"They are the scum of the earth," answered another.

"The Master says we are all children of a Heavenly Father and that God is no respecter of persons."

"I heard Him speak of being born of the water and of the spirit. Being born of the water I can understand means baptism. Wasn't that the purpose of John's teachings in the wilderness near Bethabara? I just don't understand what it means to be born of the spirit?"

Eli, walking quietly behind the others, respectfully listened to what the men had to say. He pondered what it meant to be 'born of the spirit'. *Is that what happened to me earlier today? I felt totally immersed in that warm glow. How can I keep that feeling? It already seems to be fading away.*

Nehome dropped back to walk beside his son. "I wish I could listen to Jesus every day, but I am not one of the chosen Twelve who was asked to give up their occupations to be with him full time. So I must return to my loom and perhaps assist in his work by a monetary contribution."

"How can we afford to give money to others when we barely have enough to get by on ourselves?" asked Eli.

"I don't know, but I feel we can find a way if we show that we have faith. Your brother is becoming quite skilled in his apprenticeship, so maybe it is time to have another loom built so that two of us can be working. Is it time for you to become my newest apprentice?"

"I'm not sure I want to be a weaver, Father. No disrespect, but I think I would rather be a carpenter."

"Is that so?" asked Nehome looking at his son in surprise. "I have not heard you speak of this before."

"It's just something I've been thinking about lately. It's hard to know."

Nehome put his arm around the boy's shoulders, "Did you know that Jesus was trained by his father to be a carpenter?"

"No," said Eli glancing at his father, "I guess I hadn't thought about him having to do any kind of labor. He speaks with such authority I assumed he spent many years studying in the rabbinical schools."

"That is another amazing thing about Jesus, Eli. He didn't learn these doctrines from any man. He learns directly from God."

"You mean God actually speaks to him?"

"Well, in a way. I believe Jesus spends much time praying to His Father in Heaven and then things are revealed to his heart and his mind. Jesus always says he speaks the words of the Father."

"Many boys in the synagogue classes say God is fierce and angry and jealous. That doesn't sound like the same God Jesus is talking about."

"God is God. How we look at Him may have more to do with our own choices of right or wrong than Him, for He is unchangeable forever. If we choose wickedness, of course we are going to fear God because we know we deserve punishment. But if we are keeping the commandments, we have no reason to fear Him. We feel His blessings and are filled with love and gratitude, singing praises to Him for His goodness."

The two walked quietly for a time. Eli didn't want to say it out loud, but he thought his father had been speaking with more love since he'd been listening to Jesus. He hadn't heard him raise his voice in anger or complain if his supper was late. Is this what the teachings of Jesus did for people?

The silence was broken when Nehome spoke up, speaking to himself as much as to Eli. "Did you notice the brown robe Jesus was wearing? I can see it is quite old, maybe even a cast-off from someone else. I want to weave a new robe for Jesus. Maybe from fine wool so it can keep him warm during the winter." Nehome paused and looked at the stars which were beginning to twinkle in the darkening sky. "I will make it seamless, of the finest quality. Maybe one that will last his whole life. At least until he is attired in the robes of his

Eternal Kingdom."

"Do you think Jesus is the promised Messiah?" asked Eli.

"I do, Eli. Although I don't yet understand all that means. The witness has been born to my soul that he is the Son of God and I can't deny it. Nothing I can give, even if it might be my finest robe, will ever be worthy of the Messiah."

"I have a feeling many things are going to change, Father."

"I think you are right, son. And I hope for the better. That is what Jesus desires for all of us. To make bad men good, and to make good men better. I can't wait to tell your mother and brothers about Him. You will have a story to tell them yourself, Eli. It has been quite a day."

Eli walked on without speaking. The only sounds were the plodding of the men's feet as they picked their way along the graveled trail and the swish of the waves hitting the nearby shore. He looked up to see the stars just starting to twinkle in the dimness of the darkening sky. *I am just an insignificant speck in the wonder of God's creations, a mere twelve-year-old boy who doesn't understand much of the universe. Why was I in this exact spot today to witness this great event, yea even a form of creation before my very eyes? I suppose it started because I was willing to be obedient to my parents. Even though I was doing what was right, it wasn't easy. It was hot and the trail was rough and my feet bloody and sore. I was so hungry and thirsty. I wanted to hear Jesus preach, but I didn't really hear him say much. But I did learn from others, especially Andrew. And I guess the most important thing I learned was about the blessings that come from being willing to sacrifice.*

The number of stars seemed to multiply before Eli's eyes, the vastness of the universe above him unfathomable He thought again of the miracle of the multiplying of the bread and fish earlier that day. *Was the gospel that Jesus spoke of going to multiply as well? Was this little group on the Galilean seashore like five loaves and two fishes that would be multiplied the world over? What would it be like if Jesus's teaching spread throughout the whole earth?* It was too much for his young mind to comprehend. But Eli walked a little taller, smiled a little broader and was grateful that he had been a part of something BIG, a cause that stretched beyond himself, beyond Galilee, a part of a miracle which started with his five loaves and two fishes.

A Healing Faith

Part One

MIRIAM KNELT ON the hearth frying oatcakes on a flat stone nestled in the glowing red embers of the fireplace. Sweat dripped from her brow even though the evening breezes blew in from the nearby Sea of Galilee. It had been another hot summer day in Capernaum. The young woman frequently did the "floor work" to assist her mother Lyda.

Titus, Miriam's father, entered the small stone cottage built on the hillside overlooking the Sea. The man's garb, a leather apron, was spattered with dried grayish flecks of clay used to make the water jars common to the households of his community. Each jar was about a cubit in height, with a narrow neck so that the precious water would not slosh out needlessly. A large handle on one side allowed the pot to be dipped into the well for filling, and a smaller handle on the other gave balance for a firm grip as the women carried the full containers on their shoulders.

"You look tired, husband," said Lyda glancing up from the cucumbers she was peeling on a wooden board that lay across the small table.

"Yes, I am. The clay dried too fast in today's hot weather, so I had a difficult time shaping the jars on the wheel. Is dinner about ready? You know I have a meeting with Jonah this evening about an important matter." His eyes shifted toward Miriam, but not a word was spoken and Lyda nodded knowingly.

Several hours later, Titus quietly opened the door of the cottage and tiptoed into the bedchamber, surprised to see that his wife was still awake. With a low-burning candle on a nearby stool, it was obvious that she had been waiting for him.

"Well, how did it go?" she whispered.

"Jonah drives a hard bargain."

"You mean the dowry they demand is more than you offered?" Lyda sat up in the bed with a feeling of indignation.

"Of course; not only must we supply fifty denarii, but three goats and a dozen chickens. It seems that Jonah likes boiled eggs and goat cheese with his daily fish." He held out his palms in front of him in a "what-else-could-I-do?" gesture.

"I'm not surprised at his demands," said Lyda. "That's why he is such a successful businessman. Unlike you, Titus, who although excellent at your trade, are too kind-hearted to be as crafty as that fishmonger."

"I must confess you are right, wife." He bent over to give his wife a quick kiss on the cheek, then handing her the candle, sat on the stool to remove his sandals.

Lyda continued, "How can anyone put a price on our precious Miriam? Her ready smile, her willing hands, and her loving heart will be an asset to any man. Was Simon there with Jonah while you were dickering the bride price? "

"No, Jonah sent him down to the seashore to mend nets until dark. This is business that fathers must conduct themselves. If we let the young people attend, their emotions get in the way. Have you seen the way that Simon gawks at Miriam whenever she comes by? He's like a blithering idiot; he's so infatuated with her."

"I'm glad to know that our sweet daughter will be loved by her husband, even if he is a barrel of a man. I hope he doesn't break her ribs in his bear-like hugs. She's still so much of a child."

"She's fourteen, Lyda, the proper age when many young Jewish women are betrothed. By the time the marriage takes place, she will mature a little more and become physically stronger," said Titus as he slipped his night shirt over his head.

"So was the usual betrothal period established?"

"Yes, one year. That will give Simon time to build an extension onto his father's house for the two of them. Hopefully, this will bring about a bit more maturity in his behavior as well. He has always been such an impetuous youth, speaking and acting without consideration of the long- term consequences."

"Yes, I have worried some about that as well. I hope he doesn't hurt her feelings too much with his rough speech."

"It's what comes from growing up around all the fishermen at the seashore, Lyda. Sometimes those men have loose tongues and foul words in ready supply." Miriam's mother nodded in agreement before Titus continued. "It will also give Miriam time to weave the household linens and learn more cooking skills, although I must say the oatcakes tonight were exceptionally tasty." Titus pulled back the covers and lowered himself to the grass-filled tick mattress beside his wife.

Lyda slid back down beside her husband, pulling a light-weight sheet over them. "Miriam is already a **good** cook, but I can give her some training in the use of spices and herbs to turn into an **excellent** cook. Knowing that her time is at hand, I had better begin those lessons tomorrow. Do you think your stomach can stand her experimentations, Titus?"

"I'm sure this cast-iron stomach of mine can handle anything she prepares," he said patting his abdomen. "I've had plenty of practice over the years, my dear," the bearded man teased.

"Oh, away with you," Lyda responded in like manner tickling

him under the chin.

"We'd best get some sleep. The morning will dawn soon enough. Do you want to talk to Miriam or should I?"

"I think you should do it, Titus. I would probably blubber and cry at the thought of losing my youngest daughter."

"You've always known it would be like this, Lyda. It's the cycle of life."

"Yes, but now that the time has come it seems that the past fourteen years have slid by in an instant," Lyda moaned, tears starting to stream down her face.

"It's not like she is moving far away, woman. She will just be living down the hill and you will be able to see her often."

"I know, I know. But it will never be the same. I remember thinking similar things a few years ago when our Anna was married. But then, look what happened__Jehud was offered a position in the stables at Caesarea at steady wages. I worry about him working in that Gentile's palace, even if it is just with the horses. Then there's Caleb, the son you trained to join you in the pottery business who decided he wanted to be a scribe and has moved to Jerusalem to study with the Pharisees."

"You worry about too many things, Lyda," he said pulling her into the crook of his arm.

"There's no certainty in anything anymore, Titus. The Romans have made sure of that."

"Yes, yes, dear; dry your tears," he said as she wiped her face on the edge of the sheet. "I'm sure that Simon and Mariam will be very happy together. Jonah assures me that Simon will always have a place in their fishing enterprises, although Andrew as the oldest brother will probably inherit the business itself."

Titus pulled Lyda close and rubbed her back as they snuggled into each other. Although both were tired from the day's labors, neither fell asleep quickly as the silence hung heavy between them.

Lyda had been right about one thing__there was no certainty in their lives anymore.

Part Two

Miriam sank to the wooden bench parked near the front door of her stone cottage, pulling the fussy infant to her for a much-needed feeding. Miriam was grateful that Rachel was generally a patient baby; there were so many things that needed her attention with her busy little family. She looked down the hill toward the Sea of Galilee hoping that Simon was finding a good catch today. He spent so little time with the fishing business these days that their income was far from adequate and it seemed her young brood was always hungry. She could see Joshua and Saul playing with their cousins not far away. She wasn't sure if they were re-enacting the fall of Jericho or the slaughter of the Philistines, but their make-believe battles seemed intense. Miriam was glad that Andrew's children and her own were such good playmates, but they were certainly a lively bunch when they got together. An old, but never forgotten ache, tugged at her heart as the baby suckled with noisy slurps. Another daughter that had once been cuddled as close as this one and should have been playing with cousins was no longer present. A high fever had gripped little Mary's body and within a day she was gone from their lives forever. Miriam's mother-heart could not be consoled with the loss of such a sweet child. She had been glad that this newest baby had been another daughter, not someone to take Mary's place as some well-meaning but gossiping women had said to her, but another to keep by her side in her own place of honor and love.

It had been ten years since Miriam and Simon had made their vows under the wedding canopy. Miriam had been content and loved her husband more deeply than ever. However, the past few months had been strange ones for them. Simon was enthralled with the teachings of an itinerant preacher, a thirty-year-old man named Jesus who had grown up in Nazareth. Whenever Jesus was in the area, Simon left his boats and nets and followed after the man, as did Andrew as well. Miriam could still see the impetuous nature exhibited by her husband in his more youthful days bubble to the surface every now and then. She hoped this intense interest in the teachings of Jesus would soon pass and that their lives would settle back into the normal routine.

Miriam could understand Simon's desires for learning and trying new things. He was always experimenting with different kinds of bait or lures to see what would attract the fish to his nets most readily. But Miriam had to admit she had been surprised that Andrew, the steady, reliable older brother, was almost as enamored with Jesus as Simon. There were many times that their father, Jonah, was left to pull in the catch by himself or any workers that he might be able to hire for the day. He had originally established his fishing business in Bethsaida, a few leagues away from Capernaum on the eastern side the Jordan River where it emptied into the Sea of Galilee. But as Capernaum, which was closer to the Gentile cities, prospered under Roman rule, Jonah moved his family to the western side of the Sea. Miriam felt sorry for Jonah, now alone with his dear wife Hannah gone. The sons he had hoped to turn his business over to were now frequently wandering around the country listening to parables. Her thoughts then turned to her own father Titus, who had joined his ancestors in the great beyond, wherever that was, about five years ago. He had been traversing a familiar path up the hillside at dusk one evening, when some misguided rabbit or squirrel had darted into his course and caught him off-balance, resulting in an awkward fall that fractured his hip. Titus lay in pain for many months but could never recover from his injury and had just wasted away on his pallet. Miriam was glad that her mother still lived nearby, and as if her thoughts had somehow summoned the presence of the woman,

Miriam saw that Lyda was approaching the cottage. The gray-haired woman waved to the children as she passed and continued along the trail that paralleled the seashore. Miriam quickly switched Rachel to her other side and smiled as her mother drew near.

"Good afternoon, daughter," Lyda called out. "I hope I'm not interrupting anything important."

"Well, I guess that all depends on your perspective," replied Miriam. "Rachel and I both feel that this is pretty important. I'm grateful she was patient with me while I got the lamb and vegetables simmering for supper first. Would you like to stay and eat with us?"

"I would like that, dear," not wanting to confess her loneliness since becoming a widow, "but that's not why I came. I wanted to share some of these berries I picked earlier this morning in the highlands. They are not so sweet like this, but when combined with some honey, they make a delicious pudding."

"Thank you, Mother, that is so kind of you. I know Simon and the boys will be most appreciative."

"You expect Simon home for supper then?"

"I hope so. I never really know these days when he's gone off with Jesus."

"That is something I would also like to discuss with Simon. It seems to me that he is neglecting not only his fishing business but his family."

"I'm sure it is just a passing thing, Mother. You know how he is, always interested in something new that catches his eye, or in this case, his ear."

"What have you heard about this man called Jesus, Miriam? I hear rumors of some supposed miracles that he's performed, like changing water into wine at a wedding in Cana. We all know that is impossible."

"That's why they're called miracles, Mother. No one can explain how they happen."

"Have you heard some of the things he's been preaching?"

"Only second-hand through what Simon reports. I can't very well leave my family to go hear Jesus myself."

"I was talking with Sybil at the well yesterday morning when I went to draw water, and she says that Jesus is teaching a higher law. 'To love your enemies'__"

__"like the Romans?" Miriam interrupted with disgust.

"Yes" continued Lyda," but also anyone who persecutes us or uses us for their own selfish purposes. For that is what the prophets throughout the ages have done."

"I don't think I'm at the spiritual level of the prophets. Do you?"

"No, I think that I'm just one poor widow from the tribe of Judah that has about used up her allotment of years."

"Now, Mother, don't be talking like that."

"Well, you can't deny that I'm getting older, can you?"

"Of course not, but you know how much your encouragement and assistance is appreciated by all who know you. Please don't leave us anytime soon."

"I get to wondering every so often when I'm alone and feeling down what my life on this earth has been worth? If I've made a difference to anybody? If I've made a difference to God?"

"People have been asking themselves these questions for centuries, Mother. If the Greek philosophers couldn't come up with any definite answers, I doubt if you or I will be able to."

"I wonder what Jesus would say to those questions?"

"I hope you'll get a chance to ask him sometime, maybe the next time he's in Capernaum."

Miriam raised the now-sleeping baby to her shoulder and gently patted her on the back until a big burp erupted from her small mouth where milk bubbles drooled in a tiny stream. "I think Rachel will nap for a while now. It will give me time to cook those berries for dinner that you have worked so hard to kindly share with us.

Please, do say that you'll stay and eat with us."

"Well, if you insist, Miriam," Lyda responded, not wanting to reveal how happy it made her feel to be invited. "Maybe I can tell the boys some stories afterward."

"They would love that."

Miriam arose carefully so as not to disturb the dozing infant, then scanning the area for the nearby presence of her sons, she and her mother stepped into the coolness of the stone house.

An hour later Miriam heard voices on the path and turned toward the door to call her children into the house for the evening meal. Simon bounded into the living quarters with eight-year-old Joshua clinging to his father's back and six-year-old Saul dangling by his ankles, which Simon held tightly in his big fists. Both boys were squealing with delight, "More, Papa, more."

"Not right now, boys, I must speak with your mother," was his response. "Miriam, please prepare another plate for a guest. I have invited Jesus to join us for supper."

Miriam lifted her eyes with a challenging look, but noticing the bearded man in the doorway decided to hold her tongue until later. Didn't Simon realize that their rations were barely feeding their own family, and she had already invited her mother to stay? Of course, he wouldn't know about his mother-in-law, but she was always irritated when he did not consult her first before issuing invitations to others. Forcing a smile, Miriam turned aside from her husband, and hastily tied a scarf over her hair befitting a proper Jewish woman. Starting toward the door, she gestured for the stranger to enter. "Welcome to our humble abode."

"You are most gracious to include me in your supper, woman. Thank you for your kindness."

Miriam looked into the dark eyes of the man called Jesus and could see the intensity of his gaze, almost wistful, she thought to herself. Although she had never met the preacher, Simon had told her much about him and she did not feel intimidated. She knew he was not accustomed to the social circles of the upper classes, but frequently found himself in the company of the poor or outcasts of society. She also suspected that he longed for the companionship of a family, even one adopted for an evening.

"May I called you Master?" she inquired. "I would like to introduce you to my mother, Lyda of Capernaum, formerly the wife of Titus the Potter."

Jesus approached the older woman who was seated on a nearby stool holding baby Rachel. "I am most happy to make your acquaintance Lyda of Capernaum. I can see that you are enjoying the rewards of being a grandmother." Lyda nodded her head in quiet agreement.

"Saul, will you please arrange the cushions for your father and our guest." Miriam was embarrassed that they did not have a luxurious couch for the men to recline on but quickly pushed the thought away. Saul was quick to obey and gathered the cushions which had been neatly stacked in a corner and placed them around a small knee-high table. "Joshua, please fill the cups with wine from the skin hanging on that peg," she motioned with the wooden spoon that had been used to stir the stew, "and be careful not to spill any."

Simon poured a small quantity of water into two small bowls and set them on the table with a linen towel so that the men could rinse their hands as part of the Jewish purification rites before partaking of the food. Simon then ushered Jesus to one of the cushions nearest the small window and the men lowered themselves almost to the floor so that their knees were akimbo and their ankles touching. Miriam ladled a generous serving of lamb stew from the pot hanging inside the fireplace, realizing that there would be scant servings for her boys and even less for her mother. She herself would probably go without. Laying a thick slice of barley bread beside the stew, she carried two wooden trenchers toward the men, extending them with downcast eyes as was considered proper for a woman to do in the presence of men.

Simon cleared his throat and asked Jesus if he would say a blessing over the food. Miriam heard his sonorous voice speak with humility and gratitude, giving thanks to the God of Heaven for the bounteous fare of which they were about to partake and for the generosity of the members of Simon's house in sharing it with him. Miriam was amazed at the sincerity of his tone and the meekness of his spirit as he addressed God, as if Jesus was well acquainted with this Deity. As was the custom, men in the family were served first, but Miriam could tell that her boys were also hungry, so she dished up stew for them as well, giving them larger portions than she had originally anticipated, for it seemed that there was still plenty of food in the pot. The boys sat on cushions closer to the kitchen area so they would not disrupt the conversation of the older men who seemed to be discussing something in earnest, something about the Kingdom of God on the earth. There's a lofty subject thought Miriam, when we barely have enough to feed ourselves and not even a couch.

As the men finished their stew, wiping the trenchers clean with their last crusts of bread, Miriam stepped forward bearing two small bowls. "I have a sweet surprise for you tonight," she said, "because of the hard work of my mother picking these berries, we have a pudding for your enjoyment."

"Mama, mama," cried Saul, "Will there be berry pudding for us too?"

"Yes, my sons. There's some for you too if you eat your carrots. I notice that you have separated them from the rest of the vegetables."

"Ah, mama, you know I don't like carrots."

"But they are good for you. God would not have given us carrots as part of the bounties of the earth if they were not healthy for our bodies."

Jesus smiled as if he knew a secret, but did not say anything.

"Thank you, Miriam, wife of Simon, for the delicious supper," said Jesus as he stood. "I know that there are some in this village who are less fortunate. I now go to them to provide comfort and healing of their infirmities."

Miriam wondered how he could cure people of their sickness; Simon had never said anything about him being a trained physician.

"Master, if you need a place to rest tonight, my home is open to you," said Simon.

"Again, your hospitality is appreciated. Foxes have holes and the birds of the air have nests, but the Son of man hath not where to lay his head." (Luke 9:58) Then opening the door, paused to ask, "Would you care to accompany me, Simon?"

"Of course," replied Simon. "Thank you for supper, Miriam. We will be back by dark."

Miriam gave a little wave, disappointed that Simon was leaving for the rest of the evening. She bent to scrape the bottom of the pot to serve her mother and was surprised to find an adequate amount for both of them. "That's odd," muttered Miriam.

"What's that you said?" asked Lyda.

"Oh, it's just a little strange. I guess I prepared a larger pot of stew than I realized. There's still plenty for us." Miriam set a trencher on the work table close to where her mother sat. "You can lay Rachel in her cradle for now. If she wakes, I won't worry. She's had a little nap to keep her happy for the rest of the evening, but I hope it's not so much that she will want to stay awake and play when the rest of us want to go to sleep. It's hard to control an infant's schedule to meet that of the rest of the family."

"Yes, indeed, Miriam. That is one of the challenges of motherhood for sure. What did you think of the man Jesus?" Before answering, Miriam sent Joshua and Saul into the adjoining courtyard to feed the few chickens and the black nanny goat that supplied their household with a few edibles. Then the two women ate their stew as they discussed their interesting visitor.

Miriam threaded her way through the crowd of women thronging the market located in the center of Capernaum, Rachel wrapped tightly in a shawl that was bound to her chest. Lyda had arrived a few hours earlier bearing another basket of the dark red berries she had picked from the gnarled bushes growing on the upper hillsides. Joshua and Saul were happy to see their grandmother because she always took the time to play games with them but Miriam didn't want to burden her mother with the watch-care of the children for too long. Miriam picked up a green melon, thumped it on its side, and smelled the blossom end for ripeness. *Yes, this will do* she thought and placed it into her basket. Moving toward the stalls filled with onions and leeks, she heard the buzz of the women saying, "Jesus is coming." Then she immediately recognized the voices of her husband and Andrew, "Make way. Please stand aside and let the Master through." Simon's extended his arms trying to hold back the rush of people who always seemed to want attention from Jesus. Miriam strained to get a glance, trying to catch Simon's eye, but the gaggle of interested onlookers prevented a clear line of sight. "Please Master, can you heal my baby? He has been coughing for weeks."

Just then a louder voice boomed from the edge of the market, and everyone hushed their voices, stepping aside to let the Roman Centurion through. He strode with his usual upright military bearing until he approached Jesus, and then surprisingly fell to the Master's feet. "Lord, my servant lieth at home sick of the palsy, grievously tormented."

Jesus said unto him, "I will come and heal him."

But before Jesus could take a step, the centurion continued, "Lord, I am not worthy that thou shouldest come under my roof: but speak the word only, and my servant shall be healed. For I am a man under authority, having soldiers under me: and I say to this man, 'Go' and he goeth; and to another, 'Come' and he cometh; and to my servant, 'Do this' and he doeth it.

Simon, Andrew, James, John, and the rest of the followers of Jesus marveled at this saying. Jesus, perceiving their thoughts, said, "Verily I say unto you, I have not found so great faith, no, not in Israel. And I say unto you, that many shall come from the east and west and shall sit down with Abraham and Isaac, and Jacob, in the kingdom of heaven. But the children of the kingdom shall be cast out into outer darkness: there shall be weeping and gnashing of teeth." (Matt 8:10-11) Then Jesus reached toward the soldier as the man arose from his knees. Looking the Roman in the eyes, Jesus said, "Go thy way; and as thou hast believed, so be it done unto thee."

The crowd gasped in astonishment for they had heard of the power which Jesus had used to heal others by touching them. The buzz of conversation passed from woman to woman. "I have heard He has healed the blind by touching their eyes, but can this be so? The sick man is not even present."

"Does Jesus's power extend even over such a distance as to the Roman garrison leagues away?"

Another woman sneered, "And a servant of a Roman? They are the scum of the earth."

"What did he mean that people from the east and west will sit down with Abraham, Isaac and Jacob and the children of the kingdom cast out? Are not we the chosen people?" asked another.

Miriam wished that she could speak to Simon about it, but Jesus and his disciples were already moving away. With a sigh she hoped that perhaps tonight, her husband would stay home so that they could talk.

When Miriam returned home, she saw Lyda sitting listlessly on the bench near the door while the boys were playing in the dirt nearby, arranging pebbles in some intricate design. "Mother, are you all right? You look flushed?"

"I'll be all right soon. It's probably just the heat. I admit I do have a headache. Don't forget the berries I brought to make more pudding. Maybe Jesus will stop by again. He enjoyed the pudding so much the last time."

"Come inside the house where you can lie down and rest. Don't worry about the pudding, I'll see to it. I never know how many to prepare food for these days. Sometimes, it's just me and the children; sometimes Simon joins us, and sometimes it's him and all of the Twelve. I'm sorry I was gone longer than expected, but something very interesting happened while I was at the market." Miriam set her basket on the bench and put her arm around her mother's shoulders and led her into the coolness of the stone house. "Let me tell you about it..."

Throughout the afternoon Lyda lay on the pallet in the sleeping quarters, not moving or speaking. After Miriam had settled on what to prepare for dinner that could be expanded as needs dictated, she set the berries in a large pot over the fire to boil. It was a hot afternoon, and she didn't relish heating up the cottage with the heat from the fireplace after already baking her barley loaves that morning.

But her mother seemed set on having the berry pudding again, and after all of Lyda's hard work to pick the fruit, Miriam didn't want it to spoil in the heat.

Miriam pulled aside the curtain that separated the bedchamber from the rest of the cottage and was dismayed to find that her mother had a raging fever. She poured water onto a towel to lay across her chest and forehead in an attempt to cool her temperature. Miriam sat on the pallet next to her mother while nursing Rachel, stroking the hot skin and providing some small measure of comfort. She pondered on the many times that these roles had been reversed and it was Lyda who comforted Miriam through a childhood illness or minor injury. But somehow Miriam sensed that this time it was more serious. What could have caused the fever to come on so quickly? Her mother had seemed fine when she left her earlier that morning to go to the market. A thought flashed through Miriam's mind__*her mother had been in the highlands picking berries. Was it possible that she had bitten by a viper or some insect?* As soon as Rachel was through nursing, Miriam began to exam her mother's skin more closely for any sign of infection. It didn't take long for her to discover a small tick which had burrowed itself into the back of Lyda's neck near the hairline. She could see the redness surrounding the black body of the small beetle with golden spots on its back and the red lines starting to spread outward from the entry point. Spotted fever! Miriam knew that the bite could be fatal.

Lyda began to be restless and moan in her semi-conscious state, "Titus, I'm coming," she mumbled over and over in her delirium. Miriam was frantic. What could she do to save her mother's life? She continued to change the towels, saturating them with cool water from the firkin in the kitchen. At this rate, she was going to run out of water before evening. She called for Joshua and Saul to come in from their play in the front of the house.

"Joshua, your grandmother is very ill and I must have more water from the well. Do you think you are strong enough to carry the pitcher and bring some back to me?"

"Yes, mother. I am big and strong," said the eight-year-old flexing his arm muscles.

"Good. Please walk carefully and try not to spill it before you return."

"What about me, Mama? Do you want me to go to the well with Joshua?" asked Saul.

"No, son. I need you to search along the seashore for your father. Check with Grandfather Jonah first. Perhaps he will know where to find him. I hope that he is mending nets and not far away with Jesus."

"Yes, Mama. I will find Papa. I am big and strong like Joshua, and I can even run faster than him sometimes."

"That is good, Saul." Then to both of the boys she admonished, "Please hurry and may the God of our Fathers guide you. We need to do all that we can to help Grandmother as quickly as possible."

The boys scooted off on their respective errands. Miriam knelt on the mat beside the moaning woman and prayed for that same God of their Fathers to heal her ailing mother. Then Miriam thought of Jesus. It had been said that he had healed many people, although Miriam hadn't seen any of those miracles herself. But that is what Lyda needed__a miracle. Miriam recalled the words of the Master earlier that morning uttered to the centurion about faith. Did she have as much faith as the Roman soldier? What was it Jesus had said about faith when he had eaten with their family on an earlier occasion__that if we had faith even as small as a mustard seed that it would become a tree large enough for birds to lodge in. She didn't really understand all that meant, but it must have been important for him to have said it. Miriam prayed again that somehow Jesus would know of her needs and come and heal her mother. She had to believe it was possible even though she didn't know how it would happen.

The minutes dragged by. *What more can I do?* wondered Miriam. *I do not have the tools nor the skill to remove the tick. Perhaps if Simon were here he could use the sharp tip of his dagger that he uses to gut the fish. He is much more skilled at such delicate maneuvers than I. But will he get here in time?* Miriam checked the tick bite again and could see that the red lines of infection were spreading further down her mother's back and across her shoulders. Her mother's skin was flushed and paper-dry, and she flinched whenever Miriam touched her as if her whole body was painful. The fever was getting worse!

Joshua returned with the additional water and Miriam quickly added the cold compresses on as many areas of her mother's body as she could without indecent exposure. Joshua looked on with concern. He had never seen his grandmother so sick. She was usually smiling, telling him and Saul stories, or playing little games with them. Best of all, he liked seeing his grandmother hold his little sister and make sweet baby sounds as if Rachel could understand her babbling.

"Joshua, go to the front door and watch for Saul, and if he has found your Papa. " She didn't want to alarm the child any further by seeing his grandmother in such distress.

"Yes, Mama," he said quietly.

It was nearing evening when Miriam heard voices__first of all Joshua calling out to her that his father was coming up the path, then adding that Jesus was with him. A few minutes later, Saul, Simon, and Jesus burst into the cottage. "I found him, Mama," squealed Saul.

"Oh, I'm so glad, Saul. Thank you for being such an obedient boy," she said giving her youngest son a hug.

"What is the matter, Miriam?" Simon asked. "Saul said that Grandmother was very sick."

"Yes, Simon. She has been bitten by a tick, probably which probably attacked her when she was picking berries in the mountains this morning. I believe she has spotted fever."

"That is not good," said Simon. Then turning to Jesus, Simon pleaded, "Can you heal her, Lord?"

"Do you have faith that I can do so, Simon? Faith is the first principle of the gospel and all other things are built upon a foundation of faith in the Redeemer of mankind."

"I have seen your healing powers used on many__the blind, the maimed, and the lepers. I have even seen you raise Jairus's daughter from the dead. I know that you have the power of God to do so, if it is your will that my mother-in-law lives."

"And you, Miriam, do you have faith that your mother can be healed?"

"I have not seen the things that Simon has, but he believes you can, and I believe him."

"Some have faith to heal, others to be healed. To some it is given by the power of the Holy Ghost to know the Son of God and that he will be crucified for the sins of the world. To others, it is given to believe on their words, that they also might have eternal life if they continue faithful."

Then Jesus knelt down near the pallet and closed his eyes. After a few moments of silence, he reached out his hand to touch Lyda's burning skin. Miriam nor Simeon heard any words that Jesus might have spoken, but their eyes were fixed on the face of their kindred, praying that this moment would not be her last on earth. Lyda's eyelids fluttered; she took a deep sigh. "Master, I felt the touch of your hand and the heat left my body as surely as the dew evaporates before the sun." She bent to kiss the hand of Jesus, which still lay upon her forearm. Then raising herself to a sitting position said, "I told Titus he'd have to wait for me a little longer." With a quickness belieing her condition moments before, she arose saying, "Miriam, have you cooked those berries yet? I must make the pudding for Jesus. It is the least I can do to thank him."

Yes, preparing a meal for Jesus is the least I can do too, thought Miriam. *Him and how many others he ever wants to bring to my home. I will be grateful 'til my dying day for the miraculous healing of my mother. And it is indeed a miracle, right before my very eyes. I cannot have a greater witness than that of his healing power!*

Later, in the quiet of the evening, after the children were settled down to sleep, Jesus gathered a few of his disciples around him within the stone cottage. A few candles flickered on the window sill and the embers of the dying fire still glowed in their redness. There was Andrew, Simon's brother, Simon himself, and two other men who were brothers__James and John, who were also fisherman. Two other women, the wives of Andrew and James, joined Miriam and Lyda on the fringe where they still overhead bits of the conversation, something about the priesthood. The only priests that Miriam knew anything about were the teachers in the local synagogue.

Jesus paused in his explanation and surprisingly called for the women to bring cushions and to seat themselves near their husbands. He teased John that he needed to be seeking for a wife. John smiled but said he'd been too busy following after Jesus to pursue a maiden. Jesus said, "He who chooses to follow me will have mothers and sisters, fathers and brothers." What did that mean? Miriam wondered. There were so many things that Jesus taught that she didn't understand, but she wanted to. She especially wanted to understand the healing that had taken place before her very eyes a few hours earlier.

"John, you're of an age where you could almost be my grandson. If you don't mind, may I sit next to you?" asked Lyda. "That might help both of us feel a little less lonely."

John graciously scooted to the side allowing the older woman to sit beside him. "I would be most honored, Lyda."

All eyes were riveted on Jesus in anticipation of what he might say to them. It was indeed unusual for women to be included in any such discussion, for even in the synagogue, men and women sat on opposite sides of a partition.

"My friends, yea dear friends, it brings me joy to be gathered with you all this evening. We thank Simon and his wife Miriam, and her dear mother, Lyda for preparing the evening meal for us. Their service is not forgotten but is recorded by the angels in heaven. Those who serve in the background without public approval or even anyone noticing, are truly in the service of God. We are also grateful for the quick recovery of such a good woman as your dear Lyda," and he flashed a smile at the older woman. "Remember that miracles do not come to plant the seed of faith, but to nurture an already-existing faith." Peter's mother-in-law noddded in silent agreement.

"I call you all together this night because of the importance of the work of the Kingdom in which we are all engaged. This is the appointed day for these things to be made known unto the children of men and I cannot do it alone. You four men here have been given priesthood power that you might go forth and do the works that I have done. There will soon be others and you will be called apostles, or special witnesses of me. You will have the power to cast out unclean spirits, to heal all manner of sickness and disease, even to raise the dead. (See Matt 10:8) You will not only heal the body, but also the souls of men who are broken as to things of the Spirit. This power can only be used to bless the lives of others and can only be maintained by gentleness and meekness, virtue and love unfeigned. If you attempt to use it for your own glory or gratification, the power will be taken from you and you will be left to the wiles of the devil. You are to go to the lost sheep of Israel saying that the Kingdom of Heaven is at hand for therein you will find the greatest joy.

"I desire to explain this in the presence of your wives, so they will know of your commission and the sacrifice that will be necessary. You are not to wear the soft shoes of the rich, but the sandals of the common man, for you shall journey to whatever city or town that will hear you. You will not take a scrip, nor a stave, nor money in your pouches, but will rely on the goodness of those whom you meet to provide for your needs. Those who are honest in heart will receive you and care for you. You shall be brought before governors and kings for my sake for a testimony against them, but when you are delivered up, take no thought how or what ye shall speak, for it will be given you in that same hour what ye shall speak. It is not you that speaketh, but the Spirit of your Father which speaketh it in you.

"Your family members may turn against you, yea, you shall be hated of all men for my name's sake, but he that endureth to the end shall be saved. (See Matt 10: 8-20) This salvation cometh only as you are united in thought and dedication with your wives now sitting beside you, for in the Kingdom of My Father, neither is the woman without the man, or the man without the woman in the sight of the Lord. Yea, even for this is the work and the glory of My Father to bring about the immortality and eternal life of man.

"Miriam, Agnes, and Abigail," Jesus looked deeply into the eyes of each woman, "henceforth, you may be required to manage your households and families without the continued support of your husbands. Counsel together on how you might arrange your affairs__ sustaining and encouraging one another, calling upon the assistance of others when necessary, or being self-reliant to provide for your own needs. My work is greater than the works of man, and I must have strong and committed men beside me for my time is short."

The men glanced at one another and even though the room was dimly lit, they could see sorrow manifest upon the face of the man they called Lord and Master. "Aren't we just beginning thy work, Lord?" asked Simon. "How can your time be short?"

"No man knoweth the hour or the day, but the Father which is in heaven." (Mark 13:32) Simon was confused at the answer, but he had accepted Jesus as the promised Messiah, and there was so much more he wanted to learn.

"Simon, I have special need of you to be a rock among my followers, someone strong on whom others might rely. Indeed, I shall henceforth call you Cephas, Peter, a little rock. You can become a mighty force in the Kingdom of God if you build upon the true Rock of Salvation. You will henceforth be a fisher of men." (John 1:42)

Simon turned to Miriam with a lopsided grin and asked, "Can you get used to calling me Peter? It seems that I have just been given a new name."

"You will always be the same man on the inside, Simon Peter, the same man that I love," she answered with a smile and he took her hand his. Miriam felt his large calloused hand, worn and leathery from the fish and the salt water and the nets used in his former trade. A fisher of men? What an idea!

"Miriam, Agnes, Abigail, will you be willing to support your husbands in doing my work?' Jesus looked to each of them for an answer. Thoughts rushed through Miriam's mind. *Did I just say a few hours ago that I would be willing to do anything Jesus asked? How deep is that gratitude now that a test has really come? And I'm sure this is only the beginning? What will I and my family have to endure in the years to come? What will happen to Simon? Oh yes, it seems I must now call him Peter. That will take some getting used to.* Then she looked up at the man before her waiting patiently for her answer. Love for Jesus swelled up inside of her and she said, "Yea, Lord, I will. Be it unto me according to thy word." Agnes and Abigail also nodded in agreement.

"Lyda, I have not forgotten you in this matter. You are a widow and among those considered the least in the world, but I say unto you, that you are a woman of great compassion and will be a strength to your family. You have skills that are needed in the growth of my Kingdom if you will seek to use them for the glory of God. Will you be a part of this work that will someday fill the earth?"

With tears streaming down her face, Lyda smiled and said, "I will Lord. Whatever I may do will be a small payment for your mercy unto me."

Scanning the faces of those around him, Jesus continued, "Fear not what men may do to you, but fear God. The very hairs of your head are numbered. Take up your cross and follow me. For he that loseth his life for my sake shall find it, and ye shall in no wise lose your reward."

Miriam thought back to the beginning of the day and the changes that had taken place. *I know that this day has changed the course of my life forever. The routine trip to the market ended with lessons of faith that I never dreamed of. Even though my faith in Jesus was only in the sprouting stages, it was strong enough that I drew upon it in my own hour of need. I have much to learn, but the Spirit has borne witness to my heart that the things Jesus is teaching us this night are true. From this humble cottage, from this little town in the corner of a conquered nation, these teachings of truth will spread throughout the world. I know not what sacrifices might be required, but believe that whatever will be asked of me, I will find the strength to do. My faith will continue to grow and with faith all things are possible. Now if I can just get used to calling my husband Peter.*

What of Jairus?

Part One

ABIGAIL STROLLED THROUGH the marketplace of Capernaum, sniffing the pungent odors of the spices brought in from the East_cloves, ginger, and cinnamon. Capernaum lay along the Great Road that ran from Damascus through Syria and on to the seaports of Ptolemais, Caesarea and Joppa. It was one of several villages lining the western shore of the Sea of Galilee and most of its residents earned their living as fisherman or associated trades. Abigail picked up a melon, sniffing the blossom end for the odor of ripeness and handed it to the vendor for weighing. Could she trust his scales? Many in the past had surreptitiously attached additional lead pieces to the underside of the scales to make the produce seem heavier than it actually was. But Abigail had known Caleb, the produce merchant, for many years and considered him honest. At least she saw him attend synagogue every week and hopefully that counted for his integrity.

Eyeing her friend, Sariah, she waved and moved across the open-aired market, so she could catch up on the latest gossip. "Have you been to hear Jesus today," Abigail asked Sariah.

"Yes, and he speaks of not sewing new cloth onto an old garment. Or putting new wine in old bottles or skins. I'm not sure what he meant."

"We all know that if new wine is put into an old skin that it will cause the container to burst."

"You're right. But what did He really mean?"

"Sometimes His words are very confusing. Even Jairus says that he doesn't always understand it and he has studied the Torah since he was a young boy." Jairus was Abigail's husband and held the honored position as ruler or leader of the local synagogue.

"Then how are simple women like us who can't read or write ever supposed to understand?"

"I wish I had a good answer for you, Sariah. But His teachings a few days ago when he was on the Mount above the city were easy enough to understand. When we fast, we should not be as the hypocrites who draw attention to themselves. We should wash our face and braid our hair, although he didn't exactly say that, but you know what I mean. We should just look normal."

"Yes, and then fast and pray in a private way, believing that God will reward us openly. I also like what He said about not being able to serve two masters. We cannot serve the one true God and the god of mammon or riches."

"He certainly has the country in a turmoil with his teachings, doesn't he?"

"Yes, multitudes throng to hear him every day, Abigail."

"I must finish my shopping and return to prepare the evening meal. Jairus has a meeting with the council of the elders tonight at the synagogue and I don't want to make him late."

"Your family is honored to have Jairus as the ruler of the synagogue, Abigail."

"I know, but it is also such a responsibility."

Sariah gave a sigh as her friend hustled back to other vendors, choosing some dried figs, almonds, and fish, freshly caught that morning in the Sea. Sariah's gaze drifted out to the waters of the

Sea, which was really an inland lake, and thought how much it looked like a bowlful of glistening blue water. Sariah's husband, Joel, was a blacksmith, which was a respectable enough trade, but not one of high honor in the community like the ruler of the synagogue. Sariah had to admit that she was a little envious of Abigail's position as the wife of such an important person. She continued to ponder the words which Jesus had taught as she moved through the market place selecting the items for her own family's evening meal. Was she like the hypocrite that saw the mote in another's eye instead of the beam in her own eye?

"Mama, I don't feel well," complained twelve-year old Deborah to her mother Abigail later that evening.

"Were you out in the sun too long this afternoon?"

"No, I haven't had much energy all day. I tried doing some of the weaving that you've been trying to get me to do for weeks, but I couldn't even focus on it."

"Let me feel your forehead, dear." Then placing her palm on the girl's forehead, said, "You do feel feverish, Deborah. Go to your bed chamber and lie down on your mat."

Deborah didn't need a second invitation. Abigail retrieved a clean cloth and using a ladle, dipped a small amount of water from the large pot in the cooking area of the house, pouring it onto the cloth. She retreated toward the back of the stone house built along the rocky embankment of one of the many hills surrounding Capernaum and entered a small room where her daughter lay on the woven reed mat. She placed the cool cloth across her forehead noticing that in spite of the fever, that her skin was clammy. "Thank you,

Mama. That feels good."

"Hopefully you can rest, child, and feel better in the morning."

Abigail knelt beside her daughter a little longer, rubbing the girl's temples, and then stroking her fingers through the long dark hair. How she loved this daughter, her only living child. A son, born two years after Deborah, had died in infancy. Not only did the caravans bring spices to the area, they often brought diseases that were spread to those most susceptible, the very young and the very old. Her baby Asher was one of the casualties. And then there had been two babies that had been conceived in the womb, but did not develop properly and were cast out. Abigail had feared for her own life with the amount of blood that had been lost and it had taken her several months to recuperate. Then the fountains of her motherhood seemed to dry up within her and there were no more babies. She always felt badly that she had not been able to give Jairus a son, an heir to take his place on the Council, as he had replaced his own father.

The next morning, Deborah's health had deteriorated even further. She lay pale and limp throughout the day and refused the chicken broth that Abigail had especially prepared for her. Abigail and Jairus watched with grave concern throughout the night, fearing that their daughter was dying right in front of their eyes.

As they waited, they spoke of the power of healing which Jesus had shown many infirm persons who had been brought to him. The blind could now see; the paralytic now walked, the lepers were cleansed. Jairus spoke of the ancient prophets such as Isaiah, Ezekiel, and Jeremiah who had written of One who would come with healing in his wings, who would take upon Himself the pains and sicknesses of His people. Could this Jesus, a simple carpenter from neighboring Nazareth, possibly be the one they had been waiting for? But Deborah was too ill for them to take to Jesus. What could they do?

"If our daughter does not show signs of improvement in the morning, I will go look for Jesus and ask Him to come to her."

"You could send Micah."

"Micah is a trusted servant and scribe to me for Council affairs, but I feel that this is a family matter and that it would be better if I approached Jesus myself.

"You are wise as usual, Jairus. Would it be wrong for us to pray outside of the synagogue?

"No. God asks that we call upon him in our trials, wherever we are. Abraham prayed in the fields of Mamre; King David prayed in the caves of Engedi."

"And Hannah prayed in her own home that she might have a son."

"That is right, Abigail, and God answered their prayers. He can answer ours as well."

The outlook the following morning was even more dire than the previous evening. It appeared that Deborah was at the point of death as her face was drained of color and a thin blue line outlined her small lips. She lay motionless upon the pallet, the rise and fall of her chest barely discernable.

Shortly after dawn, Jairus prepared to leave the house. "Where will you look for Jesus? He goes to a different area to preach every day," asked Abigail.

"I will ask as many people as I can. Surely someone will know where he is."

"Go in haste, my husband. For the sake of our daughter."

Jairus quickly walked toward the center of Capernaum asking all whom he met where he could find Jesus. He was directed toward the seashore where Jesus had crossed over from Decapolis the night before. Even though the day was fresh and the sun shone brightly, Jairus perceived none of it. His thoughts were completely focused on the life of his daughter and he prayed fervently within his heart that the Master would return with him to her bedside.

At last Jairus saw a large group gathered on the shore near the fishing boats of Jonas and Zebedee, long-time Capernaum residents and business partners. Jesus was speaking to some of the former disciples of John the Baptist, whom many regarded as a Prophet, but who had recently been arrested by Herod Agrippa and thrown into prison. Trying to be polite, but impatient in his urgent task, Jairus broke through the cluster of men and threw himself at the feet of Jesus.

"My little daughter lieth at the point of death. I pray Thee, come and lay Thy hands upon her, that she may be healed, and she will live."

Jesus withdrew himself from his listeners and followed the ruler of the synagogue back toward his home. People were anxious to ask them questions of their own and thronged about him, slowing the progress of the anxious father. "Stand back and do not hinder us," he pleaded. "My daughter is at the point of death and in need of the healing touch of the Master."

"I am in need of his healing also," cried another from the crowd. "I know he can cure my twisted foot."

"Where do you get the authority to teach as you do?" called out a Pharisee.

"Show us a miracle like you did at the wedding in Cana," demanded another.

"Please, please, let us go quickly. My need is most urgent," pled Jairus.

All of a sudden Jesus stopped in his tracks and asked "Who touched me?" His disciples looked about incredulously. "You asked who touched you? Why, in the press of this crowd hundreds of people could have touched you."

Jesus answered, "I perceive that virtue has gone out of me," and he looked around at those in the crowded street.

Realizing that her actions had been detected, a woman came forward and fell at His feet, acknowledging that she had touched the fringe of his robe. "I have been plagued with an issue of blood for twelve years and suffered many things at the hands of physicians but have only grown worse. I thought that if I could but touch the touch the hem of your garment that I would be healed."

Jairus felt sympathy for the woman, but was irritated at the interruption. Jesus seemed to be in no hurry, which further frustrated the ruler of the synagogue who knew that time was short for his Deborah.

The woman continued her story, "The moment that I touched your clothes I felt the fountain of blood within me dry up and that I was healed."

"Daughter, be of good comfort; thy faith hath made thee whole. Go in peace and be whole of thy plague."(See Mark 5:25-34)

Just then, breathing heavily as if from a fast run, Micah thrust himself into the center of the crowd. "Jairus, Sir, there is no need to trouble the Master any further. I am sorry to tell you that your daughter is dead."

Jairus dropped his head in anguish, groaning in sorrow, "Too late, too late. My little daughter is dead."

Jesus reached up and put his hand on the grieving man's shoulder. "Be not afraid, believe only and she shall be made whole." Then in an authoritative voice, He indicated for the crowd to halt and give him room to proceed toward the house of Jairus. The grief-stricken father could not utter a word as they walked up the hillside, his heart breaking and his mind blaming the woman who had delayed their movement. *She had waited for a cure for twelve years, for the same lifespan as my daughter. And now she is made whole and my daughter is dead. Could she not have withstood her plague one more hour so that my daughter might be healed by the Master's touch? But Jesus said, believe and she will be made whole. Perhaps Micah is mistaken; perhaps she is still alive and there is a chance of a miracle.*

As they approached the stone house near the top of the hill, they could hear the keening of the professional mourners who had already arrived upon the scene. Usually women dressed in black, they and minstrels were hired to publicize a death with their loud wailing and mournful cries of anguish. Entering the courtyard, Jesus said, "Why make ye this ado and weep? The damsel is not dead, but sleepeth." (Mark 5:39) The crowd hissed and laughed Him to scorn in retort__"She's dead all right."

"Stiff as a board already the servants say."

"The mistress of the house would not have called us if the girl hadn't died."

Following Jairus into the house, Jesus allowed only Peter, James, and John to accompany Him. Each man paused to respectfully touch the mezuzah attached to the doorpost. The small cylinder contained quotations from Moses, taken from his second writing of the law, sometimes known as Deuteronomy, reminding them of their freedom from bondage and the covenants God made with Israel. The house was cool because of the thickness of the stone walls. There was no smell of bread baking or the sound of pots banging as there usually would be at this early morning hour. There was only the stillness of death that pervaded the atmosphere.

Jairus opened the door to his daughter's room and saw her lying in rigid stillness upon the mat. His wife, Abigail knelt beside the lifeless form, her head bowed in grief and quietly weeping. She turned and looked up at the sound of the door opening, her reddened eyes acknowledging the return of her husband and the presence of Jesus standing behind him in the doorway. "It's too late. Deborah is dead."

Jairus rushed to Abigail's side, kneeling beside her and taking her into his arms. "I'm so sorry. So sorry."

Jesus said, "Weep not. She is not dead." Then reaching down he took the damsel's limp hand in his own strong one and said unto her, "Talitha cumi; which is being interpreted, Damsel, I say unto thee, arise." (Mark 5:41)

For a moment there was not a sound, not a breath taken by anyone in the room. But then there was a fluttering of the eyelids, a twitching of the lips, and a quick intake of breath. A smile erupted as she looked up into the eyes of Jesus, then to her weeping parents who reached out to her. Straightway Deborah arose, along with her astonished parents and started to walk.

"Deborah, my daughter!" called Jairus.

"I can't believe my eyes! I thought you dead," said Abigail amidst her tears.

"I feel as if I've been far away to a beautiful place, but then I was told I needed to return home."

Jesus raised himself up smiling at the girl; Peter, James and John stood with their mouths open in astonishment. They had seen Jesus cure all manner of diseases and infirmities. But this was something way beyond a cure; this was raising someone from the dead! They had heard of the prophet Elisha who had raised a widow's son from the dead centuries earlier. Did Jesus have that same prophetic power? Was he even someone greater?

"Give the girl something to eat," Jesus admonished Abigail. "She is in need of nourishment. But no one here is to say anything about this matter. At this time, it might hinder my work more than help it."

"We will just tell people that it was a mistake. We will honor your request, Master," said Jairus.

"How can we ever repay you for this great blessing, Lord? Our daughter is restored to us," added Abigail.

"Increase in your faith and do the will of the Father."

Although Jairus, Abigail, nor Deborah spoke of this incident, the fame of Jesus increased throughout the land.

Part Two

"And Jesus spake many things unto them in parables, saying, 'Behold, a sower went forth to sow;

"And when he sowed, some seeds fell by the wayside, and the fowls came and devoured them up.

"Some fell upon stony places, where they had not much earth and forthwith they sprung up, because they had no deepness of earth.

"And when the sun was up, they were scorched; and because they had no root, they withered away.

"And some fell among thorns; and the thorns sprung up, and choked them.

"But other fell into good ground, and brought forth fruit, some an hundredfold, some sixty fold, and some thirtyfold.

"Who hath ears to hear, let him hear..."

"Hear ye therefore the parable of the sower.

"When any one heareth the word of the kingdom, and understandeth it not, then cometh the wicked one, and catcheth away that which was sown in his heart. This is he which received seed by the way side.

"But he that received the seed into stony places, the same is he that heareth the word, and anon with joy receiveth it;

"Yet hath he not root in himself, but dureth for a while: for when tribulation or persecution ariseth because of the word, by and by he is offended.

"He also that received seed among the thorns is he that heareth the word: and the care of this world, and the deceitfulness of riches, choke the word, and he becometh unfruitful.

"But he that received seed into the good ground is he that heareth the word, and understandeth and endureth, also beareth fruit, and bringeth forth, some an hundredfold, some sixty, and some thirty." (Matthew 13:3-8, 18-23)

But what of Jairus? Some adventure stories for children include optional endings. Which of the following scenarios would you chose for this Biblical character who followed the admonition of Jesus to never speak of his daughter's miracle to any man?

"How could I have been so deceived? Jesus came to make me look like a fool in the eyes of the people. A man who has been respected as a ruler in the synagogue would be a real plum for him to boast about."

"Please keep your voice down, Jairus. We don't want Deborah to overhear us," said Abigail interrupting his tirade. They sat on a stone bench in the courtyard as the sun dipped below the horizon in what was normally a peaceful conclusion to their day. "I thought you believed that Jesus had the power to heal Deborah."

"I don't know what I was thinking. I suppose I was just desperate for the life of my daughter. I should have known better than to fall to the trickery of a false prophet."

"How do you know He is a false prophet?"

"What else could He be?"

"You said yourself that the Messiah would be a man who healed and comforted others."

"Oh, that Jesus is a clever one, all right. He has the cunning of a fox, sometimes speaking in the smooth tones of the mourning doves, and other times with the roar of a lion. He must use some form of sorcery. I believe He is a charlatan up to no good."

"But Jairus, you have to admit that Deborah was a very sick girl two days ago, and now she is as happy as one of the little kittens she is playing with," nodding toward their daughter who was kneeling near a fountain playing with a pet.

"Yes, I do have to admit that. I just wish I knew what sort of magic he used. It wasn't potions, or incantations. Did he have some kind of ointment on his hands that stimulated her bodily systems to start functioning again? He must work by the power of Beelzebub. That is all I can say."

""Oh, Jairus, I don't know what to believe."

"Maybe it is one of his followers that has the real power and he is the showman."

"You have known Simon, James, and John since they were lads. How could they be sorcerers?"

"We will certainly follow his admonition never to speak of this again. In time, Deborah will probably forget too. If she brings it up, just tell her it was delusions brought on by her fever. I will keep an eye on this Jesus. One false move and he will not be allowed into my synagogue again."

"Your synagogue, Jairus? I thought it belonged to God."

He responded with a look of hatred and darkness that Abigail had never seen in her husband before and it frightened her.

"I don't have the answers yet, but I'm not through with him," was the muttered response before Abigail arose from the bench and walked alone into the house, tears streaming down her cheeks.

Jairus strode around the perimeter of his courtyard, his hands laced together behind his back. His head was bent and he muttered to himself as he walked, frustration increasing with each step. *Who is this man Jesus? Is he the Anointed One foretold by the prophets? Is he another imposter?*

Micah approached cautiously seeing that his master was in a contemplative mood, just has he had been for the past week. “Sir, Ebenezer the Pharisee is here to see you.”

“Oh. Oh yes, of course. Micah, show him into the house and ask Abigail to bring him a cool drink of water. He will be thirsty after such a long journey. I will join him shortly.” Jairus entered the house through a side door and went into his own chamber where he washed his face and hands before greeting his guest. He wished he could wash away the memory of the incident regarding Deborah’s supposed healing a few days earlier. Had it all just been a dream?

“Ebenezer, welcome to Capernaum. What brings you all this distance from Jerusalem?”

“It is rumors regarding a man named Jesus. We hear that he is preaching against the Law and performing miracles. I thought that you, as ruler of the synagogue, would be able to tell me the truth.”

“I wish I could.”

“I also hear that He raised your daughter from the dead. What nonsense, Jairus! “

“He did come to my home and afterward Deborah arose from her sick bed. I can’t really explain it.” Jairus let his voice trail off without offering any further comment.

“Is he dangerous? Is he planning a revolt on Rome?”

“There are some who claim that he will be the Deliverer that will free us from the bondage of the Romans. But to my knowledge He has never made that claim himself. Thousands flock to listen to his teachings although there does not seem to be a Zealot movement among them."

"What about the elders of the Council here? Do they believe Him?"

"Most do not. It seems to be the lower class of people who are drawn to him. His words of hope help them forget their poverty and servitude for a brief time."

"You know that talk such as this is could stir up the Roman governor against us. Letting the Sanhedrin exist, let alone have a voice in regulating the affairs of the Jews, puts us in a precarious position. Pilate is looking for any opportunity to squash us like insects on the ground."

"But what do you want me to do?"

"Keep your eyes and ears open, report any suspicious behavior, that sort of thing. Forget about finding out the truth. Look for anything that indicates he is breaking the Law of Moses. We cannot stand for that. The Law is supreme. Surely you, of all people, should know this."

"I can try."

"You'd better do more than try. Your position as leader of the Capernaum synagogue can easily be over-turned. It would only take a little pressure on the other members of the Council to bring a negative vote against you. Then where would you be? Out on the street begging like the rest of the riff-raff of Galilee. I once thought you were a strong candidate for a member of the Sanhedrin. But now it appears that you are as unstable as a reed in the wind."

"Oh, Ebenezer, I did not realize that you felt so strongly about Jesus. You were certainly right to come to me first. You will see no support of Him from me in the future. I realize now that I was almost duped by His power, but I suppose that it was just a ploy among my own family, to win me to His side. I will not be led astray again."

"See to it, Jairus. You must warn others through your position as the ruler of the synagogue. You cannot afford to fail us."

"As you wish, Ebenezer. I will do all in my power to rid the Galilee of this imposter."

Jairus surveyed the interior of the synagogue intently although he was as familiar with every nook as he was in his own stone house. The rectangular interior was supported by a row of columns made of finely grained cedar cut from the renowned forests of Lebanon and then planed and polished with oil until the redness of the wood shone like vintage wine. The center section was filled with backless wooden benches, the seats worn from decades of use by the men of Capernaum. The sides of the room were separated by high lattice partitions, open on the front and back. These were the areas set aside for the women who also desired to attend the Sabbath Day services. Narrow windows were cut into the sides of the stone walls allowing sunlight and ventilation in the summer months, but could be closed with shutters during the cold of winter. During those months sconces on the walls held torches made of rushes dipped in pitch providing minimal light to the interior.

At the front of the elongated room, opposite the front door, stood a chest-high lectern also made of cedar wood standing on an elevated platform. Behind the lectern were twelve high-backed chairs with wide arm rests where members of the local Council sat. Jairus' eyes drifted to the center chair, his chair. To the side of the dais was a small table with a simple straight-backed chair holding a small box containing writing tools used by the scribe, a position currently held by Micah. Beside the scribe's desk was a large ornately carved chest, which Jairus knew contained the sacred writings of the Torah and some copies of the messages of Isaiah, Jeremiah, Ezekiel, Amos, and other long-since-dead prophets.

Muttering to himself, he said, "I inherited this position on the Council from my father, who had likewise claimed it from his father, back as far as the Exile." That period was mostly likely the origin of the synagogue, which in Greek meant "a group of people." During the Second Temple period, the term came to mean the building itself where the group assembled for instruction and prayers. During the Diaspora when Jews were deported to conquering nations and no longer able to worship and offer sacrifices at the temple in Jerusalem, the synagogue became a substitute place for worship.

His eyes sought out the pile of cushions stacked against a wall. As part of his duties, he was also a teacher and during the week the building was used as a school for the boys of the village. Their curriculum consisted of the Torah, official interpretations of the Law of Moses, as they were viewed by the Pharisees, the strongest sect of Judaism. The scriptures, as they are now known, are composed of the Prophets, the Torah, and the poetical psalms of David and Solomon. *I have to admit that the Torah is given more credence than the original rules revealed to Moses by Jehovah himself.*

Jairus slowly walked into the empty room, stepped up on the dais, and then seated himself in the center chair, the designated chair of the chazzan, a position he occupied not because of heredity like his Council appointment, but because of his popularity. *This office came to me because I made friends with the right people who exerted power and influence. I know it's a sin to boast, but I can't help feeling a measure of pride in the way that people look up to me, come to me for advice, and then 'ooh and aah' as I quote some scripture to them as if I were the Law myself. Am I willing to give this all up?*

Some of the teachings of the itinerant preacher Jesus, who recently designated Capernaum as his headquarters, are beginning to sink into my own heart. Some of what I hear contradicts the Law, some seems to enhance it. Where does this man get his authority? Jesus admits that he has no formal training at one of the rabbinical schools in Jerusalem. No one is even sure of his birthplace, although he says that he is from nearby Nazareth and was brought up in the home of Joseph the carpenter. But he owns no carpentry shop, nor has a wife or children although he is certainly past a typical age for marriage. He seems to reside with one of his disciples, Simon, a local fisherman. What is there about His words that touches me? What if they are true? Can I remain a neutral observer? A bystander, of sorts, until I 'see which way the wind is blowing', so to speak? That probably won't be possible in my position. People will come to me for answers and I still have too many questions myself. Is he indeed the prophesied Messiah as he is now claiming to be? But how can our Deliverer come from Nazareth? Nothing good ever comes from Nazareth. The scriptures teach that the Anointed One will be born in Bethlehem located almost one hundred miles to the south of Capernaum in the province of Judea. They also say that He would come out of Egypt. Jesus obviously doesn't fit either of those criteria.

After pondering in silence for some time, Jairus rose from his seat and prepared to leave the building. He had come to a decision although he wasn't entirely sure it was the right one. *I can't afford to give up my position as leader of the synagogue for an unproven doctrine or way of life. If I follow Jesus, I will be cast out as a dissenter, losing respect and social standing. I will have to give up the comfortable home in which we now reside. How would I even be able to provide for my family? All I can foresee are losses, not gains, even if Jesus proclaimed that His way was the only way to gain eternal life. I must adhere to the traditions of my fathers.*

He stepped into the bright sunshine, squinting after being inside the dim interior for so long. The door of every synagogue was built to face Jerusalem as a reminder of their once-great past__the strength and unity of the Kingdom of Israel known under the magnificent King David, who made Jerusalem his capitol city after putting down all their enemies. David's son, Solomon erected the First and most beautiful temple. The one that stood there now was an inferior replica built under the administration of Nehemiah following their return from Babylon. The Roman governor, as a way of ingratiating himself with the Jews, had recently increased the size of the temple mount with porticoes and a marketplace for purchasing sacrificial animals. No, it wasn't the glory promised to the House of David forever, but that glory would come again when the true Messiah came. He closed the heavy oak doors securing the lock with a large bronze key which hung from a cord tied around his waist. He had made his choice__Jerusalem, not Jesus.

Jairus and Abigail sat on the stone bench in their courtyard at the setting of the sun, their favorite time of day. The peach, lavender, and pink hues filled the horizon with a brilliant glow behind the hills that framed the Sea of Galilee.

"How could we here in the Galilee be the favored ones to have Jesus live and preach among us first?" asked Abigail.

"The prophet Isaiah may have been speaking of that very thing when he said, 'Nevertheless the dimness shall not be such as was in her vexation, when at first he lightly afflicted the land of Zebulun and the land of Naphtali...the people that walked in darkness have seen a great light: they that dwell in the land of the shadow of death, upon them hath the light shined.' (Isaiah 9:1-2) This very region was part of the original designation for the tribes of Zebulun and

Naphtali. And because it is easily accessible by invaders from the north, it was often a land afflicted by enemies. Its inhabitants continually lived in the shadow of death."

"I wish I knew the scriptures like you do, Jairus."

"It may be an advantage or a disadvantage now that we are hearing Jesus' interpretations of them. If one is too set in what has been written in the past, we may not recognize truth when it comes to us in the present."

"You are referring to the truths taught by Jesus?"

"Yes, Abigail. I seem to have greater understanding and enlightenment concerning them every time I hear Jesus preach. I can't seem to get my fill."

"My heart too has been touched and I feel a warm spirit come over me whenever I am near him."

"You know what this is going to mean to us, Abigail? Personally and socially?"

"If you mean that I must accept Jesus as our Messiah with all of my heart, might, mind, and strength, Jairus, I have already done that."

"It has been more difficult for me to come to that recognition, but I too have come to that decision. You felt it with your heart, and I have had to weigh it out in my mind. Together, I hope we are right. It means giving up this home, my position on the Council of Elders, our social standing in the community, many of our friends and family."

"I know. I have thought of all of those things as well, but I cannot deny the confirmation of truth that has come to me."

"Me neither. How do you think this will effect Deborah? There will be fewer eligible men who believe in Jesus from which to arrange a marriage."

"Deborah has been in love with Jesus ever since he cured her fever. And hopefully with the passage of time, within a few years when she is of marriageable age, there will be many more young men who have also accepted the message of Jesus and are wanting a believer for a wife."

"I think I still have the skills as a stone mason to build us a small house if we can find a spot of suitable ground. This place belongs to the *chazzan,* the leader of the Council, and I will be ostracized from the Elders as soon as I declare my allegiance to Jesus."

"It is a high price for you to pay, Jairus."

"His challenge to his people anciently seems to apply to me today. 'Choose ye this day whom ye will serve;...but as for me and my house, we will serve the Lord.' (Joshua 24:15) I wish I had more than my allegiance to offer Him. There are many others who give of their funds and their food; the Twelve gave up their occupations. He has said we must be willing to sacrifice everything to obtain the Kingdom of God."

"In time, perhaps we will have more that we can contribute. For now, we are offering all that we have, and that is all that He has ever asked."

Jonah, Disciple of John

THE TINKLING OF metal harnesses was the wake-up call for those still huddled inside the caravansary and trying to catch a few more moments of sleep. Jonah reached over, shook his brother's shoulder, and whispered, "Enosh, It's time to arise." His companion grunted but did not move or even open his eyes.

"Enosh," repeated the elder brother, "Get up. We're both too old for me to tickle you like I did when you were a sleepy-headed boy and father called us."

"Maybe you are, Jonah," Enosh blurted out as he quickly rolled toward his brother grabbing him by the ribs," but I'm not!"

Jonah quickly crawled away, accidentally bumping into another sojourner curled up near the stone wall of the outdoor shelter, the place where travelers too poor to afford a room inside the inn were allowed to camp for the night.

Enosh jumped up with an alacrity that belied his middle-age status and with his strong arms pulled his brother to his feet, both of them laughing in merriment.

"You trickster," teased Jonah. "You always were the fastest."

The two men grabbed their scrips, which they had used for pillows, and felt inside to make sure the purses containing their few coins were still wrapped securely.

"We were protected from thieves this time, "said Jonah.

"Praise the Lord," replied Enosh. "Now we can get some breakfast before we take up our journey again. There should be fresh bread in the city of Jericho by the time we arrive."

Daylight was just breaking over the eastern hills bordering the Jordan River. Jericho was a major junction of the trade routes of the region: to the northeast lay Damascus; a steep incline led westward to Jerusalem through a barren stretch of rocks and sand; and south, the part of the trail they had traveled yesterday, led caravans along the shores of the Dead Sea and onto the Silk Roads beyond. There was a natural ford of the River near Jericho, it being one of the lowest spots on the earth, but the men had preferred to wait until morning to cross it as the spring run-off from Mt. Hermon made the water swift at this season of the year.

A short time later, after each purchased a loaf of warm barley bread and a handful of dried figs, they filled their goat-skinned water bags at the community well. "This is where we must part," said Enosh clapping Jonah on the shoulder. "I am glad we could spend this time together listening to The Baptist."

"Yea, brother; John is gaining a larger following all of the time."

"Do you think he is a prophet?" asked Enosh.

"He certainly sounds like some of the ancient ones we hear about every week in the synagogue."

"But it has been so long, "said the younger man.

"Almost three hundred years according to the rabbis."

"I have almost given up hope that God even remembers he once called us His Chosen People."

"We can never give up hope, Enosh. There are prophecies of a Great Deliverer who will come to save us all."

"I know, some Messiah. Do you think that John might be that Messiah?"

"He's never claimed to be. In fact, did you notice what he said this time? 'I come to prepare the way for one who comes after me, whose shoe latchet I am not worthy to unloose.'" (Mark1:7)

"Well, John is surely bold in calling men to repentance," grumbled Enosh. "He makes me feel about as worthy of God's love as a worm."

"I believe the Psalmist wrote that He loves all creatures, great and small."

"Maybe there's hope for me then. "

"Well, Enosh, I must be on my way. It will take me two or three days to reach Galilee. You are fortunate that you may be home by nightfall."

"You are the fortunate one, Jonah. You have two strong sons to carry on your fishing business while you are away."

"Yes, I am indeed lucky to have Andrew and Simon to take over."

"My Jesse is learning some basic skills so as soon as he gets some more meat on his bones, I will teach him some of the tricks of the tanner's trader. Is your family still planning on coming for Jesse's Bar Mitzvah?"

"Are you still planning on the ceremony after Passover next month?" Jonah responded with a question of his own.

"Yea."

"Then we will be there. Attending Passover is one tradition my Ashanti insists we keep. It gives us an opportunity to visit both of our families."

"You know that you are always welcome in our home, small as it is, any time that you come to the Holy City."

"Goodbye, Enosh," Jonah said, embracing his brother.

"Shalom, until we meet again."

With that, the two men parted but turned to wave before the dust of the trail obscured the view. Jonah hoped he could find a traveling party that he might join for a few days. There was protection in larger numbers and even though it was longer to travel around Samaria than through it, he always felt a little safer taking the Eastern road.

A few days later Jonah and his son, Simon, sat on the seashore mending their nets in preparation for the night's work ahead of them.

"Where is Andrew?" asked Jonah.

"Off as usual. Cana, I think, listening to some new preacher."

"You can't mean John the Baptist for he's on the other side of Jordan."

"No, this is a man named Jesus. Came from Nazareth, I believe."

"Well, the real preacher to listen to is John. I hope you can go with me the next time and listen to his powerful words."

"Like what?" asked Simon as he threaded the long bone needle through the torn mesh.

"He certainly isn't afraid of offending anyone. He called us a generation of vipers."

"Well, that's certainly strong language!"

"John says if we are children of Abraham, then we should bring forth fruits worthy of repentance like Abraham did. If not, we are good for nothing, but to be hewn down and cast into the fire."

"I see what you mean. The Jews are proud of being descendants of Abraham for sure. What does he say that we should do to repent?"

"Well, that's just it," Jonah paused, staring out across the Sea still glimmering blue in the fading sunlight. "He tells different people different things. That is, even though they each asked the same question 'What shall we do?"_he gave them varying answers.

"What? That can't be the true gospel. The Law of Moses is the same for everyone."

"Oh, that part is true enough, but it's like he understood the foremost sin of each particular group of society and told them how to repent. For example, to those who were selfish he said if they had two coats, they should give one to someone who didn't have any. Or if a man was without food and we had some, we should share it."

"Nothing too strange about that. What else?"

"To the Publicans, he warned not to exact any higher tax than was appointed."

"That would be a blessed relief. The Publicans always like to add a surcharge to fatten their purses."

"There were Roman soldiers in the vicinity who were also curious about this so-called wild man who lives in the desert, wears a camel skin tunic, and eats wild honey and pods from the locust trees. John told them to do no violence to any man, neither to accuse any falsely, but to be content with their wages."

"I see what you mean about cautioning people differently. Did he have any special words for fishermen?"

"Not this time," Jonah chuckled.

"It would probably be something like, 'Don't sell yesterday's fish for the same price as today's fresh catch." Both men laughed heartily.

"Oh, here comes Andrew now," and Jonah waved to his eldest son to join them on the boulders lining the shore as the sun was setting.

"It's about time you got back, Andrew. We'll be heading out for a night's work as soon as it's dark," said Simon as his brother squatted on the nearest rock. "Here, grab the other end of this net so it will be ready for casting."

Andrew and Simon worked with dexterity, folding the long net into the proper shape. There was nothing worse than trying to straighten a tangled net in the dark.

"I can see that you are bursting with news, Andrew," said Jonah perceptively.

"Yes, Father. I have wonderful news! I have found the Christ!"

"What? You mean the Messiah is on earth now?" asked Jonah incredulously.

"You saw the Messiah in Cana? This afternoon?" asked Simon in skepticism.

"Yes. The one called Jesus," he answered excitedly.

"You're trying to say that Jesus of Nazareth is the Promised Messiah? Oh come now, Andrew, you're not that big of a fool," chided Simon.

"How can you be so sure, Andrew?" questioned his father.

"It's hard to explain. Mostly it's a feeling burning inside my heart."

"But where would this Jesus get his authority? There are no High Priests in Nazareth."

That's just it. He says he got his authority from his Father."

"And who might that be?" asked Simon. "

"He declares that he is the Son of God."

"Oh, come, come Andrew. You know that is not possible," Jonah reminded his son.

"Now with John The Baptist, it's very clear where he gets his authority. His father, Zacharias, was a priest and in fact, was serving his course in the temple when an angel appeared to him telling him that he and Elizabeth would have a son in their old age."

"I know that's what you've heard, Father, and I don't disagree with you. I just wish you and Simon could come with me and listen to Jesus. You would feel the same as I do."

"I doubt it," replied Simon sarcastically.

"If there's a true prophet on the earth today, Andrew, I believe it is John The Baptist, not Jesus," said Jonah emphatically.

"Just come and see," pleaded Andrew.

"It's time to be off to work. Maybe a night out on the fresh air will clear your head of all this foolish thinking, brother." Simon scrambled down the rocks and waded into the waist-deep water to their small boat tethered to a buoy in the undulating waves and was soon joined by Andrew. Somehow Simon felt that this particular conversation would go on all night and to him it was just a Big Fish Story. The Son of God, indeed!

Passover had been a joyous celebration for the families of Jonah and Enosh, along with the Bar Mitzvah of Jesse, who after answering all the questions posed by the council of rabbis and going through the purification rites was now considered an adult. Before returning to Galilee however, Jonah, accompanied by his wife, Ashanti, chose to head east from Jerusalem so that they might hear the preaching of John The Baptist, who was now south of the Dead Sea near Bethabara. It was a difficult road with many sand dunes and outcroppings of rocks where thieves laid in wait for unsuspecting travelers. This particular time it was crowded as there were many returning from the Passover festivities. It seemed that a good many were also on their way to hear John, and some were even planning on being baptized by him, including Jonah and Ashanti. The conversations buzzed among the travelers regarding this new prophet in Israel.

Some asked, "Is he the Christ?"

"No, he denies that he is that long-awaited One."

"Do you think he is the promised Elias who will restore all things?'

"He also denies that he is that prophet."

"Well then, who is he?"

"The only title he claims is that he is 'a Voice of one crying in the wilderness to make straight the way of the Lord.'"

"That is a quotation from Esaias; God rest his soul," answered a priest.

A Levite traveling with the group added, "When the Pharisees asked why, if he was not the Christ or the Elias to restore all things, was he performing baptisms?"

"What was John's response?"

"He said, 'I baptize with water: but there standeth one among you, whom ye know not. He it is of whom I bear record, for he is preferred before me. He shall baptize not only with water, but with fire, and with the Holy Ghost.'" (See John 1:26-27)

"Who was he referring to?"

"None of us knows. Perhaps when we see him tomorrow we can ask him."

A large crowd gathered on the banks of the Jordan whose rushing current a few weeks earlier had now slowed to a gentle stream. The spring leaves of the willows had emerged providing shade for those eager to hear the words of John The Baptist. All of a sudden, John halted his preaching as he observed a man coming toward him. "Behold the Lamb of God, which taketh away the sins of the world," he said pointing toward Jesus. "This is he of whom I said, 'That after me cometh a man which is preferred before me: for he was before me'." (John 1:29-30)

The man was apparently known to John, but a stranger to most in the multitude. They wondered who could be so important that John would cease preaching and wave to the newcomer, someone who appeared to be about John's same age. Speculation buzzed through the crowd until it was learned that the man's name was Jesus.

"This is the man that Andrew claims to be the Christ," whispered Jonah to his wife.

"He doesn't look like someone claiming to be the long-awaited

Deliverer, "she answered. "Even if he were, why would he come to John?" Jonah shook his head unable to give an answer.

"Will you baptize me?" Jesus asked The Baptist.

"I have need to be baptized of thee, and comest thou to me?"

Jesus replied, "Suffer me to be baptized of thee, for thus it becometh us to fulfill all righteousness." (See Matt 3:13-15)

Why would John need to be baptized? Did he need to repent? Was John saying he would be a disciple of Jesus? Jonah was confused. I thought John had priesthood authority already. Does Jesus have a different authority? If I was baptized by him today, would it be acceptable unto God? What did it mean that the two of them were fulfilling all righteousness? I have so many questions.

A few words passed between John and Jesus which Jonah, Ashanti, and others nearby could not hear. They looked at one another with questioning countenances as the two men waded into the waist-deep water. One man called out, "Let him wait his turn to be baptized like the rest of us." But neither John nor Jesus paid any heed to the heckler.

John immersed Jesus in the River, then as Jesus rose with rivulets streaming from his face and hair, they both looked heavenward as if listening to an unseen voice. Then to the amazement of all observing the tenderness of the moment, watched as a single white dove flew down and landed upon Jesus' shoulder. (See Matt 3:16-17)

Jonah wondered, *Is this some kind of sign? What is so special about Jesus? There does seem to be an aura of light around the man that I haven't noticed before.*

Simon, Andrew, and Jonah sat on the shore of the Sea of Galilee, also known as the Sea of Tiberius in honor of the Roman Emperor, it recently having been so named by The Tetrarch Herod Antipas, always trying to ingratiate himself with the monarch. The night's catch had tangled the net and the three men patiently worked to unravel its twisted knots.

"I feel like my thoughts are as tangled as this net," said Jonah to his two sons.

"Why so, Father?" asked Andrew.

"Ever since I witnessed the baptism of Jesus, I cannot get the man out of my mind."

"Ah, yes, Jesus. He is certainly a man to confuse our thinking," replied Simon.

"I find no contradictions in anything he says," defended Andrew.

"How can you be so sure he is the Christ, brother?'

"All I can say is that God has born witness to my soul."

Jonah intervened with "That is why I am so confused, my sons. One of you is as sure about Jesus as the other is skeptical of him."

"So where do you stand, Father?" asked Simon.

"I have not come to a conclusion yet. I desire to know the truth, but what is the truth? Isaiah says that the Lord will come from the stem of Jesse and Micah says he will be born in Bethlehem. Zechariah calls him a BRANCH and King David calls him a King and a priest. Hosea says that God will call his son out of Egypt. Yet Jesus fits none of these. How can he be the Promised Messiah?"

"I will pray for God to reveal the truth to your mind, Father, so that your soul may be at rest," said Andrew as he twisted the twine and loosened one of the knots, "just as easy as that," and he smiled at his father.

"If he is an imposter, he is certainly a clever one," added Simon. "How can he trick so many people into following him? The crowds become more numerous every day. Some claim to have been healed of diseases or blindness or had devils cast out. Is it by the power of

Beelzebub that he performs such magic?"

"It is not magic, Simon. They are miracles performed by the Son of God. Would you expect a God to do less?'

"That's just it. How can a mortal man be the son of God?"

"I do not know, Simon. I only believe that with God all things are possible. "

"Enough of your wrangling, my sons. Cast the net upon the water and see if all the tangles are out," said Jonah. Simon and Andrew carried the net and waded out from shore before casting the net into a circle above their heads. It floated smoothly upon the waves. "Good work," called Jonah from the shore. "It will be ready for tonight's work." Andrew and Simon tugged at the net as they pulled it back to shore. They climbed out, dripping with water when Jonah raised his head and said in a quiet voice, "He of whom we have been speaking is approaching."

The brothers looked up as they saw Jesus walking toward them along the edge of the sea. "*Andrew, Simon, I am he of whom it is written by the prophets; follow me, and I will make you fishers of men.*" (Matt 4:19)

Both brothers looked to their father, who gave a nod. "Go and learn what you can and then come and tell me."

So Andrew and Peter straightway left their nets and followed Jesus, Andrew with eagerness in his eyes and Simon with skepticism. Going further along the shore they soon saw their cousins, James and John, sons of their Uncle Zebedee, likewise mending their nets for they were also fishermen. Jesus called to them in the same manner. They immediately left their ship and their father and with a jovial clap on the back, this second set of brothers joined Simon and Andrew as they all tread the well-worn path toward Capernaum. (See Matt 4:21-22)

The young men were gone for several days and Jonah toiled alone in his boat every night, often with only a skimpy harvest of fish. The dark hours alone gave Jonah much time for thought, but no matter how he cast his net of questions toward God, it seemed to come back empty as well. *Why would Jesus want my sons? I am getting to be an old man and I need my sons if this business is to survive. Let him choose someone else. Why are my two sons so different_Andrew so believing and Simon so unbelieving? Didn't I raise them both the same? Where should I cast the net to obtain fish? I need a whole school of tilapia swimming toward me right now. Why would Jesus want fishers to catch men? Is he trying to recruit men for an armed rebellion against Rome? Where does Jesus get his power to heal? Why does John direct people toward Jesus instead of enlarging his own flock? What did John mean when he called Jesus the Lamb of God? Does Jesus belong to John's flock? Or does John belong to one being created by Jesus? John fasts often, but Jesus doesn't seem to fast at all. John lives a solitary life in the desert, but Jesus socializes with all kinds of people. Yes, that is even part of the problem_Jesus looks upon publicans and harlots as lovingly as any parent would. On the other hand, some of his strongest accusations are against those like the Pharisees who follow the Law of Moses with exactness. What can he see that the rest of us can't or refuse to see?*

When Andrew and Simon returned, they could not stop talking about their experiences with Jesus. Jonah was amazed at the change that had come over his younger son, who now seemed to believe in the divinity of Jesus as much as Andrew did. The young men shared all the teachings of Jesus with their parents as they sat in the courtyard of Peter's humble home. Peter's wife, Rosa, held his youngest child Amos on her lap and two others, his oldest named after his grandfather Jonah and Susanna, his only daughter, played with a valued collection of colorful stones in a nearby corner.

Andrew related how the crowds multiplied daily and followed Jesus from place to place. One day Jesus, whom they now called The Master, had the multitude sit on the hillside while he stood above them so that all could hear his voice.

"It was a beautiful scene indeed," interjected Simon. "We will have to show you the spot someday when we journey to Capernaum."

"Yes," agreed Andrew. "The view of the Sea and the mountains were beautiful, but the words of Jesus were even more wonderful."

"What do you mean?" quizzed Jonah wanting to learn more.

"Jesus taught a higher law."

"You mean more rules to add to the six-hundred and nine we already have?" asked Ashanti.

"No, not more laws, but a higher and holier application of the laws we already have. Let me give a few examples. We all know that we shouldn't kill, but Jesus says we should not even get angry. The Law says we should fast and pray, but Jesus wants us to do it secretly and not publicly where we will be praised for our righteousness."

"Ah, yes, I have seen how the Pharisees like to pray in the streets so that everyone will take notice," said Jonah.

"But here's the hardest one of all," added Simon. "Moses taught us to love our neighbors and hate our enemies, but Jesus says we are to love even our enemies."

"Do you mean that Jesus is saying we have to love the Romans who oppress us?" asked his mother.

"As difficult as it may seem, yes that is exactly what he means."

"But won't that just give them license to exercise more control over us? When they demand it, we already have to walk a mile and carry their packs. What does Jesus say to that?" questioned Jonah. "Walk with them two?"

"Exactly," replied Simon.

"That is indeed a hard saying, my son."

"Yea, Father. But if we are filled with the love of God, then we will find the strength to do it. We must seek to be filled with this kind of love and we will be blessed," added Andrew.

"Speaking of blessings, Jesus gave a long list of ways that we can be blessed. For example, if we mourn we shall be comforted; if we hunger and thirst after righteousness, we will be filled; if we are poor in spirit, we will obtain the kingdom of heaven."

"Well, we are getting poorer every day," grumbled Jonah. "The fishing has been scant indeed. "

"We will go out with you tonight, Father," said Simon. "I promise. But before we leave, I want Rosa to tell you about her mother."

"Yes, Rosa, how is your mother? I heard that she had been ill with a fever," said Ashanti.

"My mother was indeed very ill, and I was very worried. But Jesus came unto her and reached out and touched her hand, and the fever vanished. Immediately, she arose from her bed and prepared The Master a meal. It was a miracle indeed."

"And you saw this yourself?" asked her mother-in-law.

"Yes; Simon, Andrew, and I were all there with her when Jesus healed her. It was almost unbelievable how quickly she revived."

"And she wasn't pretending to be ill?"

"Oh no, she was near the point of death."

"I'm so glad for you and your mother, Rosa. Does this mean now that you are also among those called the Believers?"

"Yea, I believe with all my heart."

"So do I, Father," declared Simon.

"I can see that a great change has come upon you the past few days. You left here a skeptic and returned as a believer."

"I know. Isn't that the greatest miracle of all?"

"Miracle indeed, Simon. But the sun has set, and we must now get about our business. Hopefully, there will be many fish swimming into our nets this night."

The men arose and walked down to where their boat was tethered to a large boulder. Loosening the rope, their images soon faded into the darkened night.

Ashanti stayed a little longer to help Rosa get the children ready for bed by singing lullabies. Then they sat quietly talking of the miracles of Jesus.

"And it came to pass, that as the people pressed upon [Jesus] to hear the word of God, he stood by the [Sea of Galilee] and saw two-ships standing [nearby]. But the fishermen were gone out of them, and were washing their nets. And he entered into one of the ships, which was Simon's and [asked] him that he would thrust out a little from the land. And he sat down and taught the people out of the ship. (Luke 5:1-3)

"Now when he had left speaking, he said unto Simon, "Launch out into the deep, and let down your nets for a [catch.}"

"And Simon answering said unto him, "Master, we have toiled all the night, and have taken nothing; nevertheless at thy word, I will let down the net."

"And when they had this done, they [enclosed] a great multitude of fishes, [insomuch] that their net [was breaking]. And they beckoned unto their partners, which were in the other ship that they should come and help them. And they came, and filled both the ships so that they began to sink.

"When Simon saw it, he fell down at Jesus' knees. "Depart from me; for I am a sinful man, O Lord". For he was astonished, and all that were with him at the [large quantity] of the fishes which they had taken. And so was also James and John, the sons of Zebedee, which were partners with Simon." (See Luke 5:4-9)

All the men worked rapidly, sorting the fish according to variety and size, marveling again at how with a word from Jesus their nets were miraculously filled. Jesus approached the group, and squatting down spoke quietly to Jonah. "I have a greater need of your sons than you do. The gospel seed must be sown and the laborers are few. The harvest will be bounteous for it is a great and marvelous work. If you have desires, you are also called to the work and every man who plants will reap. And great shall be his joy with me in the kingdom of my Father."

Jonah looked up into the face of Jesus, whom he had never seen this close before. The clear dark eyes seemed to penetrate to Jonah's very soul and he bowed his head in shame.

Jesus reached out, touching Jonah's shoulder and Jonah had never felt such love. The older man raised his head in sorrow. "Depart from me Lord, for I am a sinful man." Then with tears streaming down his face, Jonah looked upon the face of Jesus and said, "Help thou my unbelief."

"Fear not, Jonah, for whosoever giveth his life for my sake, shall receive an hundredfold in the world to come. I am come to do the will of my Father, and whoso believeth in me shall not perish, but have everlasting life. "

Jonah felt a warmth growing inside that he could not explain, but it was something greater and more magnificent than he had ever felt in his life. *It is the baptism of the fire and of the Spirit that John The Baptist had foretold! That prophet was right all along! He served as a forerunner preparing the way for the King. They were not competitors, but companions. I can now understand and believe as Andrew and Simon had. Truly this Jesus is the Son of God!*

"All that I have is thine, O Lord," and Jonah was clasped in the arms of The Master.

"Is that the last?" asked Simon as Rosa tied the final bundle of cooking pots onto the side of the old wooden cart. A donkey stood harnessed swatting flies with his tail and twitching his long ears.

"Yes, just let me sweep the house one last time," she answered.

"You already swept yesterday," he chided.

"I know, but I don't want the next occupants to think that I was a slovenly housekeeper," and she laughed as she ducked through the low door into the house. "But will you hold the baby while I do so?"

Simon reached out one of his strong arms and took the wriggling Amos while clapping his other hand on his father's shoulder, who standing nearby had observed the scene. Young Jonah was patting the donkey's neck and feeding it some fresh grass he had pulled with his stubby six-year old hands. Four-year-old Susanna already sat perched on top of the load of household goods they were transporting to Capernaum. "You may sit here for now," said Simon addressing his daughter, "but when we start, you will have to get down and walk. This poor donkey will already have a heavy load to pull without a big girl like you."

"You are a good father, Simon. I should have helped Ashanti more when you and Andrew were younger," replied Jonah. "Now that I can see a better way of living taught by Jesus, I am realizing that many of our traditions were..." he stammered, "not correct."

"Don't be ashamed, Father, we're all learning new things from Jesus. It is part of the beauty of the principle of repentance that Jesus talks so much about. We are free to change, not held back by the mistakes of our past. I'm sorry that I cannot take over the fishing business as you always planned. Bethsaida has been your home for a long time."

"Yes, I thought I would pass on the boats and nets to you as my father did for me," admitted the older man. Then with a sigh continued, "But all things will turn out for the best, I suppose. It will be hard for me to get used to living in a city again after the open air of Galilee." Jonah's bald pate was glistening in the summer sun, and he wiped the sweat from his brow with the sleeve of his homespun tunic. "We are fortunate that we found a buyer for our business, as well as Zebedee's, in such a short time. Though I suspect that Joab's connections with Herod's steward may have something to do with that. It rankles me to think that my boats and nets will supply the tables of the Romans."

"You'll just have to let that go, Father. You ran an honest business all of your life. You can't control the actions of others after you've sold it."

"You are right, Simon," said Jonah stroking the dark curly head of his namesake. "I hope that Zebedee can also find peace with the decisions that James and John made to forsake him and follow Jesus. He is having a harder time accepting it than I," speaking of Ashanti's brother.

"Maybe he just needs more time," Simon said trying to support his father's life-long business partner and closest friend, as well as being his brother-in-law. Then trying to change the subject, he said, "I'm glad that Uncle Enosh has given you a spot in the tannery for the time being," responded Simon shifting little Amos to his other shoulder.

"I guess it's trading the stink of rotting fish for the stink of tanning leather," grimaced the older man. "But Ashanti will certainly enjoy living closer to her family again."

"I will miss our daily connections," said Simon with a lump rising in his throat. "But I too am glad that Rosa can live close to her mother now as I expect that I will be gone a great deal of the time on The Master's business. Of course, we are all so grateful for Jesus when he healed Rosa's mother from her fever. "

"Jesus seems to recognize your leadership skills, Simon, and I'm proud of you as my son." With the baby between them, the three generations impulsively clung to one another.

"We promise that we will come to Jerusalem for the festivals," said Simon, breaking the embrace.

"And bring these little ones," ordered Jonah. "Your mother will never forgive you if you don't."

"And you plan to visit John the Baptist in prison?" asked Simon.

"Yea. A few of us are trying to arrange some kind of a release with King Herod."

"Good luck with that. The Tetrarch is a very unpredictable man."

Rosa emerged from the house carrying her sagebrush broom which she tossed on top of the loaded cart. Then holding out her arms, she took the baby from Simon. With tears glistening on her cheeks, she lifted her chin and eked out a faint smile, "I'm ready."

Turning to her father-in-law, she gave him an affectionate hug. "I will miss you and Ashanti", she murmured. "The two of us said our good-byes yesterday, but here is one more kiss that I ask you to give to her from me. We will see you on Yom Kippur."

"Yes, your husband has already promised that."

"I guess there's no more reason for delay. It will take us the rest of the day to get to Capernaum," said Simon. "Shalom, Father."

"God be with you till we meet again," Jonah almost choked on his words, "'til we meet at Jesus' feet."

The Centurion

POLONIUS SAT ASTRIDE his twelve-hand bay stallion staring at the Roman parade ground near Caesarea. The red plume perched on the top of the horse's bridle waved in the breeze blowing in from the Great Sea. The centurion assumed a similar one on top of his metal helmet was swaying likewise, but it didn't bring any coolness to his sweat-streaked forehead. The horse's ears flecked the pesky flies away and the swishing of its long black tail kept up a steady rhythm for the same purpose. Polonius wished he had similar helpful appendages as he muttered something under his breath about the unbearable summer sun.

Polonius squinted trying to get a clearer view of the soldiers under his command as the dust swirled about them all. He rubbed a gloved hand across his eyes trying to clear his vision, but it was more of an irritant than a help. He wanted his men to look sharp when King Herod came to review the troops, so he barked an order to straighten their lines. He immediately regretted his brusqueness knowing that the soldiers were just as hot and uncomfortable as he was, and even more tired standing than he was sitting on his horse.

"Sergeant," called Polonius to his sub-commander standing nearby. "Find out from one of Herod's officers when the Tetrarch plans to arrive. Our men and those of the other regiments have been waiting for more than an hour. If His Excellency doesn't arrive soon, they'll be dropping like stones cast from a mountain top with this heat."

"Yes, Sir." responded Darius as he trotted off toward the garrison's headquarters closer to the palace.

Until he returned, Polonius decided to give his men a short break. "At ease," he called out and the men relaxed their rigid posture and moved their stiffened limbs. "Water boy," he again barked and a lad about ten years of age appeared with a bucket and gourd ladle and began passing through the ranks giving each man a drink of fresh water to slake their thirst. Polonius glanced at the via duct nearby, a cement trough constructed on top of stone arches with just enough slope to carry fresh spring water from the Galilean highlands to those residing in the southern provinces. *I have to give the Romans credit for their engineering skills*, the centurion thought to himself. *But I'm sure the native population of Jews isn't nearly so appreciative.*

A short time later Darius returned at a trot, "The Tetrarch is on his way now," he blurted out between gasping breaths. Polonius didn't waste any time in commanding the men back to full attention. His cohort needed to be as impressive as any of the others lined up similarly on the parade ground. He didn't want Herod to see one slouched shoulder or one loose shoe latchet. The haughty King Herod prided himself on the precision of the troops under his jurisdiction, ready to squelch any Jewish uprising that might be fomenting among the zealots who frequently called for a liberation movement against their foreign oppressors.

Polonius and his century composed of one hundred men were normally stationed near Capernaum or Kaper Nahum as some of the orthodox Jews referred to it by its ancient name. He would be glad to get back to the relative quiet of the village where the cooling breezes off the Sea of Galilee made the summer heat more bearable. Thinking of the large inland lake he recalled that Herod had recently renamed it the Sea of Tiberius, trying to ingratiate himself with the Roman Emperor who would probably never see it. *It was just another thing to rankle the natives* according to Polonius' train of thought. *No wonder the locals kept trying to revolt.*

The eye irritation which had bothered Polonius during the Caesarean military review grew worse as the week progressed. Each morning when the centurion awoke, his eyelids were matted shut with dried yellow pus. He would immediately call for William, who lay on a pallet nearby, and the loyal servant was by his side in a moment. *Was the man a light sleeper or was he already awake ?* wondered Polonius, who himself slept like a bear hibernating in the mountains of Dan.

"Yes, Master", said William at the bedside.

"My eyes, my eyes!" Polonius screeched, "I can't open them! I'm blind!"

"Calm yourself, Master. Just lie still and I will have water warmed very soon, and then I will wash them."

"Be quick, William. I must be about my duties."

"Yes, Sir,"

Although a small brazier heated a pot of water quite quickly, Polonius thrashed irritably on his bed, moaning in pain. William took a soft piece of cloth, dipped it into the water, and gently began softening the dried matter on Polonius's eyelids. With tender strokes, the slave cleared away the crustiness until the man slowly eased each eyelid open a fraction at a time. The brightness of the morning sun blinded him temporarily, as he flung the bed covering to the floor and clawed the air.

"William?"

"I'm right here, Sir. Just take it easy. Sit here on the edge of the bed for a moment until you regain your sight."

Polonius, out of fright and frustration, obeyed his servant's suggestion. Then making another attempt to open his eyes, this time he adapted more quickly to the sunshine.

"Get my sandals."

"Yes, Sir."

William knelt on the floor and laced the leather thongs of the footwear up the centurion's hairy legs, tying a knot beneath the knee cap. Looking up into the Roman commander's face, he carefully chose his words before saying, "Sir, if I may say so, your eyes still look bloodshot and sore."

"They feel like they are on fire, William. I don't know what to do."

"If you desire, I can go to the marketplace today and ask among the locals if there are any herbs we can use for a medicinal poultice."

"Yes, that is a good idea. It would be unseemly for me as a Roman commander to appear there obviously ill. It would indicate weakness when we must maintain our show of strength. But it would not seem out of place for a slave to be in the market. I pray to all the gods from Jupiter to Zeus that there might be a cure. If not, I may scratch my eyes out with madness."

"I'll go as soon as you've eaten, Sir. I will have some porridge ready for you soon. Or perhaps a few grapes while you wait? It is too early in the day for wine, don't you think?"

"Thank you, William. I'm sorry for being in an ill temper this morning."

Holding his head in his hand, Polonius was still sitting at the large wooden table where William had left him less than an hour earlier. Despite his best intentions, Polonius had not had the strength to begin his duties. The slave entered the centurion's living quarters and held out a small wooden box toward his master.

"What's this?" Polonius asked as he opened the lid.

"On good authority from the rabbi's wife, it is a mixture of aloe, frankincense, a few secret ingredients, and beeswax. When it is heated slightly, it softens to a pliable gummy consistency. One spreads it over the eyelids and it should provide relief from the pain and promote healing."

"You say this came from the rabbi's wife? Eliezer's wife?"

"Yes, Sir." Then clearing his throat, he continued, "It was quite expensive, Sir."

"How much?" grumbled Polonius.

"Two denarii, Sir," confessed William.

"Why that's two days' wages!" thundered the Roman. "For this small amount? It's robbery, that's what it is. The Jews are trying to get back at us any way they can."

"The woman didn't seem like she was trying to cheat us, Sir. In fact, she apologized that it was as expensive as it was. She said it was the frankincense which has to be imported, besides the taxes which the Romans place on everything that passes in and out of the country. Plus she travels into the neighboring hills to locate the plants she calls her secret ingredients. Surely her time is worth something as well."

"Humph," was the only reply.

"There's one more thing necessary for the medicine to work, Sir."

"What's that?"

"You must lie still in a darkened room for seven days, from Shabbat to Shabbat."

"And how am I supposed to command my regiment laying in

bed for a week?"

"That is your decision, Sir. But may I remind you that Darius is a loyal sergeant and could probably keep the province in order for a short time."

"He's no commander," growled Polonius.

"No Sir, not like you, Sir. But maybe with a little more practice, he could improve his leadership skills. I guess it's really up to you and how badly you want to get better."

"It looks as if I have little choice in the matter, William. Call Darius to report to me at once. Then we will begin this treatment plan. At two denarii, it had better work."

Although it was against his nature, Polonius agreed to the second part of the treatment as well as the medicinal salve. He lay quietly on his bed in a dimly lit room, William having covered the window with the commander's cloak. The heat during the day was stifling without a breeze coming off the inland sea, so the evening's coolness was welcomed when the curtain was removed for the night.

William brought him food from the commissary and Darius reported the state of affairs with the regiment on a daily basis. So far, there had been no revolutionary outbreaks as the populace seemed to be conserving its energy from the relentless sun.

Day by day, the itching and burning subsided and Polonius was tempted to be up and about his duties. But William reminded him of the seven-day rest period also prescribed, as if the Rabbi's wife thought there was some magic in the number seven, or in honoring Shabbat.

The enforced rest gave Polonius a lot of time to think and he reviewed the course his life had taken. He had grown up as the son of a Roman officer, so it was no wonder that as a boy he wanted to follow in his father's footsteps. It wasn't until Polonius was eighteen and excited about joining an expedition to Britain that his father had taken him aside and revealed for the first time in his life an experience he'd had about twenty years earlier. Lucanus, the father of Polonius, had been assigned to the Fortress Antonia in Jerusalem, not far from where Polonius now served. King Herod, the father of the current Roman Tetrarch bearing the same name, was approached by three travelers from the East who had come seeking an infant who according to their beliefs was born to become King of the Jews. The men explained that they had seen a star which was a sign to them of this newborn King. Of course, this news made Herod very angry, thinking that a revolution would take place to displace him and his own heirs from the throne. Herod called the wise men from his court to search the sacred writings about such a sign, and it was reported back that indeed an ancient prophet had said that a new king would be born in Bethlehem, a village about forty furlongs south of Jerusalem.

The travelers soon departed, but jealousy took root in Herod's heart, and when the King realized that the three travelers had no intention of returning to report back the whereabouts of the babe, his anger exploded. Herod commanded the regiment under his command to march to Bethlehem and slay all of the babies under the age of two as a means of ridding himself of a future usurper. Lucanus was one of the soldiers assigned to that grisly task. He tried to explain to Polonius the atrocity of the situation__mothers running in a panic trying to hide their children; screams of anguish as the babies were snatched from their mothers' arms and pierced with a sword, then dropped like rubbish on the ground. Lucanus was sickened by the heinous deaths he had been required to carry out. He had nightmares for years afterward. It was only through the instrumentality of close friends that he had been transferred back to Rome, acting as a guard on Palatine Hill.

Lucanus wanted Polonius to know the horribleness of innocent killing before his son committed his life and loyalty to Caesar. Polonius was shocked to learn of his father's experience, whom he had always looked up to as a great soldier and defender of Rome. But the lure of adventure overshadowed the cautions of his experienced father. Polonius soon found himself on a transport ship sailing the Mediterranean, out of the Straits of the narrow opening into the mighty ocean beyond, and eventually landing on the shores of a northern island.

Polonius had been grateful for a few months to mature in body and mind in the strict training of the cohort of young recruits before participating in actual battle. It was on a foray into the interior of the southern end of the island that they met the greatest resistance and engaged the natives. It was here that he had first encountered William, a young boy about ten or eleven years of age, and obviously, an orphan after the Roman invasion of the small recalcitrant village had left his parents dead. Polonius had claimed the boy as part of the spoils of war and the lad had proven to be loyal and dependable. William probably realized that without Polonius he would have ended up being sold as some galley slave or left on his own to die of starvation.

After Britannia, Polonius had moved up in rank and served in Gaul, a major defensive outpost that lay over the mountains northwest of Rome. When Lucanus died, Polonius took upon himself the responsibility of caring for his mother and two younger sisters. With his mother's encouragement, he arranged marriages for his sisters and paid the dowries from the funds left by his father. Although Polonius was promoted to a higher rank with more prestige and was a fine specimen of manhood, he had never made marriage a high priority for himself. What respectable young woman would want to be left alone for months at a time while he was out on campaigns? When his mother died from the fever which was rampant in Rome every summer, he lost all ties with his family. There was only him and William, and a small inheritance from the sale of his boyhood home.

An appointment as a Centurion was the culmination of a dream Polonius hardly dared entertain as an exuberant eighteen-year-old. Now, as someone approaching his third decade of life, he knew that the rank meant little, especially when he and his men had been assigned to the backwater province of Palestine. Polonius knew his chances of ever returning to Rome were slim and he had reconciled himself to spending the remainder of his military career under the jurisdiction of another Herod, who appeared to be touched with the same madness as his royal father.

The most recent case in point for such insanity, if Polonius had gleaned the information correctly, was of the beheading of a local Jew, one whom the people had called John the Baptist, even known to some as a prophet. Herod had been celebrating his birthday with a large feast and of course, everyone had consumed too much wine. When Herod's daughter Salome danced for the guests, he had rashly promised her anything her heart desired. The girl, too young to decide for herself, consulted her mother, Herodias. The Queen was fiercely angry with The Baptist for condemning her divorce from Philipp and marrying her brother-in-law, Herod. When the chance came to get rid of her nemesis, Herodias was more than eager to demand the head of the prophet. Herod could not back down and save face, so the dastardly deed was carried out and the severed head was delivered to the King on a silver charger.

The thought sickened Polonius, and he realized anew the anguish his father had felt at such a useless killing. It was one thing to loyally defend one's homeland, even to fight against the enemies of Caesar, but it was another thing entirely to be a part of the murder.

Polonius was glad his current assignment was to keep the peace in the small town of Capernaum and as he lay on his sickbed he pondered on the tactics of other leaders for maintaining a quiet way of life. There seemed to be two courses of action__a show of strength and force, ever on guard quelling any hint of rebellion, or a steady vigilant presence that allowed the Galileans to pursue their individual lives without too much interference. Polonius was no coward, but in the present circumstances, he thought that honey might be a more powerful defense than vinegar.

When the week's respite was concluded, Polonius was eager to see his men and survey the province again. It wasn't that he didn't have confidence in Darius or the daily reports that all was well; it was that he had missed the camaraderie of his troops. The medicine and the week's relief from the bright sun had worked their magic and he felt like he was ten years younger.

The cohort was quickly assembled and they started on patrol of the countryside always keeping the Sea of Galilee on their left as they paraded through Magdala, then up the hills into Nazareth, where they camped outside the village for the night. The next day's circuit took them through Cana as they returned to Capernaum. Everywhere they went were rumors of another prophet, a man from Nazareth itself who was performing miracles.

What is it with these Jews anyway? wondered Polonius. *The Romans, after they initially conquer a region, are known to be quite generous in allowing the native population to continue worshipping their own gods. What's one more deity to the plethora of gods already accepted in Rome? But the Jews are a little different__they claim there is only one true God, Additionally, they believe in the reality of prophets as well as God, albeit most of their prophets have been dead for more than three hundred years. I know that many called John the Baptist a prophet, but that man is now dead as well.*

So now a new prophet seems to have emerged, a man *named Jesus. Some claim that he is John risen from the dead, but those who saw and heard the Baptist squelched that rumor. No, this Jesus appears to be someone even greater than John, for certainly the Preacher John never performed any miracles. I've overheard the gossip in the markets__Jesus changing water into wine at a wedding in Cana; sending evil spirits exorcised from madmen into the bodies of swine; the animals then turning wild and running headlong into the sea near Magdala. Everywhere there are stories that Jesus has healed the blind, the lame, and cured the lepers. Even from my base of operations in Capernaum, I've heard that the mother-in-law of Peter, a local fisherman, was cured of a fever and rose within minutes to prepare a meal for her benefactor. Some are even starting to call Jesus a King of the Jews. If that is the case, I will have to be extra vigilant to ward off any simmering revolt.*

The troop returned to Capernaum near dusk and the men, weary from their two-day march, were glad to be safely settled into their barracks before a tumultuous wind assaulted the town. Sudden storms were not uncommon on the Sea of Galilee, as fierce winds churned the waves into a frenzy. Polonius hoped that all of the fishing boats were tied securely to their anchors on the shore; it was certainly no night for the local men to be out on their customary fishing expeditions.

The next morning Polonius learned in a report from Darius that a large tree had split apart in the storm and crushed the local synagogue. Polonius went to investigate, taking only William with him.

The young Brit walked just to the right and two steps behind his master, carrying a long staff, and his eyes continuously scanned those they passed. Most of the Jews ignored them; a few flipped their shawls over their heads to block the view, but none dared spit or call out derogatory comments. Past lessons had taught them the futility of such actions as punishments were swift and harsh. Still, William was always on the lookout for any potential trouble and prepared to act swiftly to protect the Centurion if the need arose. He knew that he owed his life to the Roman and they had developed a mutual respect and trust for one another.

As they approached the synagogue, Polonius could see that Darius' report was somewhat exaggerated, as only a section of the synagogue had been destroyed, but already men were at work sawing the large tree branches that had caused the damage so that they could be carried away.

"Good morning, Rabbi," said Polonius to the gray-haired man supervising the clean-up. "I am sorry to see the damage to your place of worship."

"'Tis a great loss to us. We will be forced to meet in the out-of-doors for a while until it can be repaired."

"At least it is summer. You should be able to have it fixed before the winter rains."

"I hope so," replied the rabbi. "Rebuilding the outer walls will only require labor, but it is the supporting poles inside that will be expensive and difficult to replace. The cedar must be obtained from Mt. Tabor or Mt. Moran, then fashioned into columns," the old man sighed deeply. "I hope I live long enough to see it."

"Are you unwell, Eliezer?" asked Polonius.

"Alas, yes. My strength diminishes by the day."

"Too bad your wife can't conjure you a medicine to cure your ailments."

"Oh, she has tried, God bless her soul, but mine is an internal malady of the bowels that no salve or ointment can penetrate."

"Well, her salve was certainly a cure for my eyes. Convey my thanks to her."

"I will be happy to do that, Centurion," said the Rabbi as he looked into the man's eyes. He had never dared look into a Roman's face before, perhaps afraid that some pagan curse would fall upon him. But now he saw something entirely unexpected, a hint of compassion.

Polonius turned, waving William to follow him, as they continued on through the village to see if any more damage had been wrought by the storm. But already new thoughts were stirring within the centurion's mind, thoughts of honey and keeping the peace.

A few weeks later on another patrol, Polonius and William dropped by the construction zone. Eliezer was supervising as usual and the centurion recognized the gravelly voice of the old rabbi. "Be careful there, Johann," he called out to a man with an extended hand holding a glob of mortar heaped on a trowel, stretching to a stone just beyond his reach. "We can have Reuben do that section when he comes on duty tomorrow. I would hate for you to fall."

"Yes, Rabbi," called Johann from above their heads.

Eliezer saw Polonius approaching and raised his arm in salutation, "Good morning, Centurion. What do you think of the construction?"

"It appears to be progressing nicely," replied Polonius.

"We can't thank you enough for your generous offer to beautify our place of worship," said the Rabbi, bowing his head slightly, his long gray side locks bobbing in agreement.

"The columns should be ready in a fortnight," said Polonius.

"We will be the envy of every village in Galilee," bragged Eliezer, but hastily repenting of his pride added, "for the glory of God, of course."

"Of course," said Polonius trying not to smile. He knew that the Jews would never accept an actual offer to help in the construction of their synagogue because as Gentiles or foreigners, our contribution would render the building ritually "unclean". However, arranging for the cutting and delivering of cedar columns from Lebanon at his own expense would not contaminate it. Even King Solomon had conferred with King Hiram of Tyre for the cedar wood used in the first temple built in Jerusalem centuries earlier.

"If there's ever anything I can do for you, Centurion, I would repay you a hundredfold."

"Just keep the peace, Rabbi. Just keep the peace."

Polonius bade the man "Good Day" and continued on his patrol through the village. He sensed that the residents were not as disdainful as they'd been in the past. In fact, a few of the Jewish maidens seemed to be giving the young Brit wistful smiles. Polonius suddenly realized that his slave was developing into a strong and handsome young man.

As the two approached the seashore, they saw a small crowd gathered and Polonius thought he should check on its purpose. As they drew nearer, they could see that the people were seated around a man, who appeared to be teaching them. After listening for a few minutes, and hearing nothing that sounded seditious in nature, Polonius was about to continue on, but William seemed to be riveted on the teacher and Polonius patiently waited a little longer. *There's no need to hurry on such a fine day*, he thought to himself. Polonius and William listened as the teacher told stories of sowing seeds, and how some grew and some withered. *Nothing too remarkable in that tale; so what is it that keeps the crowd so attentive? Is it the gentleness in his voice? Is it the way the man looks at the people with sincerity and love?*

It wasn't until the crowd broke up that Polonius learned that the man's name was Jesus. So this was the man who had performed miracles? He didn't look like anyone extraordinary. Just then, a man who Polonius recognized as Jairus, one of the rulers of the synagogue, rushed forward. Falling at Jesus' feet, Jairus besought him greatly, saying, "My little daughter lieth at the point of death; I pray thee, come and lay thy hands on her, that she may be healed; and she shall live." Jesus departed with the man, and many people followed after him. (See Matthew 9:18-19)

Polonius and William continued on their way, finding nothing amiss in the village. Later that afternoon, as Polonius was polishing his armor, William came rushing into the barracks. "Sir, remember this morning, the man Jesus? And how Jairus begged him to heal his daughter?"

"Of course, what about it?"

"I must confess, Sir, that I was so interested in Jesus that I returned to the village," said the slave breathlessly.

"Another story **from** Jesus, William?"

"No, a story **about** Jesus. Maybe not even a story, but something that actually happened."

"Well calm down and tell me what has you so excited?"

"You know that Jairus claimed that his daughter was at the point of death,"

"Yes, yes, William, go on."

"As Jesus was on his way to the home of Jairus, you saw how the people thronged about him. It was difficult for him to make much progress. Then all of a sudden he stopped and turned, looking around at the crowd as if searching for someone in particular. Then a woman dropped down at his feet, confessing that she was the one who had touched him."

"There's nothing too unusual in that when there are crowds of people around."

"But the woman said that she was healed of an issue of blood which she'd had for twelve years just by touching the hem of his prayer shawl."

"That's impossible, William. Don't be led astray by the exaggerated stories of these Jews." Polonius rubbed his metal armor a little harder as if to emphasize his point.

"But it isn't just a story, Sir, I was nearby and saw it all happen myself."

"And you believe she was actually healed?"

"Well, I don't know the woman personally, so I can't be positive she has been sick for twelve years, but that's what she said, and Jesus believed her."

"Well, whatever the circumstance, I suppose we can be glad she at least thinks she's been healed."

But that's not all, Sir," continued William.

"You mean there's more to this story?"

"Oh yes. As Jesus bade the woman to go in peace, a servant from Jairus's house came running. Speaking to the ruler of the synagogue, the servant tearfully cried out, "Thy daughter is dead. Why troublest thou the Master any further?"

"That's too bad that Jesus was delayed in getting to the girl. Perhaps he might have given her a blessing of healing as some claim he has the power to do."

"But that's not the end of the story," said William.

"Oh?"

"No, Jesus told Jairus to not be afraid, but to believe. Then he told all the people to go home,"___

"Something he should have done in the first place," interrupted Polonius.

"Jesus only allowed Peter, James, and John to continue with him and they went into the ruler's house. A few moments later all the women who had gathered to keen for the dead girl were ejected from the house. Jesus had told them that the ruler's daughter was not dead, but was just sleeping."

"I'm sure that made some of those women angry," grinned

Polonius. "They like to earn a few shekels from their side business of mourning for the dead."

"But that's still not the end of the story, Sir."

"Oh my goodness, William, be done with it. Was the girl dead or not?"

"No one can say for sure, Sir. The women were positive that she was dead, as was the servant who had run to Jairus. But a short time later, it was reported that the damsel was up walking around and eating."

"Well, then she obviously wasn't dead, was she?"

"I don't know, Sir. It is all so very strange."

"As I said, William, don't believe all of the wild stories you hear from these Jews. They are superstitious people and persons of a sound mind can only rely on logic, not superstition."

"Yes, Sir," said William dejectedly as he turned with drooping shoulders and left the room.

Somehow, Polonius's armor didn't seem to shine as brightly as it had a few moments earlier.

Despite Polonius' advice to William, he found his own mind returning again and again to the things that he had heard about Jesus. *Who is he? Are his miracles genuine or the tricks of a magician? Some call him a king, but he doesn't seem to be instigating any revolt against the Romans. In fact, he tells people to make peace with everyone and to love their enemies. What are his motives? He doesn't seem to have any means of livelihood, yet he doesn't look like he's starving as the commoners flock around him in ever-increasing crowds.*

Whenever Jesus was in Capernaum, which was unpredictable

as he traveled from one village to another without a set schedule, Polonius and William went on patrol just so they could eavesdrop on the fringes of the crowd and listen to what the Master, as most now called him, had to say. Some were even calling him the long-awaited Messiah, some deliverer-image that was part of the Jewish folklore.

One day William rushed into his headquarters, as usual breathless with the latest news. "The Rabbi Eliezer is dead," he reported.

"I am very sorry to hear that," responded the centurion. "He was a good and fair man." In spite of their political, religious, and social differences, the two men had come to respect each other.

William nodded in silent agreement.

"When will the burial take place?"

"Tomorrow, Sir."

"I think we should "go on patrol" again, William, and pay our private respects."

"Yes, Sir."

As planned, the two gathered in the vicinity of the newly completed synagogue but stayed out of the flow of mourners streaming into the building. Polonius was glad for his contribution to the reconstruction of the house of worship so that it would be a fitting place for a funeral honoring one of the beloved of the town.

After the service, Eliezer's widow, being comforted by her children, emerged from the building. Despite protestations from her companions, the old woman, recognizing Polonius in the background, started toward him. Neither reached out toward the other, but the widow said, "Eliezer thought highly of you. Thank you for acknowledging him with your presence."

"He was an honorable man and I will miss him. Besides, I never had the opportunity to thank you for the eye salve which you prepared a few months ago."

"It was helpful I see," said the woman looking up into Polonius's face for the first time.

"Yes, you are skilled in the healing arts. May you continue to bring comfort to many."

"Well, I'll try, but it won't be here in Capernaum. I am moving to Jerusalem to live with my daughters," and she gestured to two younger women standing at a distance. One could tell from their expressions that they were not happy with their mother conversing unescorted with this man, and a Roman officer at that! "I cannot bear to live here alone now that Eliezer is gone," and tears again came to her eyes.

"May the gods go with you," replied Polonius. "I mean, may your God go with you," he corrected himself so as not to offend her. "Let us be on our way," the centurion motioned to his slave so that he might prevent any more discomfort to the grieving widow who turned toward the burial site.

A few weeks later, William reported that a new rabbi had been sent by the Sanhedrin in Jerusalem to fill the vacancy left by Eliezer's death. Polonius and William again set out for a walk around the village in hopes of meeting the newcomer. Near the synagogue stood a half-dozen villagers talking to a stranger dressed in the rabbinic robes. Jairus, one of the rulers of the synagogue, recognized Polonius and appreciating the fairness with which he administered the Roman affairs, invited the centurion to come and meet the new rabbi.

It only took a few moments of conversation for Polonius to realize that the new religious leader was not the same open-minded conciliatory man that Eliezer had been. Rabbi ben Hanoch pulled his robes closer to his bony frame so they would not accidentally touch the Gentile and become ritually contaminated.

"The first thing we must curtail," declared the rabbi speaking to his Council of Elders, "is the preaching of this imposter, Jesus. He will bring nothing but trouble to our community."

Polonius and William looked at each other with a knowing raise of an eyebrow. The synagogue's rulers imperceptibly stepped backward putting more space between themselves and their new religious leader. "The people are very fond of the Preacher," one ruler ventured to say.

"He has done nothing against the Law of Moses," contributed another. "He has brought comfort and healing to many people," added Jairus without fully explaining his personal beneficence from Jesus.

"Well, things will be different, nonetheless," said the rabbi, starting to walk away without acknowledging his companions or the Romans.

"Indeed, things will be different," said Polonius to William as they continued on their patrol. "Somehow I feel like I almost need to send soldiers to guard Jesus against the rabbi. Not that he would agree to that, but somehow I sense that Jesus' life will be in greater danger."

"I could be his guard," volunteered William. "I am strong and can use my staff to defend him."

"I'm sure your heart is in the right place, William, but I simply couldn't get along without you!" Polonius clapped his hand on the younger man's shoulder as they moved away from the center of town back toward the military barracks.

The winter rains returned to Galilee as dark clouds hung low over the Sea of Tiberius obliterating the mountains around them. These were miserable days for soldiers on patrol, and Polonius could never fathom why King Herod routinely scheduled a military review during December, the month the Jews called Tebeth Nonetheless, orders were orders, and his men marched over the trail to Caesarea once again, this time slogging through mud rather than dust. Polonius recalled his last journey there, his eye irritation and subsequent cure, and was grateful again for the Rabbi's wife and her healing salve.

The day after their return, William felt miserable, with an aching head, fever, and sore throat. But he was never one to complain and went about his duties as usual. The whole regiment was preparing to celebrate *Saturnalia,* probably the most popular Roman Festival beginning on the 17th day of the month. It honored the god Saturn, an agricultural deity whom humans placated with favors, hoping to reap the bounties of the earth without labor.

One of the traditions connected with *Saturnalia* was a role reversal, where the slaves were treated as free men and served dinner prepared by their masters. Polonius was away in the kitchens helping with the meal and William sat near the brazier with a blanket around his shoulders trying to warm his aching body. Between coughs, he stitched two red *pilleus,* cone-shaped felt hats generally worn by a freedman, but which both slave and master donned for the celebrations.

The day of the festivities arrived and even though William felt ill, he could not bear the thought of missing one of the most enjoyable holidays of the year. Shouts of *io Saturnalia! Ave, Caesar!* rang out in salutation as the men greeted each other. The first event was to choose by lot the *Saturnalicius princeps* or "Ruler of the Saturnalia", who presided as master of ceremonies for the remainder of the day. The pseudo-monarch delighted in issuing capricious demands that had to be obeyed. Darius, the Sergeant in Polonius' regiment, was selected King for the festivities and he relished his new role by dressing in colorful robes decorated with tassels and feathers. All the men dined together, enjoying a dinner of roast pig, an "unclean" or forbidden food in the Jewish Law of Moses.

Part of the frivolity was the *Saturnalian* license to freedom of speech, which allowed the slaves to speak disrespectfully of their masters without fear of punishment. Comments such as "Draconius snores like an old bear" or "Master Julius stinks" were bantered across the table as the men consumed firkins of wine. William felt too miserable to join in the teasing, although he really couldn't think of anything rude to say about Polonius. There was more of a brotherly relationship developing between them since they'd been listening to the teachings of Jesus.

Following the banquet, the gambling games began with master and slave kneeling side by side, shaking knucklebones in a cup. The stakes were generally low, composed of nuts, colorful stones, or a few pennies. Great laughter filled the barracks as evening approached and the men became more and more intoxicated.

Polonius noticed that William wasn't participating in the games and moved to his side. Looking at his companion, the centurion noticed the glazed eyes and reached out to touch William's forehead. He was burning with fever! Grasping the young man around the shoulders, he gently guided William back to their private chambers. Then removing his red felt cap, laid him out on his cot, covering him with a blanket when the Brit began to shiver. He had never known William to be sick before; it had been William who had always cared for his commander in the rare times when Polonius had been ill. *What shall I do for him ?* the centurion wondered. *How I need the Rabbi's wife! She would know what herbs or medicines to prepare.*

Throughout the night Polonius sat next to William, bathing his forehead with cool cloths or rubbing his limbs when the shivering replaced the lethargy of the fever. William often seemed delirious, calling out for his mother, his arms outstretched toward heaven. *The days preceding the winter solstice are the darkest of the year and I feel similar darkness and dread filling my heart now. I can hardly bear the thought that I might lose William. We have become so close in the past few months. I know that William still looks up to me, but I actually feel that he is the younger brother I never had.*

Polonius glanced at the carved wooden box sitting on a nearby table, highlighted in the soft glow of the candlelight. It was meant for William on *Sigillaria,* the day of gift-giving two days hence and the culmination of the Saturnalia festival. Most men gave their slaves inexpensive wax figurines, pottery or gifts meant as a joke. Polonius had considered a comb carved from a ram's horn, a new tunic, or even a colorful parrot. But with the increased respect he was feeling for William, he wanted to give something more meaningful. He had purchased the olivewood box in the Capernaum marketplace made by a gifted craftsman.

As the hours passed, however, he knew that he needed to give William an even more meaningful gift; he must give him his freedom. Polonius vowed to call upon a magistrate the next day and draw up a document of manumission. That is if William survived the night. Polonius called upon the favors of all the Roman gods he could remember to spare the life of his young friend. Then, remembering the words of Jesus, he humbly called upon the God of Israel to bless William. Then the thought came to him—Jesus had the power to heal! Was the man even in Capernaum? He hadn't seen or heard of him for days. The thought remained with him throughout the night, and he knew that somehow he must find the Master Healer.

The storms that plagued the area for several days passed and rays of pale sunlight were now filtering through the thin clouds. Polonius must have dozed off sometime during the night, but he didn't know how that had been possible as William's raspy breathing was interspersed with deep coughs as loud as a wolf-hound's bark. Polonius dared not leave his servant's side to go search for Jesus. He did the next best thing he could think of you.

Going to his doorway, he hollered for Marcus, the slave which attended Darius in the chamber next door. It took repeated calls before the door was opened slowly by the squinty-eyed servant, obviously suffering from the effects of the previous evening's revelry.

"Marcus, awaken your master at once. I need him," barked Polonius in his most authoritative voice.

"But Sir," began Marcus in a whining tone; Polonius cut him off with the single-word-command, "Now!"

A few minutes later the sergeant appeared with bloodshot eyes and an unsteady gait.

"Reporting for duty," mumbled Darius.

Without preamble, Polonius declared, "Canvas the town for the Elders of the Jews, especially Jairus if he can be found. Tell them that I seek Jesus. Do not come back until this mission is accomplished. Report to me the minute you return."

Darius saluted and turned toward the door, hiding his look of disgust from his commanding officer. The sergeant thought Polonius was too soft in his treatment of the Jews. Returning a short time later, Polonius thanked Darius for his quick service. The officer hoped to go back to his bed and sleep off the effects of the prodigious amount of wine he had consumed the night before, but Polonius squelched that thought with, "Stay nearby and be ready to carry other messages if the need arises."

"Yes, Sir," grumbled Darius.

An hour passed, although it seemed longer to Polonius. William lay listless on the cot, bathed in sweat, his breathing shallow and irregular. "Go and see if Jesus has been found," he ordered the sergeant.

Darius returned shortly reporting that Jesus was on his way to the Roman headquarters.

The centurion was torn between his concern for his servant and his own undeserving self. He again sent Darius with a message. "Intercept Jesus and the elders before they get to the fort. Tell them that I am not worthy for him to come to me, nor for me to approach him for my own benefit. However, I desire that Jesus will bless my servant. He knows that I command and soldiers obey. I know that he has exercised power over many who have been ill and that they have been healed. I believe that he can do the same for William."

"And when he [Jesus] had ended all his sayings...he entered into Capernaum. And a certain centurion's servant, who was dear unto him, was sick, and ready to die. And when he [the centurion] heard of Jesus, he sent unto him the elders of the Jews, beseeching him that he [Jesus] would come and heal his servant. And when they [The Elders] came to Jesus, they besought him earnestly, saying that he [The Centurion] was worthy for whom he should do this [for they reported] He loveth our nation, and he hath built us a synagogue.

"Then Jesus went with them. And when he was now not far from the house, the centurion sent friends to him, saying him, "Lord, trouble not thyself: for I am not worthy that thou shouldest enter under my roof. Wherefore neither thought I myself worthy to come unto thee, but say in a word, and my servant shall be healed. For I also am a man set under authority, having under me soldiers, and I say unto one, 'Go', and he goeth; and to another, 'Come', and he cometh; and to my servant' Do this', and he doeth it.

"And when they that followed him [Jesus] heard this, they marveled. And when Jesus heard it, he marveled, and said to them that followed, "Verily I say unto you, I have not found so great faith, no, not in Israel. And I say unto you that many shall come from the east and west, and shall sit down with Abraham, and Isaac, and Jacob, in the kingdom of heaven. But the children of the kingdom shall be cast out into outer darkness: there shall be weeping and gnashing of teeth. "And they that were sent, returning to the house, found the servant whole that had been sick." (See Matthew 8:5-13, Luke 7:1-10)

Spring! The smell of pines from Mt. Ebal and Mt. Gerazim filled the valley. The foothills were bursting with the red poppies and white lilies that grew wild, nourished by the winter rains. It was Polonius' favorite time of year in Palestine and he had been here long enough to enjoy many such seasons. It was hard for him to imagine he'd spent such a big chunk of his life in this province on the far eastern rim of the Roman Empire. He rode his bay horse ahead of his troops along the main route from Caesarea through Samaria on what King Herod had termed a peace-keeping tour. It was a week following the spring equinox and the semi-annual military review for the monarch. Before allowing Polonius to return to Capernaum, Herod had ordered the centurion to take a longer way home. Herod expected the roads to be jammed with Jewish pilgrims heading to Jerusalem for Passover and he didn't want any mischief developing along the way. Herod forgot to take into account that the animosity between the Jews and Samaritans was so strong, that most traveling to and from the Galilean area preferred to take the more lengthy route on the eastern side of the Jordan through Decapolis than tread on the tainted soil of Samaria. Therefore, Polonius found the trek easier than Herod had anticipated. Still, it was good to be alert; the Samaritans were not labeled thieves and robbers for nothing.

Polonius thought back on the miraculous healing of William a few months earlier. Jesus had not even come to his house, nor touched William, but nonetheless, William had been healed instantly at the word of the Master. Polonius was grateful beyond measure and true to his word, the centurion had granted William his freedom. A scribe accompanying the magistrate and Darius had acted as the legal witnesses when the document was signed, sealed, and delivered to the young Brit. But all parties involved felt that the matter should be kept confidential, rather than stir up animosity or unrest among the other Romans. William had stayed on in his customary role, but now earning a wage every week which he tucked away in the olive-wood box that Polonius had given him for Saturnalia, and said box was hidden in what he hoped was a safe place within the fort.

William and Polonius had listened to the teachings of Jesus as often as possible. William was present when another miracle occurred_Jesus had multiplied five loaves and two fishes and fed five thousand people! There was still no viable explanation and Polonius had given up trying to see the logic behind such reported events. He simply had to accept them on faith. That had been a difficult leap for a man who relied on logic, weapons, and his own strength to survive as a Roman soldier.

Jesus was now claiming to be the Son of God. *Was that really possible?* Polonius wondered. He knew Roman legends were filled with stories of heavenly deities spawning human offspring, but for the Jews to accept such a concept was even more confusing.

Not all Jews did so however, for Polonius heard Rabbi ben Horach decry such blasphemy often. The new rabbi sent from Jerusalem had not been well accepted by the citizens of Capernaum and Polonius had heard enough rumblings among the citizens to know that the majority did not agree with their religious leader.

Polonius almost wished that Herod had assigned his regiment to join with several others that were sent to Jerusalem to monitor the Holy City when its population more than doubled. He knew that Jesus had gone to Jerusalem for the annual Passover celebration and he would have liked to have heard him teaching in the temple courtyard. Of course, Polonius, as a Roman was only permitted into the outer section of the temple precincts, but from what he'd seen of the additional courtyards leading up to the golden doors of the temple itself, he knew the building was magnificent. The original temple constructed by Solomon had been destroyed centuries earlier when the Babylonians had conquered both Jewish territories__the Kingdom of Israel to the north, and the Kingdom of Judah where the temple was located, in the south. A generation later King Cyrus of Persia, who had defeated the Babylonians, not only allowed, but encouraged the Jews to return to their homeland and rebuild their temple.

But the second structure was not nearly as large or elaborately furnished as the original. When the first King Herod had taken over the governorship of Palestine, he inaugurated a massive building project to enlarge the Temple Mount and build extensive courtyards leading to the religious shrine. The construction had been ongoing for as long as Polonius had been alive and probably wouldn't be finished before he died the way things were going. But to make sure the Jews didn't even get out of his sight, Herod constructed the Fortress Antonia even higher on the mount so that he could look down on the temple grounds.

The second day into the patrol, William suddenly appeared next to Polonius who was riding at the front of the column. The young man was panting as usual; although he had exciting news to share, he had a downcast demeanor.

"Sir," said William who still addressed him formally when they were with the other men. Polonius bent low, his head almost touching the neck of the horse. Then speaking in undertones that wouldn't be heard by the other soldiers, the servant went on, "I heard rumors as we passed through Sychar that Jesus was crucified in Jerusalem yesterday."

"What? Are you sure?"

"I'm not positive, but it is what I heard." Polonius reached down and pulled William up to sit on the rump of the horse so that they could converse in private.

"What else did you hear?"

"That he was arrested by the temple guards and taken for a trial by the Sanhedrin."

"I wonder how much influence Rabbi ben Horach had in that?"

"Maybe quite a bit from the outcome, Sir."

"Go on."

"The Sanhedrin does not have authority to order crucifixions, so they had to get Pontius Pilate to sanction their decision. They hauled Jesus before the Prefect who could not find any legal means to condemn the Master. But the Elders of the Jews were adamant about his death. They even chose Barabbas over Jesus when given a choice as part of a Passover Custom."

"Barabbas! Why he's a scoundrel and a murderer if there ever was one," replied Polonius.

"I can hardly bear to tell you the rest, Sir. It is too awful to even contemplate."

"Was Jesus sent to Antonia for whipping?"

William nodded, tears streaming down his cheeks.

"Was he forced to carry his cross to the place of crucifixion?"

Again William nodded affirmatively.

"I can imagine the rest. The Romans have perfected the ultimate, most torturous way for a human being to die__nail them to a cross and let them hang there for days until they die from strangulation or dehydration." Polonius groaned with disgust at the cruelty with which men treated other beings.

"Why didn't God reach down and save Jesus? He has the power to save his Son doesn't He?" sobbed the servant.

"I'm sorry, William; I don't have a good answer. I wish I had been in Jerusalem; perhaps I could have saved him." Polonius's eyes filled with tears, but he quickly wiped them away with the back of his hand. He couldn't allow his men to see him weeping over the death of a Jew! But inside, his heart was breaking.

Epilogue

The pleasant flora and fauna of spring disappeared with the heat of the Mediterranean summer, but life at the Roman outpost in Capernaum continued as usual. In the privacy of their own quarters, Polonius and William often talked of Jesus, his teachings, and his miracles. Polonius could still recall the gentleness of his smile and the way his dark brown eyes could penetrate to one's very soul.

William reported gossip picked up from locals in the market that some were saying that Jesus had risen from the dead. Some of his followers even testified that they had seen and touched the Master. But of course, those tales were so obviously fabricated that even a simpleton would not believe them.

As the months approached the Autumn Equinox, one day there came a knock on the door of the headquarters. Polonius nodded to Darius sitting nearby to answer it.

"Is Centurion Polonius in?" asked the stranger.

"Yes. Is he expecting you?"

"No, but I have good news to share with him."

Darius stepped aside and let the strange man into the room. Polonius glanced up from his ledger, to see who it was, but didn't recognize him. As the visitor had not given his name, the centurion was left to wonder what the man's business was. As the stranger let down the hood of his cloak, it was Polonius who was the most surprised because obviously, the man was a Jew. Polonius grew suspicious, wondering what favor the man was so in need of that he was willing to risk the religious ramifications of coming into the presence of a Gentile.

"You said you had news to share with me?" queried the centurion.

"Yes, Sir. If you wouldn't mind, I'd like to speak to you in private." Polonius gave a nod and Darius willingly left the room in haste.

"You probably don't know me, Polonius, but I know of you. I am Simon ben Jonah, and was a fisherman here and in Bethsaida for many years before I became a follower of Jesus." Polonius relaxed slightly and indicated for the man to have a seat across the table from him.

Speaking in a hushed tone, Simon went on, "I am now called Peter, and before His death, Jesus appointed me to carry on His work."

"So there are those among his followers who are trying to keep his memory alive by sharing his teachings?"

"It is much more than that; however all that has transpired will have to wait for another time, that is, if you are interested. I was led to believe that you and your slave had heard Jesus teach many times."

"Even more than that, Peter; Jesus healed my servant when he was at the point of death. I am very grateful to the man and miss him. I know that probably sounds very strange to you coming from a Roman."

"While Jesus was alive," Peter continued, "He said that His message was for the House of Israel."

"Yes, I am well aware that I, as a Roman, cannot be numbered among the "Chosen People" of your God," Polonius commented with a hint of bitterness.

"That is the good news that I want to share with you, Polonius. A few weeks ago while I was residing with a tanner in Joppa I had a vision." Then seeing the surprised look on the face of the man across the table, Peter went on, "Don't look so startled; the day of spiritual gifts has not ceased. In that vision, it was made known to me that the Christ, for indeed Jesus was the very Christ, our long-awaited Messiah___"

"I thought your Messiah was supposed to be a deliverer," interrupted Polonius.

"Oh, He is, to be sure. Just not in the ways that many people expected Him to be. His mission was to deliver us from the curse of Adam, from the effects of mortal death and personal sin."

"What does that have to do with me?"

"As I was saying, it has been made known to me by a vision from God that this gospel, which means '*good news*', is now available to all mankind__Jew and Gentile, bond and free, male and female."

Polonius looked deeply into the man's eyes trying to determine the validity of his words. Peter seemed to be sincere; in fact, he was almost bursting with excitement.

Not knowing what all that meant, but with the faith to pursue the matter, the Roman replied, "Yes. Peter. I would like to hear more. But this probably is not the safest place to discuss these matters." Peter nodded in agreement.

"We will be meeting at my home on the first day of the week, the day after the next Shabbat. You are most welcome to come that evening after the sun sets. And bring your young friend, the servant that was healed, if he desires to hear more."

"Oh yes, William will be most eager to come. But are you sure that you want a Roman officer in your home?"

"If Christ has opened the door for all people, who am I to turn you away? It's not so much that the Jews are the Chosen People any longer, if we ever were. It is that we are now chosen to do His work.

Ultimately, it is for each of us to choose to be a follower of the Master."

"That is indeed '*good news*'. Shalom, Peter."

"Until we meet again," and Peter extended his hand.

Although he had never shaken hands with a Jew before, Polonius gripped it eagerly. "I can't wait to share this good news with William! The day of miracles has not ceased; it has just begun. Even for a Roman centurion!"

Jude, Brother and Disciple

MARY CARESSED THE long dark curls as she gently slid the brush through her daughter's hair. Thoughts of Sarah as a child rushed through her memories__her laughter, her songs, and her nurturing touch with growing plants. Where had the years gone? Before her sat this young woman clothed in her bridal gown and wearing a smile almost too large for her dainty face.

"Mama, if you keep brushing my hair it will turn gray before I'm ever a bride," chided Sarah as Mary lingered over her task. Mary knew she had dominated the bridal chamber well beyond propriety; it was just so hard to let go. She sighed and laid the brush aside.

"As you wish, girls," speaking to Sarah's friends and younger sister Rachel who were gathered in a giggling cluster, holding a translucent silk veil in their hands. Mary stepped back and allowed the bride's attendants to place the veil over the curls Mary had so recently caressed.

"Don't smash her curls," Mary pleaded.

A long circular golden chain with several Jewish coins was placed on top forming a headpiece to hold the veil in place. The coins were part of the dowry which Jude had arranged with Dov's father. Mary's heart was saddened as she again thought of how her husband, Joseph, would have loved to have seen his daughter as a lovely bride. Although Joseph had been dead for several years from a plague that had swept through Nazareth, Mary's heart still longed for her husband. *Kind Joseph who had not condemned her publicly when he'd learned that she was with child during their betrothal; protective Joseph who had sacrificed his carpentry business in Nazareth when it had become expedient for them to flee to Egypt, hiding her and her child, Jesus; provider Joseph who had taken care of the growing family for more than twenty years.*

After Jesus, children of their own soon filled the small house in Nazareth_Judah, Sarah, Rachel, and then James. The twins, Joses and Simeon, had died shortly after birth. Additional rooms of the house were added as the family expanded, but with Joseph's skills and plenty of rocks nearby for building materials, they had lived as comfortably as anyone else in the small village located in the North Country near the Sea of Galilee. She had hated leaving that home when Joseph died, but it could not be helped since it was attached to the carpentry shop where Joseph had spent his days. At one time Mary and Joseph thought that Jesus would take over the shop as the young man had an aptitude for working with wood. But Jesus had reminded them many times that he must be about His Father's business. His earthly parents never fully understood what that meant, but they also knew he had been born for greater things than being a carpenter. Judah, whose name was shortened to Jude, perhaps because he was also the smallest in stature of their sons, was more bookish and wanted to study to become a rabbi. The youngest, James, loved working with animals more than wood and spent most of his days with his flocks. So when Joseph passed away, Mary sold the shop and adjoining house and moved to the neighboring town of Cana to live closer to her sister where she could assist with their weaving business to help provide for her family's needs.

Bringing herself back to the present, Mary reminded herself that she was not going to cry anymore, at least until the ceremony started. She blinked away the tears that were welling up and joined in the ceremonial chant traditionally sung to a young woman on her wedding day, reminding her of her responsibility to fulfill her womanly role as a daughter of the chosen people, Israel. Mary hoped that Dov, who was the size of his Hebrew namesake__a bear__would be gentle with Sarah tonight and for the years to come.

Everything was ready as the sun began to set on a Tuesday evening in the late spring as the month of Iyyar was commencing. Traditionally Tuesday, the third day of the week, was seen as the most fortuitous day to be married because in the ancient traditions of the Creation the phrase "God saw that it was good" was repeated twice. They would wait here for Dov with his family and friends to march up to the house with their torches glowing to collect his bride. Then in the courtyard of Dov's home where a canopy had been erected, the rabbi would conduct the wedding ceremony with the intertwining of the ribbons and the lifting of the veil. When the wine was drunk and the goblets broken, the groom would escort Sarah to the bridal chamber, a newly constructed upper room of his father's home.

The rest of the guests would then begin feasting, calling out in more raucous laughter as the festivities wore on for the bride and groom to come and join them. But perhaps the couple had more important things on their mind and would not make an appearance until morning. Some wedding feasts were known to last for several days, but in a small town like Cana, the festivities would probably only last until dawn.

The darkness deepened and still the women waited. Sarah began to fret that Dov would never come, saying that she would never be able to endure such an embarrassment and her life would be ruined forever. The betrothal ceremony had taken place almost a year earlier so she was legally considered his wife; however, the wedding would finalize the contract and they would begin living together. During the past year, Dov had not only helped in constructing the new room for his bride but had completed his apprenticeship as a cooper, shaping wood into barrels for the transport of oil and wine, the two major crops of the area. Sarah had refined her weaving skills and provided sheets, towels, and the linen tablecloth used for the weekly Shabbat meal. Mary knew that Sarah and Dov respected each other and hoped that a strong love would develop between them in the years ahead. That was the way with most Jewish marriages. Although Mary was somewhat sad that Sarah would no longer be under her roof, she rejoiced in the righteous desires of her daughter, hoping that she would soon be able to fulfill he role as a Mother in Israel.

Soon a shout was heard and flickering light from the torches was seen as the wedding party made their way through the narrow streets. Townspeople came to their doorways, clapping and cheering the group onward. There was a flurry of excitement inside Mary's home as the veil was lowered over Sarah's face and she was at last allowed to rise from the small stool where she had been required to sit during the preparations. The women quickly grasped their small lamps which were sitting on a nearby table, checked to make sure there was adequate oil to light their way to Dov's house, and waited for the fateful knock on the door, the knock that would change their little world forever.

Tables surrounded by low couches were set up in the courtyard of Dov's family home and servants soon began placing large platters of roasted lamb, dates, pomegranates, cucumbers, and melon slices on the tables. The most important guests were invited to sit on the upper terraces, which tonight included Sarah's immediate family. Mary looked around for her firstborn son, for Jesus had promised that he would attend. It should have been Joseph who was the governor or master of ceremonies for the feast, representing the bride's family. With Joseph's demise, the responsibility fell to Jesus. However, Jesus had been so secretive lately, going off by himself into the hills surrounding the inland Sea, often absent for days at a time. He told Mary that he could not take on the familial responsibility, for the time of his ministry was drawing near and he must commune with His Father. So Jude, the next oldest, was the one to oversee the distribution of food and drink to the guests.

Mary spotted Jesus chatting with people on the perimeter and waved for him to join the rest of the family. He passed slowly through the crowd, patting a man on the shoulder, shaking hands with another as he moved up the terraced steps toward his family. He first embraced his mother before settling himself on a fat cushion next to Jude. "I trust that the ceremony went well", he commented to no one in particular.

"Sarah was such a beautiful bride," sighed Mary.

"I hope I can have a wedding just like hers," Rachel piped up.

"Oh please, dear, wait a few more years. I could not bear to lose both of my daughters in one season."

"The groom didn't back out or Sarah didn't trip on her robe or any such disaster then?" Jesus asked playfully.

"No, no, everything was wonderful," said Mary, choking back an unwelcomed sob.

"There's certainly a large crowd here," commented Jesus as he surveyed the guests assembled around the tables.

"Yes, it's more than Dov's father told us to plan for. I hope there will be enough food and wine."

"It's so hard to know how many people who were sent invitations will actually show up," said Mary."

"It looks like the whole village of Cana is here," said Jude apprehensively and he gave his mother a questioning glance. "Maybe I will go check with the steward and see how the supply is going." Jude excused himself and Jesus turned to his youngest brother, James.

"How is your flock this spring?"

"The ewes have been most productive and we've had several sets of twins, and only lost three that were too weak to survive."

"Your flock is increasing then?"

"Oh yes, these hills are great for grazing sheep and with the early rains there has been plenty of grass for them to feed upon," said James.

"Yes, God has blessed us greatly;" Jesus raised his eyes heavenward in an attitude of prayerful thanksgiving.

The family filled their plates with food brought to them by servants who were circulating with large trays. They all commented on the delicious food as they sampled each item. Jude soon rejoined the family with a furrowed brow. "The steward says that the supply of food seems adequate but that over half of the wine has already been served and it is still early in the feast. He asked if I had a reserve supply nearby. Of course, I had to confess I did not. How was I to know the whole village would be here?" Jude plopped down on his cushion, putting his head in his hands. "How embarrassing for our family," he mumbled to himself. "I instructed the steward to have the servants pour smaller portions and not provide refills at present."

Jude's wife, Suzannah, reached over with a reassuring hand to her husband's shoulder.

"Would you like me to go to a wine merchant and buy some more?" asked Jesus.

"Any merchant who isn't here will already be in bed by this time of night," said Jude.

"Look among the guests, brother. Do you recognize any wine merchants here?"

"No, no, Jesus, you don't understand. The supply is already limited at this time of year until another harvest comes in the autumn.

The merchants have sold their surplus already and are measuring out their product by degrees to make it last. Even if there was any to be had, the price would surely be doubled knowing that we were in such great need." Then Jude moaned in frustration, "I will never be able to live with this great disgrace." Mary looked worried; Rachel and James hung their heads not speaking, but knowing that this embarrassment would surely be inflicted upon the rest of the family.

Mary rose from her cushion and said quietly, "Jesus may I speak with you privately?" Jesus also got up and without comment followed his mother behind a nearby column.

"Jesus, you do not say much about your **work**, as you have come to call it. But I know that you are a special man. Can you not use your gifts to bless your family at this time? "

"What would you have me do? I already offered to go in search of a merchant."

"You have said that God has given you power. I don't know what all that means, but if you have any ability to save us from shame, can you do so?"

"Mine hour has not yet come, woman."

Mary looked longing into her son's dark eyes. "Please." She did not move, as Jesus bowed his head. Had she violated some sacred relationship she didn't understand?

Jesus was quiet for a few moments, thoughts swirling through his head. *Yes, I have the power; I used it to create this very earth. But if I use that power now, my ministry must become public. Is it the right time, Father? It will be the beginning of the long road from which I can never return. What is Thy will?* Then raising his head slowly, he made eye contact and placed his hands on his mother's shoulders. "The answer has come to me through the Holy Spirit. I will do as you wish."

Mary threw her arms around Jesus, saying, "Thank you, thank you, my son."

Then turning away she caught a servant by the sleeve who was about to enter the house and said, "Whatever this man," indicating Jesus, "says to do, do it." Mary gave Jesus a nod and left to rejoin her family.

"And there were six waterpots of stone, after the manner of the purifying of the Jews, containing two or three firkins apiece. And Jesus saith unto the [servants], 'Fill the waterpots with water.' And they filled them to the brim. And he saith unto them, 'Draw out now, and bear unto the governor of the feast'. And they bare it." (See John 2: 3-10)

Jesus rejoined his family and a few moments later one of the servants who had witnessed the miracle approached Jude carrying a silver goblet. "Sir, a new supply of wine become available. Would you like a sample before it is distributed to the guests?"

Jude took the goblet into his hand and raised it to his lips, then taking a sip, he looked up at the servant in amazement. "This is the best wine I have ever tasted!"

"Yes sir."

"Where did it come from?"

"I am not at liberty to say, sir."

"Usually the best wine is served at the beginning, and when everyone has 'well drunk' shall we say? __ then that which is of poorer quality is served. But tonight, the best wine has been held in reserve." Jude passed the goblet around the table and everyone, including Jesus, took a sip agreeing to its superior quality.

"Is there adequate to serve all of the guests?" asked Jude, now worried that the quantity might be very minimal.

"Oh yes, sir."

"Then let them all be served. Only the best for our sister, Sarah!" he laughed loudly clapping James on the back. But Jesus became somber throughout the rest of the celebration.

"This beginning of miracles did Jesus in Cana of Galilee, and manifested forth his glory; and his disciples believed on him" (John 2:11)

Jesus had instructed the servant to "tell no man,", but of course, it was too big of a story not to share. The tale of Jesus turning water into wine spread like wildfire on a summer day. Jesus departed from the village, moving northeast along Galilee's seacoast to escape the publicity, eventually disappearing into the mountains where he remained for several weeks.

But Jude couldn't get the episode out of his mind. *How had it happened? Had some secret cache of wine been discovered? Had one of Dov's friends or family, wanting to save the groom from an embarrassing situation, delivered a new supply? Or had the wine really been kept in the water pots all along, perhaps due to a shortage of other storage containers? Or had Jesus truly performed some miraculous feat of turning water into wine as the servant claimed? How was that even possible?*

Over the next few days Jude continued to muse about his older brother, his mind distracted from his study of the Torah outstretched on a table in front of him. *Jesus has always been nice to me; in fact, sometimes too nice. Jesus never instigated a quarrel, and if someone was mean to me, Jesus was quick to intercede on my behalf. But Jesus was also quick to forgive the instigator of the conflict.* Jude remembered scenes from their childhood__ how his brother was always kind and patient and willing to share. *Unlike the other children, Jesus immediately responded to requests from our parents to help. There is nothing to dislike about Jesus, but sometimes I have to admit to myself, that I do just that. It's hard to live with someone who is perfect, especially if I always felt like I am falling short of the same standard.*

Jude had read enough of the scriptures to know that ancient prophets had performed miracles__an ax floated to the top of a river for Elisha; fire consumed water when Elijah confronted the priests of Baal; and of course, the parting of the Jordan River when the Israelites under the command of Joshua entered the Promised Land. *Was Jesus a prophet? Did Jesus have special powers from God? Is that what made him different? Jesus hadn't started calling people to repentance like prophets of the past had done. What else did prophets do? Somehow the multitude of rules, added to the Law by the rabbis over the centuries and now written in the very copy of the Torah I now hold in my hand, don't have much to say on the subject of prophets.*

Jude unrolled the scroll, scanning the Hebrew characters for the word prophet. Some were men of position in the royal court like Isaiah; some were common men like Amos, a shepherd. He knew one thing for sure__prophets were never welcomed in their own country, and their words were rarely accepted by the populace. *How did someone get to be a prophet? Did Jesus receive some "calling" from God? He'd never spoken of a vision or a dream, and no priest had come to anoint him. How could a person you'd known for your whole life become someone so special?* Jude had many questions and few answers as he tried to rub away the throbbing pain in his temples. He knew that further study today was not going to be profitable, so Jude rolled up the scroll, sliding it vertically into the large pot with similar parchments, and with hands clasped behind his back, quietly turned and left the synagogue.

More than a year passed and Mary saw little of her eldest son, although news of his teachings and miracles spread throughout Galilee. They heard of him curing all manner of disease and of providing bread and fish to over five thousand people, although that must surely have been an exaggeration. When James married, an invitation was sent to Capernaum where Jesus had centered his ministry, but Mary's oldest son did not come. She later learned that he had been further north near Caesarea Philippi.

As much as Mary tried to postpone Rachel's departure from the household, her mother's heart could not deny her youngest daughter her well-deserved future happiness when Daniel's father approached Jude with a marriage proposal. Of course, Jude consulted his mother, but Mary owned no property and only a small dowry had been collected over her many years as a widow, so Jude felt they should accept the offer. *What if there weren't any other forthcoming suitors and his sister was a spinster? That would bring great shame upon the family. Daniel seems like a nice man, but in my opinion, the potter is rather lazy. He seems content to sit staring into his own creative vision, slowly twirling his dangling sidecurls. I hope that marriage will spark greater ambition within the prospective groom so that he can provide well for Rachel.*

The betrothal ceremony had taken place and the marriage would transpire in a few months hence. Mary wondered if a personal invitation to Jesus would mean more than a written epistle, so she convinced all of her children and their families to journey with her to Capernaum to see Jesus. She also had a premonition that perhaps it might be the last time they would all be together and being the matriarch of the family wondered if the time of her own death was approaching.

Although Capernaum was less than 20 miles from Cana, with their small caravan it took more than a day's travel. On the first day of the journey, they walked to Malaga and set up a small camp outside the village. As they walked, Mary sang songs or told stories to her grandson_Jude's five-year-old, Nathaniel, or carried Asaylah, James's daughter of only a few months. They arrived in Capernaum about mid-day and it didn't take long for them to find out where Jesus was preaching. As they approached the house, they discovered that a large crowd of people was gathered around the doorway, pressing forward trying to catch the words of his message. Jude whispered to a bystander, "Send word in to Jesus that his mother and brethren are without and would like to speak to him."

The stranger nodded and spoke to a man standing in front of him, the latter turning to stare at the newcomers. Mary gave an embarrassed wave in return. The family watched as the message was passed quietly forward. They could hear Jesus' voice from inside the house, then a pause as the message was apparently delivered. Then Jesus spoke again, a little more loudly so that those outside the door easily heard his words.

"'Who is my mother? And who are my brethren?' Then stretching forth his hand toward his disciples said, "Behold my mother and my brethren! And he gave them charge concerning her, saying I go my way, for my Father hath sent me. And whosoever shall do the will of my Father which is in heaven, the same is my brother, and sister, and mother. (See Matthew 12:46-50)

"Is there a message we can give to Jesus on your behalf?" asked one man standing nearby. "Is there anything we can do for you?" Mary shook her head, turning away in sorrow, not able to hide her tears. She knew it would do no good to invite Jesus to Rachel's wedding. The journey had been in vain.

Jude was offended that Jesus could not spare a few minutes to speak with them when they had made such an effort to come to him. "Who does he think he is?" muttered Jude. "Some high and mighty preacher with no interest in his family?" Suzannah cautioned Jude to not make a scene among strangers, but Jude stomped off obviously angered. James put one arm around Rachel, comforting his sister whose feelings were hurt and Sarah clasped Rachel's hand. James too was disappointed, but in better control of his emotions than his older brother. The small group turned southward, retracing their steps toward Cana.

Rachel's wedding took place without a hitch, with no shortage of wine this time; Jude made sure of that. But only a few months later it was apparent that Daniel had not changed his ways. Rachel tried not to complain about her husband's lack in providing for their basic needs. Mary then knew that the time had come for her to act upon ideas that had been brewing in her mind for quite some time.

A few weeks later a tearful farewell was shared next to a loaded cart in front of Rachel's house, where the day before Mary's loom had been delivered. Mary's hands were becoming arthritic because of her many hours spent at the loom and the pain slowed her weaving. Mary used her disability as a reason to give the loom to Rachel so that her daughter might use her skills to help provide for her family's needs. Mary herself would join Jude's family in a move to Jerusalem where Jude would continue his rabbinical studies under the tutelage of the scholar Nicodemus.

"We will surely see you next spring for Passover in Jerusalem, won't we?" pleaded Mary to both Rachel and Sarah who were standing nearby. "We will try, mother," the girls said, enfolding her in a warm embrace.

"I know this is the right decision, but it is still so hard to leave Cana. This has been my home since your father died."

"We know," comforted Sarah. "It has been a good place for us. But since Aunt Beulah moved to Jerusalem to care for a distant relative of their cousin Elizabeth during her last days on earth, it hasn't been the same for you."

"You're right", Mary sighed nostalgically. "How I wish I could have spent more time with Elizabeth. She was a great comfort to me during a difficult time in my life," said Mary choking back a lump in her throat. Elizabeth had given birth late in life and her son had become an itinerant preacher known as John The Baptist. Mary had hoped that Jesus might have an opportunity to meet John before the latter had been imprisoned by Herod a few months earlier. It seemed that John and Jesus had much in common, so Mary hoped that the same fate would not befall her son.

Jude interrupted the women, "Come mother, we must be on our way."

Mary gave each daughter one more hug, then tucking her few personal belongings into a corner of the heavily-loaded cart, followed Jude, Suzannah, and Nathaniel southward toward Jerusalem. Every few rods, she would turn and wave until Cana disappeared from sight.

Surprisingly over the next few months whenever Jesus was in Jerusalem, he stopped by to visit his mother. Mary didn't know what had brought about the change, but she welcomed him enthusiastically whenever he came. Jude, however, was still angry at the offense they'd suffered and about to forbid his elder brother from stepping foot into his house. But the rabbinical student thought it prudent to ask advice from his teacher, lest he break one of the six hundred rules of the Torah. Jude was surprised to find that Nicodemus was quite open-minded about the teachings of Jesus. He cautioned Jude to let the situation play itself out. Perhaps Jesus would just disappear from Mary's life again as he had in the past and it would prevent bad feelings within his household.

In addition to the crowds that flocked around him wherever he traveled, it seemed Jesus always had a special group of twelve other men who continually accompanied him. Jesus called them apostles. Most were from the Galilee, so they and members of Jude's family, had mutual acquaintances, and Mary enjoyed visiting with them to catch up on news of old friends. Three, namely Peter, James, and John, all from Capernaum, seemed to be especially attached to Jesus and called him Master.

One day Jude returned early from Solomon's Porch, a colonnaded area on the Temple grounds, where religious discussions often took place. He again found Jesus at his home and scowled at his brother as he entered the courtyard.

"You again?" grumbled Jude. "Why don't you get a place of your own and stop mooching off the goodwill of others."

"Foxes have holes and birds of the air have nests, but the Son of Man, hath not where to lay his head." (Matt 8:20)

"Exactly what I was saying," said Jude as he passed through the crowd and entered his home.

Suzannah immediately followed after him saying, "May I get you some cool wine to drink, husband?"

Holding the goblet his wife had prepared for him, Jude stayed inside the house but stationed himself near a window so that he might hear what was being said outside. "All things are delivered unto me of my Father; and no man knoweth the Son, but the Father; neither knoweth any man the Father, save the Son, and they to whom the Son reveal himself." (Matt 10:27)

What is the man talking about? He speaks in riddles; fathers and sons? Jesus' father has been dead for years.

'The Father loveth the Son, and hath given all things into his hand. He that believeth on the Son hath everlasting life: and he that believeth not the Son shall not see life; but the wrath of God abideth on him." (John 3:35-36)

"Master, we believe that thou art the Son of God," called out one of his apostles.

"What blasphemy!" muttered Jude, "thinking he is the Son of God. I want that man out of my house immediately."

But before Jude could get to the doorway, he heard these words, "For God sent not his Son into the world to condemn the world, but that the world through him might be saved...for light is come into the world and men loved darkness rather than light, because their deeds were evil. For every one that doeth evil hateth the light, neither comes to the light,...but he that doeth truth cometh to the light." (John 3: 17-21) Some force stopped Jude in mid-stride. *Were these words of darkness or of light? Was he himself walking in darkness while the light of God was sitting in his very courtyard?* He lingered long enough to hear, "For God so loved the world that he gave his only begotten son, that whosoever believeth in him should not perish, but have everlasting life." (John 3:16) *Everlasting life! That's what I am seeking. But doesn't the religious pathway I am already following lead to that life? What about the scriptures which consume my time and attention? I thought they would lead me to eternal life. What is truth? Where do I go to learn the truth?* Jude sunk to his knees in private prayer for the first time in his life.

That evening after the crowds had dissipated and Nathaniel was tucked into bed, Jude sat withSuzannah and Mary quietly discussing the things that Jesus had taught. "How can he call himself the Son of God?" Jude asked. "He's my brother, just like James. Or little Simeon and Joses, the twins that died."

"Not quite," said Mary softly.

"What do you mean?" asked Jude with apprehension in his voice. *Was Jesus a bastard? Was his mother a whore? Unthinkable!*

"Let me tell you a very special and private story that happened to me about thirty years ago," began Mary. After recounting the visit of the angel Gabriel, her marriage to Joseph, the birth of Jesus in Bethlehem, and the flight into Egypt, Mary concluded with "So yes, Jude, your brother Jesus is the Son of God."

"This is unbelievable!" the man exclaimed. "If anyone but you would have told me this story I would have called him a fool, a liar, a blasphemer. But you, Mother, whom I've known my whole life as a woman of integrity and truth, I cannot use these names."

"I agree, it is a strange story," admitted Mary. "If it hadn't happened to me, I wouldn't believe it myself. But I know it, and I know that God knows it, and I cannot deny it."

"Do they," Jude fumbled for words, "they, his apostles, everyone know this?"

"No, son. And it is not the right time to tell the world. Jesus has important work to do, and this knowledge would only hinder him. Can you keep this confidential, for my sake as well as his?"

"Better keep silent than be called a fool or a liar myself," exclaimed Jude. "I make a solemn promise to you not to reveal your words. But I am going to have to think about what you have told me. If it's true, this changes everything!"

"Yes, Jude. Jesus changes everything!"

Jude could not contain his excitement; he was almost a different man from the normal somber scholar, soon-to-be-ordained rabbi. "Just think, Mother! That means he is the Deliverer we've waited for so long to free us from Roman oppression."

"Calm yourself," cautioned Suzannah, "we don't want to wake Nathaniel or have the neighbors overhear our conversation."

"I hope I have not made an error in judgment in confiding in you, Jude. We must wait for Jesus to take the lead in all these matters. I do not understand all of his ways, but I am trying. That is why I listen to his teachings whenever I can. I would exhort you to do the same."

Jude's mind continued to whirl despite his mother's admonition, "Tomorrow I will begin a search of all the scriptures prophesying of the coming of the Son of God. I recall Isaiah had some things to say about him, probably others did also. I wonder if Nicodemus knows more."

"Jude, Jude, we must be careful. Do not speak of this to anyone outside of our family. You could ruin everything for Jesus."

"I won't forget my promise to you, Mother. But it's so hard to contain myself. Just think, my very own brother!"

Two days later Jesus was preaching on a street near Jude's home as the latter man returned from his studies with Nicodemus. When Jesus sighted his brother approaching, he quickly concluded his parable and dismissed the crowd.

Jude guided Jesus into the courtyard of his home, where he invited his brother to sit in the shade of a sycamore tree. He lowered a gourd into a clay pot bringing up some cool water and offered Jesus a drink.

"Thank you. It has indeed been a warm day for the month of Tishri. I was thirsty."

"Jesus," Jude swallowed a lump in his throat, trying to gather the courage to continue the apology he had been practicing ever since his conversation with Mary a few days before. "Jesus, I'm... I'm sorry" he said, choking on his words.

"It's all right, Jude. Mother has told me of your change of heart. I am glad you know that I must be about my Father's work"

"That's what I don't understand, Jesus. But I'm willing to learn."

"You a student of the Torah and you don't understand?"

"Well, I thought I did. But now I think there is more than just the written word."

"You're always the student, Judah. Humility and a willingness to learn is a gift of the Spirit, your gift. If you exercise that gift you will learn many of the mysteries of God. He has a plan for the salvation of every man on this earth that they may be saved in the Kingdom of God."

"That's what I want to help you with, Jesus. To overthrow the Romans and establish God's kingdom on earth."

"The kingdom of God is already here."

"What? I don't comprehend."

"Whosoever puts away the things of this world and follows me is part of the Kingdom of God. My kingdom is not of this world, Jude, but in heaven. I have come to show man the way to obtain **that** kingdom. I am not come at this time to overcome the oppression of Rome, but the oppression and bondage of sin. The establishment of a kingdom here on the earth will come later after people have learned to have faith and be obedient to God's commands."

"You have not come to deliver us from Rome? I've always thought that that is what our Messiah would do. Are you that Messiah?"

"I am the Anointed One, it is true. But I am come to save people from their sins."

"You can do that?" Jude asked incredulously.

"Yes, but only if I am able to accomplish my mission here on earth. I must be lifted up that I may draw all men unto me."

"You talk in riddles, Jesus. Please speak plainly so that I may understand."

"I cannot tell you everything at this time. You must have milk before meat. But if you are willing to become my disciple, you will learn line upon line, precept upon precept."

"I recognize those words; they come from the prophet Isaiah."

"I see you have been diligent in your studies, Jude. That is good. The prophets have all testified of the Son of Man."

"Son of Man? Son of God? Which are you?"

"I am that I Am."

Jude looked up in shock to hear his brother utter the sacred title, the one Moses had learned on Mount Sinai.

Jesus reached out to touch his brother's shoulder. "I must leave Jerusalem for a time, Jude."

"Oh no, you can't go. I am just beginning to learn."

"I must spread the gospel to as many as possible in the time that I have left."

"What do you mean, 'the time you have left?'"

Jesus shook his head. "I know that the Pharisees are stirring up the people against me. It is not safe for me to stay in Jerusalem any longer, for mine hour has not yet come. But I ask your help, Jude. You know many among the scribes and Pharisees. Some are for me and some are against me. But you may trust Nicodemus for I know his heart. If you desire to be my disciple, I wish for you to be my eyes and ears here in Jerusalem. Discern their thinking regarding me. Let me know if it is safe. I will return for Passover." Jesus gave a deep sigh, looking down across the city of Jerusalem toward the Temple Mount. "Yes, I will return at Passover, in time for the sacrifice."

"Of course, I will do that for you. But is there more you want?"

"No, Jude, not at present. Be humble, pray, and "search the scriptures; for in them ye think ye have of eternal life. And they are they which testify of me." (John 5:39)

The winter passed with its blustering winds and pelting rains. Suzannah gave birth to another son during one of the worst storms of the season, and they named him Joseph after Jude's father. Mary spent long hours cuddling the infant, remembering the days when her own children were small. How quickly the years had passed!

The month of Nisan and Passover drew near and the women began the task of scouring the house, cleansing it of all dirt, cobwebs, mouse droppings, or bread crumbs that may have accumulated in corners, unseen during the dark days of winter.

One pleasant day the shutters were thrown open to allow the light and heat from the sun to permeate the interior of the stone cottage. Mary sat on a low stool gently rocking little Joseph in his cradle; she occasionally bent low to whisper something to Nathaniel who was playing with stones on the floor. Outside they heard birds chirping among the leaves of the sycamore trees. "I feel like I should be helping you," said Mary to her daughter-in-law.

"Believe me, you are helping! Keeping the children entertained so I can clean is so appreciated."Then inhaling the fresh air from the open window Suzannah, exclaimed, "I love this season of the year, even though it is a lot of work to prepare for Passover." Dust particles danced in the sunlight as Lydia reached her broom high into the rafters which were now bare of the strands of onion, garlic, and thyme which had hung drying after the harvest.

"The sunshine does brighten our spirits," replied Mary as she coached Nathaniel in assembling smooth stones gathered from the brook Kedron in sets of threes.

"It's a good symbol of the deliverance from the bondage of winter as a reminder of the deliverance of our forefathers from slavery in Egypt." Suzannah gave her mother-in-law a sideways glance before asking, "Do you think Jesus is our Deliverer just as Moses delivered the Children of Israel? Many are calling him The Messiah."

"I do not know all things, Suzannah. I was allowed to be a small part of God's plan in providing a physical body for His precious Son, but beyond that, I am learning just like the rest of you. I have seen no sign from Jesus that he plans to organize a revolt and free us from the bondage of Rome. He only speaks of us repenting of our sins and freeing ourselves from the ways of the world. That is hardly seditious."

"Then why are the Pharisees and chief rulers so set against him?"

"They are afraid. If people accept and live the teachings of Jesus, then the rulers lose their power over us and have no influence with Rome. They're afraid of what giving up their social standing, their wealth, and their influence would mean."

"Sometimes I fear for Jesus's life," confessed Suzannah.

"I also. But I know that he has the power to call down angels to his defense if he needs to, so I try not to fret about it. But my heart aches for him sometimes. He has endured so much rejection when all he wants is to teach people a way to a happier life."

"Look, Mama," Nathaniel interrupted. "I have the stones all in piles just like Grandmamma showed me. One, two, three," he counted pointing a stubby little finger on each rock in succession.

"And how many piles do you have with three stones?" asked Mary.

Nathaniel looked at his collection again, then began counting each pile. "I have five piles."

"You're right," smiled his grandmother.

"What a smart boy you are," Suzannah responded, patting his dark curls. With one front tooth already missing, the lad grinned at both of the women as he warmed to their praise.

"Can I leave them to show Papa?"

"I guess so if he comes soon. But we would not want anyone to trip over them. And remember your Uncle James, Aunt Ruth, and little Asaylah will be arriving soon. We would not want your little cousin to put any of the stones in her mouth and choke on them now that she has learned to crawl. The house and courtyard will be very crowded with people for a few days, so as soon as Papa sees your fine work, you will need to keep them in the linen sack that Grandmamma made for you. All right?"

"Yes, mother."

"Have you been memorizing your part for the Pesach dinner?

"Yes, mother."

"You know it is the tradition that the youngest child in the family is the one who gets to ask the most important question. This will probably be the last year that you will have a chance to do it. Can you tell me what you're going to say?"

Nathaniel straightened his shoulders, stood tall, and recited in his best speaking voice,"' What mean ye by this service?'"

"Well, done Nathaniel. And after your question, then your father will remind us of why we celebrate this festival every year."

"I know," her son supplied the answer. "It means when God killed those mean Egyptians but saved the Israelites."

"You're right," she smiled. "I'm so proud of you," and Suzannah bent to hug her son.

"Oh, mama," he said, gently pushing her away as if he was embarrassed, then turning, quickly darted out the door.

"You are very patient with him, Suzannah," complimented Mary.

"Thank you. I am only trying to follow your example of how to be a good mother."

"Believe me, daughter, I had to learn over the years just like you're doing. I regret that I was not a perfect mother, even though I have a perfect son," and the two women briefly hugged each other.

"I only wish that Rachel and Sarah could be with us," sighed Mary. "Then our family would be complete and under one roof once again. It has been so long."

"I know that you miss your daughters, but I also know how happy you are that two more grandchildren will be born this summer. It's just not a good time for them to be walking the ninety miles to Jerusalem right now."

"You're right, Suzannah. Maybe next year for Passover we will all be together in Jerusalem."

The two families of Jude and James lingered over their evening meal which because of the pleasant weather, had been moved to the courtyard. Nathaniel had wandered off to look for tree frogs, and the babies were calmly resting on their mother's laps.

"There was an unexpected event at the Temple this morning," Jude brought up the subject he'd been cogitating in his mind all day.

"Oh?" asked Mary.

Jude looked at James, and his brother gave a nod, urging him to continue. "It involved Jesus," Jude said as he looked at his mother.

"I didn't know he had arrived in Jerusalem yet," she responded.

"Then he hasn't come by the house?"

Both Mary and Suzannah shook their heads. "What happened?" they asked in unison.

"James and I were in the outer court, you know the area where the moneychangers have their booths for transferring Roman currency into Temple coins?" The women nodded and he went on. "The vendors had set up their merchandise so that people can buy the animals needed for sacrifice__lambs, goats, pigeons, doves___"

James took up the thread of conversation. "Jude and I were looking for a proper lamb, you know, a yearling with no blemishes."

"Of course," Ruth joined in.

"But we couldn't find one that I considered fine enough. How I wish I could have brought one from my own flocks. They are far superior to the ones we saw__"

"Yes, brother; we all know you have the finest flocks in all of Galilee," Jude heckled James good-naturedly.

"What does this have to do with Jesus?" asked Mary.

"Well, you know how noisy it can be with the sheep bleating, and the birds in their crates, and vendors hawking their wares. And of course, the stink!" Jude pinched the end of his nose to emphasize his words.

"It's really despicable that the House of God has become a place of merchandise," added James, "even though I know it's always worse during the festivals."

"And what about Jesus?" Mary again asked.

"Well, that son of yours must have felt the same way we do, because he marched into the place as if he owned it. He grabbed some small cords and quickly braided them together into a scourge which he brandished in the air. Then he yelled, "My house shall be called the house of prayer; but ye have made it a den of thieves!"

The three women gasped! "Oh no!"

"He used the whip to split open the crates and the birds flew in every direction. The sheep broke loose with all the noise, bleating louder than ever as they ran away from their masters. Jesus overthrew the tables of the moneychangers and the seats of them that sold the doves. The coins went rolling in every direction. You should have seen those moneychangers down on their knees scrambling for every dinari." (See Matthew 21:12-13)

"Was anyone hurt?" asked Ruth.

"Only their pride," exclaimed Jude.

"It was quite the scene of pandemonium for a few minutes. Really quite comical to watch," added James clapping his brother on the back. "Right?"

"What did Jesus do afterward?" asked Mary with concern written all over her face.

"He calmly walked to the porticoes and the blind and lame immediately flocked to him, hoping for a cure."

"What did the priests do?"

"Oh, they were seething in rage. We all know they get a portion of the money earned. But there wasn't much they could do but clean up the place. They knew that Jesus was right and that they had allowed the courtyard to be turned into a bazaar."

"Did you notice how Jesus called it "my house', Jude?" asked James.

"Yes, I did. We've always called it the House of the Lord or the House of God. But if Jesus is truly the Son of God, then I guess it is his house too."

"Oh, I hope this doesn't put Jesus in any more danger," said Mary. "The chief priests are just looking for an excuse to arrest him. What can we do to warn him?"

"I'm keeping my promise to him to be his eyes and ears among the scribes and priests. There is much division among them, but you must recall that Jews are always known for their love of debate on any question," replied Jude.

"Amen to that," chuckled James good-naturedly.

"From what I've noticed, Jesus has always been able to handle these situations in the past, Mother. I'm sure he'll do the same now. Sometimes he just seems to melt into a crowd and no one knows where he's gone."

"With all that excitement, did you purchase a lamb?' asked Suzannah.

"Uh, no," said Jude.

"What? The Passover meal is only two nights hence and we must have a lamb to roast."

"I know, I know," apologized her husband. "But you realize the high standards that James has, and we did not find anything at the Temple Court that he was satisfied with. So we will go to Bethlehem first thing tomorrow morning and select one from the temple flocks there. We should be back in plenty of time. Then it can roast all day Friday."

"I hope you can find what you're looking for at this late date," she sighed.

"Where is Jesus staying now?" asked Mary, coming back to her favorite topic.

"I heard from his disciples that he is in Bethany, at the home of Mary, Martha, and Lazarus. That is probably a much safer place than here in Jerusalem," said Jude trying to reassure his mother.

"Is this the same Lazarus that we heard about? The man that was raised from the dead?" asked Ruth.

"Yes," answered James. "That is probably his greatest miracle yet! Can you imagine after the man was dead for four days!"

The conversation turned to the many miracles that Jesus had performed as the sky darkened and stars twinkled in the distant heavens. Everything seemed so peaceful.

The plans that Jude and James had made were successfully carried out the next day, except that everything took longer than expected. Not only was Jerusalem crowded, but the roads connecting it to other towns were as well. Bethlehem lay about five miles to the southwest of The Holy City and was the traditional grazing site for lambs dedicated for use in temple sacrifices. From them James finally selected one that met both the ritual specifications and his own high standards. Leading the small lamb back up the road of the steep hillside proved challenging, for if the lamb had stumbled and broken a leg, it would have been unacceptable as a sacrifice. James finally just picked up the lamb in his strong arms and carried it on his shoulders the remainder of the distance.

Jude pushed open the gate to the courtyard and James gently set the lamb down. Immediately Nathaniel burst from the house, "Did you get it?" asked the boy enthusiastically. "Did you get the lamb?"

"Right over there," pointed Jude to the lamb who was nosing its way around the perimeter of the wall. "I'm sure the lamb is thirsty by now, son. Please get some water in the bucket and let it have a good drink, but don't get too attached to it. You know it will only be with us for a few days."

"I will, Papa. I mean, I won't," he giggled. "I will take good care of the lamb," he called back as he skipped toward the small animal. "Here, little lamb, come to me. I will take good care of you."

"I always hate this part of Passover," Jude admitted to his brother who was still standing nearby watching the interchange between a father, a son, and a lamb.

"I know what you mean, Jude. It was always hard for me too. Father would bring home one of these small innocent creatures for us to care for. Then a day later they would be snatched away and sacrificed. How were we supposed to be able to choke down the roasted meat later that day knowing we had played with it and treated it as a pet?"

"Father always cautioned us, just like I did Nathaniel. But it never did any good, did it?" Jude's voice caught with emotion as he looked at his brother.

"Nope," replied James, his own eyes filling with tears. "I think that might have been a reason that I chose to be a shepherd myself. I just felt this inner need to protect and care for them."

"Remember what King David wrote in one of his psalms?"

"You mean about the Lord being our shepherd? "

"It's one of my favorites," replied Jude. "Also the one that says we are the people of his pasture and the sheep of his hand. It gives me comfort knowing that God is protecting and nurturing us in the same way." (See Psalms 23 and 100)

The two men watched as Nathaniel lugged the heavy wooden bucket, sloshing water with every footstep. "It will be a wonder if there's anything left for the animal to drink," muttered Jude.

James clapped him on the shoulder, saying "I guess for today I'm glad my firstborn was a daughter. I am spared this ritual a few more years."

"It truly makes the sacrifice more personal, doesn't it?'

"I suppose that is the whole point, isn't it," replied Jude.

"Oh Papa, Uncle James, come, feel how soft his wool is. And how curly on his head. The lamb loves me to scratch behind his ears."

"So much for my words of caution," confided Jude to his brother. "It happens every year."

Of course, the next day there was an emotional scene as Nathaniel clung to the animal, begging his father not to take it away. But with the firmness of his father before him, Jude led the lamb to the slaughter. Finding an available priest during this extremely busy time was the next goal, and the brothers waited until almost sundown. After the lamb was presented at the altar, the three men laid their hands upon the head of the animal, dedicating it to the Lord according to the laws given to Moses, and then gave thanks for the deliverance of their forefathers from Egyptian bondage. This lamb served as a substitute for their own firstborn sons, in remembrance of the firstborn of all that were smitten by the angel of death. Only the Hebrews who had obeyed the voice of Moses and smeared the blood of a lamb on their doorposts were passed over in the tenth and final plague. This was the origin of the Passover which was celebrated annually on the fifteenth day of Nisan.

The priest handed the sacrificial knife toward the men and James nodded toward his elder brother. With experienced hands, James held the sheep in place, while Jude took a deep breath, plunged the knife deep, and slit the lamb's throat. The priest and James then turned the lamb to its side so that the blood could drain into a basin at the side of the altar. In a burnt offering sacrificed on other occasions, the shoulder portion, considered the choicest piece of meat because it was veined with fat, was donated to the priest. But on

Passover, the lamb was to remain whole, symbolizing that one's dedication to God must be complete and sincere.

Picking up the slaughtered lamb, they carried it to Jude's home where in the courtyard they skinned it, gutted the entrails, and washed it with water brought in large pots from the neighborhood well. The next morning they would skewer it with a long metal pole and it would roast above a steady fire throughout the day. Jude's senses were primed__the tantalizing aroma, the juices dripping into the flames below with a sizzle and a pop, and finally the savory taste at the meal. All of the meat had to be consumed by sundown, for none could be saved.

The morning of The High Day dawned with a few puffy clouds blocking out the brightness of the sun. It was doubtful they would form into thunderheads, but one never knew with the changeableness of the weather at this season of the year.

James and Ruth left to visit some other relatives in the city so Jude sat in his courtyard, his son at his knee, where he had long strands of leather thongs spread out on his thigh. "Now, watch closely, Nathaniel, this is how you tie a knot. See how this long piece twists and loops around to form a shorter piece."

"Yes, Papa,"

"Then take the second strand, lacing it through the loop, and pull the two ends in opposite direction."

"Let me try."

"That's right...no, loop it in...the other direction."

"Mine doesn't look like yours, Papa."

"Try again."

Earlier that morning, Suzannah shooed Jude and Nathaniel out of the cooking area telling them that she still had many of the special foods to prepare for the Seder meal and they would just be in the way. It allowed Jude to spend some time with his son, something he realized he'd been neglecting of late when his Torah studies kept him on the Temple Mount later than planned. All studies and discussions with the scholarly rabbis had been canceled due to Passover Week. So it was with great surprise that he greeted his Master Teacher, Nicodemus, when there was a knock at the gate.

"Welcome, Rabbi."

"I'm glad I found you at home, Jude."

"I'm just surprised to see you. Am I late for class or something?"

"No, Jude. But I have come with news."

"Oh? Good news or bad?"

"Well, some of each."

"Pray tell, sir. It must be of great importance for you to journey to my home instead of waiting until we resume classes next week."

"Yes, of great importance," Nicodemus paused to take a breath. Then mustering up the courage to begin, he said, "I will relay the good news first."

"Go on..." Jude waited in apprehension.

"There is a position for an assistant rabbi which has just come to our attention. The chief rabbi from Thessalonica who arrived yesterday told me that his assistant had suddenly died from the fever and they are in hopes that one of our brightest students would be interested in the position. I immediately thought of you, Jude."

"Thessalonica? Why that's so far away, in Macedonia."

"I know, I know. It would take you away from your kin. But think of the experience you'd gain. Something as valuable as actual experience cannot be passed over too lightly." Then giving a wan smile, he continued, "And you are one of our brightest students, Jude."

"I hardly know what to say, Nicodemus. I've just always envisioned some small synagogue in Judah or Galilee."

"I understand, Jude. But the Jews have been scattered to many lands and nations for centuries. They must also have good rabbis to teach them the word of God. I had hopes that the time of the gathering of the Jews back to their homeland was nigh at hand, but now..."

Jude, too caught up in what his teacher had just presented to him, didn't notice that Nicodemus had not finished his sentence. "Would this be a permanent assignment?"

"Nothing in this world is permanent. Perhaps after a few years; if you find that you desire a change, there might be other vacancies that need to be filled."

"When would it begin?"

"Well, the position is open immediately, but I suppose it would take you a few weeks to make arrangements for your family to move. I realize that you also care for your mother, Mary, as well as your two fine children. Is this your son?" Nicodemus asked as he noticed the lad half-hidden behind his father's back.

"Yes, this is my firstborn. Nathaniel." Jude urged his son forward, "Don't be shy. This is the great Master Teacher Nicodemus. You may bow to him."

Nathaniel gave his little body a quick bow from the waist, honoring their guest.

"Perhaps you could send your son to his mother now?" asked Nicodemus.

"Of course, sir. Although she's very busy with the Passover preparations today and wanted me to be in charge of him."

"It would be for the best right now, Jude."

"Yes, sir." Then turning to his son, he instructed. "Go into the house, Nathaniel."

"But, Papa__", he began, holding up the leather thongs in his chubby fingers.

"Later, Nathaniel," he said more firmly. Then turning the boy around, gave him a gentle push on the back, "Now."

Nathaniel plodded toward the cooking area located at the rear of the living quarters where his mother was vigorously chopping apples and nuts for the charoset on a wooden table.

Jude turned back to Nicodemus and saw that there were now tears streaming down the wrinkled skin of the older man's face, soaking into his graying beard.

"Are you unwell, sir?" Jude asked with deep concern.

"Yes and no. I'm not ill, Jude. But I am filled with pain not of the body, but of the heart. I told you that I had both good news and bad."

"Go on."

"I don't know much yet of what happened, but Jesus..." Nicodemus choked on his words.

"Jesus? I thought Jesus was in Bethany."

"He was. But apparently, he was with his apostles in some upper room here in the city last night, something to do with a Passover feast. Then sometime during the middle of the night, Jesus was arrested."

"What!" gasped Jude.

"As I said, I do not know all of the details. But what I've heard is that the Sanhedrin met in secret council during the night."

"Why that's illegal!"

'Of course, it is; but they did it anyway."

"Were you there?"

"No. Only **certain** members of the council were informed of the meeting. I suppose because I have been open-minded about the teachings of Jesus, I was not invited."

"So what does the Sanhedrin have to do with Jesus's arrest?"

"The chief priests held a so-called trial accusing Jesus of blasphemy."

"Well, that's nothing new. They've been accusing him of that for months."

"But this time they had an informer, one of Jesus's own apostles. It was quick work for the temple guard to arrest him in Gethsemane."

"You mean one of his apostles betrayed him?"

"Yes," sobbed Nicodemus. "Oh, that it were not so."

"Which one?"

"I don't know his name."

"Where is Jesus now?"

"After the council found him guilty__ yes, Jude, they hired witnesses to testify against him__and so declared him guilty and condemned to death."

Jude raised his hand to his mouth, "No!"

"That's not all, Jude. You know the Sanhedrin cannot impose the death penalty without the sanction of the Roman governor. So, he was taken to Pilate."

"Oh, this is even worse. If I'd only known he was back in Jerusalem, I could have protected him."

"'If only', 'if only'; that is the beginning of every sad tale of our nation's history," moaned Nicodemus.

"I must go to his defense right now." But then realizing which day it was, he paused, "Oh no, it is the High Day and if I enter into Pilate's palace, I will be unclean, and unable to partake of the Passover meal."

Nicodemus nodded soberly. "Can you see that that is the very reason that the Council chose this day to act?"

"But I promised that I would be his eyes and ears, that I would warn him of danger. I have failed, Nicodemus. I have failed to protect my brother!"

Nicodemus reached out and put a hand on the young man's shoulder. "I'm sorry that I had to be the bearer of such bad news on this special day."

"What should I do, Master?"

"Tell Suzannah that you must leave for a short while, but do not tell her the reason. The two of us can go toward the Fortress Antonia. We do not have to go inside, but perhaps we can find out something. You know that I loved Jesus too, although I could not publicly declare it because of my position."

"I do understand, Master. I do not hold you accountable. Only myself."

"I will wait for you by the gate while you tell your family goodbye. However, I suggest that you do not share either the good news or the bad news with them right now. No use getting them upset until we know what's going on."

"Of course,sir. I will be right back."

It didn't take long for the two men to glean the facts as they walked through the marketplace, their hooded cloaks camouflaging their identity. The name of Jesus was on every tongue.

"He was brought before Pilate twice?"

"Why twice?"

"Because Pilate sent him to Herod the Tetrarch in between."

"Is that old fox in town?"

"Yes, for the festival."

Jude leaned into Nicodemus and asked, "Did you know Herod was in town?"

Nicodemus nodded, but put his index finger to his lips, cautioning Jude to be quiet so that they could hear the rest of the conversation.

"What did Jesus have to say for himself in front of Herod?"

"The man didn't utter a single word."

"What? Not even a word in his own defense?"

The three vendors didn't notice Jude and Nicodemus standing in the shadows listening, and continued with the gossip.

"Pilate tried to let Jesus go. He even tried bargaining with the priests offering them to trade for Barabbas."

"That murdering scoundrel? They chose to free Barabbas and kill Jesus?"

"That's what I heard."

"Pilate knew the Preacher was innocent of any crime, but the chief priests kept calling for Jesus to be crucified."

"The Sanhedrin doesn't have authority to order crucifixions so they had to get Roman approval."

"Why not stone him? That's the Jewish method of execution."

"I don't know; ask ol' Caiaphas. He's the man behind it all."

"Pilate's just watching out for his own head. He doesn't want to get into any trouble with the Emperor after that last fracas with an attempted rebellion."

"Jesus wasn't trying to start a rebellion. He was the most peace-loving man you'd ever meet."

"Still, some of his followers were starting to call him Messiah, the Deliverer. You saw how he entered Jerusalem a week ago riding a donkey and people calling him The Son of David, King of the Jews."

"Yes, I was there. We waved palm leaves and some of the people threw down their cloaks for the donkey to walk over. It was quite the grand triumph!"

"Well, that's my point, man. Pilate doesn't want any local yokel being called King of the Jews."

"Jesus is already dead, at least I think so. No man can stand the kind of whipping he received and survive."

"Oh, he's alive all right, but just barely. The Romans are forcing him to carry his cross up to Golgotha."

"Did you see him?"

"No. But Zebediah, my son, saw him, an awful sight." The man clucked his tongue, repeating, "awful, awful. Zeb said the lashes had lacerated his back so badly the skin was hanging in shreds and a crown of woven thorns was piercing his head so that blood was running down his face into his beard. Jesus was so weak he kept stumbling under the weight of the cross even when the guards applied the whip. So the Roman guards grabbed an innocent bystander to do it. That's when Zeb took off. He didn't want to risk being pulled into the melee."

"If they were on their way to Golgotha, they probably have Jesus nailed up to a pole by now."

"You know how brutal the Romans can be in their executions. It turns my stomach to even think about it."

Jude whispered to his companion. "I've heard enough. I need to go to Golgotha and be with Jesus. He needs to know we still support him. I can't leave him to die alone, even though it is my fault."

"Why is it your fault, Jude?"

"I promised to help keep him safe, and I failed. So it's my fault."

"You weren't at the trial to condemn him. Don't take the blame for someone else's wrong choices."

The two men retraced the steps they had taken only an hour earlier. "I dread the idea of telling Mother. She worries so much about Jesus's safety as it is. This will break her heart. But she should hear it from me, not someone else."

"Do you think it wise for you to go to the Place of the Skull?" asked Nicodemus.

"What do you mean?"

"I'm talking about the position as an assistant rabbi in Thessalonica, Jude. Being seen anywhere near Jesus right now might have ramifications."

"Please explain, Nicodemus. My mind is so numbed with this whole mess that I may not be thinking clearly."

"The Council will check your background before approving the appointment. They will find out about your parents, your relatives, Suzannah's relatives, your friends, anyone you might know in order to determine your character. If it is revealed that you are the brother of Jesus__"

"__half-brother__" Jude interrupted. "We had different fathers."

Nicodemus looked at him with a raised eyebrow, "Whatever your relationship, it could be a mark against you."

"I hadn't thought of that."

"On the other hand, it could also be a mark for you."

"Now I'm really confused. Please, Sir, don't talk in riddles."

"Perhaps the Council will think that the best way to rid themselves of the 'Jesus-problem' is to scatter all of his followers. Sending you to Thessalonica could be just the outlet they're looking for."

"Well, it's obvious we can't predict what the Council will do. I will have to take my chances. I just know that I must be there for Jesus. I can't let him die alone."

The two men parted ways as Nicodemus did not want to be seen at the place of execution. It was with a heavy heart that Jude entered his home and broke the awful news. With two small children, it was very difficult for Suzannah to leave, so it was decided that Mary would accompany Jude to Golgotha. The last thing Mary saw as she went out the door was the paschal lamb on the spit, its bloody juices dripping like raindrops into the fiery flames.

Mother and son climbed the road upward to the Place of the Skull, nicknamed by some because of the facial characteristics naturally etched in the limestone below the hill. The Romans liked performing their crucifixions along public highways in plain sight of any who passed by. It served as a gruesome deterrent to those contemplating future crimes. Normally Mary would have paused to admire the small white flowers growing in the crevices of rock where soil and moisture accumulate. But today, her downcast eyes only saw the dark shadows of the vultures circling above.

Three crosses were erected, and Jesus hung from the center one, still wearing the crown of thorns. Blood trickled from His wounds soaking into the wood like the blood smeared on the door lintels with a Passover lamb's blood. A board attached above his head read "King of the Jews" written in Latin, Greek, and Hebrew. Mary almost fainted as she looked up into the face of her firstborn son, his features clearly showing the physical agony he was suffering. He spoke very little due to the pressure put upon the lungs by the unnatural position of the body__arms outstretched and nailed to the cross through the palms and wrists, one leg crossed over the other, also nailed through the feet by the heavy iron spikes the Romans had sharpened to a point.

As Mary stared at the lacerated body of her son, she felt like a sword was piercing her own heart. A snippet of memory flashed through her mind.

When Jesus was eight days-old, Joseph and I took the infant to the temple according to the Law of Moses. There, with two turtle doves as a sacrifice, our firstborn male child was redeemed and pronounced holy to the Lord. An aged man named Simeon happened to be in the temple at the time, he having been promised that he would not die until he had seen the Lord's Christ. The Spirit came upon him and he cautiously approached us, asking if he could hold the baby in his arms. I was astounded at the prophecies the old man delivered concerning my little son. How could he know such things? Then Simeon, handing the infant back into my outstretched arms, gazed into my own eyes and said, 'Yea, a sword shall pierce through thy own soul also.' I shook off the dreadful premonition and scurried away from the old man. But surely his words have come to pass on this fateful day. (See Luke 2: 21–35)

A half-dozen or so women gathered at the base of the cross and raised their keening voices in the traditional mournful chants of the dying. Along with Mary, there were three other women Jude recognized_ his mother's sister, Mary, the wife of Cleophas, and Mary Magdalene whom Jesus had healed from evil spirits.

Jude retreated to the perimeter and pulled his brown hood over his head trying to hide his identity. But he couldn't hide the horrible scene from his mind even with his eyes closed. He wanted to put his hands over his ears and block out the taunting cries of the chief priests who had come to make sure the ghastly deed was carried out. He knew these sights and sounds would come back to haunt his dreams for the rest of his life. Jude was sick at heart to see someone who had lived such a virtuous life as Jesus treated as a common criminal. *But Jesus is not guilty of any crime! He is as innocent as the lamb we sacrificed last night. Is this event the very thing that Isaiah prophesied of more than six hundred years ago? "He was oppressed, and he was afflicted...he is brought as a lamb to the slaughter." (Isaiah 53:7)*

Some of those who passed by reviled him, wagging their heads and saying, "Thou that destroyest the temple, and buildest it in three days, save thyself. If thou be the Son of God, come down from the cross."

Likewise also the chief priests mocking him, with the scribes and elders, said, "He saved others; himself he cannot save. If he be the King of Israel, let him now come down from the cross, and we will believe him. He trusted in God; let him deliver him now, if he will have him: for he said, I am the Son of God." (Matthew 27:39-41)

Jesus spoke loud enough for the crowd to hear, "My God, my God, why hast thou forsaken me." (Matt 27:46*)* Jude recognized the phrase as coming from one of the psalms of David.

Thoughts tangled themselves in Jude's mind. *Has God forsaken*

Jesus? The One to whom Israel was beginning to look upon as a Savior and Deliverer? A devastating darkness hangs over me and is sinking deep within my own soul. God has forsaken me as well. Forsaken all Israel. What good does it do to be called The Chosen People? It seems we have been chosen to endure endless oppression.

Then another utterance from the cross: "Father forgive them; for they know not what they do." (Luke 23:34)

Jude glanced up and noticed how dark the sky had become. The few clouds of the morning had gathered into gray globs, like cold gravy left on a dirty plate. Jude saw one of the apostles of Jesus join the women, recalling that the young man was named John. W*here are the rest of the apostles? Have they also forsaken him? Or are they hiding away in fear of their own lives like animals trapped in a snare? Why aren't they here supporting their Master? Or did perhaps Jesus instruct them to stay away?*

When Jesus, therefore, saw his mother, and the disciple standing by, whom he loved, he saith unto his mother, 'Woman behold thy son!' Then saith he to the disciple, 'Behold thy mother.'" (John 19: 26-27)

With those words, Jude's heart was wrenched in two! *Jesus recognizes my failure to protect him and is now disowning me, not even deeming me worthy to care for our mother any longer. I am cast off forever*! Jude couldn't bear the scene another minute. As he turned away, he felt the earth begin to tremble under his feet and he stumbled to the ground. *Is the very God of Nature wracked with the pains of hell, seeing this charade being carried out upon its face? I wish the ground would open up and swallow me as it did the wicked family of Korah who led a rebellion against Moses and Aaron.*

Jude was now determined to plead to the Council for his appointment to the position in Thessalonica. The sooner he could distance himself from the events of this day in Jerusalem, the so-called Holy City, the better he'd feel. But he knew he would carry the memories of the fifteenth day of Nisan with him forever.

By mid-afternoon, with the winds swirling dust, dark clouds hanging low on the hillside, and the ground quaking beneath their feet, the Romans wanted to be done with the nasty business of the crucifixion and return to the safer confines of their barracks. A Roman centurion in charge declared that Jesus was dead after this so-called King of the Jews had called out "It is finished," and given up the ghost. Just to be certain, he gave a piercing jab into the Preacher's side wherein a bloody flux of accumulated liquids gushed forth upon the ground. The legs of the other two criminals were immediately broken to speed up the process of dying, which sometimes took days for those with the determination to hang onto life.

The lament of the women ceased as they pulled their shawls more tightly around their heads and made their way back to their own homes. Assisted by compassionate friends, a downcast Mary walked slowly in quiet disbelief of what she had just witnessed. *My beloved son is dead! What about all the dreams and plans for his ascension to the throne of David? What could I have done to save him? Why didn't God rescue him?* There were no answers to the multitude of questions swirling in her head.

With all of the uncertainty, Jude was hesitant to bring up a touchy subject to his mother later that day as they sat in stunned silence. Mary had not said anything about the charge that Jesus had given to John to care for her, and Jude didn't want her to know that he had overheard their personal exchange of words. However, Jude did learn privately from his mentor, that Nicodemus had joined Joseph, a man originally from Arimathea, but now a resident of Jerusalem, in making the arrangements to carry the bruised and beaten body of Jesus from Golgotha and bury him in a newly hewn tomb belonging to Joseph.

That evening the bereaved family gathered as planned to eat the Paschal meal which began at sundown. Although Nathaniel recited his part perfectly, there was no celebrating; the Sabbath also passed in relative quiet. The young boy couldn't understand why everyone was so sad, often crying, and didn't seem to feel like playing with him.

Because Jesus's body had been hastily wrapped and put in a tomb on Friday evening, there had been no time for the burial spices to be wrapped with the corpse. Not wanting to make things worse for Mary, other women made quiet plans to meet early Sunday morning to complete the burial rites. So it was surprising to Mary when some of these same women visited her later on the day following the Sabbath, to tell her that they had seen Jesus, risen from the dead. Not only had they seen him, but he had spoken to them, and some had even touched his feet; they swore it was truly him and not just an apparition. Even though she respected these women, she considered their words as idle tales. Her grief was too deep to open up her heart again to impossible claims.

Jude soon met with the Council and his appointment to the synagogue in Thessalonica was now almost certain. Jude and Suzannah started making plans to move northwest to the region of Macedonia. It would take several weeks to travel by sea with stops along the way in Miletus, Ephesus, Troas, and Philippi. So far away! *Would they ever see their kin again? How would Nathaniel handle being on board ship for so long and not being able to run around? In fact, would any or all of them experience seasickness? What if there were violent storms? What household belongings should they take or what would they be able to purchase once they arrived?*

Suzannah was somewhat surprised on the Fourth Day of the

week following Passover when bells jingled at her gate late in the afternoon. Standing outside, were two of Jesus's apostles, Matthew and Simeon, who Suzannah recognized from previous gatherings of The Believers. She quickly pulled a scarf over her head, and invited them into the courtyard, explaining that Jude had not arrived home from the Synagogue.

"It is nice to see you again, Sister Suzannah. Understandably, we have been "laying low" the past week. We're just not sure what the Chief Priests may be up to, or whether they will consider that Christ's followers will all give up now that they killed Him," explained Matthew.

"But be assured, the teachings of Jesus will not be forgotten," added Simeon.

"We have come with an invitation for you, Jude, and Mary."

"Oh?" asked Suzannah, now curious.

"We must speak of this privately right now, but we testify that Jesus has risen from the dead!"

"I heard rumors of such things from some other women but considered them idle tales. Can it really be so?"

"On the evening of the First Day of the week, most of the apostles were gathered together in the same upper room where we ate the Passover," Matthew began. "Then just all of a sudden the room filled with light and Jesus was standing there among us!"

"What?" gasped Suzannah incredulously."You saw him yourself?"

Both men nodded, big smiles erupting on their faces. "Not only did we see him, but we also touched him," added Simeon.

"So you're sure it just wasn't a spirit?"

"No, he invited us to touch the wounds in his hands and feet, which had not completely healed from the Roman spikes. He even ate fish and honeycomb with us."

Suzannah was left speechless to think that a once-departed spirit could be seen, heard, touch, and even consume food.

"We knew that he had the power to raise the dead from the experiences with the daughter of Jairus and Lazarus, the brother of Mary and Martha," said Matthew, "but we didn't understand that he would be resurrected by the power of God, the Father."

"I guess I don't understand what resurrection means," confessed Suzannah.

"We are all just learning ourselves."

"So then this means that his work is not done, that his teachings and miracles can continue?" asked the woman.

"We're not sure; we too are increasing in our understanding of the messages he taught," said Matthew. "He said that all of this__his suffering, death, and resurrection__were all necessary." Then clearing his throat, continued, "But I'll save all that preaching for another time. The real reason we dropped by is that we want to invite you, Jude, and Mary to join us three days hence, on the evening of the First Day following the Sabbath. Peter, James, and John are our designated leaders and they are inviting many of Jesus's disciples to gather together that evening. We want to share our testimonies of the risen Lord with as many of his followers as we can."

"You're serious, aren't you?" Suzannah questioned.

"I've never been more serious in my life. Ever since I left my booth as a tax collector, I believed. But now I know," Matthew stated emphatically.

"We do hope that you all will come, especially Mary."

"It would surely bolster her spirits," said Suzannah. "You can understand why she has been so despondent this past week.

"As would we all, if we did not know the glorious news. I want to shout it from the housetops!"

"I see your zealous spirit is still strong as ever," Matthew teased Simon. "But for the time being, we must use prudence and caution. The Lord has said that we should tarry in Jerusalem until we are endowed with power from on high."

"What does that mean?" asked Suzannah.

"We're not sure. As we said, we're still learning."

"We must be off and spread the good news to some of the other disciples, Please tell Jude and Mary. And do try to come. Shalom."

"Shalom," Suzannah returned the salutation, thinking of its true meaning: 'May God be with you'. She quickly closed the gate and hurried into her house. She could hardly wait to share the good news with Mary.

A few days later the trio was on their way to the upper room. Suzannah had found a neighbor girl willing to stay in the house with the children, even though Nathaniel and little Joseph were both asleep before the adults departed. Jude was reluctant to attend, considering his state of mind__his feelings of failure, inferiority, and self-loathing building up inside of him. But he did not want the two women to venture out in the dark unescorted.

The large room was almost full by the time they arrived. But others made a way so that the two women could be seated on some benches and Jude stood at the back, trying to remain in the shadows. The door was locked and shutters closed so that their gathering would not draw the attention of the neighbors. Retaliation against The Believers by the chief priests was still a possibility, although it seemed that the tension was lessening.

Peter began by relating their experiences of the previous week and the sudden appearance of the risen Lord. "The first things Jesus asked were 'Why are ye troubled? And why do thoughts of doubt arise in your hearts?' I'm sure that all of you can sympathize with our feelings. This was so unprecedented!" There was a wave of quiet laughter that spread throughout the audience, knowing they would have felt the same way. Peter continued, "Then Jesus explained to us about the Holy Ghost that would come to us. He had mentioned such things to us while he was with us. But now it all started to make more sense; we understood what the prophets meant that he needed to suffer, die, and rise from the dead the third day."

Jude's ears pricked up; *Jesus' death was necessary? That it would not have made any difference whether James or I had been there to warn him or not? That his death was inevitable?*

Peter ceased speaking as a light suddenly filled the dimly lit room, and it was brighter than at noonday.

"Then came Jesus, the doors being shut, and stood in the midst, and said, 'Peace be unto you.' Then he saith to Thomas [who had been absent the previous week and had expressed disbelief in the so-called appearance] 'Reach hither thy finger, and behold my hands; and reach hither thy hand, and thrust it into my side; and be not faithless, but believing.'"

[Thomas dropped to the floor in adoration] and answered him. 'My Lord and my God.'

Then Jesus saith unto him, 'Thomas because thou has seen me, thou has believed; blessed are they that have not seen, and yet have believed.' (See John 20:26-31)

Everyone in the room knelt in reverent silence. Jude thought to himself__*What words could a mere man utter in the presence of such glory and majesty? I have been too much like Thomas, wanting evidence before I totally believed. I have been persuaded by fear of men. I let anger, offenses, and mistakes dominate my life and harden my heart.* Jude gradually lifted his eyes to gaze upon the brilliant figure standing before him. He had never felt such a feeling of love and acceptance in his whole life. Then the darkness which had filled Jude's mind for so long suddenly melted away. This was not only his brother, but his Savior and Redeemer!

Then Jesus spoke, "Repentance and remission of sins [shall] be preached in [My] name among all nations, beginning at Jerusalem. Ye are witnesses of these things." (Luke 24:49)

"Many other signs truly did Jesus in the presence of his disciples...that ye might believe that Jesus is the Christ, the Son of God; and that believing, ye might have life through his name." (John 20:31)

Epilogue

It was another moving day. Little did Jude, Suzannah, and Mary anticipate such a day as this when they had packed up their small cart a little more than a year ago. Today there were a few crates and bags, but no household furnishings. They would only be traveling together as far as Joppa, where the young family would board a ship sailing farther north than they had ever dreamed life would take them. A house was being prepared for them in Thessalonica where Jude would begin his duties as an assistant rabbi. But he had a greater commission from his true Master now as well. Jesus had spoken to his followers on several occasions since that evening in the upper room, once with five-hundred brethren present. He said, "Go ye therefore, and teach all nations...and he that believeth shall be saved... [if] they observe all things whatsoever I have commanded you; and lo, I am with you alway, even unto the end of the world." (See Matthew 28:19-20 and Mark 16:16) Jude, like John The Baptist, would be a forerunner in the land of Macedonia. Jude knew that as a true witness, he could now preach the word of God with greater knowledge and invite his fellow Jews to accept Jesus as their true God.

Mary would not be sailing with them, but would now reside with James in the Galilee for the time being. However, she too felt that she had a greater mission to perform. She and John both remembered the words uttered from the cross that they should love and care for one another as a mother and as a son. She did not know all that these words might entail, but her faith in the promises of Jesus was now unwavering. This special son, her son, God's Son, was her Savior as well. She did not shed tears at the leaving of Jerusalem with its haunting memories, but set her feet forward, following in faith wherever her path might lead.

"Today Thou Shalt Be With Me in Paradise"

MEPHIBOSHETH STRETCHED OUT his crippled leg trying to find a measure of comfort from the cold stone floor of the dungeon, but he wasn't about to give up his hard-fought-for-space against the wall where his back had some support. Even in this place, there were some spots more sought after than others, and the wall was one of them. He gazed at the rectangle of light on the floor, a silent indicator of the passage of time, reflected from the small window ten feet above Sheth's head. The open-air did little to erase the putrid smell of the cell, an odoriferous mixture of human waste, unwashed bodies, and fear. Sheth tried to remember how many days he had been here, but had lost track in the wondering and the waiting. Surely, help from someone would come soon! But who?

Mephibosheth's mind drifted as the afternoon sun narrowed its prescribed allotment of space and finally escaped the prison altogether. How Sheth wished he could do the same, catch a sunbeam and sail upwards, through the bars and out onto the streets of Jerusalem once again. His mind traversed those streets he knew so well__the butcher shops, the cheesemaker's lane, the central market, and of course, the Temple mount. This had been "his district" for more than a decade.

Before nightfall completely enveloped the dungeon, the clanking of metal buckets announced the arrival of the evening meal, such as it was. The men began to holler at the slowness of the guards bringing the nightly ration of soup__a greasy concoction of a scant amount of potatoes and leeks and a few grizzled strips of tough goat meat. Sheth leaned against the wall and with his good leg heaved himself upward, grabbing his tin cup from the shelf above him, and hobbled to the front of the cell. Each prisoner extended his cup through the metal bars and a guard ladled the soup, often sloshing the broth over the edge. The allotment was meager rations for the hungry men and Sheth hated to see even a drop wasted. Perhaps the soup had been hot at one point, but by the time it reached the dungeon underground the Fortress of Antonia, the gruel was lukewarm at best, the grease already forming a film on the top. The men were only allowed a few minutes to consume the food. As soon as the guard finished with the soup, he returned to the head of the line to divvy out a cup of water. If it wasn't empty of soup, oh well, the water just diluted it a little more. The men had learned quickly the routine: one metal cup issued per prisoner, filled with an oatmeal porridge in the morning followed by water; the evening's menu only varied with the soup instead of the porridge, and one more cup of water.

Darkness settled in and the men's eyes slowly adjusted so that they would not step on any of the dozen or so prisoners. Those who had been here longest could identify each man through the heightened senses of hearing, smell, and touch. Mephibosheth had been here one of the longest. He was only outranked by the boisterous bellows of a zealot named Barabbas, who had been arrested for insurrection, robbery, and murder. Being a three-offense prisoner gave him immediate precedence over the others. Mephibosheth was in for one offense__ thievery. That was not to say he had only committed the crime once, for it had indeed been his livelihood for a decade now, but it was the only crime he was accused of under the Roman law.

Barabbas had made it clear from his first hours in the dungeon that he didn't expect to stay here long. He had many connections to the outside world, men who were probably even now formulating a plan to spring him from the prison. Barabbas, as the leader of a zealot band with plans to overthrow the Roman oppression, even now sought to increase his fighting force with additional recruits for the anticipated day when the prison would be stormed and they could escape. Mephibosheth had not been approached by Barabbas but it was not surprising. What good could he do as a cripple, even though his hatred of the national interlopers burned as fiercely as the others?

Sheth's mind took up his nightly thread of thought wondering about his family and how they were surviving without his income. *Who is caring for my widowed mother and younger sisters now? My sisters are now in their early teens, undoubtedly lovely, perhaps even looking at young men with eager eyes. If they are anything like our mother, they will also be pious and obedient to the Law of Moses. Ten years ago things were so different....*

I was eight and sitting on a crimson pillow in the center of the synagogue. I pulled a stylus and tablet from the lining of my robe, and prepared to write the scripture that father had designated for memorization that week, taken from a psalm of King David:

Thou art the God of my strength.
O send out thy light and thy truth:
Let them lead me:
Let them bring me unto thy holy hill,
And to thy tabernacle.'
(Psalm 43)

This was the last scripture my father, who was also the rabbi of our village, ever assigned me. Within a week the summer fever had taken him, and he was buried in the cave of our ancestors. Here I was, the 'man of the house', so to speak, but also a cripple. How were we going to survive?

At first, it seemed like things were going to work out because my Uncle Absalom, my father's brother, invited us to move in with his family in Jerusalem. He was a decent man but not the equal of my father. Absalom's wife? I can't think of one good thing to say about that woman. She was jealous of my mother from the beginning; accused my sisters of stealing food from her own children; and me, she mocked me for my uselessness. Absalom could have taken my mother to wife according to the Levirate Law, but Aunt Grisel would have none of it.

I often went with my uncle to his cheese-making shop, but it was soon obvious that I was of no help to him. So I started to wander the streets, my crutch under my arm, hopping along the best I could.

With my uncoordinated movements, I frequently bumped into people. This caused a purse, often carried within the folds of a robe, to be dislodged. At first, I quickly told the owner, and if I was lucky, he would reward me for my honesty. Sometimes though, the owner had already disappeared into the throng and did not hear my shouts for him to return. With my crutch, I could not move quickly enough to overtake him. I remember the first day I returned to my uncle's home and gave a purse to my mother. She was so proud of me!

The situation at my uncle's house soon became unbearable and we needed to find a small dwelling of our own. It wasn't much more than a hovel with the most meager of furnishings, but my mother was resourceful and set up a loom to weave the thin cloth used by the cheesemakers to strain the whey from the curds. My uncle promised he would purchase all that she could produce, so she worked day and night to weave the cheesecloth. Sometimes I would watch my little sisters while my mother worked, but as the girls got older they were soon able to care for themselves and I was left again to wander the streets.

Then an idea started to form in my head__ if it had been so easy to dislodge a purse accidentally, how would it be if I did it intentionally? It would be so simple and would most likely increase my chances of a reward. As I grew taller and stronger, it almost seemed effortless and I became even bolder. In the confusion of an encounter, I could deftly slide my free arm inside the folds of a robe and snatch a purse before an unknowing man could know what was happening. I knew it was wrong. I knew my father would be so disappointed in me. I knew that God would know of my sins. But our family needed the money and so I became a thief.

The clanking of tin cups on the cell bars awakened Sheth from a fitful night's sleep. He tried to arise quickly to grab his cup and move to the bars before he missed his morning rations, but the kink in his neck from sleeping in an awkward position hindered his movements. Mephibosheth barely made it to the end of the line in time to get the half-sized portion of porridge, which irritated him even more.

"Don't be such a sleepy-head or you won't get anything next time," warned the guard.

Sheth wanted to snap back but knew it would only get him into deeper trouble, so he muttered his discontent under his breath and gagged down the tasteless porridge.

The men settled in for the long day ahead. Some spent their time shaking bones in their tin cups in some kind of a gambling game. Sheth perceived that Barabbas was winning from the grin on his face and the greedy look in his eye. *Why do some guys always seem to come out on top even in a prison? I always seem to come out on the bottom. It has been that way my whole life;* he started down the well-worn path of self-pity.

Why was I born this way? If I existed before this life, what did I do wrong before I was born that brought about my lameness? If there is a

God why did he punish me with a life doomed to failure? Maybe there isn't a God after all, despite all the preaching in the synagogue. Did my parents sin and I was the curse that came upon them? No, I can't blame my father. He was a devout Jew, always studying the Torah, respected by the other rabbis. But even he, in his respect for scriptural names, doomed me to a life of rejection. When he saw that I was born with a club foot I was named after Mephibosheth, the son of Jonathan, who was the son of our first King, Saul. Perhaps he hoped that someone would provide for me throughout my life as King David did for Jonathan's son. But no descendent of the House of David rules on our throne, although the ancient prophets declared that a Son of David would come to deliver us.

Nor can I imagine my mother ever sinning in her whole life; she is more saint than mortal. She would be so ashamed of who I have become. I can hardly look her in the eye when I see her. Does she suspect anything?

What's taking Uncle Absalom so long to respond to the message that I sent? I was only allowed one message. Was the lad I hired as dishonest as I? Will I rot in this cell for the rest of my life? I know Absalom suspects something isn't quite right in my life, but he has never challenged me when I turn my collections over to him every week as compensation for my mother's and sister's upkeep. Even though my family no longer lives in Absalom's home, he controls the purse strings according to Mosaic tradition. I've only told him that I have "business dealings" with some of the merchants and scribes in the city. Even if he doesn't love me, surely he will come out of a sense of duty to kin and pay my legal fines. I will try to make it up to him with extra earnings in the future. That is if I ever get out of here.

The wrangling of the other prisoners brought him out of his daydream. It looked like Barabbas was no longer winning and in a foul mood, yelling and cursing in his boisterous voice. The man was obviously not used to losing. The game broke up and the men separated, most retreating to their chosen spots along the wall.

A fellow prisoner plopped down beside Mephibosheth with a

grunt and looked with disdain at his neighbor.

"What are you staring at?' grumbled Sheth. "Ain't you ever seen a club foot cripple before?"

"Not up close," muttered the man, pulling away as if the disease was contagious.

"No one ever wants to look at people like me," countered Sheth. "We're considered the scum of the earth."

"Don't bite my head off, man. It don't mean nothin'."

"Yeah, nothin'." Mephibosheth didn't pursue the conversation. He tried to wrap his tunic a little tighter around himself. He could feel his ribs protruding a little more every day as a result of the scantiness of the food. He huddled down, trying to conjure up the one good dream he ever had.

I am a lad, running in the fields, playing hide and seek with my friends. I am a youth climbing on the boulders of Mt Herman to the snow level. I am wearing a prayer shawl in a Bar Mitzvah, standing tall next to my father. I am a stonemason or a carpenter or maybe a fisherman with strong muscles rippling beneath my bronze skin. I am under a white canopy holding out my hand to a beautiful girl who smiles at me with love in her eyes. I am a father with a newborn son of my own cradled in my arms as I present him as an offering to the Lord in the Temple of God.

The dream disappeared and Mephibosheth moaned in agony; *I am nothing.* The small figure of light on the floor shriveled until it was entirely gone.

The jingle of metal armor in the dungeon annex disturbed the sleeping prisoners even before the torchlight temporarily blinded them. A quick glance at the window space assured the jailor that daylight had not completely chased away the night's darkness even outside their confinement.

"Be quick about it, man!" the centurion demanded of the warden who was trying to locate the correct key from the cluster in his hand in the flickering light of the torch. "Pilate doesn't like to be kept waiting."

The jailor finally unlocked the cell and the prisoners surged forward hoping for a chance at escape. "Back, back," yelled the Roman officer, and several swords pierced the spaces between the bars. The prisoners knew it would be foolish to contend against an armed patrol. "Which one of you is Barabbas?" the centurion called out.

"Here, sir," he said quickly moving to the forefront. "Have my men liberated me?"

"No, not your men. You can thank the mobs stirred up by the Sanhedrin for your freedom this day."

"What? Why?" the murderer stammered.

"It looks like this is your lucky day, Barabbas. The people chose you over Jesus of Nazareth to be freed according to the Passover custom."

Due to the length of his incarceration, Mephibosheth had forgotten the advent of the most important Jewish holiday. His first thought was that it would have been a lucrative time for his "business" enterprises with the multitudes thronging the city. Then he hung his head in shame again for the criminal life he had chosen. He vaguely recalled the custom of freeing a prisoner in commemoration of how the Israelites had been freed from Egyptian bondage.

"Commander Paulus," said one of his associates, "What are we going to do about the third cross already in place? You know the Governor likes to keep up the quota of executions as a warning to the rebellious Jews."

"Yes, Lucius, you are right. A convicted thief is already scheduled for crucifixion along with this Jesus. We might as well take one of these scumbags to Golgotha while we're at it."

"Without a trial?" asked another Roman standing in the darkness.

"Why not? If one Jew can be executed with such a mockery of a trial that we witnessed this morning, it won't make much difference for any of the rest of these." The commanding officer raised his torch and scanned the dozen or so inmates who had all retreated as far into the dark recesses of the dungeon as they could. Seeing Mephibosheth crouched next to the wall, he called "You, there, the one with the crutch". *Might as well rid the city of one more crippled beggar* was the Roman's warped logic.

Two Roman soldiers entered the cell and approached Mephibosheth as he attempted to bring himself to his feet. They each grabbed an arm and pulled him upward as Sheth tried to balance on his crutch. "You won't need that where you're going," grumbled the soldier and kicked it away.

"Better let him keep it a little longer," stated the centurion. "He's going to have to walk up the hill to Golgotha while carrying the beam of his cross." Reluctantly, the soldier bent over and picked up Sheth's crutch and thrust it toward him with disgust, then wiped his hand on the front of his tunic as if touching the piece of wood had somchow contaminated him.

The prisoners again rushed forward trying to make it to the opened door, but the guard was quick to slam it shut and lock it as the platoon marched down the hall__Barabbas to freedom and Mephibosheth to crucifixion.

O God; give ear to my prayer;
Hide not thyself from my supplication,
My heart is sore pained within me;
And the terrors of death are fallen upon me.
Fearfulness and trembling are come upon me,
And horror hath overwhelmed me.

And I said, Oh that I had wings like a dove!
For then would I fly away and be at rest.
(Psalm 55)

Sheth hardly remembered the walk up the cobblestone street leading to the place of execution. Each step was an agonizing effort as he tried to balance on his crutch and carry the heavy wooden crossbeam. Several times he stumbled to his knees, but the Roman soldiers just kicked him with their metal-toed sandals inflicting more pain to his emaciated body. He soon learned it was better to stay on his feet than endure their brutality.

After reaching the crest of Golgotha, he was stretched out on the ground and some bitter liquid was forced down his throat; he had no energy to resist. With the first blow of the mallet on the metal spike to his palm, he screamed and writhed in terror! The soldier placed his knee on Sheth's chest, squeezing the breath from his lungs until he passed out, his mind descending into oblivion.

When Mephibosheth came to, he was hanging about two feet above the ground from a vertical pole. Lifting his head, he turned it slowly from side to side, observing the nails piercing his palms, fastening him to a cross. *This can't be true! It's all just a bad dream. But no, I feel the sun shining down upon my naked body. I am so thirsty and I involuntarily moan for a drink. A soldier kneeling nearby lifts a hyssop sponge to my lips so that I can suck some moisture, but the foul liquid burns my throat, which brings on a coughing spasm. Any effort to suppress the cough only increases the pain in my chest as I seek for any measure of comfort. I notice another man hanging similarly on a cross to my left, but there's no movement from his impaled body.*

Sheth's attention was diverted to another man staggering up the mountain slope, but he was not carrying his cross. It appeared that someone had been compelled to carry it for him. *Oh that I could have had that bit of mercy*, Sheth thought to himself. He watched as the man's robe was lifted over the tangled mass of hair, which was topped by a crown of plaited thorn branches. *How odd*, Sheth observed. The robe was tossed aside and the prisoner was laid out on the ground and offered a narcotic liquid to dull his senses, which the newcomer refused. *You'll wish you had it when you feel what they're going to do to you*, he thought. Sheth cringed inwardly when the mallet struck the mail, driving it through the palm and deep into the wood.

"You'd better be sure of this man," called out the Roman officer in charge. "Drive nails into his wrists as well." With each thud of the hammer, Sheth wanted to vomit. He couldn't believe the callousness with which the Romans inflicted each blow. *How could one human being treat another in such cruelty?*

Soon the new prisoner, nailed to his crossbeam, was raised up and hung from the center pole. Then a wooden board was attached to the cross with writing in Greek, Latin, and Hebrew, JESUS OF NAZARETH, KING OF THE JEWS.

There seemed to be some disagreement regarding the superscription that it should read "He said he was King of the Jews", but the centurion said it would remain as written according to Pilate's orders. Mephibosheth had heard of this man, Jesus, as he had patrolled the streets of Jerusalem. Some had called him a prophet, the Son of David; some even claimed he was the promised Messiah. It was reported that he had performed miracles, such as healing the sick, curing blindness, palsy, and even leprosy. Some bragged that this Jesus had even raised a man from the dead, but of course, that was absurd. Sheth wondered if this Jesus was really a miracle healer, would he have been able to cure my own lameness? *Now I will never know.*

At least Jesus seemed to be popular based on the number of people gathering around his cross. The first to arrive was a young man and what appeared to be his mother, considering the kindness being extended to the older woman. It wasn't hard to hear what was being said even in such private sorrow as this circumstance was. The haggard prisoner, with love in his eyes, called the woman his own mother and commended her care into the keeping of the young man who had accompanied her. *What an awful thing for a woman to have to bear, to see her son executed in such an ignominious manner. For a moment I am glad that my mother isn't here to see me. Ho*wever, that thought was soon replaced by a great yearning that I have to see my mother one more time and tell her that I love her. *She will probably learn about my death through an official notice delivered by a Roman messenger.* Tears started to stream down my face, but I couldn't wipe them away.

Other women soon gathered at the foot of Jesus' cross, obviously people that had adored him during his life. They began the low keening chants lamenting the dying and the dead. The sounds only increased Mephibosheth's sorrow. However, it was not only those who admired this so-called King who were now congregating at this place of execution. In derisive tones, these newcomers taunted, saying "Thou that destroyest the temple, and buildest it in three days, save thyself. If thou be the Son of God come down from the cross." Sheth observed that a few were even chief priests, scribes, and elders mocking him with "He saved others; himself he cannot save."

"If he be the King of Israel, let him now come down from the cross, and we will believe him."

"He trusted in God; let him deliver him now, if he will have him; for he said, I am the Son of God."

The other thief hanging on the left of Jesus joined in the railings of the onlookers, "If thou be Christ, save thyself and us."

I could not bring myself to join in the blasphemous accusations.

Something about this Jesus is different. He bears his punishment without complaint. In fact, I even heard him call out to his father to forgive them for they knew not what they were doing. Who is he referring to? The Jews in general? The Romans? Who is this man that some call a King of the Jews and others call the Son of God? He looks like an ordinary man; he bleeds like a regular mortal, but somehow he is more. I cannot say how I know this but from a feeling deep inside of me.

With a dry mouth, I answer the other malefactor, "Dost not thou fear God, seeing thou art in the same condemnation? And we indeed justly: for we receive the due reward of our deeds: but this man hath done nothing amiss." I turn my gaze from the other thief to Jesus and for the first time speak to him directly, "Lord, remember me when thou comest into thy kingdom.

Jesus lifts his head with difficulty turning toward me, and with love in his eyes answers, "Verily I say unto thee, today thou shalt be with me in paradise." (See Luke 23:39-43)

What an unusual thing to say! Is he going to paradise? Where is it? Will I go there with him? I know the ancient prophets spoke of entering into the rest of the Lord. Is that the same thing as paradise?

What happened to the sun? The sky seems to be growing darker by the minute even though it can't be much past the sixth hour. This is strange indeed.

The hours drag by and still, no relief comes. Oh death, come quickly and relieve me of my pain. Is that my father standing a short distance away holding his arms out as if to welcome me? How can that be? Father has been dead for more than a decade. I must be hallucinating. Maybe the image was triggered by Jesus when he called out for his father, "Abba". Another time he called out for Elias to come and save him. But it looks like neither the former nor the latter are going to deliver him from the cross. Strange how scriptures learned long ago keep coming to my mind.

O Lord God of my salvation.
Let my prayer come before thee;
Incline thine ear unto my cry;
For my soul is full of troubles:
And my life draweth nigh unto the grave.
I am counted with them that go down into the pit:
I am as a man that hath no strength:
Like the slain that lie in the grave,
Whom thou rememberest no more.
(Psalm 88)

I am suddenly brought back to a state of full consciousness as I hear Jesus call out in a loud voice, "Father, it is finished, thy will is done: Into thy hands I commend my spirit." With that, Jesus's head slumps forward. (Luke 23:46)

The earth begins to tremble and people scream. It is as if the very God of Nature is crying out at the death of Jesus. The spectators clutch their robes more tightly and scramble to the nearby public highway which runs near the place of execution, wanting to distance themselves from the rocky mount before another tremor comes. *Earthquakes are not uncommon in the area, but there is no predicting their frequency or strength.*

The guards, who have been playing a game of chance contesting the ownership of the robe which had been removed from Jesus's shoulders earlier in the day, fall to the earth. The centurion who has been observing the gambling staggers on wobbly legs toward the crosses, apparently wanting to reassure himself that the poles are still firmly anchored in the ground. He looks up at Jesus and says, "Truly this was a righteous man." To be certain that death has actually occurred, he withdraws his sword from its scabbard and thrusts it into the left side of Jesus's limp body. A gush of watery liquid spews forth onto the ground.

Paulus, the centurion, addresses his men, "Although I do not adhere to the Jewish religion, it is Pilate's wish that we do not tread on their sacred traditions. This is Passover, a highly regarded festival from the time of Moses, and according to their laws dead bodies must be buried before sunset. Considering the situation of the elements of the earth and the skies, I feel that our own gods are telling us to move quickly. Since it appears that this one," pointing at Jesus, "has already given up the ghost, let us break the bones of the other two and hasten their deaths as well."

In my numbness, I hear more than feel the cracking of my leg bones and pass into the darkness of oblivion.

Epilogue

My next sensation is one of warmth and light. *Undoubtedly another dream.* However, as I slowly open my eyes expecting to see black thunder clouds, hear the howling winds, and feel the earth trembling, I feel none of these. I am in some kind of a dark tunnel, but seem to be approaching its end where a brilliant light is shining. Drawn to the light, I begin to run. Yes, run, for the first time in my life! And it feels wonderful! I am filled with buoyancy and speed I've never known. For the first time, I realize that I have left my crippled body behind and that my spirit is free!

As I emerge from the tunnel, I see a large crowd gathered, but again it is a sight I could have never imagined. There are personages old and young wearing white robes and emanating a golden aura from their beings. In the midst of the crowd stands a man more glorious than all the rest and everyone is gazing in rapt attention at this central figure. At that moment, the man turns toward me and stretches out his hand, beckoning for me to join the group.

I hesitate but the smile on the man's face is irresistible. It is Jesus, the same man who hung on a cross beside me hours earlier! Or was it days? I seem to have lost all sense of time and space. I inch my way forward until I reach the outer limits of the crowd.

Jesus speaks, "I have drunk the bitter cup; I have finished the work my Father sent me to do. I am the light and the life of the world: he that followeth me shall not walk in darkness, but shall have the light of life. " (John 8:12)

"I am come to preach good tidings to the meek, to bind up the brokenhearted, to proclaim liberty to the captive, and the opening of the prison to them that are bound...To appoint unto them that mourn...beauty for ashes, the oil of joy for mouring, the garment of praise for the spirit of heaviness...that [ye] might be called trees of righteousness. " (See Isaiah 61:1-3)

"'I am the resurrection and the life; he that believeth in me, though he were dead, yet shall he live.'"(John 11:25

The multitude raises its voice in shouts of Hosanna and praise for the Redeemer, Jesus Christ! I timidly join in, then break forth into full song. I am not cast off forever because of my sins. Because of the love which I feel radiating from Jesus, I have hope. Today I am with Him in paradise.

The Last Miracle

A. D 23

KEEPING ONE EYE on the pile of tantalizing oranges stacked on the table and the other on the wily merchant standing nearby, Malchus crouched behind the wooden cart pulled to the side of the busy Jerusalem marketplace. It was still early morning and the shadows hid the dirty brown-skinned body of the ten-year-old boy. He was so hungry, having eaten very little since yesterday. The oranges were so beautiful__perfect roundness, fragrant scent, and stacked so neatly in a towering pyramid. Surely the merchant would not notice the disappearance of just one. Malchus could almost taste the juice on his parched tongue. Anticipating that this might be the moment to act, Malchus crept from his hiding place toward the table as the merchant haggled with a customer over the price of a green melon held in his gnarled hand.

Reaching with practiced fingertips, Malchus plucked one of the pieces of fruit, and then on second thought decided he'd better grab another for Barabbas. That was the undoing of his chicanery, as the whole tower of precisely stacked oranges went tumbling to the ground. The merchant caught sight of the boy, yelling "Thief, thief! I've been robbed by one of those beggar rascals."

Malchus, quickly hiding the plųndered fruit inside his ragged robe, skittered down the street, dodging vendors, donkeys, and slaves carrying stacks of wood upon their backs.

"That was a close call," thought Malchus grinning to himself. "But that's the life of a street boy." He quickly exited the main square of the market into the Cheesemaker's Street. Maybe he would be lucky here too. Meanwhile, he couldn't deny himself the delicious fruit any longer, biting into the rough outer rind, puckering his lips at the bitterness. Then pulling the opening created by his sharp teeth, he dug his dirty fingernails into the crack and peeled away the outer layer. There, in perfect balance, were the twelve segments of the orange. He extracted one wedge and thrust it into his waiting mouth, savoring the sweetness of the ripe fruit. "Oh, yum, it's as good as I had hoped." Sometimes that was not always the case with the food he was able to pilfer from garbage heaps or discards at an inn. But for him, food was food, no matter where he had to procure it.

Malchus knew he should eat the rest of the orange slowly, savoring each delicious piece in the ecstasy of the moment. But his empty stomach was arguing otherwise, and soon the boy was chewing them as rapidly as possible, the juice dripping from his chin and fingers.

The second orange inside his robe was so tempting. *Barabbas would never know, would he?* But somehow the loyalty to his gang leader outweighed the desire for the second orange. He owed Barabbas a lot after all. If it hadn't been for the youth about eight years his senior, Malchus would probably have died in some dark alley, identified only as "one of those filthy orphans".

He couldn't help it that he was an orphan; he couldn't help it that he was dirty. How did self-righteous people who looked down their noses at them expect orphans to be properly bathed or clothed when they were forced to live in a cave outside the city walls?

Malchus slowly meandered through the Cheesemaker's street, pilfering a chunk of white goat cheese which he also quickly devoured. As he followed his normal routine, he moved next into the baker's street. The smell of the dark brown rye loaves freshly baked that morning assaulted his nostrils and his mouth began to water. But rather than steal, he cautiously made his way to the vendor stall of Elias, a baker who sometimes saved his leftover loaves for the poor boys who came his way. Malchus spotted the old man a furlong ahead and answered the wave inviting him to hurry forward. "Malchus, my lad! How are you this fine morning?"

Malchus grinned the wide smile which was saved for only a few trusted adults before answering the greeting with "Shalom, Elias."

"I can see from the stains on the front of your robe, that my establishment is not the first you have visited this morning," commented the baker who was wearing a flour-dusted grayed apron over his flapping robe, his feet covered by the thick leather sandals typical of tradesmen.

"No, sir. Yes, sir," Malchus blubbered, not knowing exactly how to answer the older man's question. "But I am most happy to see you, sir."

"Well, you're not the first street boy to drop by this morning either, so I guess we're even. You're lucky I still have two loaves left from yesterday's batch that you may have. Yes, I know your gang rules__one for yourself for now, and one to carry back for the group to eat tonight. Right?"

"Yes, sir. Thank you, sir. Your kindness means so much to us. I don't know what we would do without your generosity. May the blessings of the gods smile upon you. May your family…"

"Now, now, don't get carried away there, young Malchus. I recognize true gratitude when I see it. I'm glad to share with you what I can, although don't tell my wife, Gazelda, or I'll never hear the end of it. She's a tight one, always counting every farthing. But I can't blame her. It's what keeps the roof over our heads and our young ones fed. "

"Good day, sir. See you again tomorrow," Malchus smiled with a hopeful grin.

He made his way back to the cave where about eight orphaned boys slept each night. Most of them were out on their various patrol circuits at this time of the morning, so the cave was empty. Malchus placed the bread on the makeshift table, a wooden plank placed upon two rocks about eighteen inches from the floor. This was the depository where everything was shared in common from whatever could be begged, borrowed or stolen throughout the day. At the evening meal, they would recline on their left sides like the gentried class, picking food from the table with outstretched right hands. Surreptitiously, Malchus removed the orange from his robe and hid it inside his tattered blanket which he kept folded neatly near the back wall. The fruit was for Barabbas alone and he didn't want the other members of the gang to know of its existence. Perhaps the temptation to pilfer it would be too great for someone who was especially hungry.

Barabbas, the leader of the gang, ruled with an iron fist, taking his cues from watching the Roman soldiers in their daily drills. But Barabbas had no desire to be like the Romans in any other way, for he hated the invaders. He watched so that he could learn their weaknesses, as it was his dream to someday form a band that would drive out the foreign enemy. Malchus wanted to stay in the good graces of Barabbas, and he knew that the orange would go a long way in cementing a favorable relationship. Malchus could always use it as a reminder of his loyalty if Barabbas forgot and started slapping the younger boy around.

A.D. 33

Malchus rotated his neck trying to get the kinks out before giving a big yawn exposing his brown-stained teeth. His eyelids drooped crying out for sleep and he leaned heavily against his spear, before catching himself and pulling his body into the erect position demanded of a temple guard. Malchus knew he should have gotten a few winks of sleep before coming on duty at the beginning of the third watch, but the rituals of the Passover Feast had lasted longer than a normal meal. Then the jeers of his comrades had outweighed his good judgment. He had indulged in a few more cups of wine, he couldn't recall how many, which led to trying his luck at the Knuckle Bones used in games of chance, but he hadn't scored. Now he was paying the price for his lack of self-discipline.

"Barabbas would be disappointed in me", he muttered to himself. It was true, for Barabbas had been a strict leader when he had taken charge of the gang of street boys almost ten years earlier. Even when Barabbas had traveled north to the Galilee, Malchus, loyal to the end, had tagged along with him, joining up with some other Zealots who were trying to overthrow the Roman stronghold at Caesarea. But that had ended badly, as Barabbas had been charged with insurrection and murder and was even now confined to a prison cell at the Fortress Antonia just above the hill where Malchus now stood on guard duty.

After Barabbas' arrest, Malchus had stayed in the Galilee for a while trying to find some means of supporting himself. He was too old to be a street boy any longer, but his need for daily sustenance was just as great as it had been ten years ago. He had happened to be near Capernaum on a day when an itinerant preacher named Jesus had supplied bread and fish for over five thousand people. Malchus had tagged along with him a little longer, not that he was particularly interested in hearing of this new religion, but in hopes that more bread would be miraculously conjured up. When no more was forthcoming, he had decided to return to Jerusalem.

Malchus's reputation as a tough fighter, proficient with a sword, dagger, or even his fists, proceeded him to the Holy City. It just so happened that Caiaphas the High Priest, was looking for a new officer to be a member of the police at the temple. Malchus, although small in stature due to his malnourished childhood, was nevertheless quick on his feet and was hired without too much checking into his background. Temple guards were strictly controlled by the ruling council called the Sanhedrin, not the Romans, so none of his fellow officers recognized him as being involved with the revolt in Galilee. Malchus realized how lucky he was; the work wasn't strenuous, just boring, and he was now able to eat on a regular basis, something he had only dreamed about in the past. There was some sense of personal satisfaction at being honestly employed.

But honesty was not a virtue he perceived in his employer, Caiaphas, who was High Priest, thanks mostly to being the son-in-law of the previous religious potentate, Annas. Caiaphas was a member of the Sadducees, the Jewish aristocracy who recognized that their tenuous power was based on ingratiating themselves with the Roman governors. Malchus had been blasted only once by Caiaphas' sharp tongue and that was enough to staunch any criticism in his direction ever again. But there was enough talk among the other guards in the barracks to let Malchus know that there were shady dealings going on in the shadowed walls of the sacred sanctuary he now stood guarding. *What a hypocrite*, thought Malchus. *Caiaphas, posing as the highest religious figure in the temple, probably makes a tidy sum on the side from all the vendors that sell sacrificial animals within the outer courtyards or exchange the common specie for designated temple coins.*

Trying to relieve the ache in his legs from standing still so long in one place, Malchus walked five steps to his left, then turned and walked ten steps to his right before reversing directions, being never more than five feet from his sentry's post. The night was quiet and there were stars overhead, a full moon rising on the distant horizon. Looking at the heavens always brought on a sense of uncertainty. *What, if anything, lay beyond what the eye can see? I didn't have parents who sent me to Torah school, nor did I attend synagogue on a regular basis as a child. However, I've heard enough to know that there are many conflicting ideas over the existence of a Supreme Being. It is hard to imagine some Great Power in the universe, somewhere beyond the stars, that is in charge of everything that happens on earth. Here I am, a pipsqueak in the national population, barely worth a tick mark on the government census. How can a god know or care about me? If I were to die tomorrow, who on earth would even care?*

Malchus yawned and stretched some more. Too much philosophical thinking only made him sleepier. Thoughts of the Passover, the Holiest Day of the Jewish calendar, which had been celebrated the previous evening was a more joyous thing to think about. Although he had no family with whom to eat the traditional meal, the cook in the guards' barracks had prepared the special foods for them__roasted lamb, bitter herbs, and unleavened bread, and of course, plenty of wine. There had been other fellows to pound on the back in fun or over the head in a brawl, as the case might be. Overall, it had been a most satisfactory party, except for losing at Knuckle Bones.

He scanned the night sky, anticipating that he'd be off duty before dawn when he could return to the barracks and crash onto his cot for some much-needed sleep. *How much longer until 3:00 A.M, the end of the third watch? I hope my replacement shows up on time.* By the complete silence, he suspected he was half-way through his shift. Even though the city was thronged with Passover visitors, most had retired into relatives' homes or a caravansary for the night, and the pre-dawn sounds of farmers bringing their crops into the city's markets had not yet begun. Tonight there was not even the bleating of the lambs which he had listened to for several nights. The unblemished, one-year-old male sheep had been brought to Jerusalem to become the sacrificial offerings required at the Passover. *Poor lambs, slaughtered just so the Jews could remember some act of deliverance that had occurred hundreds of years ago.* For some strange reason, Malchus suddenly became teary, thinking of those innocent lambs. *What kind of weakness is a tough man like me showing? Crying over lambs?* He wiped his face with the back of his hand, determined to think of something else. It was so hard to stay alert when there was no one to talk to, so he started pacing again, five steps in either direction. *Would counting steps help pass the time?*

Then Malchus abruptly stopped his pacing. What sound had he heard? Yes, he could identify it now__marching feet. Were the Romans out investigating some disturbance? Then he heard his name being called, and recognizing the voice of his captain, he stood at attention and saluted.

"Malchus", the man barked, "join us immediately."

"Yes, sir." Then falling in with the multitude, he could see that there were not only the temple officers, but priests, elders, Sadducees. and Pharisees, the other large ruling sect who saw themselves as pious role models in living the Law of Moses. According to their traditions, more than six hundred rules had been added to the Law. There always seemed to be friction of some kind or another between the Pharisees and the Sadducees, so Malchus was curious about what brought them together in the middle of the night. Looking to the head of the gaggle of men, he saw a man next to Caiaphas that looked somewhat familiar. *Where have I seen that man before?* Malchus prided himself on his keen observation skills and rarely forgot a face. *Now I remember; I've seen this man as one of the followers of the preacher, Jesus. Hmm, that raises even more questions. What is this fellow doing in Jerusalem when the hangout of Jesus and his followers seems to be the province of Galilee? Has Jesus perhaps come to Jerusalem for the Passover? Of course, that makes sense. Perhaps The Preacher will perform another miracle. That will certainly be a way to get the attention of a massive number of people who are currently in the Holy City interested in his teachings.*

The multitude marched down from the Temple Mount, eastward across the Kedron Brook, and then up the hill known as the Mount of Olives. The eclectic company of men squeezed through an entryway into what was a large olive vineyard enclosed by a low stone wall. From the light cast by their torches, Malchus could see the olive press to his right as he passed by. Being distracted, he almost ran into the man in front of him when the group stopped abruptly. He stepped to the side as the crowd fanned out in a semi-circle facing a small group of about a dozen men in the center of the garden. Malchus, his eyes straining in the semi-darkness, immediately identified the man called Jesus and recognized that the others were some of his followers.

Jesus asked, "Whom seek ye?"

Caiaphas answered "Jesus of Nazareth."

"I am he," responded Jesus.

Caiaphas nudged the man next to him, the one that had led them here, as if it were some kind of rendezvous. The man stepped forward somewhat reluctantly, then approached Jesus, calling out "Hail, Master," and then kissed him on the cheek, a common enough greeting among close acquaintances.

"Friend, wherefore art thou come? Judas, betrayest thou the Son of man with a kiss?"

The multitude shrank back as if afraid of him. But he repeated, "I am he whom ye seek. Let these," gesturing with his hands to his followers, "go their way." (See John 18:3-10) Peering more closely, Malchus could see the Preacher's skin and clothing were covered with spots of blood and his face portrayed deep sorrow. *Had he and his men been involved in some kind of a brawl? Is that why Caiaphas was looking for him? Perhaps arrest him for starting a revolt?*

Then before Malchus knew what happened, one of Jesus's followers withdrew a short sword from the sheath that girded his ample body, reached out and attempted to attack him. Malchus, subconsciously reverting to his alacrity in street gangs, swerved just in time to miss decapitation, if that were the intended action, although the right side of his head immediately exploded with searing pain. Instinctively, he reached up with his hand to stop the flow of blood, which soon leaked through his fingers. Pulling his hand away, there in his hand lay his severed right ear! He screamed and other soldiers immediately drew their swords to attack.

But Jesus, speaking with authority said to the man at his side, "It is enough. Peter, put up your sword into the sheath. All they that take the sword shall perish with the sword. Thinkest thou that I cannot now pray to my Father, and He shall presently give me more than twelve legions of angels? But how then shall the scriptures be fulfilled, that thus it must be? The cup which my Father hath given me, shall I not drink it?" (Matt 26: 52-54) Then gesturing again, the disciples turned and fled into the darkness leaving their leader alone.

Then Jesus stepped toward Malchus and taking the ear from his palm, with a gentle hand placed it onto its accustomed place on the side of his head. (John 18: 51) The pain was instantly gone. Malchus cautiously felt the ear and it was attached as if nothing had happened! *Did I just dream this bizarre experience? But there is unmistaken evidence of blood on my palm. Was a miracle truly performed on my behalf? What kind of a man is he? He's certainly more than a preacher. Is he a prophet? Or someone even greater?*

Jesus stepped back and said in a calm voice as if nothing extraordinary had just taken place, "Ye come out against me as a thief, with swords and staves. When I was daily with you in the temple, ye stretched forth no hands against me. But this is your hour and the power of darkness." (Luke 22:53)

Caiaphas, enraged, gave the order, "Bind him!"

The captain nodded to two other guards, who stepped forward, dropped a noose around Jesus's neck, and started to lead him away. The image of lambs, led by a similar rope around their necks being led to the slaughter, jumped into Malchus' mind. *Was this an innocent man being led to a similar death?*

Malchus fell into marching formation and the multitude started down the hill. *The men around me seem pleased that the arrest took place so easily. Had they expected a fight? Is that why the temple guards had been summoned? But even I, a relative newcomer, know that it is illegal to arrest someone at night. The Pharisees, elders and priests shout as if celebrating a great victory, "We've got him now. This will be the end of his deceiving the people with his so-called miracles."* Malchus reached up to feel his ear. *No, I'm not dreaming.* The smooth skin around the appendage blended into his hair. *I was the recipient of a miracle indeed. What is going to happen to this man Jesus now? Will this be his last miracle?*

The group soon reached the palace where the aged and venerated priest Annas, was waiting in the room where the Sanhedrin normally met to do business. Malchus and the other guards stood at attention around the perimeter of the room watching that the prisoner not attempt an escape. As Malchus stared at the captured man, he didn't think any such effort was likely. The Galilean looked defeated and worn, his blood-stained clothing disheveled, his body almost limp with exhaustion.

With a nod from Annas, Caiaphas presided over the quickly-assembled hearing. One by one witnesses were brought in, although no two seemed in agreement with their stories. *How had these men been located in the dead of night? Trials held during those hours were also illegal. Through it all, Jesus just stands there with his head bowed, but holding his peace. I admire the Preacher's self-control and courage in the face of such accusations.*

The High Priest arose and shouted at Jesus, "Answereth thou nothing? I adjure thee by the living God, that thou tell us whether thou be the Christ, the Son of God."

In a perfectly controlled voice, Jesus responded, "Thou hast said. Nevertheless, I say unto you, hereafter shall ye see the Son of man sitting on the right hand of power and coming in the clouds of heaven."

Then the High Priest rent his robe and shouted, "He hath spoken blasphemy! What further need have we of witnesses? Ye have all heard his blasphemy; what think ye?'"

The cry went up from the assemblage of priests and elders, "He is guilty of death! " Then it was if all hell broke loose, and men who saw themselves as the nobility and upright leaders of the Jews began to spit upon Jesus, and mock him, striking him with the palms of their hands. "Prophesy unto us, thou Christ, who is it that smote thee?" (See Matt 26:65-68)

Malchus almost turned away in disgust. He had seen plenty of street fights, been involved in them himself. He watched in wonderment as Jesus suffered the physical and verbal abuse without flinching. Never had he seen an innocent man so besieged by hate as he now saw exhibited by this mob. "Death! Death to this deceiver!" rang out the cries.

"But our laws only allow us to put him on trial," reminded others.

"We cannot condemn him to death without sanction from Pilate."

"Then let's take him to Pilate!"

"Better to wait until the Governor has at least had his breakfast." And with that, the cock began to crow.

Malchus was relieved that his shift was finally over and he staggered toward his own barracks. *This has been the strangest night of my life. It seems that a fortnight has been crammed into the past few hours. I just want to forget it and get some much-needed sleep. No, I really want to always remember it and the healing touch of the man called Jesus.*

The next morning

In spite of his earlier tiredness, the officer's attempts at sleep had left him more restless than refreshed. He hadn't been able to get the images of lambs and Jesus with a rope around his neck out of his mind and he immediately felt his right ear. Yes, it was still there just like it always had been. Except for those few minutes last night when it hadn't been. *Maybe it was all just a bad dream after all.*

Glancing through the opening into the courtyard of the officers' quarters, Malchus noticed it was dusk. Had he really slept all day, after all? He wandered toward the cook's shack, hoping to get a decent meal. But his desires were curtailed with the offerings of a scanty portion of left-overs from Passover. The serving maid explained that since he had missed the mid-day meal that he would now have to wait until dinner. So, he surmised, it wasn't evening after all in spite of the darkness of the sky. Perhaps there was a storm brewing. Obviously, the maid was too busy to offer him any explanation, so Malchus wandered over to where a few of the other maids were gathered, chopping vegetables for some kind of stew. Malchus didn't want to be too obvious in asking questions about what had happened to the Galilean Jesus. So he stood aside and tried to piece together the situation from the gossip he overheard.

"Taken before Pilate, he was, then up to that old fox, Herod, and then back to Pilate."

"Herod didn't even get the satisfaction of hearing his voice. Jesus spoke not one word to him."

"Yes, but one good thing came out of it."

"What's that?"

"Herod and Pilate are now on speaking terms again."

"I heard Pilate's wife had a dream and told him to have nothing to do with that man."

"Oh, that's just her deranged mind. Everybody knows she's half-crazy with those headaches she complains of all the time."

"Pilate stood right there on the balcony and washed his hands in front of the whole crowd. Said he couldn't find any fault with Jesus. As if that would wash away his guilt."

"So why has he been crucified?"

Malchus cringed at the word. *Getting rid of Jesus was one thing, but the cruelties of death by crucifixion seem excessive for the crime of blasphemy, which in fact, wasn't even a crime punishable by Roman laws.*

"That's what happens when a man claims to be a King of the Jews. Pilate wanted to put down any insurrection before it could start a real rebellion. His crown is none to secure some say."

"Can you believe they let that murderer Barabbas go free instead? Talk about someone worthy of death by crucifixion; he's the one who tried to stir up a revolt with the Zealots."

Malchus' ears pricked up at the mention of Barabbas' name. *My old leader is free? What strange turn of events brought that about?* He listened more carefully, keeping to the shadows so as not to draw attention.

"Well, the way I heard it is that Pilate tried to make a deal with the mob and pacify them by reminding them of their Passover tradition to allow some prisoner to go free. He was hoping that a scourging for Jesus would satisfy their demands for justice, and then he could send the Preacher on his way, commanding him to never return to this so-called Holy City again. But that didn't satisfy the priests, who sanctioned the release of Barabbas and continued to demand death for Jesus. Caiaphas had the mob so riled up by that time that they kept chanting, "Crucify Him! Crucify Him!"

"I can't imagine the people of Jerusalem participating in such a spectacle."

"You never know the riff-raff you can pick up from the street gangs these days. They'd be willing to join any mob with the promise of some bread or a coin in their purse. Probably some of the people there didn't even know what was going on. They just got pulled in, and a few instigators egged them on to demand crucifixion. It wasn't any skin off their noses."

"Did you hear that Jesus was too weak to even carry his own cross beam? The soldiers grabbed a man from the observers that lined the street and made him carry it." (See Luke 23:8-23, Matt 27:15-31, John 19:4-16)

"You're making that up."

"No, I swear it's true. Leastwise, Ezra swore it was true when he told me."

"Oh, you're just sweet on Ezra, Rachel. Has his father been to talk to your father about a betrothal?"

Malchus could see that the conversation was taking a different turn, so he turned away from the women. *So, an innocent man is condemned to death and Barabbas let free in his place. Should I seek out my old leader? Not right now. I have a mind to go to Golgotha and see this for myself. I still don't understand this darkened sky in the middle of the afternoon. What strange things are happening today?*

He strode northward through the Upper City toward Golgotha, a hill that stood outside the city wall, but along one of the main thoroughfares. The Romans liked to conduct their executions in public settings where they could display their supreme power and hopefully discourage other criminal activity.

Malchus saw a large crowd gathered at the site, which held three crosses. On the center one hung the man Jesus whom he had helped arrest last night. He felt a sense of guilt at being involved, even if it was at the order of the High Priest. Again, his hand reached up to his right ear. *I always see the importance of things when it's too late. I had a chance to learn about Jesus months ago. I even saw one of his miracles. But I was too hard-headed to listen to his teachings. Now he's about dead and I'll never know what I might have learned from his lips.*

Scanning the crowd, he saw a group of Roman soldiers throwing dice in a cup, gambling over a robe which had previously been owned by the prisoner. Pharisees continued to harangue Jesus, as it seemed he had called upon one of the prophets, Elias or Elijah, to come. Further taunts rang out, that if he were the Son of God to call down angels to rescue him. *Can't they leave the man to die in peace,* Malchus wondered. *The High Priest and elders have already accomplished what they wanted__his crucifixion.*

Clustered at the base of the cross was one of the men Malchus recognized as a disciple, probably the youngest of his chosen followers, from what he could recall from previous encounters. There was a group of women keening the traditional chants for the dying. Malchus heard Jesus groan and a soldier lifted up a sponge saturated with gall and vinegar to quench his thirst, one of the common side effects of this type of torture, in addition to constricted breathing and an extended belly as the body filled with excess fluids.

Jesus cried out, "Father, forgive them for they know not what they do." *Who was Jesus referring to? The Roman soldiers who were carrying out their duties? The Pharisees themselves? Who was this man who had enough love to ask God to forgive his enemies while hanging on a cross?*

Not being able to read, Malchus did not know what the signboard posted above Jesus' head said. *I would give anything to be able to learn to read and write,* he thought to himself. Not wanting to publicize his ignorance, he casually asked another man standing close by what was written on the sign. The man answered, "It says, 'Jesus of

Nazareth, King of the Jews', written in Aramaic, Latin, and Greek. Guess they want everyone to be able to understand, written in three languages like that," mumbled the man.

"Was he someone who was trying to become a king?" asked Malchus.

"Apparently, you don't know much about this man named Jesus, do you?"

"No, sir."

"His kingdom was not a political one; he never tried to overthrow the Romans. He claimed a spiritual realm in order to establish God's kingdom on earth. Some even thought he was the prophesied Messiah."

"I'm not a religious man myself," responded Malchus, "but I do know the Jews believe that a Messiah will come to deliver them from oppression. Looks like this one failed."

"Yes, unfortunately," the man muttered under his breath.

Malchus moved away, not wanting to get into a debate about the injustices brought on by the Roman invaders. Sickened by the gruesome spectacle, and doubtful he could learn any more, Malchus turned, trudging back toward the Temple Mount and his sleeping quarters.I *will be a little wiser today than I was yesterday*, he thought to himself, *and get a nap before going back on guard duty. That is if I can get the thoughts of Jesus hanging on the cross out of my mind.*

All of a sudden the earth shook and he stumbled, only his skill at being quick on his feet as a street marauder, kept him from completely falling. As it was, he had a nasty scrape along his left leg and he limped onward in throbbing pain. *How could I have such bad luck__two injuries in two days? No Jesus around to heal this wound as quickly as the last, however. The air feels so heavy, like the ever-increasing darkness of the sky is going to crush us. This is only a fluke of the weather, isn't it? There can't possibly be any connection with the death of a so-called King of the Jews and these unprecedented natural phenomena.*

Still slightly limping from his leg wound, which he had cleaned and wrapped when he had returned to his barracks, Malchus again paced in his ten-step circuit while on sentry duty near the western gate of the temple during the night. The stars twinkled as the moon shone brightly just as it had the night before. But so much had happened within the last twenty-four hours and Malchus was still trying to process it all.

Now that Barabbas is free, do I want to rejoin my former leader and try to bring down the foreigners? Is Barabbas perhaps a real Deliverer after all and will succeed in his second attempt? There could be real glory if Barabbas is successful and I one of his chief supporters. That would be quite the tale to tell__two street boys hailed as national heroes! But what if Barabbas fails again? Is arrested? I might not be so lucky to escape next time and be arrested as well. Is it worth the risk? Or maybe Barabbas has learned his lesson while in prison and decided it isn't worth the risk either. Maybe the two of us could strike out for some distant city, like Athens or Alexandria, and start a new life together. Doing what? I have to admit that I don't have any education and few skills beyond those needed for daily survival. Maybe I'm better off staying in the employ of the High Priest, as much as I personally dislike the conniving man. At least now I have a roof over my head, adequate food, and a few coins in my purse. I'm not sure of anything anymore.

The next night, that of the weekly Sabbath, brought Malchus a change of assignment. Caiaphas had petitioned Pilate to provide a guard over the tomb where Jesus was buried. The High Priest knew of the Preacher's claims that he would rise on the third day, and the old man didn't want to take any chances that some of his disciples would come and steal the body, then publicly announce that Jesus had risen from the dead. That would only complicate the volatile situation. Caiaphas hoped that with the death of the ringleader that this whole sect would return to the hinterland of the Galilee and their ridiculous ideas would all fade away.

However, since Pilate had "washed his hands of the affair", he would not provide any soldiers and told Caiaphas that if he was so concerned that he would have to provide his own watch from his temple guards. (See Matt 27:62-66) Therefore, Malchus was transferred along with another man to guard the tomb. He didn't know how anybody would be able to break into the tomb anyway; it had been sealed and a huge stone rolled in front of the doorway. The shadows were darker here in the recesses of the burial grounds. Malchus tried not to think of the spirits of the dead who might be haunting their own sepulchers. He would sure be glad when the month of Nissan was over and he could be off this night watch and onto a day shift.

The night was quiet and Malchus's fellow officer, slumped next to the stone blocking the sepulcher, and was soon snoring loudly. Although a little jealous that the other man was getting some much-needed sleep, Malchus didn't bother him. *There will be time enough to wake him if anything unusual happens. This is all just a crazy notion from Caiaphas anyway. How can anyone rise from the dead? Dead is dead. I watched Jesus myself until the man was nearly so. There is no way that that man, even if someone rescued him from the cross before he gave up the ghost, is going to rally sufficiently to publicly stand in the temple courtyard on the third day and claim he has risen from the dead. It would be physically impossible.*

Eventually, Malchus saw a hint of light emanating from the eastern horizon and knew that dawn was not too far away and thought both he and his partner should be found alert when their replacements arrived. He kicked at the fellow guard, who with a snort and a jerk, staggered to his feet, muttering incoherently. Malchus chided him, "Some sentry you are. The whole burial ground could have been invaded."

"So, nothing happened? You know, like while I was dozing for a few minutes?"

"No, you lout. Nothing happened. And it wasn't a few minutes; it was more like a few hours. Now, look alive man, before we both get into trouble."

At that instant, two beings clothed in white, shining brighter than the noon-day sun descended from above. The two guards shrank back into the shadows, falling to the ground in fright, too startled to speak. *Spirits of the dead? Angels?* Malchus didn't think such beings really existed; that they were just the figments of deranged imaginations. However, he rubbed his eyes to make sure he hadn't fallen asleep and was dreaming. But no; the pain on his injured leg was too real for this to be a dream.

Without a word, the two angels rolled the stone of the sepulcher to one side and then perched themselves upon it. The doorway leading downward into the burial chamber itself was now open, but no bodies, dead or alive, emerged. The angels looked as if they planned to stay for a while, although Malchus wasn't about to stand around any longer waiting to find out. Grabbing his partner by the arm, they quietly edged themselves around the perimeter of the cave until they were out of sight, and then started running as fast as their legs could carry them. They wanted to get away from that haunted place as quickly as possible.

Still gasping for breath when they reached Caiaphas private chambers, they told the High Priest's personal guard that they needed to see the ruler immediately. Sensing something was amiss, the lackey knocked on the nearby door of the priest's bedchamber and then stepped inside. There was a roar of an incensed man awakened from sleep, and then Caiaphas stomped to the door.

"What is the meaning of this? Why did you desert your post?

Did anyone come to steal the body of Jesus? Speak up, or I'll have you flogged."

Malchus saluted, which token of respect Caiaphas gestured away. "Just tell me," the priest growled.

"We were on duty all night, sir, as you commanded. A few minutes ago, just before dawn, two__ uh, uh___ beings appeared."

"I knew some of those disciples of his would try something. Why didn't you apprehend them and bring them here?" demanded the priest.

"Sir, they weren't men. Not actual men anyway. I would describe them more as__ angels__, sir."

"Bah! There are no such things as angels."

"Well, I thought that myself, sir, until I beheld them with my own eyes."

"What about you?" Caiaphas snarled at the other temple guard. "Have you also been deceived?"

"I too saw them," stammered the man. "I've never seen anything like them before in my life. Bright and shiny they were, like the flame from the lampstands upon the golden temple doors, like sunshine glittering off the surface of still water, like moonbeams on newly fallen snow, like__"

"Oh shut up, man. Let me think." Caiaphas paced in the antechamber and then returning to the two guards asked, "You're sure no one came during the night? No one saw you leave the tomb?"

"Not if you don't count the two angels," responded Malchus.

Muttering to himself, the High Priest made a few more loops around the enlarged hallway. The temple guards stood at attention, with only darting glances toward one another. Malchus realized he didn't even know the other man's name. But before he could ask, Caiaphas returned to stand in front of them.

"This is how we will handle this matter once and for all. You will both be relieved of your duties as temple guards immediately."

Malchus frowned; *I should have expected something like this. There goes my source of income, food, and shelter. Gone as surely as if I'd gambled them away.*

"Don't panic," Caiaphas continued before either of the guards could protest. "You will be compensated handsomely for your quiet withdrawal from Jerusalem and your complete silence about the matter. Go to your quarters at once and turn in your uniforms and your weapons. Collect your personal belongings, and above all do not talk to anyone. If the Romans bring up the issue, we will tell them that you fell asleep while on duty and didn't see that the body of Jesus was stolen away, so you were dismissed for your incompetence. Meet me at the Treasury in one hour and you will each receive one hundred gold coins." This time both Malchus and his partner uttered an audible gasp. "Be off with you," commanded Caiaphas.

With that admonition, both men turned, purposely neglecting to salute, and strode down the palace hallway toward the guard barracks. One hundred gold coins! Malchus was filled with a rush of excitement he'd never known. *What wondrous things can I buy with that much money? I've never seen that much at one time before, say nothing to holding it in my hands. Of course, I'll need the essentials like some clothing and sandals, and a place to stay, and food to eat. Maybe I could use some of it as capital to win more in some games of chance. Maybe I'll become even richer! What will Barabbas and the other street boys think of me now?*

Then cooler reasoning began to prickle at his mind. *I will have to be cautious and use the money carefully. I don't know how long this state of unemployment will last. And what did I tell myself while at the cross two days ago__has all of this happened in only two days?__yes. I told myself that I wanted to learn to read. Perhaps with some of the gold I could hire a tutor. Being able to read and write would open up many more opportunities for me. And how will my relationship with Barabbas figure into all of this? Do I even need or want to see the man? So many questions and it looks like now I will have all the time in the world to think about them.*

But first of all, I want to scout out that youngest disciple of Jesus I saw at the cross. I have a lot of questions I want to ask about the Preacher known as Jesus, King of the Jews. I can't deny that I was healed by a miracle which he performed. Has Jesus really risen from the dead? The angels didn't say that as a fact, but why else would they roll the stone away? To allow someone to come in as Caiphas feared? Was rising from the dead the same thing the elders of the synagogue call resurrection? Does it mean Jeus will have a second life and die again or that he will live forever? Does it mean he can never be killed? What a champion against Rome he could be. I would surely chose his side over Barrabus. Oh, it's probaly all just a big fairy tale. No one has ever come back from the dead before. Still... perchance... if Jesus has risen from the dead, that would be a miracle. The greatest miracle of all!!

CPSIA information can be obtained
at www.ICGtesting.com
Printed in the USA
LVHW081647200921
698273LV00014B/593